Nimbus

Nimbus

a novel

A.C. Miller

To those who believed in me, this is for you.

22 August 2191

Sam

Fourteen. That's the age of nearly certified death in Nimbus. It's the age you're sent away from your home—kicked out into what the Elites call, 'the outside.' Really, it's just a name for the world beyond the wall, a world beyond the steel that encircles us each and every day.

For all I know, there's nothing beyond the wall. I just don't think teenagers are meant to live on their own at such a young age, but in this world, we have to. For eleven years, we have to survive. We have to fight against nature, against ourselves, against others to be re-allowed back into Nimbus on our twenty-fifth birthdays. Eleven grueling years in which we're put to the test against things we've never seen, cruelties we've never imagined. At least that's what the professors say. All I really know is that I won't get to see my family again until I turn twenty-five.

I like to think I'll be fine on the outside. After all, they're always telling us that when a male elephant reaches puberty, he leaves his herd to live on his own. Apparently if an elephant can do it, then so can we.

It's almost as if they're calling us animals. Us. Kids.

There's no pleading with the Elites; there's no begging for you to be the one outlier who doesn't have to go outside. The law of Nimbus states that everyone has to test him or herself to become an Elite and if you're incapable of doing so, you don't belong here. It's an absurd way of life, but it's how our society works.

"Sam," calls a muffled voice in front of me. Brushing off the noise, I close my eyes as I tuck my head in between my arms.

In this world, being Elite is the only thing that matters; at least, according to MacMillan. Through our schooling, we're given scenarios about what could happen during eleven years of seclusion, but we're not trained to handle death; we're not prepared to fend off any unwanted attention. We're not taught enough about how to survive. Sometimes it seems as if they don't want us to come back. It's almost as if they would rather live in this crudely structured society than one where everyone lives in peace. It's strange.

"In harmony we live. In peace we thrive." That's the motto of Nimbus—a false one, if you ask me. There's no harmony behind this wall. It's a thick veil hiding us from reality. It's a world in which we grit our teeth and smile through the pain. We know what our future holds. We know there's no such thing as peace. Everything we do behind this wall is child's play and everything we do outside of it is a game designed for those fourteen and up.

And for what? To be called 'Elite' when we turn twenty-five? It's pointless. We're alive now. We're Elite somehow; we all have a purpose. We shouldn't have to take part in this game just to prove our worth.

I itch the back of my neck and slump further forward.

With my head pressed against the cold wood of my desk, I sigh. The rain drips down the windows. Incoherently mumbling in front of me, the professor continues to speak nonsense.

". . .don't forget that participation is voluntary" is the only vague sentence I've gathered. *Of course it's voluntary*, I think. *What other choice do we have?* I'm four days from my separation and it's gotten to the point that I could care less about anything related to school—especially this class.

Each day, the professor reiterates the same points. *Physical fitness is your top priority*. Not survival, not mental or emotional strength, not even being able to defend yourself; physical fitness is of the utmost importance. The professor claims we'll run into vagrants who've been outside for a few years, but haven't adjusted to the speed of the outside world. If we don't have the physical capacity to hold our own, to run, we'll end up just as they have. In your eleven years outside, the last thing you want is to fall into the depths of the forest and its mind games. . .or so we're told.

But it's just a forest, I think. It can't be capable of playing tricks on me. After all, there aren't any walls and I'm in control. It

8

just feels like they're trying to scare us, like they want us to realize how important Nimbus is before we're kicked out.

I mean, the professors tend to mention that if you go beyond the wall without adept speed, strength, and agility, you'll end up just like those who wander aimlessly—perpetually lost in a world you're too afraid to discover. But, the difference between those in the past and me is that I want to discover it. I want to see everything. It's a desire that makes the rhetoric that much less believable.

Though, I do believe fate is an inescapable thing. No matter how strong you are, you can't truly survive amidst a new world if the odds are against you from the start. On top of that, if you don't believe in yourself, you're probably better off dead.

"Sam," calls the voice again—loudly in my ear this time.

Standing up from my seat, I wait for the question. It's the last class of the day and whenever the professor calls your name, you have to stand up and say why you'll be one of the few to be re-admitted in eleven years.

Of course, I know why I'll be re-admitted. Both of my parents survived their separations and my brother made it back in one piece. Casually taking glances out the window, I say, "I'll be Elite in eleven years because I have the ability to work, think, act, and do as an Elite would do."

Despite its worthlessness, that's ultimately what every professor wants to hear. Especially those who teach *Elite Exit: Standard Elite Protocol About Relative and Timely Insertion Outside Nimbus.* Or S.E.P.A.R.A.T.I.O.N. for short.

"Very good, Sam."

Quickly sitting back down, I turn toward the window once more. The storm's grown; trees are bending toward the glass. Taken aback by the sudden uptick in weather, I keep myself from resting my head upon my arms. A crack of thunder erupts outside, waking up a few kids in front of me—causing the girl with the dark brown hair and ponytail beside me to chuckle. I awkwardly smile before shifting my attention back to the storm. She giggles. I blush.

Shivering, I brush my shoulders and lightly close my eyes. Almost simultaneously, the professor whacks her ruler against the chalkboard. "Now class. . ." she mumbles as I turn my focus back to the comfort of my sweatshirt.

Separation is supposed to be about preparing us for the outside. By giving us a professor who barely seems to care about the subject matter, I'd say they've just about done my bleak future some justice. With a 10 percent return rate and nearly thirty kids in this class, I feel I'll be one of the few to make it back. Yet, the odds don't seem to agree.

24 August 2191

Elise

I gently glide my fingers down the curve of my wooden bow—my thumb slowly reaching for the frayed string—while I wait for one of the two wandering rabbits to cross my path. I don't care that the animals are scrawny like myself; I just want something to eat. *I need something to eat.*

Perched on a rock like a crow atop the wall, I watch as one of the emaciated animals hops across the field twenty yards in front of me. *C'mon, c'mon,* I think as I pull my arrow back, my fingers shaking against the string. Slowly meandering through the field with occasional stops to look around, the rabbit seems lost—void of any real purpose. As I watch it roam, I hold my arm back firmly. *C'mon,* I think, tightening my grip. My arm trembles; light spasms make it hard to hold any longer. I release my first shot. . .over its head.

Veering from its transient path, the rabbit starts to sprint away while the other darts farther into the woods. With limited time to recover after my miss, I grab another arrow and take a breath. I slightly shift my aim downward. The moment starts to crawl. The animal's path becomes clear as it scrambles to find safety. With a quick release, I fire again. This time, my shot pierces its neck.

Forcing myself between a tight pairing of trees, I toss my bow around my shoulder and hurry toward the wounded animal. Lying on its side, crying for help, it screams to escape. *I hate this part.* I hate the sight of a wounded animal even when it's by my own hand. It reminds me too much of myself: struggling to survive when everything around it wants it dead, when the environment's impetuosity strives to prevent its happiness.

With the sun climbing into the sky behind me, I stop my run and crouch down. Rays of sunlight shine through the trees and onto my catch—temporarily blinding me as I agitatedly observe my surroundings in search of others. *I see nothing.* Though, in the past when someone's tried to steal my food, they haven't gotten too far. With a lack of protein in their bodies, most stragglers can't fend off the hunter. Some I fear, but when someone is basically crawling toward my catch, it's hard to be worried. Then again, right now, I'm virtually the same as those who struggle: weak, hungry, and on the verge of giving up. *But I won't quit. I've been here before.*

Hurrying out into the opening, I rush toward my catch as my quiver rattles against my back. With a dying cry, the rabbit writhes, awaiting an end to its misery.

Quickly yanking the bloodied arrow out of its neck, I force it back into its head. "Ugh," I mutter as the animal falls silent. *I wish Sean were here*, I think. *I need his strength.* The agony of killing something so undeserving doesn't suit me; I almost ache. If only there was another way to do it, but there really isn't. This world is about survival of the fittest and, regardless of how little I enjoy killing something innocent, I need to eat. *I can't let myself become the rabbit*, I think. *I can't expect Sean to come back and do it for me.*

Whether it's a rabbit, a deer, or even a handful of berries, it doesn't matter. Food is food on the outside and if I can conjure up a meal without exhausting myself or ending up with nothing, it's a success. You never truly learn the amount of days you can go without eating until it's your only option, until you're lost in a sea of nothingness, struggling to survive. *Stop it, Elise*, I think to myself as I pull the arrow out of the animal's head—a gross red mush clinging to the end of the blade.

Burdened by constant headaches, I can't allow myself to bury my conscience in the mud. The outside is full of difficult choices and strenuous moments, but if you allow yourself to cave to the negativity of your mind, you'll break. If you can't avoid the evils of eleven years of isolation, you're not cut out to return to Nimbus. With only one year left, I have a lot to prove. I have to shake off the shadows around me that prevent me from finding happiness, that provoke the negativity stressing my aching chest. I know I'm strong enough to go home and to survive anything thrown at me, but then again, anything can happen in a year. Darkness isn't easy to overcome.

I've seen kids die on their first day outside of Nimbus. It's as if they never listened to the main piece of advice the professors behind the wall preach: once the doors close, move. If you think whining about being separated will allow you to go back home, you're wrong. The longer you cry about your separation, the easier it is for you to break. If you allow yourself to crack instantly, the pressure of surviving for eleven years will become too much for you. . .and that's when you lose yourself. Being fourteen and alone isn't something anyone should have to endure, but it's something everyone has to deal with. There's always some semblance of life in the forest if you at least give yourself a chance to find it, if you don't allow yourself to become the rabbit.

Still, it's unfair how poorly we're prepared for our exile. I remember each class always spoke about knowing your surroundings and knowing who you can and can't trust, but they never showed you how to fight. If you can't defend yourself, you're worthless and that's disheartening for too many of us. I wasn't shown how to fight until I met Sean. If I had never met him, I wouldn't be alive today. There's no doubt in my mind about it. *Sean saved me.*

There comes a point where you have to get over your fears and realize that survival is the most important thing. Moping will get you nowhere; crying about what you once had won't change your fate. You just have to keep moving and believing in yourself. If you give up too quickly, your life will be over before you even get a chance to learn your worth. You won't get a second chance to know who you are.

As I quickly thrust my knife into the rabbit's side, my forehead starts to pulse. The more I maneuver the knife through the animal, the faster the throbbing in my head. *Not again*, I think as I release my hand from the blade and dig my fingers into my scalp.

With each new day, my headaches refuse to settle. My mind has been bothered by the constant ache of my last click—the same click that has happened every year for the past ten years that notifies us how old we are. It's really the only way to know you've survived another year. Yet, each time I get mine, my headaches worsen.

Ever since I fought a vagrant over a rabbit I killed, the pain in my head and abdomen hasn't subsided. Each time I find a moment

13

of clarity, it's trounced by the discomfort of that night several years ago. Closing my eyes while my nails gently glide against my head, the incident sharply flashes through my mind.

It had been days since I'd eaten so much as a few berries. I had passed several camps, but was too afraid to ask if I could join, too afraid to be harshly kicked away from a meal. I struggled to hunt, to scavenge, and even to sleep. Then, one morning, I found a shack next a railroad. I hid there for a couple days before trying to find something substantial to eat.

One morning, I awoke to leaves being tossed against the exterior of my hideout. I thought it was an animal rustling the leaves outside the shack, but when I went out, there was nothing in sight. I kept walking and walking until I found a few berries to eat. Unfulfilled and insatiable, I kept moving until something furry jumped into the corner of my eye. I immediately pulled out my bow and fired several arrows—most of which became lodged into nearby trees. Eventually, I managed to hit the rabbit.

I quickly headed toward my dinner—my lips salivating with each step. Then, as I reached down to claim my catch, a straggling vagrant lunged at me. Something sharp dug into my stomach and the pain of starvation lifted from my mind only to be replaced by a crude opaqueness—a surreal darkness. Next thing I remember, I was being carried away.

Clutching my stomach, I lift my shirt and glide my fingers across the scar.

I remember waking up a few days later with Sean there taking care of me. His dark, vulnerable green eyes analyzing my wound—he wished he could do more. He looked at me with a sense of desire—a sense of empathy I had yet to see outside of Nimbus. Two days after that, I had my first click. He thought it was just a re-occurrence of the pain I had felt days earlier, but after I kept complaining about my head, he knew what I meant. Each time since, the clicks have re-aggravated that moment; they've made me relive the torment of one of my weakest nights.

I just want my last year to be one of solitude, of peace, but that's unlikely. I've gone ten years without a clear head. I think I can manage one more.

The throbbing refuses to settle as the sun shines heavily on my neck. "Elise," I hear from behind me. Hoping it's Sean, I turn

14

around to see nothing. Once again, it's all in my head. Just like the pain from the click, it's something I haven't gotten used to no matter how many times it happens.

As I pull the knife back out along with my cut, building a fire is the only thing on my mind. If the sun could cook this rabbit for me right now, I could finally rest and try to soothe this headache. Yet, that's impossible. Not a day goes by where I don't wish Sean and I were the same age. "Elise," I hear again in the back of my head, but nothing comes of it. There's nothing behind me, and Sean isn't here. That's just something I need to get used to for one more year.

Sean

Two days until Sam goes outside the wall. After not seeing him in eleven years, getting to spend only a few weeks with him is tough. I feel like I'm leaving Elise all over again. I know she's capable of surviving on her own for one more year, but the outside is ever-changing and one year might feel like a dozen. But for Sam, that first year will feel like an eternity. No matter who he's with or what he does, the first year will seemingly never end.

"This area's secure," I mumble to a passing guard as I stand, overlooking the vast woodland outside the wall. Another guard passes by; I turn my focus to the trees curling in the wind beneath me.

With a Separation nearing, more Elite guards have been added to the wall. It's the time of year where those outside know winter is coming. They may not know what month it is, but the first gust of winter pushes them back toward familiar territory—back toward the wall. It's impossible to regain entrance, but kids still try to do it each time. And sadly, it's my job to make sure they don't succeed—even if it means shooting them. I knew what I was getting into when I joined the Guard, but sometimes I hate what I *have* to do.

I've only been atop the wall for a week now, but several kids have approached the gates with their emaciated faces drooping, their sunken eyes watering. No matter what shape they're in, there's a set of rules we're supposed to follow. The Guard teaches us that if an outsider slams on the wall ten or more times, we're to start shooting at their feet. If they continue to scream aggressively and pound again after we stop firing, we're told to shoot them in the shoulder. And if that doesn't do any justice, the cleanup crew will be out the next day to dispose of the dead.

It doesn't matter if you want back into Nimbus; you're not allowed back in until eleven years from when you were sent out.

16

Eleven strenuous years trying to survive on what little you were taught. Tucked in a world encircled by the skies, you're never given a proper lesson on a different world. School can't prepare you for life on the outside. Nothing can prepare you for the chaos that is created when you're immersed in pure anarchy. You might think you're mentally and physically strong enough to survive, but even the strongest weaken over time, even the brightest get senseless.

That was the best thing about Elise. She knew she wasn't the strongest and she knew she wasn't the weakest, but she knew how to survive. Her hunting skills weren't top notch, but despite her headaches, her mentality was stronger than anyone I've ever met. She never wanted to give up. She'd never settle for misery. Instead, she'd tighten her stance, look at me—with her beautiful eyes and vibrant smile—and tell me it wasn't enough. Not a day goes by when I don't wish she was here, but I know I'll see her again in less than a year.

"You kill any outsiders today, Sean?" comes a deep, raspy voice from behind me.

"None so far, sir."

"Keep your eyes peeled. Separation Day will be here soon and I don't care if that means you have to shoot your family. You keep this wall protected."

"Will do, sir," I say begrudgingly.

Captain Eldridge MacMillan. He's probably the toughest son-of-a-bitch I've ever met, but he's also the most deluded. One of the eldest Elite members still alive since the founding of Nimbus over eighty years ago, he never fears to tell you what's on his mind. Whether he sees someone as a threat or not, he feels violence is the only way to keep Nimbus safe.

Since he patrols the top of the wall every day, his macabre ways have ingrained themselves into the minds of all the Guard. We know our place. We know we're beneath him. Hell, we're all held in less regard than those who founded this place. At least working up here allows me to see that; it opens my mind up to the delusion that built this world.

Having taken off his hat, MacMillan's bony fingers poke into my back. "Yes?" I reply.

"Look," he quietly mumbles.

Turning my head back around, I can see a boy, about the age of sixteen, sitting in a tree seventy-five yards away. Barely visible, I can see his left eye while the right half remains hidden behind various yellowy leaves.

Despite being in his mid-eighties, MacMillan still has the eyes of a hawk. "You gonna do somethin' about that?" he asks.

"Not unless he becomes a viable threat, sir," I reply.

"Shoot him," says a stern-faced MacMillan.

"But. . ."

"No buts, shoot him."

Lifting the scope of my rifle toward my eye, I gaze into the weary eye of the kid whose name I don't even know. As he continues to mindlessly sit in the tree, I place my finger against the trigger.

"Do it!" shouts MacMillan.

I don't want to, I think, my finger sliding down the trigger. *I don't need to.*

"NOW!" he yells as spit flies out beside me.

Without a second thought, I pull the trigger.

26 August 2191

Sam

My Separation Day has finally arrived. After fourteen years behind the wall, I get to be thrown out past it. I get to see the outside and experience the rush of nerves that comes with being pushed away from everything I've known. I'm afraid but excited to see something more than these dim walls. However this game plays itself out in eleven years, I'm sure I'll have a newfound appreciation for the protection offered within Nimbus, but I doubt my stance on MacMillan will change.

Sean's always despised Captain MacMillan and not just because of his strictness, but because he's the only surviving founder who still has his grip on Nimbus. The others just stay at home, no longer willing or able to show up at even a few separations a year. Sean always tells me that Separation wouldn't exist if MacMillan wasn't in charge, but it's hard to believe something I don't know to be true.

All I know is that, the longer I'm at home, the less I can learn about our world and the one before it. That's life in Nimbus—you get fourteen years to learn what you'll forget in eleven. We all end up in the same place in the end, so why we can't learn more about this game and why it exists is beyond me. But, I guess none of it matters now. Separation is a blank slate, one that's making my hands a little clammy the more I think about it.

Wiping my hands on my pants, I glance out the window. The sun hovers above a few passing clouds as the birds sing in the distance. Their songs roll through the window, helping me feel better about today. Separation Day isn't a day of rejoice nor is it a day of sorrows; it's a day of self-discovery and probably unwanted sweat. It's a day to find out who you are, who you want to be in eleven years, and how comfortable you are without the amenities you've been adjusted to for so long. *I just hope I get eleven years*, I think to myself.

If one thing's certain about today, it's that when I near the gates my emotions, coupled with those of my parents, will be so jumbled that no real word will be able to define the sensation. *Now I'm getting nervous*, I think before lightly slapping myself in the face. *You got this*.

Sitting on the end of my bed with my feet dangling off the side, I throw on my ankle-high socks while my mind dives into the memory of the last Separation Day I watched. It was six years ago. Six years ago, the biggest class to exit Nimbus was up. It was in September. Apparently there were a lot of September 14th birthdays that year because exactly twelve kids turned fourteen on that day. Since no one is forced out until the day of their fourteenth birthday, it was a big deal that a group bigger than three or four was up to exit.

My group only consists of three of us: Me, Abby, and Phil. I don't think there are any the day after us, but I know there are a few more at the end of the month. Six years ago, there was something so interesting about a group of twelve kids that nearly all of Nimbus was there to watch the sending off. A typical ceremony consisting of an Elite reading off the students' names followed by a cannon shooting into the sky became anything but regular.

When the cannon fired, over half of the kids tried to run from the group and hide back somewhere in the village. Despite their efforts, they failed miserably and the kids that tried to escape were all shot right in front of their families—in the kneecap. The Elites wanted to show why running off on Separation Day was a bad idea and how doing something so unruly would end painfully. After they were wounded, the doors opened and the Elites threw the six or seven kids out in front while the remaining ones who didn't try to flee were sent off to go wherever they pleased on the outside.

Since then, I've refused to attend another separation. We have over a hundred per year, but today's different. Today's my Separation Day.

I pull a black hooded sweatshirt over my head and immediately roll up the sleeves. I know I'll be hot in this today, but

I'll need it for the future. The same goes for these jeans. I put shorts on underneath, but I can't imagine how often I'll want to carry my jeans around. But, the more I layer up, the more options I'll have for temperature changes.

For some reason, upon Separation the Elites only allow us to bring one thing to the outside. It can literally be anything. I could bring my baseball bat or an extra pair of shoes, but that doesn't make much sense. Layering up doesn't count as an extra thing since we're allowed to wear enough to survive. I've seen kids bring knives and the Elites don't care. Sean brought a large fishing hook, so he could hunt almost any size of animal. The hook had to be at least three inches tall and a quarter of an inch thick. It wasn't your normal hook.

Though, when he came back a few weeks ago, he didn't have the hook with him. He said someone else had it and that I should take something else, so I'm taking my dad's hatchet.

Slowly pulling the heels of my shoes over my feet, I head downstairs as Mom prepares the table. With an apron draped over her shoulders, she turns around and smiles—her dark blonde hair covering one of her eyes. "I've made some eggs, Sam," she mutters just as Dad comes around the wooden post and latches his arm around my shoulders.

"Have you thought about what you want to bring, Sam?" he asks, his deep voice echoing around the room.

"Yes," I say pointing toward the hatchet on the wall across from the dining table.

"Good choice," he replies before walking toward it and lifting it off its hooks. "Make sure you bring it back in eleven years."

"Don't worry, Dad. You'll be able to put it right back there before you know it."

"Of course I will," he nods, handing me the hatchet as we both approach the table.

Lightly holding the hatchet in my hands, a glint of sunlight bounces off the blade—causing me to shift the handle enough that the chipped wood splinters my hand. "Ouch," I mutter under my breath. The sharp pain starts to course through my hand as I set the hatchet onto the table next to my plate.

Gently removing the small shard of wood and pressing my right palm into the other, I can't help but think how such a small thing could cause such pain. If I'm bothered by something like this, I can't imagine what the physical stress of the outside is capable of—especially after I've felt so high and mighty all morning.

"You alright, Sam?" asks Dad, clearing his throat after swallowing a big helping of eggs.

"Yea, it's nothing," I lie.

From behind me, Mom puts her hands against the back of my chair. "Are you ready for your big day?" she asks before leaning in and kissing me on the head. Pulling away, I shake my head side to side; she pulls out the chair next to me.

"I think so," I mutter.

"You go out at ten hundred hours, right?" asks Dad as he ingests another big helping of eggs, his words nearly blocked by his hunger.

"Yea," I mutter as I jab the end of my fork into the spongy yellow blob in front of me.

"How many kids exit with you, Sam?" comes a strong, familiar voice from behind me.

"Sean?"

He doesn't reply.

I turn around and sure enough, there he stands dressed in his gray Elite Guard suit with his arms out. With a slight bit of sweat trickling down his pale-skinned forehead, Sean wipes it off with a half-smile. I release my fork and hop off my seat before wrapping my arms around his back. "It's nice to see you, too," he says.

Squeezing as tight as I can before letting go, I sit back down at the table. Putting his hand on my head, Sean forcefully moves it side to side. "No noogies," I laugh.

"It wouldn't be right if I saw you and didn't give you one."

I toy with my food—not hungry enough to eat when I should eat. Mom stands up to give Sean a hug behind me. "Hi, honey," she says with a kiss before pulling him away into the kitchen. Hidden behind the cabinets, I can barely hear their conversation. Leaning awkwardly in my chair, I try to listen. "How long do you have?" mutters Mom.

"Just a few minutes," he replies.

Their conversation fades. I look over at Dad. Polishing off his plate, he smiles—a piece of bacon hanging off his bottom lip. I manage a half-smile back just as Sean steps back into the room.

22

Switching my face, I turn around and frown at Sean.

"It's okay, Sam. I'll see you when you leave. I'll be atop the wall and don't forget whenever you need me, I'll be right up there watching you."

"But Separation class taught us that if we're too close to the wall, we'll get shot."

With a light grin, Sean kneels down next to my chair. "That is what we're supposed to do, but there's no way I'll shoot you. I'll shoot one of them before I turn my back on you."

"Wouldn't that get both of us killed?"

"Yea, but at least in that scenario neither one of us killed each other," he responds innocently, a soft smile on his face. "Well, I gotta get back to the wall. I'll see you guys after work," he says before hugging Mom again.

Taking a small bite, I look at Sean. I can feel my face starting to warm, my muscles tensing up. "I'll see you in e-eleven years," I mumble. Clasping my arms around his back, I squeeze with all I can muster. My eyes start to well up.

Caught off guard, Sean grins and squeezes back. "With that strength, I'm sure I'll see you sooner."

"That's not possible," I joke. Turning back toward the table, I pick up my plate and move into the kitchen—the eggs bouncing with each step. *You should eat more,* I think. Heading into the kitchen, I set my plate down on the counter atop a bunch of dirty dishes. Simultaneously, Sean grabs onto my arm.

"Sam," he says firmly while leaning toward my face. "Just remember, you're not alone out there. Find Elise and she'll teach you everything I taught her. Stay away from vagrants and most of all stay away from the wall."

"Okay, I can do that."

"I know you can." Standing upright, Sean places his callused hand atop my head. "See you soon, little bro," he mutters before turning his hand into a fist and burrowing it into my scalp.

"At least I won't get any more of those for a while!" I cry, trying to remove his hand from my head.

Sean laughs and I half-smile back, trying not to think of the cruelty of being exiled from my family for eleven years—especially from the one man I know could protect me on the outside.

"See ya, Sean," I quietly say as he maneuvers toward the door. Stepping into the warm, summer air, he turns around and smiles. His gray Elite wristband brushes against the wood and becomes the last part of him I see before disappearing outside.

"Well, are you ready to go?" asks Mom, a piece of bacon between her forefingers. She takes a bite.

"Is it that time already?" *It feels like it's been ten minutes.* "I guess so," I say. Grabbing my hatchet from the table, I take one last look around before walking toward the front door.

Pushing the screen door open, Dad grabs his ball cap and holds the bulky wooden door for Mom.

"C'mon, Sharon. Let's go," he says.

"Coming, dear," she softly responds. Quickly clearing the table, she takes the plates into the kitchen before coming out and throwing her apron over a chair.

The moment I step outside, the moisture clings to my shirt. The smell of freshly cut grass wafts through my nostrils as our neighbor, Tom, sits on his front doorstep wiping the sweat off of his forehead.

"Great day to mow, huh?" shouts my dad, his hands focused on locking the front door while his eyes glance at the next yard over.

"Couldn't be better," answers Tom as he slowly stands back up—his hands on his back—to head inside.

I hope that's not me when I come back, I think. Eleven years is probably enough time to develop stiff joints and other unwanted problems. But, at least those are better than not coming back at all.

Slowly working our way off the sidewalk and into the stone-laced street, a gentle finger pokes into my shoulder blade. "Sam," says the soft voice.

"Yes?" I reply as I turn around.

Standing there clad in a pair of black jeans with a gray fall jacket draped over her white shirt, Abby Young happily looks at me. "Are you ready for our big day?" she asks, my mind failing to understand the simplicity of the sentence. Instead, it's too focused on her uniquely braided brown hair. Woven back and forth atop her head, her hair looks nice compared to the plainness of my buzzcut.

"Umm, yea," I awkwardly mutter. Even though I'm ready, I still don't want everyone to think I'm full of myself. "Are you, Abby?" I ask, trying to shift my focus to her chestnut-colored eyes.

24

"I think so," she replies as her parents walk ahead of the two of us and start conversing with mine.

"Hey there, how are you?" is all I hear before turning my attention to Abby.

"So, what did you end up bringing as your one token?" I ask.

Rolling up her pant leg, she reaches into the top of her knee-high white socks. Pulling out a glittery red Swiss Army knife, she holds it toward me.

"That's awesome," I say. It really is. Abby was always one of the quietest girls in our Separation class, but she was always really nice to me. We didn't speak often since socializing in class was frowned upon, but whenever we did, it improved the day. Even the one time she asked me for a hair tie during a lecture and got me in trouble for laughing was worth it. Anything was better than listening to the professor talk about types of trees.

"Yea, my dad said I should take it. It's the same one he used during his eleven years on the outside."

"That's cool," I reply, shifting my line of sight to the walking path as the sun warms my face.

Putting the knife into her pocket, Abby moves a little closer to me. "I don't really know how to use it though. Do you?"

"That's okay, I'll teach ya," I say without thinking. *I've never used one either.*

In school, they kept us in shape with occasional drills, but they never taught us how to fight. So, I never actually learned how to use a weapon, but I figured it was something I would be able to teach myself outside of Nimbus. With so much time, we should be able to learn how to fend for ourselves. If we can't figure that out in eleven years, maybe we don't deserve to be in the 10 percent who make it back home.

"Thanks," she mutters. Lightly rolling her sleeves up, Abby tucks her bangs behind her ears. "Do you know where to go when we get out there? Do we just kind of walk away and hope we can find shelter or build it ourselves?"

Unsure of how to answer, I continue to stare at the sandy stone beneath my feet. Full of coarse pebbles and unnecessary holes, the street appears defeated. There haven't been cars in use since before I was born and the Elites don't seem to care to fix something that's only used for walking purposes.

"Sam?" comes her voice again.

"I don't know," I answer, the sun warming my scalp.

"Do you mind if I stick with you then?" questions Abby.

Lifting my head back up as I step over an uneven patch of stone, I nod. "That's fine. It's better to be with someone else than to wander out there alone."

"Thanks," she replies, her fingers lightly grasping onto mine. "Hey Sam," she shyly says.

"Yea?"

"It was pretty funny when your face got all red yesterday when Melanie looked over at you after that loud thunder."

I can feel my face getting red, but not from the sun.

Abby smiles, "It was kinda cute."

I don't answer; my mind hasn't told my mouth what to say. I probably look like a robot to her.

"Sam Martin?" calls a loud voice from in front of me—one that jolts me out of my trance and subsequent confusion.

"Yes?" I reply as I pick up my pace and step between my parents.

"Stand over here," says the man dressed in the same Elite Guard attire Sean was in this morning.

Casually stepping to my left, I stand on a small, black 'X' etched into the ground. Directly in front of the spot, the dark gray steel of the exit doors stand beaming in the sunlight. Standing at twenty-two feet tall, the doors look like those of a bank vault.

"Over here, Miss Young," says the man, directing Abby to my right.

As we stand still in our places, Phil arrives and is placed to my left. Instantly, the man opens a yellowish document in which he has to adjust his glasses to read.

"It is here, on August the twenty-sixth, twenty-one hundred and ninety-one, that I send Phil Gordon, Sam Martin, and Abigail Young outside of Nimbus to complete their eleven years of seclusion. By decree of Eldridge MacMillan, you are now excluded from re-entry into Nimbus until you pass the Earliest Nimbus Trial for Returning Youth or E.N.T.R.Y. Said test will take place if the individual is alive and if the individual is in a functioning mental state in exactly eleven years. Now, the parents will have one minute to say their goodbyes before the three fourteen-year-olds will be exiled awaiting future re-entrance into Nimbus."

Upon folding up the paper, the man pushes his glasses up the ridge of his nose before he lets out a slight exhale, as if he doesn't even care about what he just read.

Lightly smirking, I turn around—the sweaty, exhausted hands of my parents force themselves around my torso. "You got this, Sam," mumbles Dad.

"You'll be okay, Sam. We believe in you," cries Mom while wiping her face on a handkerchief.

"I'll be okay, guys, really," I reply, a subtle tear sliding down my cheek. "Just like what Sean said, I'll see you guys soon."

"Very soon," smiles Dad. "Love ya, buddy."

Still clinging onto my body, my mother kisses me on the cheek and whispers a soft *I love you* as the doors open and the guards lead us out.

"Go, go, go," yell a few of the guards while others enter outside in front of us with guns pointed in all directions. "The coast is clear. No viable threats," says one of them as we step beyond the wall. It's almost as if they're protecting us—that our exit is the last time someone will care about our safety. But, it's short-lived. The guards quickly retreat as the bright light shining so heavily on the inside of the door fades to black and the shade from the trees consumes the area.

27 August 2191

Elise

Standing beneath a thicket of trees, I shiver in the mist as a light rain falls upon my shoulders. Tightly clinging to the string of my bow around my chest, I lean my body against the trunk of the biggest tree I can find. I look around, but see nothing. No animals scurry in front of me; no berries hang from a stem nearby. There's nothing. Ever since Sean took his return test a few weeks ago, I've struggled to find much more than a rabbit or two.

I've gotten by, but the hunger pains never fade. *Maybe Sam will magically have food*, I think. *Maybe as his one token, he brought food.* After all, there's no rule against it. It's not smart, but if Sean told him to find me, he would know he at least has my bow as protection.

All I know about Sam is that yesterday was his birthday. Sean told me to wait a couple hundred yards from the wall for Sam, but I have no idea where he'll end up or if he'll even know how to find me. He doesn't know what I look like and I don't know what he looks like. My only hope is that he's a spitting image of his brother. If not, he may end up on his own forever and I would hate myself if that happened.

The rain trickles down the bark and sticks to my shirt— forcing me away from the tree. I could head farther into the woods to look for shelter, but there's not much out here. Not to mention every step on the outside is a risk. Plus, Sam would never know where to find me. I can't take a chance on fate when I promised Sean I would protect Sam for his first year outside the wall.

I step out from underneath the trees and into an open dirt path; the clouds begin to lighten as the rain comes to a quick halt. *I swear it just started*, I think. As I slowly walk down the path, a deafening thud cracks in the skyline above me, sending my head into hysteria.

The pounding in my temple picks up with each step, refusing to lessen as I move. My legs buckle and I fall to my knees. The left side of my head aches like I've just had another click, but I haven't. *I've already had my click this year.* There's no way I could have two in one year and I'm not deluded enough to think a year has already passed. This can't be in my head; the chip implanted in my skull is messing with me. If there's one thing I hate near as much as being out here, it's this chip; it's a nuisance.

I'll never understand why they find it necessary to track our every move on the grid. They must know I'm not too far from the wall, but they also have to know I have no desire to try and escape farther than allowed, *so why is my head throbbing? Why am I in so much pain for something I haven't done or even thought of doing?* Whoever is in charge of the grid can't control my thoughts; they can't control my brain. They don't own my every desire. They can only track me until I hit the invisible barrier that blows up the chip a hundred miles away from Nimbus. Then, nobody can track me.

And until that moment—which, I'm not crazy enough to wander toward—the Elites have no reason to try to weaken me. That is, if they have the ability to do anything more than track us. If they did, I'm sure they'd do a lot more than just make my head hurt here and there. *Maybe my chip was put in wrong. Maybe it's defective.* Whatever the cause of my pain is, I can't help but think it's beyond my control. I just have to deal with it for one more year.

Forcing the palm of my hand into my head, I try to massage the ache as another crack of thunder resounds throughout. With birds flocking from the trees around me, I throw my quiver over my head—hoping that a bird won't be so scared it drops something on me.

With all this time to myself near Nimbus, I can't help but think I may never cross paths with Sam. Even though he doesn't have many ways to go and I'm directly north of Nimbus, I have an odd feeling he'll sneak by me in my sleep or forget what his brother was supposed to tell him. If he's anything like me at fourteen, he'll think he's tough enough to survive on his own without anyone's help. Then again, if he's anything like Sean, he'll be smart enough to pair up, but I don't know him one bit. I don't know what he wants out of his Separation.

Continuing to sit in the dirt as the aching refuses to subside, I scoot backward into a patch of wetted grass and toss my bow to my side. Propping the quiver up against a tree, I place my head against it and close my eyes, hoping that if I can't find Sam, he finds me.

Sam

"Sam, where do you think we should go? We've been walking through nothing but trees since yesterday," mutters Abby.

I'm not sure. Everything's just as new to me as it is to them. Sean told me to find Elise, but he didn't tell me where she was. I was kind of hoping she would find me, but I don't know if she knows to do that either. "I don't know. Just keep walking," I muster.

"Hey, Sam, maybe we should get onto that dirt path up there," says Phil. Pointing ahead to a withered path tucked away behind a row a trees, Phil itches his chest underneath his white zip-up jacket and smiles.

"That sounds good," I reply. Upon our Separation, Phil asked if he could stay with us and I couldn't say no. The larger our group, the safer we'll be. Plus, he's taller than me with a bit more athleticism. His lanky frame allows him to see around the forest better than Abby or I can. Not allowing him to stay with us just didn't seem right. "I'm kind of hungry. Are you guys hungry?" Looking back at me, they both shake their heads as their eyes linger around the forest—Phil's eyes, in particular, seem entranced by the sky. *I should have eaten more at home.* "Do either of you know much about hunting or foraging?"

"My mom taught me a little about picking the right berries," mumbles Abby. Casually leaning over, she picks up a dandelion and proceeds to tear off its petals one by one. The petals softly fall into the dirt, only to be stamped into place shortly after.

"What did she teach you?" asks Phil. Stopping in his tracks, he stretches out his neck before resting against a tree. Breaking a dangling branch from its side, he snaps it into a few more pieces across his knee. "I really don't know much about this stuff," he mumbles. Looking around the forest, he whips the end of the stick against the tree.

"She said, 'yellow and white may put up a fight. . .purple and blue are good for you' then something about red. . ."

Surprisingly, I know this rhyme. Chiming in, I say, "Red, could be edible, could be dead-ible or something like that. It never really made sense."

Laughing, Phil rips off another branch and starts pulling off a few leaves. "So you're saying blueberries and grapes are all I can eat? I don't think I've ever seen a wild grape and what about blackberries?"

"I don't know. I guess you could try one if you wanted to," responds Abby before throwing the crippled stem of the defective flower onto the ground.

"Maybe we should just stick to finding blueberries or something of similar color," I say while looking around the area for any brightly colored fruit. The two of them move in opposite directions—each stepping out of my peripherals.

While they wander around in search of food, I remain still, looking at the dirt path across the way. *I just want some meat,* I think.

I've never actually eaten a freshly picked berry before, probably due to the fact that Nimbus grows everything within the confines of the wall, essentially forbidding us from experiencing outside food. We're only allowed to eat what's grown locally and half the time, there's not a big selection. Nimbus just isn't big enough to expand our taste buds.

Abby calls me over.

"I found these red ones," she shouts. Quickly throwing a combination of discolored berries onto the ground, Phil walks toward us. "They kind of look like raspberries to me," she continues.

"They look like raspberries to me, too," replies Phil. Eyeing the bush, he starts to pluck a few—simultaneously placing more in his pockets while accidentally smearing a few onto the sides of his jacket.

Unsure of what they really are, I avoid grabbing or eating any until I know we're in the clear. It's almost as if they're my lab rats and I'm willing to let them suffer if they're not raspberries. It feels rude, but I don't want to get sick.

I hover behind the two of them as the sky grows a dark shade of gray. "Are either of you willing to see if they are raspberries?" I ask, my focus mainly on Phil.

"Go ahead, Phil," says Abby. With her eyes focused on the palm of her hand, she rolls a few berries off into the dirt—leaving just one.

Looking down into the mudded palm of his hand where three bright red berries loosely sit, Phil picks one up with his right forefingers. Gently squeezing the berry between his thumb and index finger, he moves it toward his mouth, his pupils enlarging. Slowly pressing the berry against his front teeth, he bites down.

"Tastes a little funny," he says before he takes another bite.

"Funny in a good or bad way?" asks Abby.

Wincing his left eye, Phil contorts his face and says, "They're sour raspberries." Yet, he continues to chew.

"Can't say I've ever had a sour raspberry," mumbles Abby. Toying with the berry in her hand, she idly stares at it almost as if it were a detonator.

"Neither have I," I say.

Coyly glancing up at me, Abby takes her first bite; her face cringes and her lips pucker as she sucks on the sour fruit. At this point, I don't think I want one. They're seemingly enjoying them and are quick to move onto eating a few more, but I just don't know. I'm not really partial to sour fruit and I can't say I want my first meal out here to make my face looks like theirs have.

"Are you going to try some?" asks Phil.

"I don't think so, Phil. I don't really like sour fruit."

"Suit yourself," he responds. Rolling up the sleeves of his light jacket, he puts a few more into his mouth. This time, his face distorts even more than the past few times. His right eye spasms while his jaw moves closer to his neck.

"Maybe we should just keep walking to see if we can find something better or maybe something with some meat on it," I say knowing we don't have any way to capture a live animal, let alone knowing what to do if we found a dead one.

"But we don't know how to hunt," says Abby. Pulling a few more raspberries off the bush, she aligns them in her hand by size, but doesn't bother to eat them.

"There's no better time than the present to learn how," laughs Phil as he tosses a few more raspberries into his mouth before shoving a few more into his pockets.

"I agree," I answer. Meandering toward the dirt path, I look back at Abby. She smiles. Each step out here makes time feel nonexistent. It's like the world's been handed to us, but we have no idea what to do with it. I'd almost rather give it back for a home-cooked meal.

The sky starts to become gray; a light rain begins to trickle down through the leaves. I slow my strides once we all get into the clearing, knowing that we have no reason to be in a rush since the unbroken path leads us God knows where.

It reminds me of three years ago when a kid named Wesley brought in a hand-drawn map of what his eldest sister said the outside looked like. She had passed her re-entrance exam a couple weeks prior and she knew he was due out in a few years, so she wanted to help. Well, Wesley brought the map to school to show it to the rest of us, but the moment word got out about the doodles, everything stopped. Wesley no longer showed up to class and his sister was sent back outside with no timeline as to when she would be re-allowed back into Nimbus. Since then, no one's even tried to help us out. The only knowledge you grow up with of the outside is that it's a vast forest. That's it. That was also the last time someone was sent back outside. *And for what?* Nothing.

By the time we reach a larger clearing of trees, the rain has picked up its pace.

Turning my head to the side, I ask, "Have you guys seen any small animals yet?"

"Nothing yet," says Phil with a cough.

Abby shakes her head beside me.

"Keep your eyes peeled, I'm getting pretty hungry," I say.

"Maybe you should've had some of those raspberries then, Sam. They were quite delicious," grins Abby. Leaning down toward another flower, Abby picks it up and begins to tear off its petals. One by one, she discards them behind her.

"It's okay, I would rather have something a little more filling."

"They were filling enough for now," replies Abby. Bringing the dangling remnants of the flower up to her nose, she smiles and

34

looks at me. "I love the way these smell; it sort of makes you forget for a split second that you're out here and instead you're back wandering through the Garden of Nimbus."

"Did that garden have much variety?" I ask.

"Not a lot, but enough to make me eager to find something new out here."

I smile. "I'm sure we'll find a lot of new things out here."

"I hope so," she says before pulling off another petal.

As we continue to walk down the path, the dirt turns to mud while Phil's footsteps start to disappear. I turn around. Grasping his stomach, his every move starts to stutter as he slows to a complete halt.

"Are you okay, Phil?" I ask.

Looking up at me, his face turns white. "No," he faintly says as he falls onto his knees. Quickly losing color, his pupils grow lighter. He falls onto his hands. With his gaze on the dirt, he opens his mouth, but nothing comes out.

"Phil!" I yell, but he doesn't respond.

Shaking his head back and forth, he tries to rid the sour look from his face, but nothing comes of it. His arms grow weak as he falls limp onto the ground.

"PHIL!" screams Abby, simultaneously dropping the single-petal flower into the mud. "HELP, HELP!" she continues to scream as she sprints toward his writhing body.

Taken aback, neither of us knows what to do. With each second, Phil becomes weaker—the only movement from his body being the slight quiver of fear. "PHIL!" I yell. I sprint toward him, my eyes continually wandering in circles as uncertainty grabs ahold of me. "What do we do?!" I shout just as Abby reaches toward his motionless body.

"I don't know!" she answers. Attempting to move him onto his back, she pleads, "PHIL!" His eyes start to roll back.

At this point, all I can think about is the fact that Abby had some of the berries, too. At any moment, she could end up just like Phil if she doesn't do something.

"He's dying," she weeps, her hands pounding against his chest. "Phil," she cries. "PHIL! WAKE UP!"

"Abby, he's not g-going to make it," I stutter, reaching for her back. *What do we do?* I think, the voice in my head reaching higher volumes of confusion.

"Why the hell not?" she shouts as she wipes tears from her eyes. "Why wouldn't he make it when I'm still here? I'm still okay and I had some of the berries, too. When will I end up just like him?"

"You won't, but we have to get that poison out of your system before it gets you, too." Extending my hand toward her, I lift her to her feet. Though, I'm not entirely sure how to go about it. I guess, throwing up could be the easiest way to do that, but nobody wants to force themselves to throw up. That's not a pretty thing to do and knowing Abby, she'll be too terrified to even consider it.

"And how in the world do I do that?" she asks.

"You're gonna have to vomit."

Instantly pulling my hand away, she angrily steps back. "I'm not going to do that."

"You're gonna have to," comes a voice from the trees. "If you don't throw up, you'll die just like him."

Trying to catch a better glimpse of the woman in the shadows, I mumble, "Elise," beneath my breath. The faint tone of my voice instantly alerts the woman.

". . .Sam?" she asks.

"Elise?" I respond, tears welling in my eyes.

"I can't believe it's you, but we'll catch up shortly. You have to throw up," says Elise. Motioning toward Abby, she furrows her brows, "You don't want to end up like him, do you?"

"No," cries Abby, her voice trailing off as more tears soak her eyes. "I-I-I'm scared," she stutters.

"It's going to be alright. You can go over into the trees and do it on your own. We'll be right here."

Heading off the path and into the woods, Abby kneels down beside a fallen tree and starts to stick her finger into her mouth. I look away.

"Sam, did you eat whatever they ate, too?"

"No. When they said the raspberries were sour, I made sure not to eat any. I hate sour foods."

"That was a good decision on your part. Now, what's the girl's name?"

36

"Her name is Abby."

"And how do you know her?"

"I took Separation class with her and she met me on my walk to the door and said that we should stick together."

"Sounds like she's a smart girl, aside from the fact that she ate some poison berries," smirks Elise.

"Yea, she's not too bad," I say. I turn my head back over at Abby crying as she sits over a pool of red. I want to console her, but I'm just as grossed out by the situation as she is.

"It's all going to be okay," says Elise. Turning to face Abby, she grins. "I've been there, too."

"When did you get poisoned?" I ask as Elise moves toward Abby.

"It's a long story," she replies, patting Abby on the back. "You're going to be fine, Abby." Lifting her up from her knees, she helps her walk back toward me.

Abby sniffles and itches her cheek. Her eyes wander away from mine.

I want to say something, but I don't know what. I feel out of place, uncertain of my emotions. *We barely knew him,* I think.

Abby coughs and looks up at me. She doesn't speak.

I open my mouth to say something, but nothing comes out. *We barely knew him.*

"Are you going to be okay?" asks Elise, her stare focused on Abby.

Abby nods.

Even with what just happened, I can't help but feel safe. I'm confused and disoriented, but I don't feel scared or sad. I just feel like things can only get better. Even with only three of us, there's something about the presence of an experienced outsider that makes me feel invincible. I'm starving and need some sleep, but there's an aura around Elise that is undeniably safe.

"Where do we go from here?" I ask as I drape my arm around Abby's back as she wipes her mouth.

"Nowhere," responds Elise.

29 August 2191

Elise

It's been two days since I found Sam—two days in which we haven't accomplished anything. We've discussed the clicks and what life is like on the outside, but that's nothing in the grand scheme; that's hardly an introduction to this world. Nor is the fact that we've only caught two squirrels and found some fresh blueberries. That's barely enough for one person, let alone three.

"So are you ever going to tell us how you were poisoned?" asks Sam as he lies on his back in the ankle-high grass. "I'm just curious why it's such a long story. I mean, our story wasn't that long. They ate some berries and got sick. That's really all it was."

I want to lie and say mine was the same way, but it wasn't. It's not that simple. Sam's still fourteen and I feel if I tell him the real story, he'll want to explore the city and that's not something he's ready to do. It's not something anybody should ever want to do, but it's something you eventually learn about whether you want to or not. That's how the outside works; that's how the city works. Everything finds a way to creep into your life.

I itch my shoulder, the grass digging into my neck. I know I should advise him against doing what I did, but at the same time I can't keep the reality of the city out of his future. He has eleven years in this ridiculous wasteland and it only makes sense for him to learn everything there is to know about it—even if it pains me to recall that moment.

Slowly opening my mouth, I close it as a light breeze rolls through the area. "I'm not really sure how to start this story," I whisper aloud to myself.

"Start from wherever you want to," mutters Sam, his eyes closing, the sun beaming across his cheeks.

"Well, I was in the city."

Instantly, Abby cuts me off. "There's a city? I thought there were only woods out here."

"Nope. There's a city, too. It's not a place I recommend that you visit, though. It's full of vagrants who are looking to rob, hurt, or murder you. From what I was taught, it used to be a major city over a hundred years ago."

"You were taught about a city?" interjects Abby. "We weren't."

"Really?" I ask.

"Really," replies Abby. "We weren't taught much of anything about this forest."

I roll over and look perplexed at Abby. "That's odd."

"I guess so," mutters Sam. "Though, if it's not a place you would recommend then why did you go there?"

I knew he was going to ask that question. It's not my fault I was just as naive as any other fourteen-year-old ten years ago. I had no idea what I would encounter out here.

"I was curious," I respond. "I was out on my own since I didn't think about partnering up like you two." Pausing, I take a deep breath. Something about just starting this story irritates my stomach; it makes me a bit nauseous. "I ended up walking for days and saw nothing more than trees everywhere I went. I knew that if they sent us outside for eleven years that there had to be more than just the forest outside of Nimbus. I knew that there was something beckoning us to come, so I kept walking until I found the city."

The city was a nasty place, too. Every building was run-down and covered in vines and moss while trees were growing into broken windows everywhere. The streets were overrun with dirt-laced cars, cracked pavement, and a putrid scent that I can't even begin to describe. Yet, as appalling as it was, something about it was compelling enough to make me want to explore it more. *Something wanted me to explore.*

"When I got to the city, I met a guy named Arthur. He was sitting on a park bench on the first street I stepped onto. Right when I walked past him, he got up and he came to me asking if I knew what I was doing. I told him I was just exploring and he told me to turn around. Naturally, I didn't listen and I kept walking."

"Sounds like you probably should have listened to him," says Abby. "Did he at least seem nice?"

I probably should have listened, but something deeper in the city was calling my name. A metaphoric phone was ringing in my head waiting for me to answer, so it could tell me to stop. But once I picked it up, nobody answered and I kept going. "He did."

Gently rolling onto my side, I look at Sam and Abby as they lie next to each other with their pinkies entwined. Abby's eyes latch onto mine. Seemingly attempting to read my expressions, she half-smiles and nods for me to continue. Rolling back over, I brush a stray hair from my forehead while my lips almost unwillingly dive back into that abhorrent nightmare.

"I probably should have listened, Abby, but something was calling my name." I pause. The subtle chill of the breeze makes the hairs on my arms stand up. I exhale and speak again. "And the more I walked, the darker it became. The farther I got, the quicker the sun faded behind the buildings. With what little daylight I had left, I searched for a spot to hide—somewhere I could see. That's when I saw the silhouette of flames in an alley."

"Elise, this story is already starting to get pretty scary. I don't even know why you would stay in such a bad place for longer than ten minutes," says Sam. "Also, why would you look for light, doesn't that spell trouble?"

"Yea, it should," I mutter to myself. "I don't really know what I was thinking, but something was pulling me in. Something in my head kept telling me to walk farther." It felt like someone was holding my hand and guiding me toward the fire, like they were leading me to safety.

"Keep going. I want to hear what happens next," chips in Abby as she inches closer to Sam.

Taking a deep breath, I stare into the sky. A part of me wants to stop now while the other insists I continue. I know if I stop, they might end up in the city someday. If I stop, they'll never stop asking me to relive it. *Keep going*, I tell myself.

"I started walking toward the fire when a voice from ahead started calling my name. I don't know how anyone knew my name other than Arthur, but he was miles away. There's no way he could have made it to that same location that I was at unless he had been following me. Plus, he told me to leave, so why would he be there? It didn't make much sense to me at the time—nor does it now—so I kept walking."

My head starts to throb. I bury my thumb in the ridge of my nose between my eyes. The aching slows the harder I press, but it ceases to flee. I grab a blueberry from my pocket and start to suck on it. Quickly, the taste of the succulent fruit soothes me. I reach for another.

"'Elise,' came the voice again. I then asked if it was Arthur and the voice didn't respond. He just kept calling my name and when I reached the fire nobody was there. I spun in circles, but I couldn't find anyone and then all of the sudden everything went black."

Just reaching this point in the story makes my body ache; it makes the pain resurface and I can't push it away. Sean's the only other person whom I've told about this and even he was unsure what exactly drew me to that place. In his eleven years out here, he was never in the city more than a couple times. He struggled just like I did when he was sent out, but he never dared to venture toward the fire. He was smart enough to hide.

"What happens next?" asks Sam.

Drawn back to the throbbing in my head, I gently caress the sides of my temple with my thumbs. I tell him to wait for a moment before I jump back in.

"Okay, Sam. The thing that happens next is the whole reason why I don't want either of you to go into the city. What I'm about to tell you should be enough of a reason to keep you out. Now, I want both of you to promise me that you will never ever go there," I say, emphasizing the 'ever.' Rolling over, I lock eyes with Sam before switching to Abby.

"I promise I'll never go to the city," says Sam; Abby nods simultaneously.

"Good," I mutter. "When I awoke again after passing out, I was in a dimly lit room. The walls were littered with incoherent writings and symbols, while a stray journal sat propped up against the wall behind me. There was a torch against the wall to my side and I was sitting on a very damp floor in nothing but my underwear. My hands were tied up in some sort of twine while my legs were wrapped in the same thing. There was nothing in my mouth, so I started to scream and plead for help, but nobody came."

With their mouths agape, Sam and Abby stare in awe while my mind wanders in all directions. I don't want to say any more, but I have to. I have to ensure they never enter that city and this. . .this is the hardest part to tell. I almost want to stop now. *Keep going.*

"Eventually, a man came in through a steel door to my right. He was wearing all black and I couldn't make out his face. He mentioned my name and then he said that they had stolen my things and that there was a poison coursing through my body. He said that I had less than ten minutes to live and then he went back out the door, leaving me in that room."

"Wh-what happened next?" stutters Abby, her eyes diverting away from mine as if she's thinking about her own experience, her own horror.

Give me a second, I think.

"Naturally, I freaked out and started biting at the twine on my hands. Like a rabid dog, I chewed right through it. Once I got that off, I untied my feet and knew what I had to do. I made myself throw up. It hurt at first, but I knew that it was the only thing I could do if I wanted to make it out of there alive."

The memory becomes tangible. I can feel the veins in my neck pulsing, the sweat dampening my forehead, and the spit trying to force itself past my lips. I take a breath.

"After that, I grabbed the torch off the wall and tried to find a way out of the room. All I could see were the words, 'Shadow Lurkers,' written on the wall in all black next to the door. I started to pound on the door begging for them to let me out, but nobody responded. Strangely enough, I tried to pull on the door to unlock it and it worked. Apparently they don't lock it when they poison people because they feel that nobody will get out. At least that's the feeling I got from it," I say. With another breeze rolling through the open field, the grass lilts in the wind around us.

"Are these people a cult? Is there more to it?" asks Sam.

"They're something. . ." I mumble as I wipe my forehead. "Once I got the door open, I ran into another dark room where my clothes were sitting on a wooden table. I set the torch down and put my clothes back on before I ran back out into that same alley with the torch in hand. I didn't hear my name again and I didn't see a burning fire. The sky was gray and it had to have been a day or so later. I ended up throwing the torch back into the room and then I sprinted to the end of the alley until I saw a hill and started running up it. After that, I ended up back in the woods by myself, hoping that there was nothing else in my system."

"I can't believe that happened. That's really what the city is like?" asks Abby, her eyes bewildered. Clenching her hand into a fist, she sits up. "Why would anyone bother to go there?"

"I'm not sure, but that's exactly why I don't want you two to ever wander that far away." Sitting up, I curl in my knees. I tuck my hair behind my ears and look off to the side. "Whatever exactly happened that day, I'll never know, but I know for certain that something isn't right in the remnants of that city and something is wrong with those who trust it."

6 September 2191

Sean

In the eleven days since Sam's departure, MacMillan has had us kill at least twenty harmless kids who've tried to get past the wall; eleven days of constant watch hoping that nobody else will try to break back in. When I was first separated, I had no desire to come back. The thought of returning to the one place that kicked me out without any justifiable reason never crossed my mind. I missed my family, but we're taught what happens if you try to return too early. This year, nobody seems to understand the consequences of tempting the fate of Separation.

"Keep your eyes peeled," says MacMillan from behind me as he makes his rounds. "Don't hesitate to shoot anyone or anything you see. I don't care if they're just waltzing around hundreds of yards away. If you can see them in your scope, they're too close."

"Got it, sir," I reply firmly.

With my gun at my side, I peer out over the wall and into the forest below. I aimlessly squint at anything that looks like an appendage or the makings of a face, but nothing stands out. Even if I do see someone, I'm not going to shoot. The only time I'll kill someone who's not a threat is when MacMillan is looking directly over my shoulder telling me to pull the trigger. Even then, I don't want to do it, but risking my place in the Elite Guard for something so foolish is hardly a good idea. Concealing my disapproval is easier.

Sometimes I wish I didn't work for the Guard. Sometimes I wish I worked as a carpenter or a blacksmith. The simplicity of a life void of murder seems like the greatest reprieve after surviving my eleven years. *It's not like I had a choice*, I think as I shake my head.

44

The Guard was the best fit. Even with my ability to shoot, fight, and survive, I'd almost rather spend more time out there than any more time up here regretting every time I pull the trigger.

"You going to shoot that?" whispers MacMillan, his fragile shoulders leaning next to mine.

"Shoot what, sir?"

"That little girl prancing over there a few hundred yards away," he says as his teeth start to grind against each other. "Shoot her."

"She's hundreds of yards away, sir. She's not a threat. She's moving even farther away," I say, knowing that he won't care.

"That's an order."

Pulling my sniper rifle up toward my eyes, I close my left and hold my breath to steady my shot. With the girl's chest between my crosshairs, I gently lower my barrel. I intentionally fire near her feet. She flees deeper into the woods.

"What was that bullshit?" MacMillan shouts.

"Sorry, sir, I figured I should scare her away rather than kill an innocent girl."

"I don't care what you figured. You pull that kind of crap with me here again and you'll be off perimeter duty immediately. You hear me?" he says, his veins tightening in his old, wrinkly neck. He's staring hard enough that it looks like his eyes will pop out of his head at any moment.

"Loud and clear; it won't happen again."

"It better not or you'll be the furthest thing from the Elite Guard when I'm through with you."

Unsure of what exactly he means, I lower my weapon to the side and lean against the wall once more. MacMillan slowly strides away as he keeps his expressionless gaze on me before nearing another person.

By the time he's out of sight, two more errant outsiders walk within a hundred-yard range of the wall, but I don't even consider pulling up my weapon. MacMillan's murderous ways are the way of the Elite Guard, but they're not the way I want to work. Killing harmless, defenseless outsiders is not my way of showing my power. Killing MacMillan would be the easiest way to do that.

10 September 2191

Sam

Small red birds fly overhead as a mild wind brushes through the field. Whenever the cardinals pass, a storm is sure to follow. Fluttering nearby, they swarm toward an old oak tree behind us before carefully landing on one of its longer branches. Like the birds, I feel that we're in search of something better, something stronger than ourselves.

Though, I'd just prefer a day without rain and intense heat. Even hiding in a canopy can't keep you away from the flare in the sky.

I look back at Elise and Abby conversing while I stray around plucking the tops off the wheat around me. An impulse to duck beneath the plants and sneak up behind the two of them consumes me, but I shake off the idea as Elise calls my name from behind.

"Sam," she says.

"What?"

"What do you want to do today?" she asks. With her black jacket wrapped around her waist, her arms stretch freely above her head.

"What can we do? We've done nothing but wander around for what has to be at least a week," I say as I pick another head from its stalk.

"There's an old railroad a few miles ahead if I remember correctly. I had my third click when I was walking down it. Fell and hit my head on the rocks. Wasn't a solid seventeenth birthday by any means," she laughs, her bright blue eyes widening the more she thinks about it.

"Let's go there," agrees Abby, her eyes looking into the distance while her hands playfully brush alongside the wheat.

"That sounds like a good idea to me, too."

Bringing her arms downward, Elise sarcastically says, "Onward!" before tilting her head down and walking forward.

At least a dull trek through an endless field of wheat is better than lying down in it, starting a relentless itch. I look above; the clouds swarm together as the gloomy sky takes shape ahead of us. With a constant wind, the heads of wheat rub against my jeans as I walk toward the storm.

Despite what's coming, Elise's positive attitude has kept my mind clear; it's allowed us to just be kids. After all, that's what we are.

MacMillan may want to take that away from us by sending us out here, but it's not something he has the ability to take. He thinks he always has the upper hand because he's instilled fear, but that doesn't mean he's killed us. That doesn't mean he's right and we're wrong. All it means is he's won the first eleven rounds, but round twelve is when we win—when we get the knockout. It's when we get to see everyone who knew what we were capable of—what he figured we'd die trying to fight.

Then again, MacMillan might be too old now to even survive his next eleven years. I guess, maybe we do have the upper hand after all. Maybe being a kid is good for something.

But none of that matters because I will always miss growing up behind the wall regardless of who's in charge. I itch the back of my neck. *I wonder what it's like back home right now.* Sean. Mom. Dad. *What are they doing without me? Is it like I never existed or are they just trying not to think about me as I try to not think about them?* The thought of home is painful. My head twinges with the image of playing catch in the backyard with Dad, dinner conversations over Mom's lasagna, and running through the streets of Nimbus without a care in the world. If only I could turn back right now and go see them—but that's impossible. Dying to go home isn't worth dying to get home.

Taking my hatchet out from my belt, I start slicing nearby stalks until a clearing of trees presents itself ahead of us.

"We have to be getting close," says Elise. Taking a few steps ahead, Elise looks around the area. Abby's eyes catch mine as she steps beside me. I manage a soft smile.

"I like her," mumbles Abby. "She's really cool."

"She's pretty great. I don't know where we would be without her right now," I reply.

"Probably in the city," says Abby, an expression of dread crossing her face.

"I wouldn't be surprised," I mutter.

"Neither would I, so it's good that's not the case. I can't imagine what it'd be like there with just us. . .if we were still together," she cuts off. I catch her eyes with mine before she drifts her stare to the right.

"We would be."

"Anything can happen out here," replies Abby. "There aren't any guarantees."

I don't reply. I just keep my focus on the ground, nodding alongside her; my hands lightly sweat. Without Elise, Abby could've died like Phil. Without Abby, I wouldn't know what to do. Two weeks ago, I thought I would be fine on my own, but if I didn't have these two with me right now, I'm certain I would be nearing in on the city. . .if I was still alive.

Abby steps closer to me with each step; her fingers dance in the wind. Time seems to speed up as more trees shadow our walk.

"I remember it was just past a pair of oak trees growing into each other in the shape of a half diamond," says Elise. With her eyes glued to the forest ahead, she pulls out a small ebony-handled knife and shushes us behind her.

Lying low as we crouch behind her, she lowers her right hand, motioning for us to remain still. The faint sound of leaves cracking echoes in the distance.

"I think there's someone ahead," whispers Elise. "Stay low and keep quiet. We'll try to get around them."

Slightly peeking my head up, I can vaguely make out a soft crimson scarf wrapped around a girl's neck while a man cloaked in all black tags along behind her. Yet, the closer I look, the clearer it becomes. The man's tugging on the end of her scarf while her hands tremble at her sides. I gently rub my eyes, hoping to see the situation better. Elise whispers for us to keep moving.

We continue to slowly move along as the woman shrieks. Faded cries of "help me, help me" echo through the trees as Elise motions for us to look away. "Keep moving, you two," she softly says.

"Shouldn't we go help her?" clamors Abby.

"No. We have to move along as if it never happened."

"Why?"

"It could be a setup. That whole incident could be staged and there could be more of them surrounding those two. We have to keep going forward."

They're too far away to even consider helping at this point, but Abby can't stop staring at the helpless woman as she falls onto her knees. I reach for her fingers, but before I can get ahold of her hand, she jolts. Fumbling with her small knife, she sprints toward the pair.

"Ab–" I yell before Elise cuts me off. Pulling out her bow, she stands up and drags an arrow back toward her ear. With a calm breath, she releases. The arrow sails through the trees and strikes the man in the neck. Before Abby can approach the woman, another bolt flies just over her stray curls of hair forcing the woman face down in the dirt next to the man.

"I told her not to go," says Elise sharply. Wrapping the bow around her shoulders, she runs toward Abby.

I stand up and follow. Just ahead, Abby flings herself onto her knees. *Why didn't she listen? Why couldn't she just understand that Elise knows more about this world than we do?* She must've thought there was a way she could prevent seeing another person die. She had to have thought she could avoid experiencing such harsh emotions for a second time already. *She didn't even know them,* I think.

Glaring behind Abby, Elise asks, "Why did you move when I told you not to?" Short of breath, her cheekbones raise toward her arched eyebrows.

"You didn't have to shoot her!" yells Abby.

"I couldn't be certain she wasn't a threat."

"She was being strangled by him," cries Abby, her eyes darting toward the man on his side. "She didn't do anything wrong!"

"Abby. You can't trust anyone outside of us out here. I've seen setups like this happen where innocent kids get lured into trying

49

to be the hero and they end up the victim sooner than you can snap your fingers. You have to listen to me when I tell you not to move. If you don't, you could end up like both of them."

"Maybe that's where I belong."

"Don't say that, Abby," I chime in from behind them.

"Why not? Everyone out here dies at some point. Everyone behind the wall dies at some point. There's about a 3 percent chance that I'll make it out of here alive and be allowed re-entrance into Nimbus. There's a 3 percent chance I'll get to see my family again. I'm just going to end up like these two people I don't even know in the end anyways," she cries.

My body tenses up; my mouth starts to dry. I want to say something helpful, but I can't. This is uncharted territory—just being around girls this much is new. I don't want to say something stupid. And I definitely don't want to bring up the fact that the odds at least give us all a 10 percent chance.

Looking over the crimson scarf loosened on the woman's neck, Abby starts to unwrap it. Pulling it along the dirt, she sniffles as the last of it slides across the nape of the lady's neck.

"What are you doing?" I mutter.

"She doesn't need it anymore," sniffles Abby, her nose reddening to an identical color of the scarf.

Lifting up the cloth, she folds it in half and throws it over her shoulders. Tucking the loose ends into the hole formed in the middle of the strip, she tightens the scarf around her neck.

"Are you going to be okay, Abby?" asks Elise.

"I don't know. I don't want to see anyone die anymore."

"Nobody does," I say, knowing that it's something that can't be stopped. Thousands of kids are on the outside trying to fend off death just as we are, even when they know it can't be avoided. Eventually, the darkness grasps ahold of all of us whether we're ready or not. "You just can't do that again, Abby. I don't want to lose you, too."

"Let's just keep moving," she says.

We oblige. Nobody speaks.

Time may have shifted slowly before, but now it seems eager to move. The darkened clouds hover above the trees while we move forward; a burst of blinding lights streak across the sky illuminating various creatures burrowing into the night.

50

I remember the first storm we experienced on the outside. It was surprisingly cold for this time of year and my shoes are still recovering from being soaked. There's nothing I can do to dry my sneakers; I can just hope this storm doesn't compare to that one.

"I think I see the tracks just up ahead," says Elise. With her hands gripping the string of her bow, she slowly moves forward.

Finally. Ever since we stepped into the woods, I was unsure if we would find the railroad. I trust Elise, but you can't memorize everything out here in ten years. With the damp air nagging at my chest, I peel my shirt outward from my wet skin. Holding it there, I start to lightly fan myself.

"What do we do when we get to the tracks? I think the storm is about to start," says Abby, her hands aimlessly playing with the loose ends of the scarf.

"We'll have to find shelter. I remember a shack nearby. If there's no one in it, we can stay there for a while," responds Elise.

"Okay," I reply. Another bright stroke of yellow highlights the sky.

The more we walk, the more Elise's statement about the tracks being just ahead seems like a lie. My feet begin to slow as the weight of mud accumulated on my shoes starts to thicken. Kicking off the clumps, I stop at a tree and begin to wipe off my shoes. The clouds start to pour. Ugh.

"We better get moving," shouts Elise, the rain muffling her voice in the distance. I guess wiping my shoes off has become a useless tactic at this point. "I see the rails," she says.

Nodding beside her, Abby shouts above the rain, "Me too."

Still unsure what they're looking at, I nod my head. I take a few steps toward them—Elise unraveling her jacket, Abby pulling her hood above her head—when the rusty track presents itself several yards away. We jog toward the rails as the mud thickens on my shoes, the rain continually washing into it. My socks start to cling to my soles.

"We need to find somewhere soon or I'm going to lose my shoes," I say as Elise pulls her jacket up and over her already-wetted hair.

With a few more steps, I make it out of the mud and onto the rocks surrounding the tracks. Still, I feel like I'm walking in complete mush.

"This way," says Elise pointing down the right side of the rails.

Her eyes waver as she makes herself certain that that's the right way to go. Sticking to what she said, she starts to work her way down the railroad with Abby and I trailing behind her.

With each step on the splintered wood beside the rocks, I can't help but feel that something is going to make its way through my shoes and into my foot. I don't want to push my luck, so I hop onto the rail and begin to slowly balance my walk.

As the sound of rain clatters against the rusted steel, vast streaks of light consume the sky while powerful claps of thunder continue to shake the ground.

"Do you know where you're going?" asks Abby. Squinting forward, she tries to focus on Elise.

Her eyes still shifting side to side in search of the shack, Elise quickly looks over at us. "You two should probably get off the steel," she says. "It's probably not a good idea to be walking on it with all this lightning."

I look over into Abby's eyes—her pupils dilate and she jumps off onto the rocks. I step off, too, knowing that there's a slim chance I make it out of this with two shoes. The rain continues to reverberate off the rails, muting my attempt to ask if I can walk between the rails. I don't and instead try to find the shack. With nothing but more trees in my line of sight, a small piece of white makes its way into my peripherals.

"Is that it?" I ask. Elise nods. It looks like something you would read about in an old mystery novel from the twentieth century, not something you would want to venture into. "I think I would rather just stay outside," I joke.

"You're more than welcome to, but if you want a place to dry off, that's our only hope for now," shouts Elise. With her hands held against her hood, she speed walks toward the place.

I move toward Abby. My hand grazes hers.

"What if there's someone in it?" asks Abby.

"Then they'll have to get out," replies Elise.

Abby glances at me with a cold look of despair as we near the rundown shack.

"Who's going in first?" I ask, stepping closer toward the blackened wood of the front door.

"Not me," replies Abby as she maneuvers behind me and gently lays her fingers into the palm of my hand. I clasp my fingers on hers.

"I think we all know the answer to that question," Elise says. I hold her stare as she pulls a knife from her belt. "You two wait here."

Elise

I don't know what Sam and Abby were so afraid of. There's nothing in this place outside of a few spiders. Just a few black, eight-legged creatures that are more terrified of me than I am of them. At this point, I'd rather bunk with them than head back into the rain.

Turning around, I slightly wedge open the front door and signal for Sam and Abby to come in. The sooner they get in, the sooner I can start a fire to warm us up—one that will make our new roommates scurry away.

"Are you sure there's no one in here?" asks Abby, shivering as she leans against Sam.

"I'm certain. If someone is, then they're very good at hiding," I joke. "Now, take off whatever you want me to dry and I'll start a fire, so we can warm up."

Just beside the entryway lies a soot-covered fireplace. As dark as the night sky, the soot consumes every inch of the brick. Grabbing a lighter from my pocket, I ignite the two pieces of firewood already in place.

"Where did you get that?" asks Sam, motioning toward the lighter while he takes off his sweatshirt.

"Your brother gave it to me," I say.

"Where did he get it?"

"I have no clue. He just knew I would need it, so he gave it to me before he got pulled out to take his return test."

Casually nodding as his eyes wander around, Sam pulls his shirt over his head and places it a few feet away from the burning logs. After spreading out the sleeves, he slowly starts to sit down and cross his legs. He positions himself, lightly sighs, and blankly stares into the flames. I open my mouth to ask him what's bothering him, but before I can speak, a clap of thunder erupts.

"Were you going to say something?" asks Abby as she takes a seat beside Sam. Stretching out the scarf to her left, Abby simultaneously pulls her damp bangs from her eyes.

"Nothing important," I reply.

Slowly resting her head into the palms of her hands, she turns toward me and asks, "So, what happened after you got out of the city?"

Unsure how to really answer the question, I head toward a broken chair in the back corner of the room. Sitting against a dust-ridden table, the three-legged chair seems useless, so I kick off one of the legs—instantly causing Sam and Abby to turn around.

Placing my hand on the seat of the chair, I yank off the broken leg. With the splintered wood in my hand, I step between them and toss it into the fire.

"That's when I met Sean. Well, a few days after that," I say.

"Then what happened before you met him?" asks Abby, her eyes mirroring the dancing flames.

A lot happened before I met Sean when I got out of the city. I found out what exactly happened to me inside that egregious room—something I won't elaborate on—and I almost died trying to scavenge some food, *but do Sam and Abby really need to know my struggles? Do they really need to know how I've almost died numerous times on the outside?* I don't want to frighten them to the point that when I leave they can't survive, but there's so much they need to know—even if it's not what they want to hear; even if it's not what I want to say.

"What do you want to know first? What happened the day I met Sean or what happened right when I escaped from the city?"

"What happened after you escaped them?" questions Sam. Turning his neck, he looks at me with a sense of intrigue—one not common out here. "What happened when the Shadow Lurkers figured out you didn't die in there?"

"I don't really know what they did, but I knew something wasn't right. I kept feeling like someone was still following me," I say as I bend down and cross my legs next to Sam.

The more I think about that moment, the more the nightmare retraces its steps, forcing a slight headache to pound against my forehead.

"Was there someone following you?" questions Abby.

"I'm not sure. No one has ever appeared and tried to take me back," I say. Unlatching my quiver, I lay my arrows down beside me. "At least, I hope somebody isn't following me." Suddenly, the once-innocuous throbbing begins to press harder above my eyes.

"So what happened then?" Abby asks with a random shiver as she scoots closer to the fire. "Nobody followed you out, so what did you do?"

"I just kept running. I ran as far into the forest as I could," I say, the fire crackling loudly, mimicking the storm. "I came here."

Shying away, I stare directly at the fire. As I allow the heat to warm my aches, the memories flood in like a volcano. This place was just as unclean the first time around; the floors were a little less muddied though—I blame that on Sam and Abby. The fireplace had two pieces of wood in it from the last person who hid here and after I ran through those, I put two more in. Each time I come back, two pieces of fresh firewood await me, presuming no one else enters. So far, it appears no one has found my favorite place to hide.

The last time I was here, it was just Sean and I. Not so much as a dust bunny accompanied our stay. Aside from my arrows and the clothes on my back, I didn't have anything. Sean at least had a knife, hook, and lighter. Other than that, we had virtually nothing, which is why we had to leave the shack again.

"What?" asks Abby. "You've been here before?"

"A few times before," I say.

"Have you ever run into anyone else here?" asks Sam as he begins to fall back into the palms of his hands next to Abby.

"Not yet," I mutter.

Despite being alone my first time here, I had Sean with me every time after. We would come back a few times a year for a week or so then venture out to find different sources of food, clothes, and weapons. We typically struggled to find weapons, but we would always find a new berry—sometimes inedible, but new nonetheless. Every second outside of the safety of this shack tightened our bond; it helped me see light in a world of shadows.

As I fidget with the end of one of the arrows, the ache continues. Gently rubbing my hands against the sides of my head, the pulse shifts around.

"That's good," he says. "That makes me feel much safer. Maybe we should just stay here for a while then."

56

"I suppose we could. At least then we would have somewhere to hide out until this storm passes."

Right as I speak, a deafening crack of thunder echoes throughout the atmosphere as the firewood quakes in its path. Soot begins to fall from atop the fireplace, dropping onto the fire, instantly putting out the heat.

Fumbling with the lighter in my hands, I reach toward the hot ash as I try to relight what uncovered wood might still burn. After a few failed attempts, the timber starts to heat up. The flames slowly emerge in front of us.

Shaking off the thunder, Sam rolls onto his side. Staring at the split floorboards momentarily, he closes his eyes briefly and looks at me. "What happened the day you met my brother?"

"A lot," I say as I stand up to break another leg off the useless chair. Trying to discern the chair from the table in the faint light, I throw my arms in front of me like Frankenstein's monster. Eventually locating the back of the chair, I pry off another wooden leg. Turning back toward the fire, I gently toss it into the yellowy pit.

"Like what?" asks Sam.

"First off, I woke up right there where you're sitting now. I knew since I hadn't eaten in days and anything I had eaten before had been expelled from my body, I had to leave this place to find something to eat."

The sound of the rain begins to slow as the clouds outside the window turn from a dark gray into pitch black.

"I was very weak when I first woke up. I don't know how long it had been since I had last eaten, but I knew if I didn't eat soon, I would probably die."

Sam picks up his shirt and pulls it back down over his head.

I itch the top of my head before running my fingers through my scalp. My hair is beginning to dry, but it still clumps together in my hands.

"Elise," I hear as I start to pull my hair up above my head.

"What?" I respond.

Tilting his head, Sam looks at me confused. "We didn't say anything."

I must be hearing things again. I haven't heard the faint whisper of my name since before I ran into Sam. Yet, there it was again, finding a way to be annoying.

"I must be hearing things. It's okay though. It's nothing," I say with a hint of sarcasm.

Keeping his head crooked as his puzzled eyes stare at me, Sam itches his cheek. Re-positioning himself, he settles his head into the palm of his hands with his elbows propped up on the floor.

Jumping back into where I left off, I start to speak again. "Once I got up, I went outside to find some small game or some berries to eat. I came across a few blueberries a couple hundred yards away from this place, so I ate those. But they weren't that filling. I could feel my energy coming back a bit, so I tried to find something with some meat on its bones. That's when I saw a rabbit."

At that moment, I felt a sensation course through my body like I hadn't seen meat in years. I'll never forget how every glimpse of the small animal turned into nothing but a piece of meat. It was as if I was chasing an already braised turkey, just waiting for me to catch it and savor it.

"Right when I saw it, I pulled out an arrow and started creeping toward it. But, I was insatiable, so the closer and closer I got without scaring it away, the more irrational I became. When I was within a dozen yards or so, I aimlessly started shooting arrows at it. I missed several, but one caught it in the neck. When I got to the dying animal, I leaned down to pick it up and that's when a sharp pain pierced my stomach. Everything went black after that."

Thrusting my hand toward my waist, I place it on my abdomen. As I press the palm of my hand against the scar, the pain resurfaces. Like it just happened, the sheer agony of the sharp stick progresses through my stomach and into my thighs.

"Are you okay?" asks Abby.

Shaking my head, I say, "I'm fine. It's just that. . .that was when I saw the face of the man I saw in the city. That's when I saw Arthur."

Sam and Abby's eyes light up. I close my eyes; the pain fades away.

"After that, I don't remember much. I woke up the next day and Sean was there with me. He had patched up my wound and he had cooked some rabbit meat for me."

"What happened to Arthur?" questions Sam.

"I don't know. Sean never really told me. He just said that he hurt him, but he got away. Sean had a few scratches on his arms, but he was fine."

"Have you seen Arthur since?" asks Sam as he sits up.

"I haven't, so I don't know where he is or what he's doing, but I can't help but think it's his voice that I keep hearing say my name; it's him who could be following me. But why?"

"I don't know. He seems to have it out for you since you got away from him the first time, but no worries. You have us here too and it's been years since you last saw him, so he's probably long gone by now anyways."

"You're probably right, Sam."

Trying to rid my mind of the visual of Arthur's greasy charcoal black hair and his wandering eyes, I can't help but think he's still out there, still chasing what he couldn't kill the first time.

20 September 2191

Sam

Days pass in an instant; nights seem never-ending. With constant darkness, this cramped shack steadily feels like it's getting smaller and smaller day by day.

"I'm tired of it always being so dark," says Abby.

"I am, too," I mutter. I feebly stand up, my ankles cracking in the process, before walking to the back of the room. Breaking off the remaining leg from the wooden chair, I snap it in half on my knee. I throw the smaller portion of it into the fire as I spin the other half in the palms of my hands. "Maybe we should try to find a lantern or something. There has to be some way we can brighten this place up."

Rolling her eyes, Elise says, "Getting more lights would attract unwanted visitors. You don't want that, do you?"

"Not really." I guess I just want what I had back in Nimbus. I miss electricity. I miss the freedom to roam at night without having to worry about being captured or murdered. I miss safety.

"That's what I thought. You should probably get some sleep, Sam. The sun will be up before you know it, so you won't have to worry about all this darkness bothering you."

"You're right," I say to Elise as she rolls onto her back, the decaying floorboards creaking beneath her.

But I'm not tired, not in the slightest. All we've accomplished in the past few days is catching a few rabbits while managing to find a few dirtied sleeping bags. It's not much, but it's something. Though, I don't like this constant sitting. It's like we're waiting for an answer that's avoiding us. Standing up, I head toward the door. Elise's sweaty hand grabs my ankle.

"What are you doing?" she asks, her eyes making frightening eye contact. Enough to make me think twice.

"I'm just making sure the door is locked," I say, even though I was kind of hoping to go outside into the fresh air for a bit regardless of how uncomfortable it is. It hasn't rained in a few days, but the humidity continues to ravage the area. Every minute outside feels like you're being sucked into an inescapable vacuum of moisture. Back at the shack, the holes in the glass don't help secure much freedom from the elements either. Just, something about being outside seems more appealing than lying in a damp sleeping bag hoping to fall asleep.

"It should be locked already. I locked it when we came back from hunting a few hours ago."

Nodding my head, I ignore Elise's exhausted eyes and step back into bed.

"It's okay. I can't sleep either," whispers Abby. Rolling onto her side, she continues, "I'm too hot. It's hard to sleep without a blanket of some sort, though."

"I know what you mean. I'm sweaty, but I feel like I have to keep at least one leg in this sleeping bag."

"The fire's dying, so maybe then this room will cool down a bit." Propping her arm up onto her elbow, she looks back at the deflated fire.

"Maybe," I mutter. "This heat makes me think of the Nimbus Founding Festival and the giant bonfire. It sucks that we have to miss it this year." The thought of missing the festival hadn't crossed my mind until today. With the flames slowly fading into the logs below me, the heat pressing against the bottoms of my feet starts to disappear. As a cool breeze finds its way through the cracks in the window, the dark orange of the fire vanishes. "I really wish we could be there."

"Me too. I'm going to miss the cotton candy and the games. I love playing Nimbus Nuisance at my parents' tent," says Abby, her rosy cheeks lifting toward her eyes, her mood seemingly improving.

"Is that the one where you shoot the water gun at the stick figures?" asks Elise as she rolls onto her side and into the conversation.

"Yea. It was MacMillan's idea for us to host that game, but it always drew in a lot of people," says Abby. "My brother was the best at it."

Everything's MacMillan's idea, I think. No family had a say in what tent they hosted at the festival; MacMillan chose everything. My family was in charge of the funnel cake stand every other year. Thankfully, I never had to work; I just got to run around.

As the smoke lifts into the air above me, the familiar scent of warm cider drifts into my nostrils. Lifting my head up to smell the air once more, I take a deep breath and inhale as the dry, smoky cloud wafts into my nose. Instantly coughing, I wipe my face. Still wishing the crisp apple scent was real, I close my eyes, but it doesn't come back.

"I don't know if anyone was better than me at that game, Abby," chortles Elise. "Actually, I was pretty bad at that game. I wasn't anywhere near as good at shooting then as I like to think I am now. I would be lucky to even graze one figure!"

Laughing, Abby and I shake our heads.

"I'm pretty sure I could at least hit two!" laughs Abby.

"How many did you have to shoot to win?" I ask.

"I think there were eleven. I remember MacMillan saying how he wanted everyone who played to know the value of that number."

"He has a point," says Elise sarcastically.

"True," I chime in. "I hate that number."

The smoke starts to clear from the room as a light rain begins to fall. The faded scent of ash expels itself from the shack. I lift my nose once more—hoping to smell cider or funnel cakes—only to smell the wormy scent of fresh rain in the ground.

"The festival has to be a few weeks away at this point," says Abby. "If only we could go back for that one day."

"That would be nice. Then, I could show you two how it's done at Nimbus Nuisance," smiles Elise.

"Sure you could. Sean would totally beat all of us," I grin.

"I'm telling you guys, my brother was the best. We had all the time to practice before the events started since it was our tent, so we would play it for hours before everyone showed up. I think he got all eleven five times in a row once. He was unstoppable, but then again that's all he would do. He sort of had an obsession with it," says Abby as her once-cheerful expression turns into a grimacing one.

"Why is that such a bad thing?"

"I don't know. He was just a little controlling about it when he talked about it. When the festival wasn't going on, he was always burning insects with a magnifying glass or trying to shoot down birds with his slingshot. He sort of had an obsession with beating down on something weaker than himself."

Confused by her changing tone, I watch as her head droops down and onto the cushion. By the time I lift my lips to respond, she's rolled onto her side facing the wall. My throat trembles as I consider speaking, but I don't. I'm afraid to ask Abby about him, afraid to bring up the past if it hurts her in any way.

Sitting up on her knees, Elise peers at Abby. "Are you okay?" she asks.

Quiet and still, Abby doesn't make a sound. Reaching for her shoulder, I clasp my hand onto the top of her shirt. She brushes it off.

Her voice shaking, Abby starts to murmur, "I'm fine. I'm fine." Still facing the wall, she continues, this time almost inaudibly. "He didn't hurt me. He. . .he killed our dog when I was five. I don't know why and I don't want to know why. He did it the day before his separation. I haven't seen him since and I don't care to see him ever again."

Staying still on her side, Abby pulls the sleeping bag above her head. Tightly wrapping it around her body, she becomes quiet.

"I'm sorry," I mutter—once again reaching for her shoulder, only to be denied. "We'll make sure you don't have to see him."

"We promise," says Elise softly. "You'll be safe with us."

21 September 2191

Elise

Out here, life doesn't have a true meaning. Life is about the buoyancy of the ship you're on. If you overload it with too much thought, your ship will sink and it will take you down with it. If you act naturally and let yourself be free then the thought of sinking should never cross your mind. Out here, life is what you make it, but if you try to do too much, you'll get pulled under.

I always try to avoid overthinking or overdoing, but whenever my headaches arise I can't help but feel that something outside of my control is causing it. Not an illness, but a person or a being of some sort. Every time my head hurts, the throbbing in my abdomen follows suit; it's almost as if Arthur is always with me. It's like he's trying to weigh me down until I collapse, until I sink into the abyss.

"Are you two up?" I ask, albeit muffled while I press my forehead into my sleeping bag, hoping the pulsing will disappear.

"No," comes a hushed voice from Sam.

"That's fine. You two keep sleeping. I'm going to go get us some breakfast."

Slowly standing up, I can feel the blood rushing into my head. The pain that was subsiding while I was lying down comes full steam ahead the instant I'm standing upright. I thrust my hands into my scalp and dig my nails into my head. *Go away!* The slight pressure somewhat relieves the tension as I try to relax. I inhale. I exhale. I wish the pain away.

Reaching for the door handle, a brownish-yellow spider scrambles across it. Swatting at the creature, I hit it onto the floor before I thrash it with my foot.

"What. . .what was that?" exclaims Sam. Rolling onto his back with one eye half-open, he awkwardly looks around.

"Nothing. Go back to sleep."

"O-okay," he says as he rolls back onto his stomach, taking his shirt off and using it as a pillow in the process.

Swiping the spider corpse out the door in front of me, I turn around and quietly pull the door shut. Softly dragging the wooden frame into the lock, I release the handle and turn around. The sun falls heavily upon me, the rays warming the cotton of my sweatshirt.

For once, the humidity is low as the sky shines bright. It's a perfect autumn morning in what has to be September by now. I can almost envision the festival taking place in the fields just behind the shack.

The vast canvas of blighted grass could host the soaring black and white striped tents while the food and game vendors set up shop around them. As the stakes slowly eased into the dirt, the area would transform into a one-of-a-kind event. An event so extraordinary, it makes life outside of Nimbus even more painful. If it wasn't bad enough, the thought of the only fun night in Nimbus makes it worse. If only the outside had a Founding Festival, but one without MacMillan, one without boundaries.

I casually start to stray away from the shack, my eyes locked onto the shaded forest. With wilting flowers and limp tree branches shaking their leaves everywhere, there's no doubt in my mind that it's September. The festival must be nearing. To think, in a year's time, I'll be back at the gala dressed in something much prettier than torn jeans and a jacket. Maybe a beautiful one-strap red gown with silver sequins dispersed throughout; something that would make everyone envious; something that would make Sean's jaw drop.

Being with him out here for several years, I never had the opportunity to truly impress him. I could hunt, I could fight, I could do anything to keep myself alive, but I couldn't change. The harsh reality of living outside limited our intimacy; it became an invisible barrier that made falling in love difficult. Everything about Sean—his dark green eyes, his smile, his attitude, his heart—captivated me from the day we met. Still, what Nimbus did to us put us both on edge; it made us fear being close to anyone, let alone each other. But, Sean was different; he saved my life.

Slowly making my way through the forest, I continue to stare aimlessly into the empty field. The farther I walk, the more I hope the pungent odor of freshly squeezed lemonade would just waltz into my nostrils, but it never does.

I turn away from the field. Trying to stave off the depressing thoughts of a lost life, I head a little farther into the forest. Looking every which way in search of some berries or even a squirrel, I squint around the area in an attempt to find something, anything really. At this point, anything edible would be considered a victory regardless of its flavor or lack thereof.

The more I walk, the less I see. There aren't any berries or any small animals; there isn't even a creek to collect rainwater from. The forest seems to be empty and unaware of its uselessness—the embodiment of MacMillan.

Strolling past a collapsed patch of branches, I press my palm into my forehead. The pulsing hasn't completely left and the beams of the nagging sun don't do much to soothe the irritation. Wiggling my hands on the side of my head, I take refuge near a giant oak tree hoping that the pain will prance away into the woods. Trying to force the throbbing out, I close my eyes.

***

Spinning into a whirlwind of black, the lights shine heavily upon the trapeze artists flying across the sky. The broken spotlight illuminates fragments of the pair, yet each face is obscured by the shadows. Effortlessly spinning and twisting through the air like it's water, the acrobats fly across the arena. Swimming through the sea of black, the woman flips as the man grabs her outstretched fingers and pulls her up to the bar.

Slowly lifting her waist above the bar, she sits on the swing as the man jumps onto the platform behind her. Closing her eyes, the woman kicks her legs back and forth until the swing becomes nearly horizontal over the ground. Standing up on the bar as it levels back out, she thrusts her arms outward, appearing ready for a dive onto the ground below. With her arms out, she falls forward toward the netting. Yet, before she plummets, her ankles wrap around the ropes

66

while the tops of her feet cling to the seat. Hanging upside down, the woman closes her eyes once more. She takes a deep breath; her arms loosely suspended beneath her.

Mesmerized in the sheer artistry of her movements, I quickly rub my eyes in sync with the acrobat. Slowly opening them back up, a nagging pressure starts to form atop my head. As I reach for my scalp, my arms instantly flail below my head. *What's going on? Where am I?* Agitated by the stress sinking further into my head, I look up. My feet rest—albeit a bit more tangled—atop the black beam the woman was hanging so beautifully from.

I try to shake my feet enough to loosen them from the rope, but they won't budge. My legs are locked in place while more artists fly freely above me. I'm stuck and no matter what I try to move, nothing happens. The throbbing pain grows stronger while I dangle without any control. I open my mouth and try to scream, but nothing comes out. My voice is empty and my body has become completely immobile. I'm trapped in a world of art as if I'm just a mere painting in a museum of sculptures. The odd one out, I'm unable to function as my surroundings. I try to scream once more, but nothing happens. The world keeps moving around me while I remain stuck in a painful mind game. I close my eyes.

***

"Elise, Elise, are you okay?" comes a familiar voice from behind me.

I open my eyes. Sam and Abby stand just above me. "What? I'm okay," I say.

"Why were you screaming?" asks Sam exhaustedly.

"What are you talking about?"

"We could hear you screaming from the shack. We thought you were in trouble. It sounded like you were dying," softly mutters Abby as she kneels down in front of me.

My hands tremble. "I just had a nightmare," I reply. Pulling myself up from the dirt, I look down as my feet sit perched atop of fallen tree trunk. "I was in some sort of circus. I was a trapeze artist and I couldn't move. I could feel my head aching, but I couldn't do anything about it. It was horrifying."

"Maybe you should head back to the shack and get some more rest and we'll search for berries today," says Sam.

"That's probably a good idea." I press my palms into the dirt, feebly getting to my feet. My legs are weak and my heart is racing while the thought of being trapped in that world sends shivers down my spine. *It was just a dream,* I think. Turning around, I slowly start to walk back toward the shack as Sam and Abby start to scavenge for the breakfast I was too lost to find.

4 October 2191

Sean

The sky is overrun with a vast blue that encompasses everything in sight—not even a stray cloud wanders into my peripherals. The sun is beaming down upon my neck, forcing the back of my suit to cling to and dampen my back. In an attempt to avoid overheating, I pull my shirt out of my pants and start to fan myself. *This feels great*, I think as I tilt my head back and enjoy the subtle breeze.

"You might want to tuck that back in," mumbles a voice from beside me.

"Why's that?" I ask.

"MacMillan's on his way up."

Quickly tucking my shirt back into place, I turn around toward the forest. With my gun at my side, I gaze through the empty outskirts of Nimbus while my shirt tightens against my skin. "This sucks," I mutter under my breath. I exhale and wipe my forehead.

If only it was colder.

Weather is something you never truly fear until you have nowhere to go. I know the lighter I left Elise will prove its worth throughout the changing seasons, but if they're without shelter, it'll be tough. And if Sam's without Elise, I don't know how long he'll make it. The cold can make a man go mad.

People fight for warmth and shelter wherever they can find it, and hundreds die trying to get back inside Nimbus. MacMillan always says that December is the busiest month for the Elite Guard because a lot of kids separated earlier in the year don't prepare for freezing temperatures. The kids sent out in November, December, and January are all ready for the weather, but the summer separations are never prepared. They're ill-advised by the warmth they're sent out in and aren't ready to freeze when cooler temperatures roll around. It seems their parents don't even have the heart to tell them to prepare, that the only person in charge of that kid's fate is himself or herself. And when you're fourteen, you're not ready for that much control—control that can be taken away in less than a day.

The upcoming months are full of screams as kids pound on the frigid steel, hoping their parents will hear their cries and bring them home. It will never happen. We have the ten-hit rule when it comes to slamming their fists into the wall. Kids should know that after we start firing, they should run. Sometimes I wish the rules weren't so strict—maybe switch it to twenty or thirty hits on the wall before we fire—but there's nothing I can do when MacMillan's always watching. I'm surprised he hasn't changed it to one-hit. Now, we're supposed to shoot if we see anyone within a hundred yards, so why he would let so many get close in the winter is beyond me.

It probably has something to do with a quicker cleanup. With fewer bodies in the fields, kids will think that area is safe. They'll linger. They'll rest. They'll die. All because MacMillan loves to limit the amount who get to take the re-entrance exam.

With his wretched stare constantly nagging the Guard, each new day increases my hatred of this job. I was specifically recruited due to my willingness to do anything in my power to survive on the outside, but I don't know how much more of it I can take. Killing innocents outside of Nimbus was different than killing them from the inside. Out there, I had to kill if I was going to make it back home. Up here, I don't have to kill because it doesn't impact me personally, but according to MacMillan, it does.

He insists that if I don't kill, the outsiders will never learn. They won't understand that Nimbus needs to be protected. The halo wrapped around this region is as big as his ego and if every inch of this wall isn't covered, then we're just as weak as them. *Them*. If we're not killing kids, we're weak. His logic never sits well with me. Killing fourteen-year-olds doesn't make you stronger; it makes you as weak as them. It shows that you're just a bully in a self-delusional world you created. It makes you evil. According to that logic, I'm becoming just as evil as him even though I kill against my own will. I kill because if I don't, I'll be killed.

There's no quitting the job you're assigned. Your skills outside dictate your work inside. If you so much as complain, the odds of your survival behind the wall are as low as they are outside. If you're not with MacMillan, you're against him and that doesn't reside well in his thick skull no matter the case.

"The colder months are coming, Sean," says MacMillan's bone-chilling voice from behind me.

Dressed in his all-black Elite Guard jacket laced with golden buttons up to his neck, he reeks of gin.

"Are you looking forward to December as much as I am?" he maliciously smirks.

"Sure," I mutter.

"Just sure? I figured you would be l-lookin' forward to killing all those stupid k-kidss," he drunkenly slurs.

"I don't want to kill them." Right as the words slip past my lips, I wish I could reach out and pull them back.

"What?" he says as his voice straightens back out. "You have to kill them. I don't care if you don't want to. You have to. Don't be such a coward."

"I don't think I'm being cowardly, sir."

"You're being a huge coward. You're trying to avoid doing your job. You know why we hired you here, right?" he says as his stench befouls the air and wafts into my nostrils.

"Because I think, act, and function as an Elite. Therefore, I belong in the Elite Guard, sir." Even though I don't mean a single word of it, it's what he wants to hear. The code of the Elites is worthless to me; it's just another way for MacMillan to get what he wants.

"That's correct. You passed the Return Test without so much as a blink. You're exactly what this wall needs, but if you're going to be too much of a coward to do your job by avoiding following my explicit orders, then we'll kick your ass back out there. That is, if you would rather have that," he says, the veins in his neck pulsing with the final syllable.

"I would almost prefer that," I whisper, hoping he didn't hear.

"What was that?" he instantly responds like he has the ears of a man a quarter of his age. "Did you say you would rather live outside Nimbus with those kids? With those cowards?"

"No, sir," I say.

Inching closer to me, he burps. "I think that's what you said."

With my back against the wall, the sweat on my shirt starts to stick to the steel. The closer I get, the more the heat from the wall starts to burn through my shirt. "I didn't say that," I mumble.

"Don't lie to me," he says as his teeth clench and the putrid scent of gin becomes palpable.

"I wouldn't lie, sir."

His eyebrows start to furl; his knuckles crack; his hand forms into a fist. Reaching his arm back, he throws it toward my nose. I reach my right hand up and catch his fist, quickly thrusting my forehead into his. He stumbles backward into the railing.

"You shouldn't have done that," he sneers. Patting his fingers against his face as blood drips down, he purses his lips together and whistles. Right away, nearly a dozen guards come running toward me.

Quickly settling all around us, two guards throw me onto the ground. The men handcuff me and pull me back up. "Sorry, Sean," whispers one of them.

With blood dripping down his face, MacMillan laughs. Unwilling to wipe the blood, he steps toward me—his boots rattling on the grates beneath us. Cocking his arm back, he jams his fist into my stomach. The pain instantly envelops my body, forcing me to bend forward in agony.

"I hope you regret what you've done for the rest of your pathetic life. . .even though that won't be too long. You're a worthless coward and you don't deserve to call yourself Elite." Thrusting his bony knuckles into my stomach once more, he grins unapologetically and snaps his fingers. The men start to carry me off the wall and away from him.

With each step away from MacMillan, the shame of the crime I've committed against Nimbus digs further into my stomach. I've committed something I can't escape from, something that might not have been necessary. I've put myself into hell, but it was almost worth it to see that smug bag of bones get what he deserved.

After all, he threw the first punch.

10 October 2191

Sam

As each new day passes, we spend more time inside and less time out. The weather is still pretty warm during the day, but Elise insists that our safety is more important than our desire to explore around us. She wants us to survive eleven years, but being cooped up in a small shack for months doesn't seem ideal to me. It's cramped and uncomfortable.

"Elise," I say while we sit in an odd-shaped triangle next to the fireplace.

"Yea?"

Fidgeting with the zipper of my sleeping bag in between my thumb and forefinger, I ask, "Do you think that, maybe today, you could teach us how to fight. . .or just how to defend ourselves?"

Without hesitating, she nods her head. "Sure. You two should probably learn at some point. I can teach you everything Sean taught me."

"Awesome," I whisper to myself.

Hurriedly standing up, I'm the first to the door. Eager to get out of the shack and into the heat, I twist the handle. The moment I step outside, clouds barrel in; the sky turns from blue to gray. *Can't we catch a break?*

Hopping out behind me, Abby yawns. "I swear it was sunny two minutes ago."

"It was," I laugh. "We're just not allowed a lot of sun apparently."

"You'll get used to it," says Elise from behind us.

"I don't know if I want to," mutters Abby.

Stepping ahead of us, Elise smiles back at Abby. "It's better to deal with the changing skies than to always see black."

Abby pushes her lips together to the side before looking over at me.

"She has a point," I say.

"I guess so."

Guiding us through a clearing of trees and into an empty field of dead grass and dirt, Elise turns around. "What would you guys like to learn first?" she asks, draping her quiver over her shoulder.

"Arrows," Abby instantly replies. "I want to learn to shoot arrows like you."

"Arrows it is." Elise shrugs her shoulders as she looks around the area for something for us to shoot at. "Sam," she says.

Giving up on trying to scout out a bottle or something in the empty field, I turn to Elise. "What?"

"I think there are some empty cans back at the shack. Could you run back and grab a few? I think I left them there from several years ago when Sean was teaching me how to shoot."

"I'll go look," I say.

Moving back in the direction of our camp, I faintly hear Elise laugh and say, "For finding the shack at fourteen, I think it's a little crazy I didn't notice the rails not too far away until seventeen!"

Abby's slight laugh disappears behind me as I move forward.

A gust pushes through—tearing dangling leaves from withered branches. With each step, a crunch howls underneath my shoes. If anything, this slight annoyance could make me a target. We haven't seen anyone around here yet, but anything is possible; there are a lot of kids out here and it's odd that we haven't seen too many more. Trying to avoid loudly walking across the field, I sprint toward the shack. At least this way, my crunches will be quick.

Hopping across the tracks near the shack, I step silently toward our hideout where for some unexplainable reason the door is hanging wide open.

Maybe someone's there. Maybe Abby or Elise accidentally left the door open when we left. I can't help but think someone went in there after we walked away. It almost seems right that I would have to fend someone off the first day we start training when we haven't actually begun.

74

A chilled shiver runs through my body as a breeze meshes with my uneasiness. I slowly creep toward the open door, my stomach twisting and turning with each step. In turn, forcing my hands to lightly shake upon reaching the door. Nervously, I peek in. To my right, I see nothing but our sleeping bags and the burnt logs from the previous night. I turn left. Only the crooked table and broken chairs sit next to the cracked window.

What felt like a potential trap turned out to be nothing. *It must be in my head,* I think. Shaking off the impulse to run back without grabbing anything, I grab four rusted cans at the back of the room beneath the table. Each one's empty and overridden with a smell of manure.

I step out the door, holding the cans against my body in my left arm. Pulling the door shut behind me, a cold touch brushes across my shoulder. I know that if I turn around, I will regret it, so I keep walking. I slide my hand toward my hatchet as I start walking in the direction of the rails with the cans rattling in my arms.

"That's my shack," comes a hoarse voice from behind me.

Ignoring the man, I keep walking to the field where Abby and Elise are standing and chatting.

"You better not come back," says the voice again.

Without thinking, I yell for Elise. "ELISE! ELISE!" I cry, my lips shaking.

She instantly turns around and points her bow toward me. Pulling the string back toward her cheek, she stands still. Nudging her head to the left, she motions for me to get out of the way. I veer diagonally.

"You shouldn't have done that, kid," mutters the voice, forcing me to panic and drop half the cans. Pulling out my hatchet, I sprint toward Elise. I still don't know what the man looks like or who he is, but I don't care to associate a face with his voice. I just don't want to hear him speak again. I just want him to be gone.

Quickly approaching Elise and Abby, Elise drops her arrow. "What was that about, Sam?" she asks.

Trying to regain my breath, I say, "There was a man. Didn't you see him? He said not to go back to the shack."

"What are you talking about? I've never seen someone else near that place. Are you sure it wasn't in your head?"

I turn around to see if I can spot the man whom I know nothing about. Though, I don't know what he looks like, I'm certain that if I saw him I would know. "I don't think so," I say. I could hear him moving around behind me; there's no way someone wasn't there. "I never looked, but his hand grazed my shoulder back at the shack. It was cold. Almost like it had no blood flow whatsoever. I've never felt something so icy in heat like this."

Squinting, Elise continues to look behind me. "I don't see anyone, Sam. He must've gotten away."

"I don't want to go back there," I mutter.

"We don't have a choice. There's nowhere else to stay," says Elise.

"Then let's find a new place," says Abby. "I don't want to get killed over that place."

Elise shrugs off Abby's remark. "Nobody does, but it's going to start getting colder at night and I don't know anywhere else to go. We have to go back. We have sleeping bags and fire there. That's more than I ever really had with Sean. You guys don't want to sleep outside when winter rolls around. It's not worth it."

"Anything's worth it to survive," I say, not realizing until after that we wouldn't survive sleeping in snow. I look at Elise as she takes a deep breath and reaches for her forehead. Digging the tips of her thumb and pointer finger into her skin, she shakes her head from side to side.

"I'm sorry, but we have to go. We'll devise a plan to make sure the place is safe, but that's our only shelter and we can't lose it—especially if it was all in your head, Sam."

It wasn't, I think. *I felt it.*

"What do you suggest we do?" I ask. While the wind starts to die down, the stillness of the air brings out the hidden sounds of nature: rabbits hopping around in the distance, leaves falling to the ground, high tree branches cracking. Still frightened of going anywhere near that shack, my arms start to twitch as the last can falls into the dirt—silencing the rabbit as it runs further into the woods.

"I think we slowly walk back and we kill him. We look every which way and if we see someone, I'll shoot. I don't care if it's the right or wrong person. If someone's trying to steal our home, they're worthless to me."

76

"What about us? We haven't even had a chance to practice today," says Abby.

"You two will be my eyes. Once we take out this guy, we can come back and train tomorrow."

Standing without resolve, I stare at the ground. The wind briefly stops and everything goes silent—the only sound is my heart rapidly beating against my skin. "Let's do it," I mutter.

Elise

"Where do we go from here?" asks Abby anxiously. "We can't just go straight back to the shack. What if they're sitting around it?"

"We don't know if there's a group or not, Abby," I say. "I think we have go in thinking there's just one and then we have to trap him." Whether I want to believe what Sam experienced was real or not, I don't think he would lie about what he felt. He's been a little shaky ever since he got back.

"And how do we do that?" asks Sam as he bends down to pick one of the cans off the ground. Blankly staring at it, he starts to pick at its wrapper.

"I'm not sure. I think we'll have to use you as bait," I say, not thinking about the negative effects of such an idea.

Lifting his head up, Sam drops the can. "Hell no. I want to help, but I'm not going to be bait." His panicky eyes wander back toward the can as it rolls across the dirt.

"I'll do it," whispers Abby from behind me.

"No," I instantly reply. "I'm not letting you do that, Abby. A lot worse things could happen to a girl your age out here than what could happen to Sam." Turning back toward Sam, he remains still with his head down. "Sam, I promise you won't get hurt."

"How do I know that's the truth? How do I know that he won't just kill me?"

"You just have to trust me. Have I lied to you yet?"

"No," he almost-silently replies.

"Then you have to trust me."

He doesn't respond. Abby steps closer to him. "You'll be okay. We'll have your back," she whispers. She grazes his hand with her fingers. Sam shyly pulls them away.

"Fine. What's your plan?" he asks worriedly.

78

As convoluted as this idea may be, I can't help but think Sam is overreacting. Yes, it's scary, but I haven't gotten them hurt even once. For all Abby and I know, what Sam experienced could be a false reality; he could be struggling with the same thing I am. "I think we surround the house and peek through the window to see if he's there first."

"What if he's not?" asks Abby.

"Then we go back in, lock the door and cover the window to prevent anyone from coming in while we're there."

"That just sounds like we're locking ourselves into danger," murmurs Sam. Bending forward, he takes a seat in the grass. Looking up, he speaks again. "If the door is locked and the window is boarded up then they'll probably just burn it down with us in there."

"I don't think they would want to do that with the possibility of losing their shelter." *They. Since when did the single become a plural?*

"I don't know. It's just a thought," he says.

Shaking off his thought, I pitch my idea. "If he's there then we'll see him through the window. I say that we have Sam knock on the door to get him moving toward it. Then, as he's about to open the door, I'll fire an arrow through the hole in the window and kill him."

"Sounds fair enough, but why don't we just shoot him initially rather than waiting for him to stand up and come to the door? If you just shoot him at first then I don't have to worry about getting hurt."

"I agree with Sam," mumbles Abby before taking a seat next to him. Curling the ends of her hair around her forefingers, she stares intently toward the ground.

"If I don't have a clear shot then it'll just make him aware that we're there. If he stands up then I will have a clear shot at his whole body."

Void of a response, they both sit there in silence as Sam starts to pick the faded red casing off another can. With his head down, he picks and picks—his nails nervously chipping off the label. Dropping the silver can back onto the dirt, he remains silent while Abby stares aimlessly into the woods.

"Is that okay, Sam?" I ask.

"Sure," he mumbles.

I hate that word. Every time he says it, I just know that he doesn't mean it. It's as if he's forcefully doing something against his will just to satisfy someone else. I'll never force either of them to do something they don't want to do, but at this point, there's more at stake. I have to give up making him feel better and make him realize that survival comes first.

"Let's go then," I say.

"Right now?" he retorts.

"Do you have something better to do?" I ask firmly.

"No."

There's no time to waste, regardless of where his mind is. He's already seen someone he knows die and now this; the outside is destructive, but you have to toughen up. Life isn't always easy, but when you're a fourteen-year-old away from home trying to survive, life almost equals death. Every aspect of what you do can come back to haunt you, but if you don't do something necessary to keep yourself alive, death will always ring louder than life.

Reaching out, I help Abby to her feet. She stands up and brushes the dirt off her jeans. Sam gets up and does the same. "Are you going to be alright?"

"I think so," he faintly replies.

Pulling my bow over my chest, I lead us back to the pallid shack we call home. Looking every direction for any movement, I keep an arrow in place against the wood of my bow.

"The area looks clear so far," I whisper as Abby inches closer to me while Sam slowly falls behind, his gaze focused on the ground.

Constantly wary of the environment, I look up. The skies darken with each step; a faded crack of thunder erupts in the distance. *We have to hurry.*

"C'mon Sam," signals Abby. Reaching for his fingers, she gently grasps the ends of his hand and pulls him toward us.

For a moment, it seemed he was going to wander away at the pace he was moving. Though, he's probably too distraught to consider such a thing—especially since he's seemingly growing wearier of his surroundings each day.

The shack sits just ahead. The lightning moves toward us, but remains out of focus deep into the forest. With a slight mist starting to fall upon us, my fingers slip on the end of the bow.

"Come with me," I say, maneuvering toward the back window. A light smoke peeks above the trees, drifting past us deeper into the woods. "Someone must be there."

"Sh-should I go knock?" stutters Sam.

"Not yet. Come with me first."

Nearing the broken window on the left side of the shack, I duck and signal for them to do the same. Stretching out my neck, I lift my eyes just above the windowsill. The orange of the fire illuminates a pasty male who can't be much older than Sam. His thin figure suggests cold-bloodedness, thus, why he felt cold according to Sam. He looks like he hasn't eaten in days, maybe weeks. He sits on the floor just in front of the fireplace with his legs crossed and his hands outward while the cotton of one of the sleeping bags is draped around his waist. I drop back down.

"What did you see?" whispers Abby.

"There's someone in there. I think I might be able to get him through the hole without having to make Sam do anything," I quietly reply.

Pulling the bow and arrow up toward my shoulders, I slowly drag the arrow back. The mist trickles down my fingers and into my palm. A heavy clap of thunder shakes the area, throwing me off balance, causing my fingers to slide off the string. Re-gripping the end of the bow, I pull the arrow back and release.

Taken aback by Mother Nature's wrath and the arrow protruding from the back of his neck, the man starts to panic. Reaching his hands back, he struggles to pull it out. His hands continually slip as he tries to remove the arrow; his skin grows an even lighter shade of white. With blood pouring down his back, he falls onto his side, convulsing. Still reaching for the object as his movements slow and his muscles spasm, his hands fall to his sides while his body writhes in pain.

I can't watch the agony anymore, so I fire again. This time, the arrow pierces the back of his skull.

Dead and unknowing of what struck him so quickly, the man lies limp in front of the fire. The orange of the flames loom large over his corpse.

"Is he dead?" asks Sam.

"Yes," I say. "But I think we have a bigger problem than that."

"What?" asks Abby.

"We have to run."

"What? Why?"

"No time to explain. Just run!" I yell.

With my hands upon their shoulders, I push Sam and Abby farther away while we run. Steadfast and hurried, we start to get farther and farther from the shack. I glance over my shoulder to see the flames engulfing the area. The once predominantly orange fire has grown to a mixture of red and blue as the heat scalds the trees next to it.

"What happened?!" yells Sam out of breath as we reach the end of the field.

Hungrily gripping ahold of the sky, a dark bank of clouds starts to rush in above us. The mist quickly turns into a sheet of liquid as the rain attempts to cease the flames from expanding.

"The cotton on the sleeping bags. . .it-it caught fire," I stutter.

"But how did it become so big so fast?" asks Abby.

"I don't know. I saw both the bags burn up next to the man and I just knew we had to get moving."

"What the hell do we do now?" shouts Sam as he wipes the rain from his forehead, only for more rain to slide down his face.

With the rain muffling our conversation, I say, "We keep moving." I know there's nothing else we can do; there's nothing more I can do. I had to kill him, but had I known that would happen, I would've done it another way.

"Keep moving where?"

Sighing, I pull my already-dampened hood above my hair and start walking toward the trees—hoping they'll follow—but understanding if they don't.

19 October 2191

Sam

I can't stop thinking about the fire. The flames went up fast enough that the rain didn't have a chance to put it out. Now, nothing but a pile of ash sits where we once lived. I can't get the bright orange out of my head; I can't escape the chill of his hand mixed with the short-lived heat against my back. He's dead, but a part of me thinks there's more to what happened than just him.

I wipe the moisture from my forehead while sitting against a fallen tree. "What now?" I ask as a tiny, green lizard runs across the trunk against my back.

"I don't know," mutters Elise, her eyes momentarily fixating on the sky before drooping back down to the dirt.

We haven't done anything since the fire. We've spent a few days exploring the land to see if we can find a new place to stay, but nothing's jumped out. It's gotten to the point that it feels like they're about to give up. I know they won't, but their limited effort to stave off the anger that comes with sleeping outside is almost enough to drag me down, too. *Keep going,* I think.

The thought of leaving Elise and Abby to fend for myself has driven itself through my mind a few times, but not enough to make me actually consider it. I know there's more out here, more to explore, more to see, but it's not worth going alone. We're not supposed to go into the city if we find it, but a part of me wants to; a part of me is pulling me into it.

It can't be all bad. A city has shelter. A city is just as limitless as a forest. There's probably more to find there, too. Everything about it is enticing; I just wish I knew more. I wish we were taught about it or at least given a history on its existence before we were forced out. Yet, we weren't. Apparently learning about the history of Nimbus was more important because somehow knowing that MacMillan's father, Aldous, was a police captain in the old world is useful knowledge.

For the next few hours, Abby and I hover around the clearing while Elise searches for food. Every time I think of disappearing and wandering off on my own, a sharp pain pulses through my head. It's as if my body differs from what my mind wants because it knows I'm not capable. I'm not as strong as Elise.

I'm further reassured that I shouldn't disappear when Elise comes back from a walk with two rabbits tied on opposite ends of a rope draped around her neck.

"I hope this is enough," she says. Casually taking a seat next to Abby, Elise starts to skin one of the rabbits. The white fur of the animal flakes onto the dirt, only to be blown into the forest with each slight gust—drifting into the sky, aimlessly floating into someone else's path.

"Any food is enough. I'm starving," I say. The thoughts of the city wander away with the fur as I watch Elise pick tufts out of the skin.

"Abby, can you go fill up the canteen at the pond over there?" points Elise.

"Sure," she replies.

Ever since the shack burnt down, Elise hasn't been the same. She seems more preoccupied with her headaches than with us. I know they're not enjoyable, but neither is any of this. We couldn't have anticipated that fire just like we can't always be prepared for a crappy day. The world's choices aren't controllable; the downfall of society isn't a blame one person can shoulder. There's no reason our worries and anger should eat away at her. We've moved past it. *I think.*

Yet, at times, it feels like she'd rather venture off on her own for the sake of her sanity. At least, maybe then, the headaches would disperse. Maybe then she could find peace of mind without us holding her down. Then again, I know she wouldn't do that, and neither would I.

If there's one major takeaway from my time at home, it's that being alone for eleven years is a lot harder than surviving for eleven

84

years. If you spend too much time with yourself thinking about your future, you'll die before the time's up. However, if you focus on getting by and you keep moving, time will befriend you. Dad taught me that. Makes me happy that Abby and I share a birthday.

I look over at her filling up the canteen. Crouched down, she drowns the canteen and scoops the water into it. Her chocolate hair falling against her cheek, her eyes intent to fill the bottle to the brim, she looks better off than I do. I smile knowing she can't see it.

Holding the rabbits up by their tails, Elise pulls off a few remaining hairs. As she shakes off the last clinging tufts of fur, I start to salivate. All I want to do right now is eat. I can't remember the last time I had so much as a berry. Even then, it wasn't enough. I feel thinner than when I first got out here, but hopefully that changes soon.

Slowly walking back, the canteen moving back and forth like a pendulum beside her, Abby asks, "Anyone need a drink?"

I raise my hand. Abby tosses it to me—her throw landing the canteen at my feet. "C'mon," I laugh.

"My bad," she smirks.

I smile.

Tossing back the canteen, the unfiltered water glides down my throat. The instant sensation of the water is great, but the aftertaste isn't the best. I set it down.

Shoving the meat onto the ends of two separate arrows, Elise looks over at me. "If only we had some salt," she says, handing me one of the arrows.

Holding the hairless rabbit over the fire, I spin it in circles in an attempt to cook all sides of the meat equally. "That would be nice."

***

I wipe the sweat from my forehead. The heat from the fire mixed with the humidity start to make me feel weak. My eyelids droop; my hands tingle; my shoulders slump forward. The arrow in my hand shrinks while the rabbit starts to squirm on the end of it. As if it's still alive, the small piece of meat shakes and shakes until I'm forced onto my back.

"Sam!" comes a voice from beside me.

85

I close my eyes and drag the back of my palm against the sweat on my forehead only to open them in an empty room. The arrow in my hand disintegrates. The fire looms over the tops of the walls.

"He's coming," whispers a voice from behind me.

"Who's coming?" I respond. Trying to quickly turn around, my feet feel stuck in mud. Shifting crookedly like a ticking clock with a defective hand, I stutter before locking into one position.

"You know who," says the man once more, his shadow becoming more apparent in front of me.

I gently rub my eyes in an attempt to see the man's face, yet nothing but a blur covers the spot where his face should be. I squint, but I see nothing. No eyes, no mouth, no nose; the man has no face and everything around him is on fire.

I try to reach out for him, but I can't. My arms have become glued to my sides as the walls around me start to crumble. A thick cloud of smoke jumps from the collapsing room into my eyes— instantly blinding all of my senses. I can't cough; I can't see; I can't breathe. Suddenly, the forest reappears and I'm alone.

I can see the railroad tracks and the open field where we were going to do training, but nothing else. I'm standing on a heap of embers as the sweltering heat boils against my feet. Unable to move, I try to turn once more, but can't. I'm stuck.

"He's right over there," says the voice. I motion my eyes left only to see dense fog barreling toward me. I look right and the fog consumes me. The gray cloud briefly blinds me. The embers beneath me fade away, allowing my feet to cool down. The fire is gone and there's no sight of it ever existing, yet I'm covered in its remains.

"WHO?!" I scream.

The fog grows darker and darker until I can't see anything. Lost in absolute darkness, a hand grazes my spine. "Sam," says the voice.

"What do you want?" I silently ask. I can feel my body shaking, but I can't move. I want to run; I want to cry; I want to escape, but I can't.

Drawing for air, the deep voice speaks once more. "I want you."

Shaking uncontrollably, I can feel my arms loosening from my sides. The cold fingers run across my shoulders.

86

"NO!" I scream as the smoke disappears and a mass of liquid smears across my face.

"Sam!" shouts the voice from in front of me.

"NO!" I shout once more.

"It's me, Sam. It's Abby," says the voice.

Rubbing the water from my eyes, I notice that I can move my arms and my legs. I'm no longer stuck in place, but instead I'm lying down. I'm not entirely sure what just happened.

"What?" I say as I try to sit up.

"What happened?" asks Elise from beside me.

"I don't know," I say.

"I think you're dehydrated and exhausted," says Elise. "You need to eat something and drink lots of water. You can sleep after that and we'll keep watch. You need it."

"I don't want to go back there," I cry, my hands trembling.

"Go back where?" asks Abby.

"Wherever I was. I think it was the shack. I saw the railroad and the field, but that was it. It was really foggy and someone was talking to me. I couldn't see him and I couldn't move. I guess it was like your dream, Elise. I was stuck."

Shuddering, Elise nods. "Get some rest."

My heart's pounding and I feel more awake than I've been since we got out here. I can't help but think, *what if that dream meant something? What if that man with the blurred face was the kid that told me not to go back to the shack? Who was saying that he wanted me?* If something exists outside of Nimbus that can get into my head like that, then I don't know how much longer I want to be out here.

26 October 2191

Sean

The fluorescent lights shine through my eyelids, impeding any attempt to sleep. It doesn't matter if I'm lying facedown or faceup—the lights find a way into my head. They're never off, like a consistent eye on me is important when I have no chance to escape. No matter how many times I ask them to dim the lights, they don't. Each time I so much as open my mouth, the guard walks away. Most of the time I won't even get a look, let alone any acknowledgment.

I sit up. Surrounded by a mass of white on the floor, walls, and ceiling, I can't help but think how fast everything changed. One minute I was on top of the world, the next, I'm trapped. Nimbus has always been my home; albeit, an undesirable one, but now it feels empty, void of hope. It's as if I'm stuck in a nightmare I can't wake up from. One so intense, no pinch could bring an end to the madness.

Every breath MacMillan takes, Nimbus remains as dangerous as the city beyond the wall. With him in charge, there's no hope. *I need to get out of here*, I think.

I stand up and hopelessly straggle toward the bars at the front of my cell. A guard stands watch at the end of the hall, his eyes fixed on the bearded man sitting quietly in the cell across from mine. Day in and day out, he remains still, an empty look about his face. I doubt his reason for being here is the same as mine, but I like to believe he has no right being here. I like to think he'll make it out better than I will.

It gets to a point where the one thing you learn in this place is that the only thing you have is yourself; your thoughts consume you whether you want them to or not. This man appears unbothered by his surroundings, which is why he never ceases to move; he stares as if the world around him is crumbling and there's nothing he can do about it. He just acquiesces to his fate. He shows no desire to live.

I stumble back into my bed, the dull mattress stiffening upon my arrival. Each way I roll, the springs refuse to budge. Lying on my back, I wipe my face before sitting up against the wall. I close my eyes and wish myself away from here, hoping that the bars will disappear and this room will fade away into nothingness. At least when I'm buried in my thoughts, I can escape. Even if it's not physical, it'll suffice. Anything is better than being trapped in this misery; anything is better than indulging MacMillan's thoughtless torment.

My spine presses into the wall, forcing me to wince. A passing guard laughs.

Inching myself forward, the grinding sound of ceramic gliding against the tile reverberates throughout the room. Shaking off the noise, I keep my eyes closed while I imagine somewhere else: somewhere with her. I know that if I open them, a mixture of slush and some form of processed meat sits just inches from my bed and I don't care to eat that garbage right now. All I want is solace regardless of how unattainable it is.

"Eat up," says a voice just outside my cell. The clattering sound of the slit at the bottom of the door makes me jump, but I keep my eyes closed. The footsteps walking away bounce off the walls with each step.

I keep my eyes shut and focused on the back of my eyelids until I can't hear anything. Eventually, the lucent fixtures creep into my vision, forcing me to lie on my stomach with the pillow over my head. Immersed in a slight darkness, I envision life without MacMillan.

***

As I run through Nimbus, the lampposts illuminate the cobblestone paths between neighborhoods. At the end of the street, she stands— her eyes glued to my movement. With her hands at her sides and a widened smile spread across her cheeks, she waits for me. Nearing her with each step, her cheeks raise. I lose myself in the beauty of her smile and stumble forward.

She takes a step toward me. Our eyes sync; time dawdles, unwilling to briskly move forward. Her eyes widen; mine widen. She smiles and jumps into my arms, immediately pressing her lips on mine. I hold her against my body as her hands brush against my shoulders. "I missed you," I whisper.

"I missed you, too," replies Elise, tears slowly rolling down her cheeks.

"I'm so glad it's over," I say. "I couldn't go another day without you."

Resting her head on my shoulder, she wipes her eyes. "I love you," she sniffles.

"I love you, too."

I hold her as if MacMillan never existed, as if the world was still blossoming before us. With our whole lives ahead of us, nothing could interfere; nothing could force us away from each other. While I look into her vibrant blue eyes, she brushes her hair to the side and smiles. I squeeze her tighter as the world around us enlivens. Cyclists bustle past, pedestrians hurry down the street, the sun shines like an incandescent bulb enlightening an alive world—one not afraid of death, one not consumed by a dark shadow at every step. Afraid to let go, to let this moment slip away, I embrace her as our passions grow deeper. I gently swipe her bangs to the side and kiss her forehead—forever refusing to let her slip away.

***

"Looks like you're starving yourself tonight, Martin," says the guard, his voice slightly muffled by my pillow.

Rubbing my eyes and turning around, I watch as the guard pulls the bowl of mush out of my cell. I nod, but don't care that he's taking the food away. I'm more surprised at the fact that MacMillan has even allowed me the possibility of food. I figured I would be starving in here for days until he eagerly called for my execution.

Rolling back over onto my stomach, I cover my head with the pillow once more. Closing my eyes, I try to fall back into the disparate world where she longingly awaits me.

5 November 2191

Elise

Wandering. Fleeing. Lost. No matter how fast we move, we end up with nothing. There's nowhere to go, nowhere to run, nowhere to escape the outside. Everywhere is a dead end.

I quickly hop over a flooded creek as we continue to move through the woods and away from Nimbus. Yet, no matter how far away we get, the lingering thought of my nightmare in the city casually slips itself into my mind. The inscribed walls, the faint drops of water softly falling onto the cement beside me, the metallic scent of drying blood—everything I wish to forget.

Will we eventually near the city? Possibly. Will we enter it? No. The moment I see so much as a fogged window, we'll be turning around faster than I can snap my fingers.

Though the frailty of the city is tempting for newcomers to the outside, it's not worth your life; the decrepit buildings laced with ivy are attractive at first glance, but they don't solve the desire for shelter. Instead, they keep you on edge, longing for a comfortable night of sleep that's unobtainable.

When I first saw the city, it looked like everything I've read. It was an early 21st-century novel thrust into the open. The vastness of its expanse immediately drew me in; it made me want to explore it for the rest of my time out here. Though, the closer I got, the more noticeable its emptiness became. There weren't any people or animals walking around, no moving cars, no signs of life. Literally everything about it was dead. Ever since our people left that area in 2105, it has become a wasteland for disease, infestations, and history incapable of being rewritten. That city is a dead zone overrun with mystery, but its seclusion is seductive. It makes you want more; it makes your thirst for its history impossible to quench. The city is an enigma.

"You guys remember what I said about the city, right?" I ask.

Tilting their heads simultaneously, Abby and Sam nod as Abby responds. "Yes. We're not supposed to ever go near it."

"Good."

"Why do you ask?" asks Sam. Taking a drink from the muddied canteen, he grimaces as he swallows.

I look puzzlingly at him.

"There was a piece of mud under the cap," he says wryly.

I laugh. "I just wanted to make sure you remembered. It's getting cold and we could be nearing it for all I know and I can't have you two running off on me," I say firmly.

"After what happened to you, there's no way we'll be running toward that place," declares Abby sternly.

"Okay. Just watch out for it. If you see it, let me know, so we can go a different way."

They both nod in sync.

The sun starts to descend behind the trees. A light breeze rustles through the leaves as Sam hands me the canteen. I take a quick sip and pour a small pool of water into the palm of my left hand. Lightly dipping two fingers into it, I press them into my forehead as the lukewarm moisture quickly dampens the slight pain pulsing against my skull.

"Are you okay?" asks Abby.

I keep my eyes on the ground, continually applying pressure between them. "I'm alright. My head just hurts a little."

Abby grabs my hand, signaling for me to sit down. I give her the canteen, put my arms behind me and lean into the dirt. The dryness meshes with the remaining water in my left hand, forcing a clump of mud to form. I shake it off.

"So when do you turn twenty-five?" she asks.

"In August next year," I say.

"What day?"

"The twenty-second."

"That means you'll leave four days before Sam and I have our first clicks."

"I guess so. Don't worry though, it's not *that* bad," I chuckle.

"Really?" asks Sam as he sits down beside Abby.

"Yea. I mean, it comes out of nowhere, but it won't kill ya."

"What does it feel like?" asks Abby. "Do they become less painful with each new one?

My mind drifts back to my first click and the lingering pain I've had with each new one since, but I'm certain I'm one of the few who has issues with them. What seems like such a swift prick to the head sits with me for days whether I want it to or not. Yet, Sean never had an issue. He would just shake his head and move on as if nothing had even happened. He was much luckier than me. "It's like someone comes out of nowhere and flicks you in the head as hard as they can," I deliberately say. "The pain retreated each year for Sean, but I wasn't so lucky."

"Why do yours get worse?" asks Abby, her fingers creeping up toward the sides of her head.

"I haven't really figured that out yet."

"That doesn't sound like fun," she replies. "I guess some things are just out of our control."

I press my lips together and nod. My headache begins to slide away.

"Too bad we're not as old as Elise," sighs Sam. "At least then we would only have one left and we'd know what we're up against on the twenty-fifth one."

I laugh and sarcastically frown at Sam. "I'm not old," I smile.

"Sure you are," gibes Sam.

"I prefer to call it experienced."

"Whatever you want, oldie," he responds, a slight smirk spreading across his drying lips.

I roll my eyes as I rub my head once more.

"Elise," mutters Sam.

"What?"

"I was wondering. . .what if you decided to stay out here when you turned twenty-five rather than going back to Nimbus. Can you do that? I mean, not just you, but anyone?"

A year ago, I would've said yes to that question, but when you're there when someone turns twenty-five, you learn that it's impossible to stay out here forever. Then again, *why would you want to?*

Sean didn't want to go, but that's just because he didn't want to leave me. He was just as afraid as I was that Arthur would come back, that he would chase me down when I was finally alone.

"You can't stay out here forever, Sam. When you become of age, the Elite Guard comes out here and picks you up where you stand and takes you away. Why would you want to stay out here longer than eleven years anyways?" I ask.

"I was just wondering," he shyly responds. "I guess I just want to explore everything the world has to offer."

"We have eleven years to explore," mumbles Abby.

"I know, but how far can we get in eleven years?"

"You can't really go anywhere," I say. "If you try to go too far, your head will start to hurt."

"How do you know that? Did you go too far once?" asks Sam.

I answer with a muffled voice as a stray tear begins to run down my cheek. "I didn't, but my brother Zeke did." Just thinking about Zeke, about being home, my mind runs in constant circles.

"What happened?"

"He ran too far and his chip nearly exploded."

When I turned thirteen, Zeke had just been re-admitted to Nimbus after passing his test. Every night before I went to bed he would tell me of his time outside of Nimbus. Whether it was about his first weeks surviving on his own or his encounters with the errant outsiders, he told me everything. Sadly, he also encouraged me to stay away from the city, but I never listened. That city has a power so enticing that no matter what you're told about it, it'll grab you and never let go—unless you're lucky.

"What? How? What really happened?" asks Sam enthusiastically.

"He was just like I was when I got stuck in the city. He was lost and he was scared, so he ran. He kept on running until he felt a nagging pressure in his head telling him to turn around. The farther he went, the more it hurt, but he kept going. He thought eventually it would stop, but it didn't. He ended up getting to the point that he couldn't take it anymore, so he turned around and the pain started to subside," I say, accidentally smearing the tear across my cheek.

"How do you know it almost exploded then?"

94

"When you pass your test to get back into Nimbus, they take out your chip. Once you're back behind the wall, they feel there's no need to track you anymore, so they take it out. When they took his out, they said it was bigger than normal and that if he would've gone a few more steps, he would've hit what they call the 'pop point.'"

Pop point. I can't think of a sillier name for 'your head will blow up' than that. It's happened a few times in the past according to his doctors, but they don't typically see someone get as far as he did without it exploding. Even after all that, he still managed to pass the test and make it home.

"Wow," responds a fascinated Sam. "Why do they put the chips in at birth then if they're just going to take them out when we pass the test? Why can't they just put them in before we go out?"

"You know as much as I do," I say.

"They just seem unnecessary," mutters Abby. "If they want us to learn how to survive, they shouldn't be allowed to track our every move. We should really be free."

"But we need to know when our birthday is," replies Sam.

"I'd almost be okay not knowing," replies Abby. Looking over at Sam, her eyes fall to the ground. "At least then, it wouldn't remind us of home, of enjoying that day with our families."

Sam doesn't reply. His lips tremble, but he doesn't answer.

I scoot toward Abby. "Just because you feel a click doesn't mean you have to think anything of it. Just use it as a reminder that you're alive."

"And still not home."

I cross my legs right as small droplets start to fall from the sky, ruining our comfort. The ill-timed sprinkle forces us up and away from the opening. I grab onto Abby's hand. She looks up at me. "You'll be home before you know it," I smile. "And when you get there, we'll throw you a party."

14 November 2191

Sam

    The sensation of falling followed by the irritable thud of the ground awakes me. I roll over as the dream fades into black and the shivers that once coursed through my body disappear.

    "Sam, are you awake?" asks Abby. Rolling onto her side, she tilts her head to stare into my weary eyes.

    "Barely," I reply, my vision obscured by my exhaustion.

    Closing my eyes once more, I fade back into the darkness.

***

I look down. The grass sits several feet below me. *Where am I?* I think. I rub my eyes and look through the trees, past the dying fields of wheat and into a rundown city. Crooked streets flooded with ivy and cracked pavement make way for massive holes spread randomly throughout the area. Past that, dozens of buildings fade into the distance. Some fallen, some still standing, and some covered in so much ivy that they appear as mere trees rather than former skyscrapers.

    "This must be the city," I say to myself.

***

"Wake up, Sam. Get out of there," comes a voice from behind me.

    I feel a shaking sensation as my eyes vibrate and open. Elise is standing over me with her eyes widened while her forehead is dripping with sweat.

"What?" I inaudibly say.

Appearing to have caught what I said, Elise responds. "How did you get there?"

"Get where?"

"To the city. We both heard you say it in your sleep. Why were you there?"

"I don't know. It was a dream. I don't know how they take us anywhere," I say as I sit up. "It's not like I was really there. It was just my imagination."

"I know, but if your mind takes you there then it may mean that you want to go there," says Elise. Kneeling down next to me, her stare refuses to lessen.

I don't want to go there. I know I can't conjure up a scenario in my dreams in which the city is invisible; it's always going to be there. If I could delete it from existence I would, but no matter what I think about, the dark side of being exiled from Nimbus will always find a way to latch onto me. Ever since the fire, my dreams have become nightmares and my nightmares have scared me to the point that I don't even want to blink anymore. Any moment behind the walls of my eyelids is a moment where I'm stuck in fear. I hate it.

"I don't want to go there, Elise. I don't even want to sleep anymore. Every time I close my eyes, I'm afraid that I'll see that man's face. Even if I don't see his face, I feel like I'll see him in some way. I feel like something is pulling me to the city in my mind and it scares me so much," I say as tears start to fall down my cheeks. "Everything you've told us about that city is terrifying, yet something seems to want me to be there and I don't want to go."

Reaching her arms around my back, Elise hugs me; Abby joins and wraps her arms around my waist. "As long as you have us, you'll never end up there," says Elise, her voice quavering.

"You promise?" I reply with heavy eyes.

"I promise," sniffles Elise. "There's more out here than that city that we need to explore. I'll make sure you never see that dump."

"And when Elise leaves, I'll make sure we never go there, Sam," says Abby. Releasing her grip on my hips, she sits beside me.

"Good," I say. I wipe my eyes with the end of my shirt Abby puts her hand atop mine, lightly squeezes, and lets go.

Lying back down, I gaze into the endless sea of blue floating above me. Staring blankly at the limited clouds moving slowly across the skyline, I start to imagine life without Elise. Like the clouds disappearing over the branches, I know that eventually Elise will be gone even if I don't want her to leave. "Can you just stay here for ten more years?" I mumble at the sky.

"What? Who are you talking to, Sam?" questions Elise.

Not realizing I had spoken aloud, I shake my head and pretend I don't know what they're talking about. "No one," I awkwardly whisper.

***

I roll back onto my side and stare farther into the forest. The dark brown of the crooked tree trunks mixed with the crumpled orange leaves make for a relaxing view—almost too much to the point that it makes me want to lie here all day. The cool breezes coupled with the scenery entrance me to the point that the leaves appear to spark. The bright orange emblazons with yellow and white, forcing the leaves to burst into miniscule lights. Like small candles, the leaves burn bright as the flames become one.

I turn back over, hoping Elise and Abby see what I see, but no one's there. The forest is empty. "Elise?" I say, staggering to my feet. "Elise," I yell again. Yet, no one responds. Not even a buzz or so much as a whisper resounds. "Elise!" I scream.

Shifting around, the flames grow larger as they barrel toward me. I start to run, praying that the heat won't catch me and pull me down into the abyss. With each step, I look back, hoping for a rogue wave to appear out of thin air and crush the fiery blast.

"Sam!" I hear from behind me. I turn back, only to see more fire as it runs through the forest, swallowing every tree in its path. "Sam!" I hear again. "Wake up!"

Rubbing my eyes, I stop. The fire continues to close in on me as I stand still. I can feel the slight tingling sensation of the heat. I start to shudder. "Sam! Open your eyes!" shouts the voice—a figure I can't quite make out—from behind the orange.

Wake up, I think. *Sam, wake up. It's all in your head.* The shudders increase as the flames rise above me. The towering sea of

98

fire starts to fall upon me like a collapsing ocean wave. The burning yellows and oranges turn transparent as they splash down.

***

"Sam, are you awake?" nervously asks Abby next to me.

I sit up and shake my head, running my hands up and down my arms. "I didn't get burnt," I whisper.

"Why would you get burnt?" asks Elise.

"The fire," I say.

"What fire?"

"I don't know. There was a fire coming at me and then it just disappeared," I say as my fingers tremble against my biceps.

"It was all in your head, Sam."

Not again. "I can't take this anymore. I just want to rest without having to worry about getting trapped in something I can't escape."

"I know, Sam. We need to find new shelter. We need somewhere where we can rest without having to worry about being watched or followed. We need an escape," says Abby.

An escape would be Nimbus, I think. Anywhere is better than here, though. I don't know how much more torment I can take. If I fall into that dream one more time, I'll probably lose it.

"I agree with Abby," says Elise. Slowly standing up, she throws her bow over her shoulder. "We should keep moving. There's gotta be something else around here that could keep us warm as the colder nights approach us."

"I guess so," I mumble beneath my breath. With my hands draped over my arms, I spasm and involuntarily push off the invisible embers. Shaking my head, I pull down my sleeves and step away from the tree.

With worry written across her cheeks, Abby speaks dejectedly. "Are you going to be okay, Sam?"

My eyes wander left and right, up and down, as I search for the right words to soothe her. Unable to calm my thoughts, I simply say, "I really don't know."

19 November 2191

Elise

I tightly close my eyes as a subtle pain runs through my head. The nagging discomfort stops my legs from willing to progress through this empty field, but I doubt my reason concerns them. I signal toward Abby for the canteen.

"Where are we?" asks Sam. Turning around, he halts and blankly stares at the field.

I take a gulp of water and shrug my shoulders. For once, I have absolutely no clue where we are. In my ten years out here, I can't say that I've ever been in this exact area. There's a small stream flowing about forty feet to our left—the water's echo livens the otherwise hushed atmosphere. Outside of that, nothing but endless dirt and stray strands of dying grass surround us. I'm just surprised we haven't gone too far yet. The emptiness seems like an end.

The more we walk, the more I think we'll never find an escape quite like the one we had—even if we try to go beyond where we're allowed. The broken-down shack was as good as it gets when it comes to fighting the cold. It had its flaws, but it had four walls and a roof. It was perfect. Sean and I never had an issue with it and we never encountered anyone else near it, but after a few weeks with Sam and Abby, it burns to the ground. *How does that even make sense?* I know it was my fault, but it still doesn't feel right. It's as eerie as my night in the city.

"Let's keep moving," says Sam. "Maybe there's some shelter around here. This field is huge. There could be a farm or something nearby."

100

"Seems fair enough," I say. Firmly shutting my eyes, I raise my cheekbones. The headache lingers ever so slightly—my stiffened cheeks providing me momentary relief. I feel a slight twinge at the top of my scalp as I take another step, but I shake off the prick. "How far do you want to go, Sam?"

"Until we find shelter. I can't sleep out here another night," he says nervously, his pupils dilating as he searches for a reprieve.

With each passing day, Sam's nightmares have grown stronger. He's barely sleeping; he's barely eating; he simply seems off. Being out here is supposed to be a prolonged mind game, but for him it's different. It's as if something has grabbed ahold of his head and won't let go. It's pushing out his sanity and replacing it with dread. I just hope it's not *him*.

Squinting with her hand above her brow, Abby says, "I think I see something."

Taking another drink, I ask, "What is it?"

"I don't know. It looks like a house or something."

"Let's go," I say assuredly. With the canteen held outward, I point toward a clearing in the distance when a small white square jumps into my line of sight. "Is that it?"

Abby nods.

We slowly start to move through the barren field, the sun shining heavily upon our backs. Surrounded by virtually nothing, the walk seems extensive. It's as if the terrain keeps getting longer with each step.

Void of wildlife, the area is completely deserted. Nothing more than scattered rocks beneath the shallow waters jump into my peripherals. It's peaceful. Almost too much so.

"That's definitely a farm," says Sam. His footsteps grow larger.

Following in stride, Abby and I walk toward Sam. With each step ahead of us, his discolored shoes leave incomplete marks in the dirt. He starts to run.

"Slow down!" I yell. Yet, he keeps running, picking up his pace with every stride. Abby and I look at each other, bemused, before chasing after him.

Suddenly, the decaying white siding of an old farmhouse appears just feet from him. Unwilling to stop in his excitement, Sam keeps running until he's inside the house and out of our sight.

"Sam!" I yell, but to no avail. "Stay behind me," I motion to Abby as she tries to catch her breath.

"Why would he sprint in there like that?" she asks.

He's afraid, I think. Exhaling, I say, "I have no idea. I really hope no one's in there."

"Me too," replies Abby dejectedly. "But what if someone is?"

I turn around. Abby's woeful eyes glance up at mine. "I think you know the answer to that."

She doesn't reply. Her lips tremble as she searches for something to say, but nothing comes out.

"Just stay behind me," I say again.

Slowly eyeing the scarf around her neck, she looks back at me. Her lips don't move. Her eyes don't waver. I can tell she knows what might happen inside; I can see the fear in her eyes, but we can't stop. Being afraid of what lies ahead is the definition of Separation, and the best way to learn that fear is temporary is to charge forward.

Quietly nearing the front of the house, I reach for the chipped handle on the screen door. Slowly pulling it toward me, it creaks. For every degree it turns, it loudens. Yanking it open in a fit of fear, I angrily press the door against the house. "Sam," I whisper.

Nervously clenching onto the back of my shirt, Abby squeezes her hand into a fist as she pulls the door shut behind us with her other hand. Trying to whisper, she mouths, 'Sam,' but nothing comes out.

I turn around and gently push her clammy hand away; her pupils enlarge as her knees buckle. "It'll be okay," I mutter, pulling her to her feet. Apprehensively biting her drying lips, she remains close with each step—almost to the point that her toes land on my heels with each groan of the floorboards.

Slowly stepping through the cluttered house, my eyes widen in search of Sam, but he never appears. Only remains of the past jump into my line of sight. Tattered photographs hang loosely from broken frames above the fireplace, upholstered seats with strange patterns sit crookedly, a broken table lies on its side as shards from the snapped legs poke out carelessly. Even the presumably once-dark oak floor is almost entirely scratched to the point that it's become a sickly, lifeless gray. The whole front room is a mess—a collection of disjointed memories.

"Sam," I whisper again.

No response. Silence engulfs the single syllable the moment it slides past my lips.

Abby pulls her Swiss Army knife from her pocket as we quietly step farther into the room. Grabbing one of the arrows from my quiver, I place it against the end of the bow and crouch behind a tilted armchair.

Still behind me, Abby grabs the back of my shirt once more. I can feel her hand clenching, her fingers trembling.

"It's going to be okay," I say, turning around. "But, we're gonna have to split up. I don't know where Sam went and this way we can cover ground faster."

Her hand stops. Her face grows a light shade of white, her cheeks droop while her eyes become teary. "Alright," she begrudgingly replies.

"It'll be okay." Gently placing my hands on her shoulders, I tell her to search the rooms to our right while I head upstairs. She inaudibly agrees, though her glum expression disagrees with every word I say.

Fearfully drifting toward an unhinged door into what appears to be an office, Abby disappears. I gradually head upstairs.

With my bow at my side, I tiptoe toward the second floor. As I maneuver past split floorboards and mouse droppings, a soft creak echoes ahead of me. I stop and whisper, "Sam."

"Elise," comes a faint cry atop the stairs.

"Sam? Sam? Where are you?"

He goes silent.

Hurrying to the top of the stairs, I notice Sam facedown on the floor in front of me. As he slowly lifts up his head, his wondering eyes appear bloodshot as a stale red drips down his forehead. I inch closer to him. His eyes twitch and close. "Sam!" I yell.

With my bow against my chest I pull an arrow back toward my shoulder. "Sam," I say again, but he doesn't flinch; the sweat atop his head pools onto the floor. "Sam," I softly mouth. Motionless and lightly breathing, Sam remains silent. I step toward him just as a powerful thump shakes the hallway and a chair smashes into the wall beside me. Sam still doesn't move. The creaks grow louder. "Who did that?" I ask.

Thrusting my back against the wall beside Sam, I peek into the empty room where the chair was flung. Holding my bow out firmly, the door behind Sam—to my left—opens up farther. A mangy, hairless man with yellowing eyes looks at me before reaching for Sam's feet. He starts to pull Sam into the room as Sam's arms lifelessly slide against the slivered floorboards. Before I have time to react, the door's shut and Sam's gone. *I was too slow, too confused.*

I shake my head and turn to face the door. Forcing my shoulder into the bulky wood, I push and push, but it won't budge. Violently rattling the door handle doesn't aid in my attempt either. Releasing the decaying knob from my grip, I put all of my weight into my shoulders. With one swift jump, I slam into the door, but it won't open. "SAM!" I scream to no avail.

Fumbling for the blade's handle against my hip, I pull out the knife. Wrapping my bow around my chest, I try to pry the door open, but it doesn't work.

Quickly averting my attention to the room to my right, I peek in. It's empty. Devoid of color, the lifeless room provides no relief. Sam's nowhere in sight. No one else is present either. The only sound is the innocuous gliding of the wind against the side of the house. *Someone has to be in here.* Even if they're hiding or stowed away in a closet, someone's here. Sam couldn't just disappear.

Lying directly in the middle of the room, a bleak mattress covered in soot stares at me. There are no prints on it, just unnecessary ash. Surrounding it is nothing but the scratched hardwood. *This room is disturbing.* I look right. A few feet over, a door partially hangs open. To my left, another door clings to its broken frame against the wall of the room Sam is in.

With my knife outstretched, I step toward the door beside me. Grabbing it with the ends of my fingers, it creaks open before I push it toward the wall. Cautiously, I lean into the pitch black of the room as softened footsteps echo behind me. *It's nothing.* I step farther into the dark room—the footsteps growing louder. *It's nothing.* A thud clatters behind me. Nervously turning around, my stare fixates on the yellow-eyed man storming at me with an axe held above his head. My heart tries to jump out my chest in fear. As the man's eyes widen and the axe starts to come down, I jump to the right. He swings into the shadows of the closet. Missing everything,

104

he tries to pull the axe out of the floor. Shifting behind him, I stab the blade into his back. Pulling it out, I bury the dagger into the back of his skull. Yanking out the knife once more, I pierce it into his neck. That's when I hear a scream.

"ABBY!" I yell. "ABBY!"

I push the man over and grab the handle of the axe. Luckily, he got it out just enough to the point that I can wedge it out of the crack.

"ELISE!" shrieks Abby from downstairs.

Ripping the axe out of the floor, I sprint down to the main room. Quickly rounding the last step, I see Abby cornered in the front of the house. A man, twice her size, stands above her as he laughs. "Don't scream, little girl," he says in a droll, chilling voice.

"Elise!" cries Abby.

Abruptly stopping on the last step, I stand still. The man speaks again; the awkward gaiety of his voice makes my skin crawl. "Why are you screaming? I just want to play," he says.

"Get away from her!" I yell.

Arching his back, he turns around. The rugged unevenness of his eyes is matched by his mangled nose, scarred cheek, and crooked smile. If his voice wasn't enough to instill fear in Abby, his appearance could haunt her; it could terrify anyone. I look away.

"Do you want to play, too?" he asks.

I turn to face him while he half smiles and moves toward me with his arms outstretched. Lifting the axe diagonally into the air, I swing for his stomach. Unfazed, he grabs just below the blade and pushes me into the wall. My back slams against the rotting wood; a frame shatters beside me.

With the axe at his disposal, he holds it out to his side. Burying his top two teeth into his bottom lip, he cocks the weapon back. With one quick motion, he swings it at my neck. I sink below the reddened end of the blade just before it smashes into the wall. Sliding onto my feet as he angrily tries to pull the axe out of the crumbling wood, I run toward Abby.

Struggling with the axe, he mumbles nonsense to himself.

"Get behind me," I say to Abby as I pull out my bow. Lining up my shot, I aim for his neck. Releasing the string, the arrow flies into his shoulder blade.

Angrily ripping the axe from the wall, he says, "That wasn't nice." Lifting the blade above his head, he walks toward us.

Pulling a second arrow back, I shoot it into his stomach. It doesn't bother him. I fire another into his chest. And another. And another. Yet, with five arrows sticking out of him, he keeps walking toward us with no signs of slowing down.

"Stop it!" he ferociously yells.

Trying to steady my shot, I take a deep breath. Dragging the arrow back, I shift my focus toward his head. Moving past the couch, he stops in front of us with the axe held high. I release the end of the string. His face contorts. Grimacing in pain, he falls to his knees, dropping the axe. "I just wanted to play," he mumbles as he falls face first into the hardwood—sending a puff of dust into the air while blood drips from his mouth.

Turning around, I wrap my arms around Abby. "Are you okay?" I ask breathlessly.

"Y-yes," she stutters. "I thought he was going to kill me."

"It's okay. We're still standing," I say. Though, I can't believe what happened. I've never encountered anyone out here quite like that. No one's ever taken that many arrows and refused to die. It feels like he was here to kill us, that our chances of ending up here were high.

"Where's Sam?" sobs Abby, her fingers twitching against my back.

"Upstairs, I think. C'mon."

Breaking up our hug, we both sprint upstairs. Running through the open door to the right, we quickly turn left inside the room. Jumping through the now-open door at the left end of the wall, Sam cries out, "Elise?"

"Sam?" I say, stepping close to his motionless body.

Lifting his bloodied head toward us, he frowns, "Help."

"What happened?" I ask.

"I don't know," he says. "I came into the house and then everything went black. I think someone hit me."

"Does anything feel broken?"

"I can't tell. My hand hurts and my head aches."

I grab Sam's hand. Covered in drying blood, his knuckles are swelling, but at first glance a clear-cut wound doesn't show. "I'm not seeing anything," I say. Lifting his hand closer to my face, the

106

more it jumps out, the more the red traces itself back to a darkened patch of torn skin atop his pinky. "Sam, don't look at your hand. Abby, find some rags and hand me the canteen."

"Okay," she replies before stepping out.

Uneasy, Sam keeps his eyes on mine. "Why shouldn't I look?"

"Because it'll just make you feel worse."

"Here's a rag and the water," says Abby, handing the items to me.

Reaching for his finger, I pour the water onto the open wound before pressing the rag into it. "Find me some alcohol," I say to Abby. Quickly standing back up, she runs downstairs.

"What happened? Why do you need alcohol?" he asks impatiently, his face contorting each second I press harder into to his finger.

"Do you really want to know?"

"Yes. No. Yes. I don't know," he says as he cringes.

"You're going to find out sooner or later, so I'm going to tell you." Biting his lip, he shakes his head at me. "Your pinky, just above the knuckle, is gone."

His eyes widen as he rips his hand out from underneath the rag. Spilling more blood, he screams. Storming up the stairs, Abby rushes back into the room and hands me a bottle of vodka.

"You need to give me your hand," I say callously. Tightening my stare, I reach for his wrist. He shrieks as I push the bloodied finger back into the towel. "You're going to need to bite onto something. This next part will sting a bit."

Rolling up his shirt, Sam sticks the end into his mouth. Lightly biting down while tears dry upon his cheeks, he looks back at me. With my eyes fixed on his, I twist open the bottle before I slowly pour the clear liquid onto the laceration. Instantly, he screams in agony and jolts his hand into the air. Reaching for his arm, I pull it down with what little energy I have left before wrapping the rag around it. Tying the ends together, I thrust my back into the wall across from him.

"It hurts so bad," he says in tears.

"It's going to hurt for a while. Just keep that rag on it and keep applying pressure. We need to stop the bleeding and let it heal itself. There's probably a first aid kit around here somewhere and once we find that, I'll patch it up."

"Thanks," he says. Wincing, he wipes the tears from his cheek—the blood soaking through to the top of the rag.

I half-smile and stand up before heading toward the door. "Abby, keep an eye on him," I say, stepping into the adjacent room.

"Where are you going?" she asks.

"I just need some fresh air. I'll be back in a few minutes. Keep applying pressure."

"Okay," she nods.

The second I step out of the room and into the hallway, my head starts to ache. The throbbing pressure that had been missing for days comes back full steam ahead. I press the palms of my hands into the sides of my scalp as I move down the stairs and out the front door. Upon reaching the front porch, I take a few steps and sit down.

With nothing but empty fields in front of me, I close my eyes. The pulsing refuses to lighten even as I raise my cheekbones and dig further into my skull. A breeze rips through the area —the brush of wind doing nothing to soothe the pressure.

"Go away!" I yell into the air. But, the headache doesn't budge. The pain worsens.

My eyes start to vibrate, forcing me to let go of my head and open my eyes. The wind abruptly comes to a halt. A faded black figure appears in the distance. Motionless, it stands in the fields. *It's all in your head*, I think as I close my eyes. *It's not real.*

I barely open them and squint. Yet, nothing appears; the figure is gone. *It's all in your head,* I tell myself once more. *He's not here.* I fully open them and watch as the sun starts to descend deeper into the fields, the misery seemingly starting to vanish.

26 November 2191

Sam

I slowly run my fingers down the misshapen mattress; the wrap covering my pinky drags against the discolored bed. The pain has hit a point where I almost don't notice it, but occasionally it throbs as if the tip of my finger is still there. It's strange, but at least it's not infected.

A loud caw shrieks just outside the window as Abby pushes open the door.

"How are you feeling today?" she asks anxiously.

"Alright," I smile. I'm doing whatever I can to avoid letting them know the extent of my discomfort. My nightmares haven't disappeared. I lost a part of my finger in way that I can't explain. My mind is all over the place and no matter what I do to soothe it, it refuses to listen. It's as if something else has a grip on me, something I can't grasp at.

At times it's almost like I'm alone. I've never felt this trapped and I haven't even been on the outside for more than a couple months. I still have over ten years left to fight for and I don't know if I can manage another month, let alone another week.

"Elise said we could train today if you want to. If not, that's okay," smiles Abby.

"Yea, let's do that," I nod.

"Let's go get Elise then. I think she's just outside." I roll onto my back as Abby reaches for my palms. Helping me to my feet, she bemusedly looks at me. "How do you even sleep on that thing?"

I shake my head and glance back at the dingy mattress. "I'm not really sure. I just need something better than the floor."

"You're probably going to hurt your back," she laughs.

"I don't think I'm old enough to have back problems," I say with a half-smile.

"Probably not, but you never know. I just wish we could find a place that wasn't completely torn apart already."

"Too bad that's impossible," I say as we start to walk downstairs.

"You never know," she repeats.

I quickly step over a crooked board as a mouse scurries down the steps and into a hole in the wall. Abby shrieks and jumps behind me, her hands shaking on my shoulders. I can't help but laugh because after all we've been through, it's a bit pathetic that a mouse can still frighten her. "Really?" I chuckle.

"Shut up, Sam. It's gross," she says, digging her nails into my shoulder blades.

"Are you two ready to train?" asks Elise from the front of the room. Standing there with a few blueberries in the palm of her hand, she pops one into her mouth.

"Yea," I reply, meeting up with her.

With her hand outstretched, she holds out a few berries as her other arm reaches for the door handle behind her. "I know it's not much, but it's food," she says, pulling the front door open.

At this point I'll eat anything. I've spent a majority of the past few days just sitting in that room attempting to cope with what happened. I've adjusted to my hopeless finger, but not enough to the point that I'm perfectly okay with it. It's my fault it happened; it's my fault Abby almost got killed; everything that happened in here is my fault, but I can't let it eat at me more than it already is. If I do, everything's bound to worsen.

If I had broken my leg or busted my arm, we'd be in trouble. Losing a fingernail isn't anywhere near that because it doesn't force us to be stationary. It lets us roam. Though, it further shows me what the outside is capable of. It proves to me that beauty on the outside can lead to internal darkness. Nothing's sacred out here.

Regardless, I'm still here. *I'm still alive.* Though, at times, I don't feel like it. It feels like there's a constant weight pushing me down—one reliant upon the burden I've been on Elise and Abby and the farther I fall, the more I drag them down with me. *If I never ran inside; if I wasn't foolish enough to believe this place was safe.*

110

Slipping a few berries into my mouth as we walk out onto the field, I aimlessly stare around. Trying to shake off any unnecessary thoughts, I watch as small flocks of birds depart from the trees in the distance. Flying deeper into the woods, they disappear into the blue.

Holding out her hand for us to stop, Elise pulls the bow down from her shoulders and hands it to Abby. "I've set up a few targets about thirty feet away for you two," she says.

Flashes of the shack run across my mind. Blurred images of the cans falling from my arms plaster themselves around the walls of my thoughts. A cold sensation runs against my back. I shiver. *Stop thinking about it.*

I shift my focus to the withering fence to our left. Placed atop one of the planks are several rotting aluminum cans a couple inches apart, bookended by a gallon jug on each end. The wind wobbles the cans ever so slightly, but none fall. "You call those targets?" I laugh. Placing the last berry on the tip of my tongue, I step beside Abby and smirk at Elise.

"You got something better in mind?" she retorts.

"No."

"That's what I thought." Shaking her head, Elise turns toward Abby. "Alright, Abby. All you need to do is knock them all off. It's that simple," she says sarcastically.

"Aren't you going to show me how to shoot?" asks Abby, flustered.

"Not yet. I want to see how you do without my help first. That way, I can see where you need to improve and help you with that. I know you know to pull the string back and release, so you can do it however you want right now."

Without hesitating, Abby pulls her arm back and fires the first arrow. From where I'm standing it looks on target, but it eventually flies several feet to the left of the first jug. Before the arrow has a chance to land beyond the fence, Abby's already pulling back another. Evidently desiring to knock the targets down one by one, she aims for the same piece of plastic. Once again, she misses the jug by a few feet. Disregarding the barrage of arrows sailing deep into the field, Abby continues to rapidly fire. After a few shots go awry—one dud drops ten feet in front of her—she's knocked down the two jugs, but can't manage to knock down the smaller targets in between.

111

"That wasn't too bad, now was it?" smiles Elise from beside Abby.

"It's harder than it looks," says Abby as she hands me the bow and the quiver with about five arrows left in it.

If you go that fast for no reason, I can see why, I think, but don't say.

"You ready, Sam?" smiles Elise.

Lifting the bow toward my chest, I mumble a soft, "Sure." A slight wind breezes through the area, forcing me to clench my fingertips tighter on the string. Moving the bow slightly to the left, I take a breath and try to steady my aim. But the more I slow everything down, the faster the wind goes, unwrapping my bandages. I let go. The end of the arrow takes a small piece of fabric with it.

"So close!" exclaims Elise as my first arrow flies just to the side of the first can—the dry wrap nicking it.

"I'll get the next one," I say.

Reaching for another arrow from the quiver, I place it against the wood of the bow. Refraining from moving my aim too much, I steady my feet, pull back, and release. Instantly, it pierces the middle of the first can, launching the rusting aluminum into the dirt.

Quickly reaching for another arrow, I stretch my arms out and drag the third one from the quiver and put it in place. Steadying my breath, I fire. The arrow hits the second can and drills it into the ground. Reaching for another arrow, I take out the fourth one and shoot it directly into the next can. With one arrow left, I take a deep breath as I gently pull the faded white string toward my cheek. With one quick breath, I let go.

"That was incredible, Sam," says Elise as she comes over and takes the equipment from me. "I didn't know you were that good with a bow."

"Neither did I," I laugh. I can't believe that I hit nearly every target with only five shots. *Hopefully, I can be that accurate when we need it*, I think. Smiling, I turn around to see Abby with a large grin across her face.

"Beginner's luck," she smirks, her eyes rolling toward the sky.

"Maybe it was," I laugh as we start to walk toward the fence to collect the arrows.

"Do you think you could do that again? Did that hurt your hand at all?" asks Elise.

"I don't know if I could, but it didn't hurt too badly. I have three other fingers to grip the staff with, so it's okay."

After a few minutes of pulling the arrows out of the plastic, aluminum, and neighboring trees, we head back to try again.

Following another round of shots complete with pointers from Elise, Abby and I have both gotten better at hitting the targets on our first tries. However, I didn't shoot as well on the smaller cans as she did this time. Naturally, that means she has to rub it in my face a little as we go to collect the arrows again.

"Nice shootin'," says Abby as she winks at me.

"Looks like you got your beginner's luck the second time around," I say.

Pulling an arrow out of the dirt, Abby looks back at me. With a straight face, she says, "It was all skill" before she starts to chuckle.

"If you say so," I laugh.

Yanking an arrow out of the dirt a dozen feet away, Elise throws it into the quiver. Hurriedly gathering the surrounding arrows for a third round, she places them beside the others. Then, discarding the plastic jugs, she positions the less-damaged cans on top of the fence. "Again," she says. "But, let's step back ten feet."

Abby arches her eyebrows and looks at me. "Why not twenty?"

"Think you can best me from farther out?" I ask.

She smiles. "I just want to see how many times we each miss."

"Probably more times than Elise wants us to," I reply.

"It's great to see that confidence," laughs Elise. "We'll step back ten feet each time until the targets look like peas."

Time passes in a mere instant as we lose plenty of Elise's arrows beyond our targets. By the time the sun peaks in the sky, we're nearly out of arrows and the phantom pain on my finger has resurfaced.

Throwing the quiver over her shoulder as she starts to walk back to the house, Elise says, "We can practice more later if you guys want to."

"Once I can take this stuff off my hand, I definitely want to," I say.

"That won't be for a while though," she replies.

"How much longer?"

"Not until it's completely healed."

"That could take months," I sigh.

"There's no need to rush," says Abby from behind me. "We have plenty of time."

"I know," I mutter. "I just wish things were different."

"Me too, but we'll get through," smiles Abby.

"It could always be worse, so be thankful you're still breathing," says Elise while pulling open the front door.

A slight frown stretches across my face as I turn around to look at Abby. Trying to hold back a yawn, her face contorts. Sleepily looking at me, she awkwardly smiles. *I hope it never gets worse*, I think. *I don't want to lose her.*

"I think we should nap before we do anything," she says.

"I wouldn't say no to that," I nod.

"Don't you think we should at least clean up where we sleep a bit? We could probably find a blanket or something to lie atop your crappy mattress, Sam, or maybe even one that Abby and I could use in the room we're sleeping in," mentions Elise before she heads into the kitchen.

"I guess so, but where do you want to look? I feel like we've scavenged most of these two floors already."

"Have either of you seen a door to a basement?" asks Elise.

The hairs on my arms stand up as the cold footprints of a short-lived breeze rush through the front windows. "Nope, but even if we did, I think we should just pass on that," I mutter.

Elise laughs as she looks over at Abby. "What about you?"

". . .I-I haven't seen anything and I wouldn't really want to go down there anyways," she stutters. "It's an old farm. I wouldn't be surprised if there wasn't one."

Slowly smiling, Elise looks at Abby. "True. Let's just look through the closets in these two rooms and Sam's room."

"Okay," says Abby, itching her eyes.

I thrust my upper back against the wall and push myself off the decaying wood toward the main room. Slowly turning around to see if anyone's joining me in my quest to find something I know

114

doesn't exist, Abby starts rubbing her eyes and sniffling. Quickly stepping toward her, Elise sits down and signals for me to go search without them. *I wonder what's wrong*, I think.

Abby's been much stronger than I have lately. We've connected to a point where I feel comfortable to tell her almost everything—except the depths my mind is taking me to. If something is bringing her to tears and she can't tell me why, it can't be good. Maybe the isolation from Nimbus is starting to hit her, maybe she's overwhelmed by everything that's happened lately and it's coming crashing down. No matter what it is, it pains me to see her sad just like I'm sure it bothers Elise to see my nightmares guiding me in the wrong direction.

Regardless of what it is, everything would be a lot worse if we didn't have Elise. My problems would become Abby's and hers would become mine. There's no way we'd still be alive if Sean didn't tell Elise to find us; there's not a doubt in my mind. I like Abby, but we're just not strong enough to be on our own. If what's been happening to me lately occurred with just the two of us, I'd be in the city by now. I don't know if she could stop me.

I shake the image from my mind as I approach the unhinged door into the first room. Newspapers lie scattered about while bookshelves lie on their sides with a mess of books in front of them. Ernest Hemingway's *The Old Man and the Sea* sits on its pages as the spine of the book arches into the air; Fitzgerald's *The Great Gatsby* is the only book still on its shelf, but it's entirely dusted over to the point that 'atsby' is the only legible lettering on the cover; James Joyce's *Ulysses* is torn in two, while numerous books from centuries ago are strewn about. Nearly every book I've ever learned about from my parents is on this floor somewhere.

Yet, one book stands out amongst the rest. Idly sitting faceup in the middle of the pile, a small brown book lies open. I pick it up and glance at the empty cover before wiping off a few specks of dust. As I gently open the book halfway, the spine tears slightly at the bottom. Indifferent to ruining it further, I quickly open the book all the way and skim through the first few pages. *It's empty.*

I flip through nearly every page, but nothing more than splotches of black ink lie dispersed throughout. The book is worthless; there's no value to it whatsoever, but for some reason I was drawn to it. I don't know why. It was one of hundreds on the floor, but it was the only one faceup. Granted, it has no title and I haven't seen any words, but there has to be something in it. I thumb through the first ten pages of the book again, but nothing changes.

"Sam, what are you looking at?" questions Elise from behind me.

"I don't know. This book was in the middle of all these other books and something was pulling me to it."

"What's the book about?"

"There's nothing in it. There are just ink spots in random places," I say.

"Can I take a look?" she asks as she steps over a few books.

"Sure," I say, handing it to her.

Quickly flipping through the pages a few times, she stops and looks at the front and back covers. "This is very strange. It's like someone tried to write something in here, but never got the chance. Maybe there are a few pages stuck together somewhere where the ink dried and someone actually wrote something." Narrowing her eyes, she rubs her chin and hands it back to me.

"Maybe," I say. "I didn't notice any stuck pages, though."

"It's just a thought. Just go through it slowly if you care. It seems a bit like a waste to me. It was probably just someone's journal."

"Probably. But, I think I'll hold onto it just in case you're right."

"Okay. Did you find any blankets or pillows or something by chance?" she asks, her eyes drawn to every corner of the room.

"I didn't have the chance to look," I say.

"You've been in here for like half an hour. What have you been doing the whole time?"

"What? It's been like five minutes," I mutter.

"Nope. It's definitely been longer than that. Have you been looking at that book the whole time?" she asks.

"I guess so." *Maybe we should have scoured the place when we first moved in*, I think—an attempt to rid my mind from the fact that I've wasted thirty minutes doing nothing. I've done nothing more than open the book a few times. No more than four. There aren't many pages; there isn't even much to look at—unless Elise is right. *Maybe there's a message inside*. Every book has a story; maybe this one just requires more attention.

116

I open the book again and start to thumb the edges, looking for two pages clinging together. I get through the first few pages without finding anything more than the mere scribbles that are present throughout the entirety of the journal. Yet, the further I go, the more the drawings jump out, the more Elise's guess becomes a possibility. Reaching the tenth page, a slight ridge pricks my fingers. Running my thumb up and down the edge, I signal for Elise's knife.

Gently wedging the tip of the blade into the slit between the pages, I run it down until pages ten and twelve are separated. Slowly pulling the paper apart, I try to avoid ripping the entirety of what could be hiding here. As the pages release from each other, a smudged mix of black lines runs straight across the journal. A dark blotch envelopes the middle of the eleventh page and continues onto the next one. *It's nothing more than a large rectangle.* I hand it to Elise.

"What's this supposed to be?" she asks, her eyes shifting back and forth from mine to the pages. Moving the book closer to her eyes, she squints. "It's pretty smeared, but," she sighs, "I think it's an arrow. It kind of looks like the ends of the rectangle on page twelve are pointing outward a bit, but I couldn't tell you what for."

"Maybe it's pointing to something? That would be the only thing that makes sense," I say.

"Where did you pick up the book?" comes Abby's respired voice.

"Right there," I say, pointing to the center of the pile of books.

"Sam," pauses Elise, "Turn your head to your right. There's something engraved in the wall, but I can't really tell what it says from here."

I slowly walk toward the wood-paned wall and kneel down to look at the inscription.

"What does it say?" asks Elise nervously.

I take a deep breath and read the crooked engraving. "It reads, 'You will not find solace in the hollows of night.'"

2 December 2191

Sean

It's been weeks since I've seen the outside, weeks since I've felt the heat of the sun on my neck. I've thinned and grown a beard reminiscent of my last days on the outside—one that's caused me more discomfort than MacMillan's constant presence. I feel worthless, hopeless, and lost all at once, but there's nothing I can do about my misfortune. I put myself here. And there's no bigger reminder of that than the conniving grin of Eldridge MacMillan and the surprise he claims to have for me.

Day in and day out, I sit here twiddling my thumbs back and forth hoping that at some point I'll escape, that I'll never see Nimbus again. It's a fallacy, but it's the only thing my mind can grab onto. Even if it is unrealistic, it's better than thinking about dying here. The last thing I need to further my self-pity is the notion that my parents could watch me be hanged and my little brother might not find out for over ten years. There's no way out of this hellhole I've created for myself; the only way to the outside is through MacMillan.

"MacMillan will be here in ten, Martin," reverberates a voice from outside my cell.

I tilt my head to the side to see if I can catch a glimpse of the guard who spoke, but no one's there. The man who once sat in the cell across from mine was executed two weeks ago, so now the guard comes by even less. Nothing's more haunting than being left entirely alone in a room where others have stayed for nights shorter than the ones I've had.

"Make that two minutes," says the inconspicuous voice.

Two minutes until my world comes to an end—assuming that's what MacMillan's surprise is. *It's not even a surprise at this point*, I think. Clasping my hands together, I sit on the edge of my mattress and bury my forehead into my knuckles.

"Stand up, Martin. MacMillan's arriving," says the guard.

Slowly getting to my feet, I look to my left where MacMillan's pointy nose pokes between the bars. "It's great to see you again," he sarcastically states. "Have you been enjoying your stay?"

I don't reply.

"I bet you're just loving it here. It's definitely where someone of your stature belongs," he jokes. "Lucky for you, I have a great idea in mind for what we can do with you."

"Oh yea?" I say bitterly.

"You were one of the strongest on the outside, right?" he asks.

Unsure if I should even speak, I keep my glare on him.

"I'll take that as a yes. Lucky for you, I'm going to send you back out. You've spent a month in here and you've grown weaker. I had them barely feed you on purpose; I had them make sure you didn't do any workouts of your desire on purpose. I wanted to make you thin and weak, so you would die out there just like you should have the first time around."

"Okay," I mutter, confused by his logic.

"Unless, of course, you would prefer for us to kill you in front of your parents," he jokes.

"I'll take the first option," I say.

"Good. Now grab your stuff and we'll head out. . .wait, you don't have anything," he says with an enormous grin.

Everything is a game to him. Separation is just about him instilling fear in everyone. What he doesn't understand is that he's old and weak and it won't be too long from now when everyone revolts against him. His power, his authority, his strength—they're all dying with each day he lives on.

"Let's go," I say firmly.

Reaching for the key in his back pocket, MacMillan sneers at me as he forces the end of the silver into the lock. "I'm going to enjoy this more than you will ever know," he gibes.

Yielding to his sarcasm, I stop myself from responding before stepping into the hallway. Instantly, a guard grabs ahold of my wrists and pushes me forward.

Bustling past an array of holding cells replete with men and women of all ages clamoring for release, MacMillan scoffs as we pass through. Quickly opening the door at the end of the hallway, he sticks the end of his boot into my spine—forcing me forward into the dirt. My knees slam into the ground as he kicks me once more. This time, it's into the top of my back.

"Get up," he shouts.

I push the palms of my hands into the dirt and hover on all fours. Closing my eyes, I fall onto my stomach.

"I said, get up!"

I exhale—the pain in my back making its way down my legs. Slowly moving upward, I turn to see the gray hue of the wall's exit doors in front of me.

"Turn around," grits MacMillan as he grinds his teeth.

With my back hunched over and my head drooped low, I strain my neck to stare into his beady eyes while he inches closer to me.

"I don't think this day could get any better," he wildly laughs before spitting onto my forehead. With an abundance of silence around him, he awkwardly stares at the guards. A sudden light laughter follows; one uncomfortable for even me. With an unwilling crowd at his disposal, he cocks his arm back and launches his knuckles into my chest. I buckle onto the ground. "Oh wait, it just did get better," he laughs.

I clench my fists, but don't stand up. His men surround him and if I so much as touch him, I'll be on the ground faster than I just was. *You're almost out*, I think. *You're almost out.*

"Get up, Martin," he shouts as a small crowd starts to gather just outside the exit courtyard. "It's time for your second Separation." Within seconds, the crowd has grown larger with civilians standing on their front doorsteps watching the torment. "GET UP!"

I don't move. My eyes glean hope from the weary stares of others. Distraught by what they're witnessing, the crowd moves closer. Several have their hands on their mouths, others refuse to look, but follow the movement of the group. Yet, deep in the middle of it all stands a boy. Holding onto his father's hand with his left, he holds the hand of a teddy bear in his right. Fixated on me, his eyes slowly widen.

Before I have a chance to gesture back, two guards come sprinting from beside MacMillan. Grabbing me by my wrists, they pull me up from the dirt. With each step, they pull harder toward the steel doors. My ribs are aching, my back is tightening, and I can barely manage the willpower to move. I try to rid the thoughts of death from my mind as the doors open, yet the stray thoughts of the shadows dive into my head faster than ever.

"Good luck," says MacMillan as he sweeps my legs out from underneath me with his, forcing me face-first into the dirt outside the wall. "You're going to need all the luck in the world to stay alive for more than a week."

Pained and afraid to move, I lift my neck upright. With his bear on the ground, the boy's eyes start to water. I shake my head side to side as he mouths, "Please" to his father. Turning away, I plant my face in the dirt.

The doors slam shut behind me. The Elite Guard yells at civilians to go back inside. As each door closes, the echoes of their disapproval ring loudly around me. Yet, the only thing I can hear is a voice I never heard, a cry I never wanted.

6 December 2191

Elise

"You will not find solace in the hollows of night. What does that even mean?" asks Sam, his eyes jumping from mine to Abby's in search of an answer.

"I've told you a million times, Sam. It's just someone trying to scare you."

"Do you think one of the Shadow Lurkers wrote that? They're the only ones who seem to embrace darkness," mentions Sam as he fiddles with the edges of the journal.

"I don't know. I feel like you've asked me a variation of this same question for the past few days. Can't you just forget about it already?" I ask while tossing another log into the fireplace.

"I'm sorry, Elise. I just feel like it means something."

It's been a few days since we found the engraving in the library, or what I'm calling the library, but Sam can't seem to get it out of his mind. He goes in there every morning to see if he can find another inscription, but he always comes out empty-handed. It's as if he's finding enjoyment in a dispiriting message and it doesn't make much sense. He's been horrified of darkness, of sleeping, of being alone for the last month or two, yet he's eager to seek out this trivial imprint. It's odd.

Tending to the crumbling wood, I look back at Sam. "You just need to forget about it. If the Shadow Lurkers did indeed write that, then you don't want to read too much into it. It'll just scare you more and more."

"But it doesn't scare me. I don't really know why either. . .it just doesn't," mutters Sam.

122

Pulling her knees against her chest in the armchair, Abby furrows her brows. "Why don't you know? You've had some pretty horrifying dreams and thoughts of the city, Sam. It doesn't make sense how something probably written by someone from there doesn't scare you."

"It just doesn't. I guess it sort of makes sense to me. I don't find peace or solitude at night anymore, so it's kind of relatable. I guess I want to figure out why it's there and why I haven't been right lately. It gives me a little bit of an answer. . ." trails Sam as he rips a page from the book.

"But is that the sort of answer you want? Something that tells you exactly what you already know?" I ask as I sit down.

Leaning toward the fireplace, Sam keeps his stare on the ground. "I don't know," he says softly. Throwing the crumpled piece of paper into the fire, he turns around. "It's just something."

"That's all it is," says Abby. "Which, out here, means it's practically nothing."

"Why's that?" replies Sam.

"Because every time we run into something out here, it just tries to drag us down. So, the only way to look at something is to treat it as nothing, so it can't hurt you."

"For your sake, let's hope it's nothing," I mumble before lifting my neck onto the back of the chair and massaging my forehead with my index finger and thumb. Trying to shake off the inconvenient pulsing, I close my eyes and press into the ridge of my nose.

"Are you okay?" asks Sam, a faint trace of worry in his voice.

"Yea, it's nothing," I say.

"You sure? Do you need something to eat or drink?" asks Abby.

"I'm fine. Plus we don't have any food right now."

"I could certainly go get some," says Sam.

Keeping my eyes shut, I roll my head side to side. "It's night."

"So?"

"I'm not going to let you go outside right now and find something to eat just for my sake," I say harshly. "We can find something in the morning. I'll be okay. We have water anyways."

"If you say so," says Sam.

"I do. Now, maybe we should get some rest."

"I'm not really tired though. Can't we just stay up and talk or something? You said it yourself, Elise: I've been having a lot of nightmares lately, so I would really rather just stay up and talk."

Sitting upright, I glance at Sam; twisting his fingers together against the binding, he agitatedly looks around the room. "I guess so. What do you want to talk about?"

Closing the journal, he sets it atop the fireplace. "Anything, really. We haven't really talked about what you and Sean did while you two were together. I know you stayed in that shack for a little while, but that's all we really know."

I exhale as Sam sits down next to me. "What do you want to know?"

Turning toward me, Sam's face shows an odd tinge of excitement. "Everything. What did you two do every day? Did you ever run into any people like who we have outside of the city?"

Doing little to resolve his alternating emotions, I mutter, "We did."

"How many? How often? What did you do?" he quickly responds.

"What do you think we did?"

"I don't know. Kill them, I assume, but how many people?" responds Sam anxiously.

Laughing, I smile and admire his perked-up enthusiasm. "I don't think that's something that really matters, but if I had to put a number on it, I'd say we may have killed fifteen to twenty people together. I mean, it may seem like a lot, but we had to do it to survive just as we did here."

I don't like thinking of the situations in which we had to kill others, but at the same time I feel obligated to keep Sam's mind occupied. We killed to survive just as anyone would, but we didn't just kill Shadow Lurkers or deranged lunatics, we killed someone's kid. We killed an innocent kid just like ourselves because we didn't know what else to do. . .and it sucks. No matter the threat, nothing lingers in your mind more than murdering someone because of a stupid game. That's all it is to MacMillan and that's all it will ever be.

124

Looking at me uneasily, Abby's eyes shift around the room. "That's a lot. Can you tell us a story about one of those situations?"

I could. They're all equally unpleasant, with each one being less painful than the one before it, but that didn't make it more enjoyable. Every kill, every second stolen from someone else whether that person was a Lurker or just a frightened soul, wasn't worth the initial torment. Sean always told me that nobody deserves to die for MacMillan, but someone has to. And the longer we went on, the clearer that statement became—the simpler it was to block out the agony of putting an end to someone's eleven years.

My wandering stare falls to the ground as I mutter, "I don't really like to talk about it." Slowly getting to my feet, I reach for the reddened fire poker. Hitting the logs a few times as the sparks flare, I look back at the two of them. "I'll tell you one though," I whisper. With my voice fluctuating back up, I continue, "Two murders that Sean and I will never forget."

Sitting with wide, animated eyes, Sam and Abby refuse to blink as they wait for me to speak.

"About a year before I met you guys, Sean and I were living off of virtually nothing. Times had passed where we hadn't eaten in days. We always had plenty of water, but we couldn't find so much as a few berries at times. It was tough," I say before taking a swig from the canteen.

Handing the water to Abby, I poke the fire once more before I speak again. "After several days of small portions of food, we finally spotted a deer. Not just a small, starved doe that I hated killing, but a buck. I had never seen one so big; it made my mouth water instantly. I was imagining the seasoned deer you have the day someone returns from out here and it made me a little senseless."

"Did you catch it?" asks Sam.

"Yea, but not without a price."

"What happened?" questions Abby, her knuckles cracking as she tightens her grip around her legs.

"Well, it turned out that we weren't the only ones hunting that buck. There were two other people out there with us: twins."

"Do I want to know what happens next?" asks Sam.

"You asked for a story."

This is the worst, I think. *I hate this, but they have to hear it.*

Taking a deep breath, I jump back into the story. "As I was lining up my shot for the deer, Sean said he spotted a boy pulling back an arrow just to our right. The arrow was toward us. He quickly pulled me behind a tree as the arrow flew right across our line of sight. Without even thinking, I pulled my arrow back and turned around the tree. At that point, I fired aimlessly toward the direction of the flying arrow."

"Did it hit one of them?" Abby asks with wide eyes.

"Yea. It hit the girl in the front. The boy ended up firing back and missing, so Sean fired his bow and killed the boy. It was horrible. I was so hungry that I didn't even care who I killed. They were new out here, too," I say as I wipe a tear from my cheek.

They were fourteen and they were frightened and we killed them. They tried to kill us out of fear and instead of helping them by yelling for them to stop, we killed them. That's why I hate it out here and that's another reason why I don't want to go back to Nimbus.

I can still see their faces.

Sniffling, I throw another log into the fire as Abby gets up from her chair. "At least you're still alive," she says, wrapping her arms around my waist. With her head pressed against my chest, she whispers. "It's okay, Elise. You didn't know. Someday we'll get back at MacMillan and you can put the arrow between his eyes."

Wiping the tears from my cheeks, I laugh as I gently kiss Abby on top of her head. "Thanks. I can't wait for that day."

Sitting upright, Sam scoots toward us and wraps his arms around both Abby and I. "As long as you're with us, Elise, you won't have to kill anymore. Now, that you've taught us both how to shoot, we can do the hunting so you don't have to worry about anything."

"Thanks, Sam," I half smile.

"Why did you choose to tell us that story, though?" he asks.

I clear my throat and turn to look into his weary eyes, "Because I'm glad that you two were not those kids. I see you guys as my redemption and I'm thankful I got a second chance."

126

10 December 2191

Sam

A loud, bothersome voice echoes throughout the hallway. I awake in a fright. Wiping my eyes, I sit up—my blanket sliding off my chest—only to be taken aback by the sudden cold against my torso. "What's going on?" I ask aloud.

"It's snowing!" rings Abby's voice from the hallway.

Pulling the blanket against my chest, I throw my feet over the edge of the mattress. Reaching for my icy sneakers, I slip my trembling toes inside—a choice I completely regret. Still snug in the blanket, I shiver and stand up, wishing my interior warmth would wrap itself around the rest of me.

"Have you seen the snow?!" yells Abby as she jumps into my room.

"No," I quip. "Why are you so excited about it? It's freezing in here."

With a certain gleam in her eyes, Abby smiles, "I've always loved snow, especially back home. It means Christmas is around the corner."

I half smirk and stand up. Slowly walking across the splintered wood in my frozen shoes, I step beside Abby. "Too bad we don't get to celebrate that for eleven more years."

"Who's to say we can't still celebrate it out here, Sam?" adds Elise from atop the stairs.

Moving out of the room to head downstairs, I glance at Elise. With her back against the wall, she breathes into her hands.

"I guess we could, but how? It's not like we can go to a local shop and get presents for each other. There's nothing out here," I say.

"We could just feast," suggests Abby.

Stepping down the first stair, Elise halts and turns around. Lightly biting the dry skin off her bottom lip, her eyes widen. "That would be great," she salivates.

"I think I would be okay with that, but what are we going to eat? There's not much out there, and there's nothing in here."

"How do you know there's nothing here?" asks Abby. Speeding past Elise and I on the staircase, she waltzes into the kitchen. Reaching up for the cabinets, she pulls the battered wooden cupboards open.

"We've been here long enough to know," I say.

"We've also been here long enough to find blankets, but we still searched for those the other night," sneers Abby. "But, you're right, Sam. I'm not finding anything." Loudly opening and closing every cupboard, Abby stops. "There's a knife up here. It kind of looks like a letter opener, so maybe that was supposed to be in the library." Grabbing the dusty blade from the rotting wood, she turns around and hands it to me.

Holding the blade in my hand, I run my thumb up and down the handle. Turning it over, I repeat the process until a faded engraving pricks my finger. I lick my thumb and press it into the end of the handle. Digging the moisture into the letters, the small clumps stick to my finger and eventually fall out. Scraping the last-clinging remnants of dust from the engraving, I look back at Elise and Abby. "It says, A.Y."

"What did you say?" asks Abby, her fingers trembling as she reaches for the knife.

"There are two letters at the end that are an A and a Y."

"Those are my initials," she mumbles. Carefully flipping the blade over in her hand, she looks up at me. "Those are also his initials," she whispers.

Taking the letter opener from Abby's pale fingers, Elise examines it. "Who's he?"

"My brother, Aden."

"Did he have a letter opener as his departing gift?"

Pulling her sleeves over her hands, Abby takes a seat. With her eyes fixated on the fire, she speaks toward it. "I honestly don't know what he had. I didn't go to his Separation Day because of what he did, so it's probably just a coincidence."

"Probably," I say.

"That has to be it," she replies. "There are thousands of kids out here right now and there were thousands before us. This could be anyone's."

I nod and grab a seat beside Abby. As I casually wrap my arm around her shoulders, a frigid gust of wind bursts through the broken kitchen window and puts out the fire. Abby doesn't budge.

"What the hell?" utters Elise.

"Maybe that's a sign that we should hunt now," I say as I pull my hands into the sleeves of my sweatshirt.

"Maybe it is or maybe it's a sign that we need to patch up that window."

"With what?" I laugh.

"With you. Go stand in front of the window and Abby and I will rebuild the fire and warm up," jokes Elise.

I glare back at her. "Let's just go hunt. We can build a bigger fire when we get back and we can cook up some meat. I'm starving."

"Yea, let's do that," mutters Abby. Without a glimpse back, she stands up and immediately heads for the front door before stepping into the icy wind alone.

"That's odd," says Elise.

"Very," I reply. Quickly moving for the front door, I pull it open and step into the wintry air with Elise directly behind me. Instantly, the piercing sting of the cold slaps me across the face. "Shit," I say without so much as pulling my hands up to my mouth to stop myself from cursing.

"Sam!" glares Elise.

"Sorry, it's just really cold. I don't remember it ever being this cold behind the wall."

"Yea, winters out here are brutal," replies Elise as she glances left and right searching for Abby. "Where's she gone?"

Placing my casted hand in the front pocket of my sweatshirt, I wipe my eyes with the other. "No clue. There's nowhere to go."

Hurriedly stepping forward, Elise runs out into the open. "Abby!" she shouts. "Abby!" The silence yields no vocal response, just Mother Nature's erratic gusts whistling through the trees.

"Abby!" I shout. Jumping off the front porch, I wipe my eyes. Nothing. The only sight is the light powdery snow amassing in the field. I shiver and turn toward Elise. "Where is she?"

Smiling, Elise says, "Turn around."

With shivering lips, I ask, "Why?"

"Just do it!" she laughs.

Slowly turning to my right, I blink just as a fluff of white explodes against my face. "Really?" I say angrily. "In the face?"

"Should've ducked," gibes Elise.

"How was I supposed to know that was going to happen?" I answer just as another ball smashes into my sweatshirt.

"Should've ducked again."

Finally obliging, I crouch as another snowball flies over my head.

"I think she wants a snowball fight," says Elise with a smile.

"Where is she?" I ask. On her knees forming snowballs, Elise doesn't answer.

Dropping to my knees, the wet snow starts soaking into my pants—forcing my jeans to cling to my legs. I start to roll the soft snow into weakly-padded balls when Elise gets up and runs toward the side of the house.

"Where are you going?"

"Where do you think?"

"Abby!" I yell. "Come out and face me!" Seconds pass without another snowball or the sound of footsteps crackling in the snow. My hands start to shake as my body cools and Abby remains void of a response.

Rounding the opposite side of the house, Elise glares at me, a narrow smile creeping in from the corners of her mouth.

"What? What are you smirking about?" I ask. "Where is she?"

"Oh, just turn around for once."

She's right behind me. . .again, I think. Furrowing my brows, I squint and stare at the broken clumps of snow in front of me. "Abby," I mumble.

"Just turn around," laughs Elise. "Maybe she won't hit you in the face this time."

I know there's no winning in this situation, no escape from her wintry wrath. Preparing to face my fears, I stick my hands up and turn around. Instantly, a dripping ball of slush slams into my cheek—the sting of ice spreads across my face. "Thanks," I say, wiping the water from my stiff jaw.

"You had it coming," laughs Abby as she wipes the snow from her bare hands. "You don't have to be such a worrywart, Sam. I know not to go too far away from you guys."

"I know. I just always think of the worst since we've ran into the worst quite a few times already."

"Sorry," mutters Abby. "I was just trying to clear my head and have some fun."

I'd prefer if she cleared it by talking to us.

"It's okay. I need to stop overthinking everything, anyways." Every time we run into a problem, it may not faze them, but it latches itself onto my mind and lingers for days. Every step they move away from me, the weaker I become; the less focused I am on the reality of what's happening to me.

"Sam, are you ready to go into the woods to hunt?" comes Elise's voice from behind me.

"Yea, let's go. That sounds better than my poor attempt at making snowballs one-handed."

"Does one of you want to carry the bow?" asks Elise as we start to walk toward the forest.

"I'll take it," I say. Pulling my wrapped hand from my sweatshirt, Elise hands me the bow.

"Are you going to be okay shooting with that thing?"

"Yea, I'll be fine. It'll be just like training."

The faint echo of wind whistling between the trees in the distance consumes our walk toward the woods. It almost sounds like a dog howling hundreds of feet away, but that's nearly impossible. With Abby standing behind me, Elise stands by my side with her knife gripped tightly in her left hand.

"Keep quiet," whispers Elise. "You don't want to scare anything away."

There's nothing around us. The only things in sight are icicles dangling from branches. I'm more worried that Abby has another snowball in hand.

Time flies by as we wander past hundreds of leafless trees and numerous decaying bushes without the sight of an animal. "Maybe today's not our day," I say.

"Let's just keep walking. We're bound to find something," says Abby. "Plus, I'm really hungry."

"Me too," whispers Elise. "Just keep moving."

With each step, the snow cracks beneath our feet in unison as it becomes the only audible sound in the woods.

"Does anyone hear that?" asks Abby as she stands still against a tree with her foot in the air as if she was about to take another step.

"What? All I hear are our feet slamming into this mush," I say.

"Shh," she whispers.

With an outstretched finger, Abby points to our left. Her finger trembles in the cold, following a deer's every footstep. With each trot, the deer stops, sticks its nose in the snow and then stares blankly into the forest.

"We need to be still. We need to be quiet," whispers Elise.

"How can we catch it if we're this far away and every footstep is too loud?" I ask.

"Just do as I taught you. Take a breath and line up your bow. Watch for trees and fire. As long as you have space, you can get it. It's not that far away," replies Elise.

Pulling up the bow from my side, I take a deep breath and exhale as I reach for an arrow in my quiver.

"You got this," mutters Abby. Now clinging to the tree with her foot firm in the snow, her eyes follow the deer.

Taking another deep breath, I pull the bow up to shoulder height. Reaching for the dangling string, I slowly drag it back as the wood starts to bend. With one last inhale, a loud crack comes from my left—forcing my fingers off the string and sending the bow into the snow. I'm forced onto my back with Elise and Abby screaming at my side. *What was that?*

"Who are you?!" screams Abby as she steps by Elise. Wielding her knife, Elise keeps Abby behind her.

132

Looking up, I wipe the snow from my face where I can see a man dressed in dark blue jeans with a black sweatshirt. His lips are shaking as his eyes wander about. He has a scar on his right cheek, but I can't make out its shape. I can just see the end stopping by his mouth.

"Nothing should die out here," says the man in a monotone voice—one that seems off for his appearance.

"How in the world have you lived this long if you don't hunt?" Elise fires back.

"They feed me," replies the man.

"Who?" Elise retorts.

"The Lurkers."

The moment that word slips from his tongue, I can feel my body tighten as my hands lock at my sides. I lie there motionless as Elise's pupils enlarge. Abby stays close to Elise, but her eyes dart toward mine. Stiff in place, I stare wide-eyed back at her.

Picking up the snowy bow beside me, Elise places an arrow against the wood. "You better run," she says. "You better get the hell out of here NOW!" she screams.

The man smirks and itches the scruff on his chin, unafraid of us.

"I SAID NOW!" she yells once more, her grip tightening on the string.

"They're coming," he snarls.

Pulling back the arrow, Elise fires. Thudding into the snow, the Lurker lies still while a pool of blood spreads around him.

14 December 2191

Sean

Days have passed without so much as a bite of food; hours have flown by without any warmth; seconds have drifted by without hope. I don't know where I am or where Sam is or where Elise is. I'm lost, I'm cold, and I'm weak. If only my mind would stray away from the negativity of what this experience has become. Each day, MacMillan's plan for me inches closer to succeeding. Each day, I near the one thing a majority of kids endure out here at some point. Every second, I step closer toward a warm paradise—one that sounds ideal right now, but one I should avoid. I just need to hold on. I need to latch onto what I have and hope this isn't where everything comes to an end.

I can't envision not seeing Elise again. I can't imagine the misery of succumbing to fate alone, let alone in the dead of winter. Collapsed in the snow, feeling the cold hand of death climb through your legs and into your lungs doesn't sound ideal to me. If I'm going to die, I'm going to die with her.

Despite being in several situations where that could have happened, Elise never let it. If I didn't see someone coming toward us, she didn't hesitate to shoot. Without her willingness to stay with me, I might have died alone. She might have, too.

It's been a few days since I last ate cold, leftover meat from an abandoned campfire and even longer since I've had water. It's gotten to a point where it's hard to walk, to sleep, and to even think. I need to find Sam and Elise or I'm not going to make it much longer. I just can't die before MacMillan. That would be a tragedy.

I gently brush the ends of my fingers against a gnarled trunk and lift myself onto my feet. The snow continues to lightly sneak through the trees as occasional flakes fall and dissipate upon my head.

With my fingers digging into the tree, I take a deep breath and turn around. My limbs consistently shake with each passing breeze as I try to manipulate my legs to move faster. Yet, they fail to heed my focus. With each paltry step, I can feel my muscles tightening—clinging to each other to absorb any possible warmth. The rest of my body feels cold enough that my fingers could succumb to frostbite at any point. Though it's not severely cold, the possibility lies there, burying itself in my consciousness.

The farther I get away from the tree, the more I'm able to stabilize my body as I head toward a barren field. Small animals scurry past into the open. Icicles waver on the branches behind me.

"Sam!" I cry out, hoping that he's nearby, but to no avail. "Elise!" garners the same response.

Approaching the empty field void of snow-ridden trees, but instead laced with odd bits of wheat poking from beneath the snow, I stop. *I remember this.*

The disquieted gusts of wind graze over the tops of my ears. The sky halts its motion; instead, turning its focus to me, making me feel like I'm the only one out here.

***

I look around the field; the snow oddly filters itself into the ground as the trees blossom into mixed palettes of green, red, and orange. Suddenly, the wheat pushes itself from the surface into the air and leans ever so slightly to the west. The golden-yellow tassels brush against my fingers.

"What's going on?" I say aloud.

"You're delusional," comes a voice from behind me.

Turning around, I can see her hair laid upon her shoulders with the wood of the bow draped against her back.

"What do you mean? This all feels real," I say.

"It's not. You need to close your eyes and wake up," she says.

"But I am awake. I never fell asleep. I've been standing here this whole time."

"No, Sean, you haven't," whispers Elise, remaining still in the distance.

"What happened?"

"You're growing weaker. You need to get food, water, and shelter."

"Where will I find that? Where are you?" I ask as I turn around only to see the field returning to its wintry state.

***

Quickly closing my eyes, I jolt them open to find myself rolling around in a pile of snow and muck. *What happened?* I think. Slowly tilting my head up, I look to see if she's still standing behind me, but there's no one there. What felt like the person I've been searching for has become a disheartening fantasy. She's gone and no matter how much I want her back, her presence has become nothing more than a false reality in this never-ending nightmare.

I might not make it.

19 December 2191

Elise

The gentle tapping of a branch against the glass sends my mind into a frenzy. The pure rush of adrenaline courses through my veins as my eyelids flutter and my body shakes. I can see him running toward me; the scar across his cheek is more visible than ever.

"Elise!"

"Get away! Leave me alone!"

"Elise, it's me! Sam! You need to wake up!"

Thrusting my arm forward, I grab the collar of Sam's shirt and pull him toward me. I stare into his frightened face as his pupils enlarge and quickly shrink back.

"Sorry, Sam," I say as he fixes his shirt.

"It's okay," he mutters. "Were you having a bad dream?"

"Yea, it's nothing," I say. My head starts to ache and my abdomen spasms, but I don't elaborate. Even if it was something, I wouldn't want to frighten him. Since our minds are following the same pattern, it wouldn't be right to subject him to my torment as well. One nightmare is enough; two would be hell.

"Are you sure? Was it about Arthur?"

"Yea," I mumble as I sit up.

"What happened this time?" asks Sam as he sits down on the dirty mattress next to me.

I shake my head and wipe my eyes, "I'm not really sure. I only saw a little bit of him. I guess I just feel like he keeps getting closer to me."

Days can pass without so much as the thought of him, but the moment he jumps into my consciousness, he's there to stay. He's like an open wound hiding underneath a bloodied bandage. You know you need to take off the protection and let the wound heal, but the sheer agony of ripping off something protective is painful. If the bandage is gone, the unhealed wound can breathe and even worsen. Though it might be for the best, there's always a possibility it could get worse; there's always a chance the positive could be spun into a negative.

"I know what you mean, but they're just dreams. They don't dictate reality. Plus, we killed off that crazy kid in the woods a few days ago, so if he was Arthur's messenger, he's gone," says Sam as he fidgets with his cast.

"I think we have to move," I say without thinking.

"What? Why? Nobody knows we're here. It's too cold to leave."

"I know, but what if someone does know we're here? What if *he* knows we're here?"

Neither of them responds. I wipe the sweat from my forehead and gaze out the window. No one's coming.

Sam mumbles under his breath. I turn back to face him. His eyes light up.

"What if there's a way Arthur can track us?" he quietly says. "What if there's a way he can into our heads?"

"The only thing in our heads is the chip. Only those behind the wall have access. No one else," I say.

"But what if someone else does?" murmurs Abby. "What if Arthur does?"

"I don't see how he could," I reply.

"Neither do I, but couldn't that be a possibility?"

I itch the top of my head. "It could be, but a tough one to put any belief into."

"Nothing out here makes sense," says Sam. "It's nearly impossible to dictate reality from what we see in our heads, so I don't see why it couldn't be a possibility."

I sigh. I hate to think that there's any chance in hell Arthur wields the same amount of power out here that MacMillan has inside the confines of the wall. If he does have a way into our minds, it's not supposed to be understood. It's supposed to be feared.

"I just hate to think that he has any value out here," I say. "I hate to feel that he's better than us."

"He's not," says Abby, repulsed. "He never will be."

"But he leads a group. There's more than just him and they're all just as crazy, if not more than him. It's like trying to outrun your past; no matter how hard you try, something will come back; something will catch you. . .and I just feel that. . ."

"Feel what?"

My lips start to tremble as my eyes wander toward the windowsill. "I feel that he's going to find me. That he's going to get what he couldn't get the first time. He's going to kill me."

Wrapping his arms around my shoulders, Sam clasps his hands together as he hugs me with all his might. "Not possible. You're the strongest person I know. Even if Arthur has a way inside our heads, he can't tear us apart."

"Thanks, Sam," I say quietly.

What if he does find us? I think as Sam stands up and heads downstairs. *What if safety is just something they teach you in Nimbus? What if true protection is impossible and everyone is in danger? What if Nimbus brainwashes you?*

"Sam!" I yell. He quickly turns around.

"Yea?"

"Do you think it's possible that no matter where you are, you aren't safe?"

"What do you mean? I don't feel safe out here, but I feel safe behind the wall."

"But do you really feel safe behind that? Do you feel that MacMillan is just protecting us from ourselves? From our capabilities? I mean, he really is just protecting us from kids."

Tilting his head a bit to the side, Sam's eyes wander about as he clenches his teeth together. "I guess that could be true. But how could he be protecting us from our capabilities? Don't we get to do as we please out here?"

"Yea, but he tracks our every move. He 'protects' us behind the wall from our friends, our family, our classmates. He does everything he can to ensure we don't live freely. He forces this idea that we need to prove ourselves through his vigorous standards and if we don't we're garbage. He basically tries to wipe our minds and fill them with his shit. That's why the Shadow Lurkers exist. Not everyone is capable of staying sane in his ways forever."

"But aren't there more people out here like us that don't cave to his ways?" asks Sam as he sits back down on the dingy mattress.

"Yea, I think there are plenty, but there are also several that have caved, several that couldn't handle it, too. I think there are a lot of different people out here and we've seen just about every kind," I say as I clasp my hands together inside my sweatshirt.

"I think so, too, but what do you mean with all this? What do you want to do?"

I exhale. "I'm not really sure, but I think something has to be done. I can't live like this anymore. The constant fear of not knowing what's next terrifies me. I've survived out here for almost eleven years, but I can't take it for another minute."

"I don't even think I could manage being out here for eleven years, but I definitely agree that something has to be done," replies Sam.

Taking a deep breath, I turn my head to the side as I look into Sam's eyes. "I think it's time I tell you two about Sean's idea. He had a plan."

Taken aback, Sam shouts for Abby. "What do you mean he had a plan? Why are you just bringing this up now?"

"You'll see," I say as Abby reaches the top of the stairs holding the fire poker in one hand.

"What's going on?" she asks as she tries to catch her breath.

"Nothing deserving of that," I laugh.

"Sorry! Whenever I hear my name yelled I never know why, but what's up?"

"I have something to tell you two," I say, gesturing for Abby to sit down.

"What is it?" asks Sam.

"Your brother had this. . .idea," I say as my mind runs in circles trying to grab the right words. "He believed Nimbus had holes, gaps where it could be brought down. He thought there was a way to revolt against MacMillan and bring down the Elites."

"Is that even possible?" asks Abby, still panting.

"Yes, but it has to be done right. Every system has its flaw; you just have to find out where it is and attack it."

"Aside from MacMillan being terrible, I can't see the flaw with Nimbus. If he's brought down then everything would be okay, right?" questions Sam. Slowly unwrapping the end of his cast around his wrist, he looks oddly at me.

"Essentially, yes, but it's not just him who's corrupt. A majority of the Elites are corrupt. That means the guards, the teachers, priests, family members, friends, just about everyone who's already survived their eleven years. Since they made it out, they have nothing to fear," I say, clenching my hands tighter in my sweatshirt.

"So you're saying that my parents would rather side with MacMillan than me if we were to revolt?" answers Sam.

"Not yours, Sam. Sean has already spoken with them, I believe. He told me when he first got out here that your parents always believed there was something wrong with Nimbus. He also said that when he got back, he would tell them of his plan. Assuming he's done so," I say as I take a breath. "Your parents know of his plan and when it will come into effect."

Squinting, Abby looks at me. Opening her mouth as to speak, she holds it, but nothing comes out. "Bu—" she says before her mouth closes and her eyes wander about again.

"I think Abby's trying to ask what the plan is and how can something like this happen from the outside with limited people? Three people can't bring down a wall," says Sam.

"No, they can't, but a lot of people can. Sean said he knows many people on the inside that are on his side, but not many out here. People hold grudges; anyone who lost someone on the outside should want revenge. However, there are only a few things I know about the plan. I know, for one, that Sean says the revolution has to happen the day before I turn twenty-five, so I don't have to take my re-entrance exam."

". . .and that's all you know?" voices Sam as his he itches the top of his head. "I guess I just don't get it exactly."

"Yea, he was pretty secretive about it even though he insisted I help. He gave me the date and told me to meet him at the wall, but that's really it. I assume he knows what he's doing because he was very adamant about bringing MacMillan down. He's always hated that man."

Smirking, the corner of Sam and Abby's lips lift in unison. "MacMillan is a prick," says Abby.

"That he is," I say as I scoot toward the edge of the mattress before standing up.

"I still don't get why you're just now bringing this up," says Sam. "Shouldn't we have known about this earlier?"

"Not exactly. You needed to experience more of the horrors of this world to see why Sean's idea is necessary."

Sam bites at the drying skin on his bottom lip before glancing over at Abby.

"Elise," mutters Abby in a calm, relaxed manner.

"Yea?"

"What if nobody's prepared to fight?"

I glance out the window as the branch gently scrapes against the glass—shedding many snowflakes in the process. "Then we go at it with what we have. Sean had a plan and I don't think he's the kind of man to give up."

As she nods her head in agreement, Abby's lips quiver. "Bu—but aren't you scared?"

"Not anymore," I softly reply.

"Why not?" she asks, still firmly holding onto the fire poker.

"We've been through hell. There's no reason this is any different."

24 December 2191

Sam

"How close do you think we are to Christmas?" asks Abby as she pokes the fire.

"It can't be that far away," I say, leaning against the chair Elise is in.

Sinking my teeth into a piece of charred deer, I pull off the end of the strip. It's chewy.

"It's probably pretty close, but there's not much we can do about it. We got our feast and we have fire. That should really be enough," says Elise as Abby hands her another chunk of meat.

Nodding, I exhale as I breathe in the cool air mixed with the waning smoke from the fire. The dry soot's so palpable that it forces me to cough.

"You alright, Sam?" asks Abby.

"Yea, I just got som—something caught in my throat," I say.

"Chew your food," laughs Elise.

Shaking my head, I take a drink from the canteen before I eat the last bit of meat in my hands. The flavorless piece slides down my throat easier than the previous chunk. I take another swig of water.

Pressing my back against the front of Elise's chair, I close my eyes and exhale. My stomach's hit a point of uncomfortable fullness that it hasn't seen since Nimbus. Taking a small breath, I open my eyes.

***

The flames start to grow larger as the once-dying orange becomes a vast, dark red. With her hair covering her cheeks, Abby pokes the front logs. The fire cracks and grows. I gaze in awe until the flames fall toward me, a wave of orange flushing against my face. "He's getting closer," comes a deep voice from behind me.

"Who's getting closer?" I reply. My hands fall limp at my sides. I try to lift them up toward my waist, but a thick, frayed rope latches against my wrists. "Elise?" I say.

A simple "no" is retorted by the invisible voice.

Sliding my hands back and forth, I try to break free from the rope. I shake, I pull, I yell, but nothing happens. The stiff texture of the rope is unbreakable.

"Just relax, Sam. It won't be long until he finds you," says the man's voice.

My eyes wander from side to side, but the empty room is all that surrounds me. Void of Elise and Abby, the fire roars in front of me while everything else has seemingly disappeared. "What do you want?" I ask. My hands grow warm.

"You," replies the voice.

"Show yourself. If you want me, show me who you are!" I yell.

An unyielding silence engulfs the room as I try to lift my hands again.

***

Jolting back up, I hit myself in the chin. My pinky throbs. I clasp my hands.

"Are you okay?!" yells Elise from behind me.

"I d-don't know," I mumble as I press my hands against my cheeks just to make sure I'm no longer trapped. "What the hell just happened?" Continuing to glide my hands across my face, I look around the room. Everything's back where it used to be. Abby's hair is tied behind her, but Elise is on the floor beside me.

"You got pulled into another dream, but this time. . ." Elise says as her voice trails off and she takes a deep gulp. "We couldn't get you out."

144

"What do you mean you couldn't get me out?" I say, a clear convulsion in my speech. "You mean, if I have another one of those dreams, I-I'm stuck until it ends?"

"I'm afraid so."

"How is that even possible? That doesn't seem possible. . .w-what did you guys do to try and wake me up?" I say as I reach for the water.

"We threw some water on you. Abby slapped you across the face once. We forced pressure into your pinky. We didn't want to, but we had to," says Elise.

"And none of that worked?"

They shake their heads together. Abby's face remains expressionless while Elise's face contorts into a frown.

How? I think as I hold my pinky tightly. *How can someone be stuck in a dream? How can reality disappear to the point that your mind becomes a false reality?*

"What can I do, Elise?"

"I don't know, Sam. I really don't know. You just have to try and force it out, I guess. . ."

"You should read a book before you go to bed," says Abby. "That way, your mind will be more focused on what you just read and it may help your dreams become less intense."

"That's true," I whisper. Shaking my head, the floor blurs beneath me.

A mix of colors blend across my sight; a circular object forms in the mess. "You'll see me in time," mocks the contorted shape.

Don't listen to the voice. Don't listen to the voice. Look around you.

"I'm sure you could find something good in the library," says Elise.

I look up at Elise and itch my scalp. Standing up from the bowed floorboards, I walk toward the library. *What's going on?* I think, my eyes wandering in circles. Stepping past the fallen door, I find myself standing in the middle of the room. Sprawling my legs out on the floor, I sit down and try to clear my mind.

"There has to be some paper around here," I say to myself as I toss a few books out from underneath me.

The thought of writing out my own escape seems better than allowing the voice in my head to control where I go. I can't envision another second behind the curtains of my eyelids in which I can't escape, in which I'm trapped and begging for everything to leave me alone.

I toss a few more books to the side before deciding to step out and grab the journal from the mantel. Quickly ripping out a few blank pages, I search the room for a pen.

Standing still in the center of the room, I glance at the engraving before walking toward a dusted-over desk beside it. Covered in cobwebs and a thick layer of grayish-brown dust, the desk appears void of any use. As if it was just an aesthetic in the past, each drawer appears empty or inoperable.

"Looking for this?" softly asks Abby from behind me. Leaning against the door with a thick, glossy pen in between her forefingers, she smiles. "I found it yesterday. I didn't know what to do with it, so I just held onto it. You can have it now that you have more of a use for it than I do."

"Does it work?" I ask as I kick a few books to the side.

"Yea, I scribbled in the back of one of those bigger books I knew we wouldn't read," she smirks.

"Thanks," I say as I take the pen. Gently moving it through my fingers, I take off the cap before emptying my misery onto paper.

30 December 2191

Elise

While flipping through the empty pages of this leather-bound journal, my fingers scrawl listless patterns throughout as I imagine a pen between my fingers. Each time I turn a page, my nails glide against the parchment as if my hands are creating a story; a story devoid of words or rhythm; a story so profound that an audience wouldn't be able to fathom the depths behind the mind of the person who wrote it. It would be my story.

Ten years away from home can eat your mind and spirit faster than anything. Five years removed from the humbled sanity of a teenager can discourage hope and force an undesired resentment of the world itself as you lie trapped. These scribbles paint my visions, my losses, my heartfelt bliss that I lost when I was sent out here. These non-linear designs define who I am and where I am.

Without myself, I would be lost. Without the presence of love, I wouldn't exist. It's these scribbles, these absurd scribbles that keep me functioning—that keep me alive.

Void of any headaches or the thought of Arthur slipping into my work, my mind feels free. . .for now.

"Hey, Elise," calls Sam from the front room.

Casually standing up from the pile of books, I place the journal back on the crooked shelf at the end of the room. "What's going on?" I ask. Stepping out of the library and into the main room, I see Sam and Abby sitting next to each other in front of an empty fireplace.

"I think we need to get some firewood."

"I'd say so."

Resting her head against Sam's shoulder, Abby holds her hands in her sleeves as Sam wraps the crimson scarf around her neck. "I'm so cold," she mutters.

"Why don't you two wait here and I'll go get some wood," I say. Stepping toward them, I grab my bow sitting next to the fireplace.

"We can't let you do that. It's not safe out there for one, even if it is you," Sam says, his words fading with each syllable.

"I think I'll be okay. You need to take care of Abby. She's freezing. If she goes outside, she'll get frostbitten in a second."

"But you won't let me go alone," he mumbles.

"That's because you haven't been out here for ten years," I state. "You two stay here and I'll be back in an hour."

Sam grinds his teeth as he stares up at me with a look of frustration sprawled across his face. "Fine," he mutters under his breath.

"It'll be alright. I won't stray too far from here. If you yell my name, I'll come back as quickly as I can. There are several trees nearby and I just need to break a few branches."

"Okay. Hurry," whispers Abby against Sam's shoulder, her voice shaking.

"I will."

Pulling the string of my bow over my arm, I kick the last fuming log in the fireplace. Instantly crumbling beneath my foot, the ashes lightly float into the air before disappearing into nothingness. The heat warms my ankle for a second—not long enough to hold value.

I pull open the wooden door and push the screen door outward.

The moment I step into the cold, the frigidity of the breeze breaks upon my face like a wave crashing into a beach. My futile attempts to shield the wind fail as the gusts blow my hair over my ears. Pulling my hood over my head, I tighten the strings as I tie them into a bow beneath my chin.

It only takes a couple minutes to venture into the woods, but with each step the wind picks up to the point that it's almost unbearable. It feels like I'm walking through a recently shaken snow globe; the snow lightly drifts above me as the wind pushes it to my right, while I have to hold on to every tree in sight just to avoid being knocked over.

With each step through the mush, my shoes start to soak. *Crap*, I think as I reach up to snag a few bending branches. Coupled with my frozen hands and icy face, my mind is yelling at me to return to the house. *I haven't even been out here very long*, I think. Unable to maneuver myself higher to pull off more branches, my body starts to shake. As I slowly become numb, a shivering sensation runs up and down my spine; my hands start to stiffen.

I long for Sean's embrace, for his persistent warmth. Even without a winter coat, the snow didn't faze him much. Sometimes he seemed superhuman—unnatural in his ability to survive. I swear he could get shot and walk it off.

"Sam!" I yell, hoping he can find me and magically bring the warmth his brother is unable to.

As I cry for strength, my body pleads for me to return to the house. The sky's once-gray color has been swept by a canvas of white to the point that it's almost impossible to see. Clinging onto the tree for dear life along with the few branches clenched in my hand, I know I have to make a run for it. I have to move before it's too late.

Pressed against the tree, I yell once more, but my words are muted by the howl of the wind. Dropping the sticks, I start to run. The snow's accumulating on the ground faster than I've ever seen it; it's to the point that each stride weakens my path. I fall.

Scrambling to my feet, I slip once again. The snow's blanketing my sight; my visibility is becoming null; my sense of direction no longer exists. *I didn't even go that far away!* I think.

I can't see the house and I can barely see my feet. "Sam!" I yell. The wind hushes my powerless cries as I keep trying to run. The blinding white obscures every which way I look. I'm trapped in a storm so uncommon that I'm starting to fear for my life. My legs tense up; my knees start to shake. I take a deep breath as I yell, "SAM!"

Muffled, I can hear the first syllable of my name. Either that or the wind is playing tricks on my mind. "I- ri' 'ere" is all I can hear as I trudge forward.

"Sam?!" I shout assuming that what I heard wasn't just in my head.

"I got you," yells Sam, his hand warming my wrist.

Pulling me out of the storm and into the house, he wipes the snow from his face as he smirks at me. "I told you it's not safe out there for one person."

Shivering, I reply. "H-h-how was I su-sup-supposed to kn-know th-that was gonna ha-happen?"

"That is true. Sit down, Elise. We got a fire going."

"How?"

"Books, duh."

Slowly removing the snow from my sweatshirt I throw it to the side and move mere inches away from the fire. The heat thrusts against my frozen hands, causing them to feel numbly warm.

"That blizzard came out of nowhere," says Abby as she sits next to me.

"Yea, I've never seen that before. I didn't think those could happen around here," Sam says as he sits on my other side.

"What books are you b-burning?" I stutter.

"Just some of the ones I didn't think we would read," he says—his eyes saying otherwise.

"Like?"

"There was a big one in there by some guy named Tolstoy, so I threw that one in there first. Pretty sure we won't read that."

"What else?"

"Don't worry, Elise. We didn't throw in anything we thought you might want to read. Plus, we're just burning the pages right now so the fire can burn longer. We threw that big one in there as a starter," says Abby as she holds her hands out.

"Okay," I mumble. My body starts to warm up, but my hands continue to shake. The heat pierces my face, but I don't budge. It scalds my toes, but I refuse to sit back. I feel as if I would rather be too hot than ever be too cold again.

The second I decide to hop into the floral armchair, Sam and Abby start to crumple more paper for the fire. Aimlessly searching the room, my eyes paint a picture. A picture so moving that it almost feels like Sean's here. I close my eyes—the scribbles of my mind draw him next to me, holding my head as I fall asleep against his chest.

3 January 2192

Sam

'. . .we freely run through the streets as the thought of fighting to survive doesn't exist; the thought of fending off vultures as we slowly crumble to the earth means nothing to us. We are the future of Nimbus.'

"What are you writing about, Sam?" asks Elise from beside me.

"Stuff," I quickly reply. Driving the pen back into the yellowy paper, I fade back into an unfamiliar Nimbus.

'We are the peaceful delegates who would never harm what we have, who would never change the flawless system we've put into effect. We are the strength Nimbus needs to survive. The more we have behind the wall, the stronger we are.'

"Just stuff?" she asks again.

"Pretty much. I'm just writing about a different version of Nimbus."

"How different?" asks Abby. Scooting beside me, she cranes her neck over my hunched shoulders.

"We aren't forced out," I reply.

'"Happy 15th birthday," exclaims Sean as I blow out the *candles of my cake. The fifteen candles can't withstand the blow and instantly burn out. Fading into the air, the smoke rises toward the ceiling before disappearing into thin air.'*

"Sounds much better to me," smiles Abby. "But at the same time, if it existed that way, would we really know each other?"

"I'd like to think so."

My response causes Abby to blush; she pulls her head away and childishly grins. "Me too. So what's so different about what you're writing?"

"It's basically the same Nimbus except we can do what we want. We have the right to do what we want back there now as long as it doesn't hurt anyone else or affect the Elites in any way. In this version, we have total control over what we do. . .and the best part is: There's no MacMillan," I say.

Laughing, Elise asks, "Can we move there now?"

"I wish," smiles Abby.

I'm only halfway through the first sheet of paper, but every time I reread it, I feel that this society could exist, that a new Nimbus would be stronger than the one we have now. Sean said that Nimbus had flaws, and this one doesn't. It would function better than what we have now and everyone would live to see his or her fifteenth birthday. Not a single soul would have to worry about avoiding torment in a wasteland outside of the wall. No one would be brainwashed by the Lurkers and have to resort to holding onto the little things, the things of the past to survive. Out here, I have to hold onto my sanity by grasping what I love. I have to be stronger than the Lurkers, otherwise I'll disappear into the darkness. Plus, without MacMillan in charge, no one would be afraid of saying no.

'The blackened wick of the candle buries itself into the wax as Dad pulls the cake away and Mom brings out the plates. "Now, who wants cake?" she asks. "I do!" I yell even though I know I'm first in line.'

Turning to the next empty page, I clip the pen onto the journal and push the thoughts of my writings from my mind. Falling back into the cold reality of the farmhouse, I grab my hatchet from the soot-covered mantle and spin it in my palm. "Aside from the possibility of Arthur watching us, do you think the Elites are actually always watching?" I ask aimlessly.

"I don't think so. Once we get sent out here, they only track us. They don't watch us," replies Elise.

"How can you be so sure?" I ask.

"I just feel like we would know. If we did something they didn't like, there would probably be some sort of repercussion or something. I'm pretty sure outside the wall is as free as it gets."

"It doesn't feel as free as it could be," I say, setting the blade down next to the fireplace.

We're taught growing up that the freedom outside the wall is enough to madden even the strongest people, but we never got an exact reason why. Maybe growing up protected entitles us. Maybe without worrying about death, we don't experience anger as much. We sure as hell never experience fear. But at the same time, I can't help but think there's an easier way to bring us down outside of sending us out. There has to be something going on out here that limits the amount of people that return each year. There has to be something watching us, something testing us.

"You shouldn't overthink what you're writing so much and how it relates to here, Sam. Create your own world," says Elise.

"I am," I nod.

"But it still involves Nimbus. For someone who's been having nightmares no one should experience, maybe it's not right. You don't want to bury your jumbled mind deeper into a world that somewhat resembles the one you're in now. I know if that were me, I would want something no one's ever imagined. A world without a wall," she says calmly.

As much as I want to, I can't pry my mind away from where it wanders. If it wants to be in Nimbus, it's in Nimbus; if it wants to be in the city, it forces its way in; if it wants to venture into this new Nimbus, it will. I'm lacking the strength to control my thoughts and it's pathetic. It doesn't make sense.

No one should be unable to control their thoughts. And the worst part of it all is that it's only happening to me. I'm the only one falling into the abyss. Not Abby. Not Elise. Just me. *Why?* I think. *What have I done? Why am I different?* No matter how much I beg or plead, the darkness won't leave. It won't latch itself onto someone else just for my sake. No. The easiest way to break us apart is for one of us to fall while the others fail trying to help. I think that's what scares me most. I think my misery is the end—and that's why I need this new world.

8 January 2192

Sean

My stomach churns as I walk along the icy railway amidst a towering canopy of trees. I've managed to find more food lately, but it's not enough. With each meal, I feel stronger. With each new day, I feel better than the previous, but there's still something pulling me down, something I can't quite grasp. Tugging on the ends of this ragged sweatshirt I found, I continue to trudge into the depths of the forest.

I've yet to see the mere sight of another person, let alone the frozen body of someone who couldn't handle the cold. Lost in the surprising tranquility of winter, I keep my eyes out for the shack as I step off the tracks and into a wooded glen.

"Elise!" I yell, hoping the shack is near and she's there with Sam.

Yet, the only response I get is the gentle dripping of snow melting above.

Where are they? I think as a clump of snow plops onto my head. Angrily wiping off the mush, I reach up for the branch, break it, and throw it into the woods.

Steadying my breath, I continue along the tracks. Seemingly heading nowhere, I cling to the slight possibility that Sam and Elise are hidden safely at the rundown shack. If not there, they have to be nearby. Elise knows it wouldn't make sense to venture too far out from the wall. After what happened to her in the city and to Zeke in the wastelands beyond it, she shouldn't be anywhere else.

The farther I walk through the forest, the quieter nature becomes. No birds, no squirrels, no deer in sight; nothing but the endless expanse of trees in front of me. It's a silence so peaceful it sends my mind back atop the wall.

Pacing back and forth, the rays of sunlight beating against my neck, I gaze deep into the woods. Nothing but recently separated kids meander beyond the sight of my scope and into unexplored territory. The air hangs stagnant as a light breeze runs through my hair, soothing my burning scalp.

Snap back to reality: I can barely feel my feet and my ears are abnormally cold; I wouldn't be surprised if they're frostbitten. "Elise!" I yell again as I step into another opening. "Elise!" Nothing. Not even a crunch from another wandering soul crosses my eardrums. The area is empty.

With no clear view of what I'm searching for, every step seems pointless. Each time I push through a clearing or pass by a crooked tree, the shack seems hidden. *Maybe I'm on another set of rails*, I think. *But I've never seen another set.* In eleven years out here, the only rails Elise and I ever found were those by the shack. *I have to be close.*

Walking around scattered patches of lifeless earth and muddied snow, the broken remnants of a small building catch the corner of my eye. I start to walk toward it as the blow of what it could be strikes my stomach harder than MacMillan's bony knuckles. *This is it.*

My mind's racing. My thoughts are jumbled and incoherent. "Elise, Sam!" I scream and scream at the top of my lungs. Just hoping, praying, and believing they're not buried amidst this pile of ash. "Please! Elise!" I cry aloud. Uncertain tears stream down my cheeks. I start to pull up boards covered in a thick mix of snow and soot as I search for something. Yet, nothing catches my stare; nothing jumps at me.

Viciously digging through the black, I find nothing. Soot buries itself underneath my fingernails as my tired arms cause me to stop. Doused in a wet mix of ash and snow, I sit back. *What happened?* I wonder as the snow melts underneath me. Searching for answers, I turn my head back and forth looking around where the shack once stood. Thrusting my hands into the muck beside me, I feel around. The mush clumps between my fingers, further lodging itself behind my fingernails. Continuing to feel around, my left forefinger grazes against a large rock.

Burying my hands further into the ground, I grab ahold of the rock and pull it out from underneath me. With one quick yank, it flies into the air and slams against the crumbling wall behind me. Lightly wiping the muck from my hands against my pants, I turn around. Perched against the wood is a chipped skull split in two.

12 January 2192

Elise

"No walls. . .no walls," mumbles Sam in his sleep. His constant exhaustive speech has gotten to the point that I feel like I'm right there with him in his made-up world. It's these ideas, these dreams, that have pulled his mind away from here. By developing a new world, he's been able to escape, but at the same time, he hasn't. His figments can only take him so far away before he has to snap back to reality. And when he does, he might not be ready for it.

"You've been talking in your sleep again, Sam," I say as he rolls over to face the fireplace.

"Really? I'm sorry. What did I say this time?" he says while he wipes his weary eyes.

"Nothing much. Just wishing away the walls again."

"My bad."

"It's okay. I'm pretty used to it by now. After all, I did tell you to write about something different."

"At least it's better than your nightmares," says Abby as she wraps the scarf tightly around her neck. Stopping, she pulls her hands further into her sleeves.

"I'd say so. Though, dreaming of that world isn't much of a reprieve from here," he sighs.

Shifting his stare away from us, Sam rolls onto his stomach before he buries his face in the discolored, featherless pillow. Disoriented by the darkened skies and the contents of his mind, Sam quickly falls back asleep as Abby and I huddle together on the armchair.

"I'm glad he hasn't been having those bad nightmares lately," mumbles Abby from beneath her scarf.

"Me too. I wish his mind could be empty for a night, though. He needs it."

If only clarity was that simple to obtain. I can't go a week without the thought of Arthur. I can go two nights, three tops, without his scrawny figure waltzing into my head, but that's about the extent of it.

"Do you think it's possible to have a world without walls?" asks Abby as she rests her head against my shoulder.

"I don't know," I whisper. "Maybe."

"We probably wouldn't be as safe as we are behind the wall. I mean, we can't be the only society left in this world. Can we?"

We could be, but I doubt it, I think. Trying to answer her question without knowing what I want to say, my lips manage a small, "Sure."

It's not something I've ever considered nor is something any of us were ever taught to be a possibility. When I turned ten in Nimbus, I was automatically enrolled in *2107: Our Existence* with about thirty others. The class taught us about the founding of Nimbus by Aldous MacMillan and his loyal followers, but it didn't teach us about others who didn't follow him. We were all young and naïve enough to never ask about others. Instead, when we learned about the founding of Nimbus, we just assumed it was true because we had no way of debating it; we had no way of knowing what was right and what was wrong. At this point, it feels like what we were taught was right. *I've never seen an outsider. Then again, they might not look any different.*

Without responding, Abby nuzzles her head into my shoulder. Closing her eyes as her body relaxes, she quickly falls asleep against my arm.

Unable to fall back into the depths of my mind as quickly as the two of them, I sit quietly as the fire crackles next to Sam's back. Blankly staring around the room, I watch as Sam's eyelids flutter and his body twitches—forcing him to roll onto his back. I keep watching as he stares at the back of his eyelids while he remains entranced in his new world. "No walls," he mumbles once again.

"If only," I whisper to myself. Resting my head atop Abby's, I try to escape.

As my eyes wander around the flames in an attempt to find an escape from Nimbus, Sam's ramblings and Arthur's violent conjurings, the light starts to heat my worried brain. Slowly closing my eyes, I try to drift into nothingness.

***

A thick mist drifts through the trees and splatters across my face, obscuring my vision. It's hard to discern the figments of my imagination from the figures of reality as the trees bend from side to side and the rain switches directions with the wind's indecisiveness. Stopping in my tracks, I look around the forest. It sits lifeless.

"Hey Elise," says a familiar voice from behind me.

I quickly turn around, only to see Sean standing still with a bundle of twigs and branches under his arm.

"What's up?"

"Where should I set up the fire?" he asks.

"Wherever you want," I say.

As long as he's here with me, my mind is unable to drift away; as long as he's near, I'm safe. His love wraps its arms around me with an aura of protection so strong, even Arthur can't find a way in.

"Sean," I mutter while wiping the nagging rain from my face.

"Yes?" he replies.

"Where have you been? I've missed you."

I wrap my arms around his waist as he looks at me with confusion. Unsure of what he'll say or if he even understands the question, I refuse to let go.

"I never left," he says as a crack of thunder rips through the skyline, scattering birds amidst the sky.

"What was that?!" I yell.

"I don't know," says Sam, a crack in his voice as he sits up in front of the fireplace.

"Is someone here?" asks Abby nervously, her hands clawing at my waist.

"I don't know, just be quiet. Sam, put out the fire," I whisper.

Sitting up from the chair, I look around the darkened room. The air starts to thicken as a cloud of ash maneuvers its way around the shadows. Slowing my breaths, I head toward the front door with my knife at my side.

My eyes rapidly search around the room, struggling to cope with the darkness. I can barely see, and what I can see is limited. The sky is void of light as the clouds cover the stars and the moon hides in the distance. Stuck in a pitch-black nightmare, I rub my eyes.

"Elise," whispers Sam.

"What?" I say.

"He's here."

Quickly turning around, I stomp toward Sam as Abby screams behind me. "Sam!" I yell. "Where is he?!"

"Too late," replies Arthur as Sam's motionless corpse falls to the ground at my feet.

"Leave me alone!" I scream. "Leave me alone!"

***

"Elise! Wake up!" cries Abby from next to me as my shoulders shake and my head twitches. "I'm right here, Elise. Sam's right there. You're okay. Everything was just a dream."

My hands are doused in sweat and I'm shaking. "What. . .?" I ask.

"You must've been dreaming. I know you haven't slept much lately, so you fell pretty deep into your dream. I heard you mumble loudly once, but I didn't know what it was, so I fell back asleep, too, but when you yelled just then, it was clear," says Abby. Reaching for my hand, she grabs it and gently rubs my knuckles.

"That's impossible, I had two separate dreams. The first was so right. The second was so wrong. How can a perfect dream grow so dark so fast?" I ask in a fright. The two of them look at me with tired eyes, unable and unwilling to fathom the darkness within these headaches.

"I don't know," says Sam.

A pang in my head spreads sheer agony behind my eyes. It feels like my head is ready to explode. It's as if I'm running away from the outside and I can't stop. With each second, the pain spikes. It's an up-and-down battle for a moment of relaxation and there isn't a clear winner. *I can't take this anymore,* I think. . .and almost yell.

"Why can't either of us get one night of peaceful sleep? One night dream-free?" I ask while looking at Sam as he wipes his eyes.

"I don't know. Something out here doesn't like us," he uncomfortably laughs.

18 January 2192

Sam

As I head into the library to get more paper for the fire, I grab the empty journal from the bookshelf. Attempting to pry it open, I slowly pull, hoping not to tear the pages. The smears of black trapped inside hold the paper together as I take a breath. Calmly peeling them apart, I start to skim the remnants of the empty notebook.

Mindlessly flipping through the blank pages, my mind hopes to catch something—to see something that wasn't there before. Yet, nothing jumps out. The journal is the same as it's always been and for some reason, a nagging part of me thinks it will change. I'm not sure why, but it's a feeling I can't shake. *Something else is in here*, I wonder as I casually look through it in search of a cryptic message, something to soothe my strange desire for the unusual.

I flip through the book from end to end, waiting for a newfound image or phrase to catch my gaze or at least to see something again in a new light. Yet, the more I turn the pages, the more my thoughts are proven useless as the pages remain just as empty as the previous fifteen times. "C'mon. Give me an answer," I say aloud to myself. My knees crack as I sit down against the bookshelf.

With my back against the wood, the dull shelves dig into my spine; my eyes wander around the room while my fingers freely wade through the depths of the hollow journal. A dark silence consumes the library. A howling wind runs along the windowsill. No longer focused on the journal, I set it down next to me.

"Sam," comes a voice from beside me.

162

"Yea?" I respond, my vision blurred by my lack of concentration. "Elise?"

Void of a response, the air tightens around my body as *his* cold fingernails dig into my arms. Attempting to clutch the bookshelf as a last grab at reality, I scream. . .or at least try to. *Elise!* yells my mind. *Elise!*

The more I yell in my head, the less my lips move and the deeper he digs into my arms. The more I squirm, the less able I am to find my voice. The more I try to break free, the stronger he holds onto me. As I hang here, shaking in fright, a black band of tape crosses my lips as darkness enshrouds my head. *I feel nothing.*

19 January 2192

Elise

"*Even a bright mind wanders into the shadows*" were the words written in the book Sam was holding before he was captured. It was the last thing he held before *they* took him from us—before they pried him into the shadows unwillingly. Not so much as a yelp could be heard upstairs; they were in and out like ghosts.

"Why? Why? Why?" I shout aloud. "Why did they take him? Why would *he* take Sam? He wants me! Not him!" I cry, kicking the crumbling logs in front of the fire.

"I don't know," sobs Abby, tears running down her cheeks. "He di-didn't ask for th-this."

Angrily screaming, I can feel my face warming, the skin reddening. With watery eyes, I grab the blade from the mantel. Holding it in my fist, I raise it above my head before violently slamming it into the wood. The initials, "A.Y." glint in the sun as the clouds quickly diminish the light from the room.

"They're in the city. . .or at least on their way," I exhale. "There's nowhere else they would go."

"Do you think it could all be a trap. . .or—or a game to him?" asks Abby as she stands up from the chair. Pacing back and forth while fidgeting her fingers, she steps toward me.

"Yes, Sam's the bait. Arthur's cast out his lure and he wants to reel me in," I softly state, trying not to allow myself to dwell on the suffering Arthur relishes.

Wedging the blade out from the wood, Abby runs her fingers down the handle before sitting back down. With her eyes glued at the engraving, she mouths, "A.Y." before looking up at me and responding to my last train of thought. "But he won't catch you," she mutters.

"He got Sam; he might get me next," I exhale as I push my palm into my forehead. "Though, he could've come into the house and taken me away right there. He could've come in and murdered us all, but he didn't. He wants to make me suffer for as long as possible."

"He wants to win," mumbles Abby.

"What do you mean?"

"He's been tormenting you for quite some time now. He must want to prove something or to win something."

"He's a murderer. Killing someone is a victory for him," I angrily reply, the pain soaring the more I visualize *his* gruesome tactics. Burying my face into my palms, I slow my breathing whilst peeking out of the gaps between my fingers.

Constantly rubbing her thumb up and down the small slit of initials written into the blade, Abby looks toward the door. "Elise," she faintly says.

"Yea?" I sniffle.

"I think this blade might be my brother's."

Slowly craning my neck to look down at her, I pause. "Why?"

"Those are his initials. My dad gave him something in a white box with a black bow on his Separation Day and I never saw what it was," she says. Looking up at me, her face shows absolute confusion. "This couldn't be Aden's though. I don't even know if he's alive or if he could have gotten out this far by himself."

"Maybe that's it," I reply. "It's small enough, but what could you do with something that size out here?"

"Whatever you want," she answers. "Anything's a weapon out here."

"That's true." I've seen a kid dead with a twig protruding from his stomach.

Seemingly trying to connect the pieces, Abby continues to speak. "He always had a thing for torturing defenseless creatures."

"What?"

"Aden was always different. He was always torturing animals that were smaller and weaker than him. Maybe this knife was my dad's way of saying he could do that out here, but to more than just animals," she says while her widened eyes wander up and down the blade.

"Why would he encourage him though? If he was already a bit odd in Nimbus, it seems strange to promote his ways even if they would be successful out here."

"I don't know. It's just a thought," she stammers.

Burrowing my teeth into the skin on my lip, I look around the room before taking a seat next to Abby.

"There's just a what-if," she says. "What if this is his? What would that mean?"

"I don't know. I really don't. Why would that be here?"

"What if he was here? What if something happened to him and he left it here?" Placing the blade on the edge of the chair, the sharp end points toward the door while the initials shine toward her. "What if he's with *them*?"

"That's a possibility. Do you think that could happen?"

"Yes," she quickly replies. "He was crazy."

"I know what he did at home, but what do you think that would translate to out here?"

"To him doing whatever he could to kill, to hurt innocent kids. He was always doing what Art said."

"Who's Art?" I ask, the aching behind my eyes dimming.

"His alter-ego," she sighs.

"He had an alter-ego? What was the difference between Aden and Art?"

"Aden liked to burn bugs with his magnifying glass, but would never hurt anything bigger than that. Art liked to bring pain to anyone and anything. He felt that Art was a tough name, so he used that whenever he hurt something. When my dog. . ." she trails off and wipes her eyes. "When my dog died, he kept saying that Art did it. That Art wanted to prove himself. That Art wanted to show he was ready for the outside."

"Do you think. . ." I stop. Turning toward Abby, I gaze into her light brown eyes. "By some crazy sense, do you think that he may have abandoned that name out here? That he may have changed knowing he was on his own?"

"I-I don't know," she stutters.

Picking up the blade, I gently run my finger down the spine of the silver. Stopping on the engraving at the end, I rub the letters

166

and blankly stare at it. "A.Y. Aden Young. A.Y. Art Young." Squinting at the initials, I hold it up into the limited beam of light shining through the door. Folding my lips, I mutter, "A.Y. Arthur Young."

"What? Arthur? What?" exclaims Abby aghast. "How did you. . .? What?"

"Slow down, Abby. You said he went by Art, so I just added the h-u-r. It could be wrong, but that connection could be there. Your brother could be the one after me. He could be the one behind the Lurkers." Exhaling I lift my knee onto the seat and continue. "Maybe he was Art when he came out here. Maybe he added the h-u-r when he saw me. Maybe he wanted to change who he was because of me. . .or because of the Lurkers. Maybe they brainwashed him further and now he's in charge."

"That's a lot of maybes."

"Yea, but we both know that Lurkers lived here before we did. Maybe he was here before and that's why that blade's still around."

"I just don't know if this could be true. It's too much."

"I know. I know that's because it is, but there's always going to be a what-if. He wouldn't take you because you're his sister. Yea, you don't get along, but you're family. Sam's not. Sam's just a victim. Sam's a pawn in his big picture."

"So why wouldn't he just go after you from the start? What does he think he's doing by capturing Sam and luring you into the city?"

"He thinks he's making up for what happened earlier. When I escaped, something had to have happened to him to do so much to bring me back. That, or he just wants me to die there like everyone else. Death outside the wall is meaningless to them. Death in the city feeds them."

Perplexed, Abby asks, "What do you mean, feeds them?"

"They feed off fear. They get into your head out here. The longer they mess with you, the more distraught you are when they capture you. The more afraid you are, the easier it is for them to find life in their ways. . .if that makes sense."

"Sort of. So, they mentally torture you out here to the point that when you finally arrive in the city, they have you right where they want you? Vulnerable, weak, and afraid?"

"Basically. They've been tormenting Sam for a while now. He's weak. We both know that. By pulling him in as bait, they're luring me in more and more. I've had headaches for years now. He's weakening me day by day. If he has us both, he wins."

"How do we stop him, then?"

"We have to do what he wants. We have to go to the city."

"But then he gets us. Then, he could kill us," she cries, her hands shaking. Wiping the tears from her face, she looks up at me. "I don't want to die there. I don't want to die."

"Neither do I, Abby, but we have to rescue Sam. We'll figure out a way around this, but we have to get moving. I don't know what they're going to do to him and I don't want them to drive him to insanity."

"Okay," she whimpers.

"Let's pack up everything we need and leave soon," I say, reaching for the blade and tucking it into my belt. "Just remember what the book said, '*Even a bright mind wanders into the shadows.*'"

22 January 2192

Sean

Elise has to be around here somewhere, I think. I've endlessly walked through the painful memories of my eleven years—I've seen everything I didn't want to see for a second time. I've stumbled, I've staggered wearily through the pain of starvation, but I can't give up. Elise wouldn't quit. Elise wouldn't stop for anything.

Aimlessly meandering through a thicket of trees, I notice dying fires sporadically ahead of me with no sight of those who set them. Not even a body is present. No clothes, no food, no trail of those who were here staving off the cold. It's off-putting. I stay away from the heat and search for a tree to climb—somewhere to get out of sight in case whoever was here comes back.

I step past a few crooked trees—some fallen, some leaning—and tuck my hands into my sleeves. Despite the soaring branches above me, nothing hangs low enough for me to grab. *I could just run past,* I think before a cold gust whips beside me lofting heaps of smoke in my direction. Pressing my back against a nearby tree, I pull my shirt above my face.

As the smoke dissipates, a clear hiding spot presents itself in the distance. I take a few strides before jumping toward a low-hanging branch. The wet bark crumbles against my fingertips; my hands start to slip down the wood. I struggle to pull myself upward and ultimately fall onto my back. Quickly standing back up, I try again, this time successfully. Pulling myself atop the branch, I slowly maneuver myself further up the tree.

Eventually finding a place to hide, I take a breath and close my eyes.

My mind wanders through the empty camps, lingering on the possibility that the Lurkers overran this area. The numerous decaying fires present around the field couldn't have been simultaneously put out on purpose. Most groups tend to knock out their fires when they leave. They wouldn't want to be traced—especially in winter. It's as if there was a camp here; one that didn't last. I bury my cold hands in my pockets.

There are too many possibilities, I think. There aren't as many Lurkers as there are kids out here; at least there can't be. Hundreds, maybe. Thousands, no. Not everyone has the mental capacity to just let go of who they were back home. It's near impossible to be as much of a lunatic as Arthur. Sanity exists even in eleven years of apprehensive exile, whether someone thinks it does or not. You just have to hold on to what kept you alive behind the wall, what little things kept your attention. If you let the thoughts of death erode your sanity, you can lose yourself in a split second.

Keeping a keen eye on the embers, I look around the tree. Nothing jumps out.

After minutes of silence, the faint crunch of snow quietly reverberates throughout the area. With each second, the crunches grow louder. With each step, the voices ring higher.

What's going on? I think as I anxiously sit up.

"He can't be that far," says a female.

"He's not here though," replies a second one.

Looking around the forest, I sit up higher in the tree. Yet, I see nothing.

"Keep your eyes peeled, there are dying fires, so maybe someone is around here," says one of the voices.

Standing up on the branch, I look around as the wood cracks beneath my feet. Gripping onto a smaller branch with my thumbs, I stare down.

The two women walk just below my tree as another small crack vibrates against my shoes. Slowly crippling underneath me, the branch gives out and snaps. I reach my arms higher, trying to grab onto another branch above me, but it fails. The icy bark causes my fingers to slip, sending me onto my back in the snow below.

"Don't move!" shouts one of the voices.

170

"I don't want any trouble," I nervously reply, my aching back only worsened by the broken stick beneath me.

". . .that's him," mumbles one of the women.

"Who?"

"Sean!" screams Elise.

"Elise!" I yell back.

"Sean! Why are you here?!" she yells before jumping onto my stomach. Wrapping her arms around my shoulders, she kisses my chin. Her dark brown hair drapes across my face as she squeezes tightly.

"I was exiled," I reply.

Leaning back, she looks into my eyes—and I, into her inimitable blue eyes. Wiping her hair from my face, her arms shake against my chest. "I've missed you," she mumbles.

"I've missed you, too," I say. "But you gotta get off me."

"I take it that's Sean," laughs the other girl—her rosy cheeks perking up.

"Yea, Abby. This is Sam's brother, Sean," Elise says.

Abby? I think. *Where's Sam?*

Smiling, Abby tilts her head sideways. Elise looks back at her. Sitting up, she grabs my arms as they both pull me onto my feet.

Tilting my head to the side, I look around the field for Sam. "Where. . .?" I ask as my voice trails off and I thrust my hand into my throbbing back.

"He's gone," says Abby. Shifting her stare toward the snow, she loosens the red scarf around her neck.

"Gone where?"

"Captured. He was taken from us a few days ago," replies Elise.

"By who?"

"Arthur."

"That bastard has my brother?" I say. Clenching my fingers into my palms, I try to regain feeling.

"We think so. We're on our way to get him back," says Abby. While she lifts her scarf above her mouth her eyes scan me.

"Where do you think he is?" I ask.

"The city," Elise quickly replies.

"How did he get there?" I ask. *The city. The one place he should never be. The one part of the outside that's more terrifying than turning your back against the doors of Nimbus.* Falling to my knees, my back starts to spasm. Spreading to my hips, the ache forces me to rotate my feet to regain feeling.

Crouching down next to me, Elise places her hand in mine. "Sean, a lot has happened since Sam came out here. Arthur has tormented him more than me. He's using Sam as bait to lure me into the city to finish what he started. I know this is a lot coming at you, but we need you. I need you."

My fingers tremble as the icy grip of the snow starts to freeze my knuckles. As the ice creeps into my veins, the pain subsides while my mind sits still waiting for a moment of clarity, a brief second of sanity. "Let's go then," I say.

Smiling, Elise pulls me back up and hands me her bow. "You were always better with this than I was."

"It's been a while," I reply.

"Doesn't matter," smiles Elise.

"Well, let's go," says Abby. "Let's go get Sam back."

I nod. Despite the pain of being beaten, of falling, of being pushed around, nothing hurts more than knowing Sam's in danger. Arthur knows we'll come. He knows the cold-blooded ecstasy coursing through his veins won't last forever. Even if he grows stronger through others' suffering, he can't prod at them forever. Eventually, someone will retaliate. And if I know Sam, he won't give in. He won't die.

23 January 2192

Elise

As we traipse through the forest, a slight breeze pushes my hair into my eyes. Yet, I find no reason to pull my hair away. It's as if the wind is shielding my eyes from what may lie ahead—from *him*.

Lost in this empty void, we wander for hours as the city strays from our path. Every step away from the farm is another step toward the unknown; every moment without Sam sends our minds farther away from bliss. In a never-ending game of hide and seek, the city of nightmares continues to win.

"It can't be that far from here," I say.

"I'm pretty sure we're heading in the right direction," replies Sean. "I remember the trees became more sporadic. I'm sure we'll see a building in the distance in the next few days or so."

"I hope so," Abby chimes in. "I hope so. . ." she repeats breathlessly.

"We will, and we'll find Sam. He's tough," replies Sean.

Nodding in agreement, I glance from side to side while branches bend ever so slightly around me. Yearning for a peaceful escape into a once-inhabited, once-functioning city, my mind plunges into the ivy-ridden buildings that now course the entire expanse. It's as if the city never bustled with businessmen, entrepreneurs looking to chase their dreams, or creatives seeking to expel their talents onto the city's beautiful landscape. It seems as if it has always been a barren wasteland, void of life, culture, or any form of habitable society. It's something I don't understand.

It's depressing how a world can disappear out of thin air, how a society can deteriorate like it was never more than a dream to begin with. Despite my hatred for what that city stands for today, the abrupt downfall of a civilization like the one before us will always baffle me. War is a terrible thing, something the Elites told us every day.

In Nimbus, our history teachers vaguely taught us the story of the city as though its presence was never worth preserving—heck, it seems Sam and Abby were never even taught about it; like the Elites figured nobody should know about it anymore. All I know is that the world fell to ruins because of a massive war, but I don't know how it started. I just know that it happened and the wall was built to start a world anew, to ensure our future is in our own hands. Without the wall, the chaos would never end. Without something protecting us, we could become endangered like the world before us. This must be why they kick us out; they want us to see what could have been, what pain and torment in a world without law feels like. They want us to struggle in a meaningless environment to make us believe Nimbus is safe. *They're brainwashing us.*

How can the Elites guarantee their society is the strongest, that theirs will outlast all those before it? They can't. Every good thing must come to an end, and everything Nimbus has ever stood for will come to an end. Forcing kids out of your society to build their strength and mentality is one thing, but killing those who don't fit your standards is another. A society without adept ideologies is like a candle. It can burn lightly with limited decay for years, but eventually it will die. Eventually, the wax will dissipate and darkness will set in and you'll die not knowing if you were right all along or if everything you accomplished was for nothing. By God, the light shining so heavily above MacMillan's thick skull will burn out and enshroud him in darkness with a thick cloud of black so terrifying it's as if he's the one out here being tormented. That'll be the day.

"Sean," I mumble, stepping under a low-hanging branch.

"Yea," he responds.

"Why are you out here?"

Lightly brushing his tongue against his cracked lips, Sean spits it out. "MacMillan," he simply says. Clenching his teeth together, he looks away before quickly turning his head back at me. "MacMillan arrested me for not killing an outsider. . .or for lying to

174

him. Either way, he tried to swing at me and I caught his fist and head-butted him."

"He deserved that," laughs Abby.

"Yea, he definitely did," grins Sean. "But, but after I did that, I was tackled by other guards and he punched me a few times. Then, I was imprisoned, fed very little, and kicked back out here within the month."

"I'm glad you're here," I say before kissing him on the cheek.

"Me too. As you can tell, I don't have much meat on my bones right now," he says while looking at the ground. "I've hallucinated once and lived off of cold meat, practically rotted meat, but I needed something."

Smiling, I wrap my hands around his back as I kiss him once more on the cheek.

"Cut it out," says Abby. "I don't want to see that."

"Sorry, Abby," I say, jokingly rolling my eyes at her.

". . .I saw you," whispers Sean.

"What?"

"I saw you when I hallucinated. You told me to wake up."

"When was this?"

"A few weeks ago, maybe. I collapsed in a field because I had barely eaten anything and I was freezing to death. You told me to find food and shelter almost as if it meant I'd find you shortly thereafter. So, I tried and tried and eventually found an empty camp with some meat and clothes," he says.

"Was the camp anything like the one we found you near?" asks Abby.

"Sort of," replies Sean. "All the fires were out, dried meat was sitting atop the ashes and clothes were scattered. It was as if whoever was there was in a rush to leave."

"Do you think maybe something happened to both those camps?"

"Maybe," he mumbles. "But what?"

Abby shakes her head and looks around the forest before biting her bottom lip. "I have no idea. It just seems odd. We haven't really seen many camps, let alone ones that look occupied, but aren't. It just feels like there's something more to it—like there is to everything out here."

"It's probably the Lurkers," I mutter.

Looking over at me, Abby's face shifts to that of fear. Her cheeks sink, her eyes wander, she scratches her earlobe, but she doesn't speak.

Letting go of Sean, I turn around and step closer to Abby. With the trees seemingly becoming more intermittent with each step, the city never presents itself. No skyscrapers lurk above the trees, no fires illuminate a path, nothing is indicative of the city's placement.

"Why is this place so hard to find?" asks Abby. Itching the back of her neck, she tucks her hands into her pockets.

"It only seems to appear when you're lost or vulnerable. At least, that's how it's been for me," I say.

"We're lost now. We're vulnerable. Where is it?"

"You seem too eager to find something I told you to avoid," I say harshly. "You shouldn't be so desperate to see that rotten place."

"Sam's there and eagerness is all I have to keep myself from being too scared," she replies, her lips remaining parted while she looks around— her eyes more focused on the ground than the sky. "If I'm not drawn to the idea of finding him, we'll never find him. If I'm not strong enough to keep moving, maybe he won't be either."

"He's strong enough, Abby. If he's anything like you, he'll survive," says Sean.

She smiles and keeps ahead of us.

"We'll find it before you know it," I faintly reply. Even though it's where we need to be, I'm afraid to see it. I don't want to see those darkened walls laced with the unscrupulous phrases the Lurkers deem logical. I don't want to feel the tingling sensation running down my naked spine nor do I desire the fear of being alone, of being trapped in the shadows. I want nothing to do with that pain—even if it's not my burden this time. *I don't want to go*, I think.

"I remember there was a road," says Sean. "The city sat at the end."

I remember a hill toward an alley. I remember aching. Clenching my fists, I try to push the woeful memory away. "I remember that way, too," I say. "It was a long, winding road mixed with cement, dirt, and weeds. It was how I found the city."

"If we can find that, we'll be well on our way."

176

Extending her strides ahead of us, the gap between Abby and Sean and I grows larger by the second. Reminiscent of Sam's thoughtless expedition into the farmhouse alone, Abby nearly starts to jog.

"What's that over there?" she inquires, pointing ahead while catching her breath. "I see footprints."

"That was easy," I say, nonplussed.
"Too easy," mutters Sean.

24 January 2192

Sam

'*Darkness is the root of all sanity*' reads the engraving on the wall beside me. Surrounded by illegible phrases amidst an overcrowded jumble of symbols, the light shines on the middle of the phrase. '*ness is the root of all*' is clear as if the beginning and ending are replaceable; as if they're unnecessary. *Lightness is the root of all*, I think to myself while I itch my scalp.

Trapped in a room layered with writings and shapes with two steel bands around my ankles, I gaze at the emptiness of this place. Two crystal vials sit just feet in front of me. One is full of a purple-green liquid, while the other sits empty. A brown leather-bound journal with the front cover ripped off lays next to me. Full of inscriptions, anagrams, and various quotes, the journal appears to be my escape. At least, that seems to be what they want me to think.

'*Visions of the endless abyss may rot your mind, but if you believe in the shadows, your eyes will see fine,*' reads the first page of the notebook. Lurkers, past and present, who've been locked away in this room had to have written everything they saw in this. Every mad, insane thought that crossed their mind probably went in here. '*Fire is the warmth of a troubled mind*' reads another. Harmless to them, this book represents everything I'm trying to escape. Yet, I can't help myself from looking through it.

The first page reads:

It's been hours since I awoke; the idea of where I once was feels like a memory. A memory lost in a world I can't run back to. . .a place I may never see again. The lights constantly flicker and even as I close my eyes to avoid them, my eyelids flutter. My arms are shaking and my body is twitching. I feel cold, yet warm. My skin is cold, but my mind is warm. These men have come in and out of this room every thirty minutes or so asking if I've drank from the vials. I say no, but they keep coming back telling me that the liquid will ease the pain. I don't want to drink their poison. . .I just want to get out of here.

Wesley

After his signature, there's a series of scribbles. It's as if something happened to him; something drove him to insanity—to what they wanted. He could have drunk the liquid to escape or maybe it was forced upon him. The scribbles don't discern a message; they just swirl around into a point at the bottom of the page. I flip the page over. The backside is empty and untouched.

Each page thereafter is as empty as the one before it. Periodic scribbles and tallies mark up a few pages in the middle, but that's it. Quickly shutting the book in an attempt to clear my mind, I lie on my back and stare at the dripping ceiling. A stretch of green runs from end to end above me as cracks in the cement leak around the room. The swaying light bounces when each drop of liquid pings against its rusted metal. The more I sit here, the more I want to escape—especially away from the dripping echo. And the more I want to escape, the more I fear my only exit is through that greenish-purple liquid.

"Thirsty?" comes a deep, throaty voice from behind the door as a man slides open a small black hatch at the top of the frame. "Drink up."

"No!" I shout back as screams from outside reverberate through the hole and into this room.

"It'll make you feel all better," he laughs before slamming the hatch shut.

The cries ring loudly outside of the room as kids scream and yell at the top of their lungs. Despite the hatch being closed, the cries echo louder with each passing minute. Every time one person stops, another breaks out. It's as if the Lurkers are bringing in multiple outsiders at once. *Maybe they snagged a group.*

I plug my ears in an attempt to mute the sobs, but it proves ineffective. Each cry vibrates louder and louder—enough that the cement vibrates beneath my legs, rattling the chains—until it

179

abruptly stops. *They're gone,* I think. I pull my fingers out of my ears right when a high-pitched shrill pierces my eardrums. Immediately jamming my fingers back into my ears, I crouch forward and tuck my knees against the sides of my head.

Suddenly, the door flings open and shut in a matter of seconds. The lights flicker more as the person bumps into the bulb.

"Let me out of here!" she screams as she pounds her fists into the door.

"They won't let you out," I say as I remove my nails from my ears.

Seeming unaware of my presence, she proceeds to throw her body against the door. With each punch, her body droops lower. With each ear-piercing scream, her voice grows a little quieter. Finally, she succumbs to her fate as she falls to her knees. Head down, shoulders up, she weeps.

"At least you're not in chains," I say.

"That doesn't help," she snarls back.

"Sorry," I whisper.

The screams eventually die out; silence engulfs the room. The scavenging cockroaches can be heard dispersing into the corners as their feet scurry against the cracked pavement.

"I'm Sam," I mutter.

"Ann," replies the girl.

Throwing her palms back toward her eyes, she continues to inhale deeply as she struggles to breathe. Choking back tears, she lets out a loud whimper before throwing her back against the door.

"Wh-why. . .why am I here?" she stammers.

"I don't know," I reply. Unable to put my thoughts into words, I briefly glance at Ann—her chestnut-colored hair hangs in front of her face; her jean jacket with splotches of dried blood on the arms sags upon her skinny frame—before looking away.

"H-how did you get here?" she asks as she wipes her cheeks and looks up at me. Pulling her knees toward her chest, she bites her lips.

"They took me from my friends. How did they get you?"

"A bunch. . .a bunch of them came to our camp and took us. They. . .they took us all."

"How many of you were there?" I ask.

"A dozen."

180

. . .and they captured all of you at once? I think to myself. "How many of them came?"

"I don't know. I didn't become conscious until they were dragging me through the hallway by my hair."

"Did you see them with anybody else?"

"No," she quickly jolts back. "I-I. . .I saw Ian dead."

"Where?"

"Out there," she says, her thumb pressing into the door.

Throwing her hands behind her head, Ann leans into them. Softly inhaling and exhaling, she sits still.

I glare back at the door, where her faded thumb imprint quickly evaporates from the steel. "We have to find a way out of here," I say.

Pulling her knees closer to her chest, she burrows her head further into her lap. Without so much as a sniffle, Ann goes quiet.

I clear my eyes and look around the room once more. Rapidly blinking at the nonsense inscribed around me, I search for a second of clarity. The loud 'ping' of the water splashing against the light doesn't help. The vials remain still, awaiting my lips. Casually stretching out my legs to the extent allowed by the chains, I try to find a gap in the wall; at least something that we can dig through. Still, nothing jumps out. The room never changes. Nothing I desire jumps out; Abby and Elise haven't barged through the door to save me.

I push against the light, hoping if it spins in a new direction, it'll show me something new: a new piece to this puzzle I hadn't seen before.

"Look up," mutters Ann. I briefly look over at her. With her chin up, the light showcases a litany of scratches and claw marks against her neck. Unfazed by the crooked lines, she continues to stare at the ceiling.

I tilt my head upward. A patch of scraggly letters instantly catches my eye as they lay centered in a surprisingly well-drawn circle. Amidst the flicker of the bouncing light, it reads, '*Darkness is for the able. Drink what's on the table and one will be unable.*'

25 January 2192

Elise

With each step closer to the empty city streets, my mind tries to run back into the forest, but my legs don't follow. Arthur knows we'll come; he knows we won't desert Sam. With everything he has, he's luring what sanity we have left into the city. Like a game of Tug of War, he's pulling us toward the center—toward an inevitable loss.

No matter where we end up, he'll be there; he's teeming with so much fury, so much enmity, that I bet waiting is agonizing him. And the closer we get to where he wants us, the sooner we could fall into his hands.

But, the farther we walk, the more fight we show. Every footprint left in the evaporating snow behind us is a sign we won't give up; they're a sign we'll fight until there's blood on our hands. Though, if it were just me, the footprints might not have made it this far. They might have stopped at the front steps of the farm. *Hell, they might still be at the shack.* I shake my head.

As I try to ward the selfish thoughts from my mind, my foot catches on a rock. Stumbling, my knees fall into the dirt. I hold my head low. "I don't know if I'm ready," I mumble.

"Elise?" cautiously mutters Sean as he stops a few feet ahead of me. "Are you okay?"

I want to say yes, but I can't. I can't lie about where my mind is. My lips muster a quick, "I don't know."

The more the snow fades, accompanied by the slight temperature increases, the more I feel my body getting colder. It's as if the darkness that lies ahead has removed the possibility of warmth from my mind. Every step chills my spine as if my body is turning

182

into ice while *he* waits miles ahead with a look of delirium on his face. Hiding in the shadows, he waits. Waiting until he can break me, until he can shatter my existence.

"I can't do this," I say.

"Yes, you can," replies Sean. His cold fingers brush against my neck while his soft lips press into my forehead. "He can't hurt you anymore."

Shaking off his remark, I remain still on the ground. The melting snow wets my knees. I try to pull my mind away from *him*, but I can't. Yielding to my physical exhaustion, I try to run away in my mind, but the footsteps in my head refuse to budge. Every part of me is worn out; every fragment of my being is tired of fighting to survive. "I can't," I mumble once more.

"You can," whispers Abby as she kneels down next to me.

I want to say something, but I don't know what. My exhausted lips can't slip the slightest of syllables out as I continue to look down, weary of stepping even an inch closer to the city. Every moment of despair that Arthur has buried in my mind starts to pull itself back out as the nightmares burst down my cheeks. I slam my fists into the dirt.

"Elise, we have to keep moving," says Abby.

"I can't. Go without me. Leave me here," I mumble. The words force themselves out of my mouth like vomit and I can't hold them back. My mind is miserable and my body is weak. I want to let go and give up, but I can't. No matter how much I try to stop, *he* keeps pulling.

"We aren't leaving you," mutters Sean, his hand on my back.

"Just go!" I yell.

"We're not going without you!" Abby storms back. "Sam is out there dying. Arthur is probably hurting him as we speak and you're just going to let him die?!"

"It's not my brother who's causing it!" I retaliate. The moment the sentence passes my teeth, I want to bite down and pull it back in, but it's too late. I've let my weakened state win. I've let *him* get the best of me. Stunned, Abby gets up and sprints down the path without so much as a glance back at me. Unable to move, I remain still as Sean stands up and chases her.

I can't take back what I said. No matter how much I want to, it's impossible. I don't know if Arthur is Abby's brother; I don't even know if the blade belongs to him, but every second I think about it, I think it's him. Even the slight gust of wind grazing my back sends chills down my sides as if his bony fingers are sliding down my body. Every little thing tampers with my thoughts enough that it feels like Arthur's near me. It's almost like he's breathing down my neck rather than the faint wind gliding across my skin.

"Abby!" screams Sean from ahead of me. Quickly catching up with her, he wraps his arms around her waist and lifts her into the air. Her arms flail as she tries to escape, but to no avail. A slight scuffle ensues as she manages to get back to her feet before he picks her up again and holds her tightly. She continues to cry. I stagger to my feet.

"Let go!" she yells.

"I can't," replies Sean, out of breath. "You can't go there alone!"

"Let me go! I'll kill him. I'll kill whoever it is!" she screams.

"Not by yourself," I say as I near the two of them. My body shivers in the wind. I cross my arms and wiggle my hands up into my sleeves. "You can't go alone, especially if Arthur is your brother."

"He's not!" Abby screams in Sean's arms. "He's not!" she yells as her voice weakens. "It can't be!"

"It might be," I say. I want to stray away from the conflict I started, but I can't. He has a grip on my mind stronger than the wall itself and there's nothing I can do to make him slip up. "I'm sorry, Abby, but it might be him. That blade has to mean something."

Kneeling down next to Sean, I hear her throat clear as she sniffles in his arms. When he relaxes his hold on her, Abby tumbles to her knees. "It's not him," she whispers.

"Why does it matter? You hate him," I say.

Sobbing, she bites her lip, trying to speak. "He's still my brother."

"Abby. He's not your brother anymore. Arthur hides in the shadows because he's afraid. . .because he has no one. . .because he has absolutely nothing. He's a coward and the only one who ever shined a light on him was you, but he didn't care. He pushed you away and he continued down his dimly lit path to nothing," I say, wiping my nose.

184

Falling onto all fours, Abby pounds her fist into the dirt as she screams. "Why?!" she wails.

"I wish I had an answer."

"But you don't," she angrily retorts. "No one can cure him. He's gone, but he's still my brother."

"Then we don't have to hurt him," says Sean. "We can talk to him."

"That won't work," I whisper under my breath.

"Why?" he asks.

"Because he's crazy. Even if it sounds like he's listening, he's not. He told me to leave the city the first time I got there, yet he was the one who imprisoned me. He'll say what he needs to say to get what he wants. It may be the right thing to say, but it's not what he means."

"I can't go," cries Abby as she sniffles against her sweater. "I can't."

I don't speak. I feel the same torment Abby feels; I know the pain of taking the wrong steps forward. I want to resolve the tension I started, but I can't. Nothing can eradicate suffering. Once something is inside of you, it eats at you forever. What you say, what you do, and how you act are the only ways to bury it. And, right now, that torment is digging its way through me. It's forcing my words. It's numbing my legs.

We sit in a semicircle of silence for a while before anyone gathers a thought to spit out. "We have to go," I say. "It'd be stupid of us to let Sam die. You were right from the beginning, Abby. I can't just let him die."

"Neither can I," says Sean. "But if you two want to stay, I'll go. He's my brother and I have to save him."

"We have to find him," says Abby.

"Who?"

"Both of them."

"What do we do when we find. . .when we find *him*?" I ask.

"We hurt him," she sobs.

"I can do it," says Sean.

Bemused, Abby glances up at Sean. "I will."

I can tell by the glimmer in her eye that she means it, that she's able to let go of their relationship in order to do what's right.

"We have to find him. We have to force him to live forever in the darkness he's so fond of. Lost, wandering the streets alone until the vagrants. . .until the people he considered friends leave him. Until he's the only one out here," she says. Instantly burying her face into her palms, she cries.

With every passing second, he extends his grueling malevolence on Sam as we struggle to move forward. I stand up and try to clear my mind. I pause, not knowing what to say as I avoid falling into the trap—as I take control. "Let's do it," I say.

Nodding her head while she continually sobs into her palms, Abby stands up. Spreading her arms, she steps toward me and wraps her arms around my waist. Squeezing with what strength she has left, she refuses to let go.

Sam

"I'm not going to drink that," says Ann.

Despite my thirst, I refuse to touch the vials. I'm afraid of what will happen if neither of us drinks, but I'm not going to hurt someone who's in the same situation as I am. I don't have a cruelty in me to willingly hurt or kill someone who's trying to survive. If anything, I'll throw the liquid at the man behind the door the next time he opens the hatch. Maybe then, I'd be doing something right. Maybe then, I could get out of here.

"Neither am I," I say.

"So what do we do?"

"I'm not really sure. There has to be a way out of here," I respond while looking around for an answer I've attempted to find at least a million times. "I know someone who was stuck here once and she said they left the door unlocked for some reason."

"I tried that when they threw me in here. It can't be that simple," she replies.

"Probably not," I mutter. *I just wish it was.*

With my back against the cold cement, I inhale as I glance at Ann. Sitting still against the door, she stares at the wall with a look of uneasiness while she fidgets with her thumbs.

"How long have you been out here?" I ask.

"Three years."

"How long have you been with that same group?"

"For about the last year. There were more of us when we started, but people kept getting angry at each other, so a bunch left. The last dozen of us haven't had any issues until now." Continuing to dig at her nails, she glances at me before looking back down. "I've dealt with conflict before, but. . .I've never been this scared."

Wishing I could agree, I bite my lip as I stare at my shackled ankles. "One of the Lurkers. . ." I mumble as my brain runs in circles.

"What?"

187

"One of them has been pulling me here for months. One of them has been in my head ripping me apart from the inside," I say. "I've been scared; I've seen what the outside can do, but something. . .something about being here has given me peace."

"How?" she asks as she inches closer to me.

Unable to turn my thoughts into words, I close my eyes as I jump into the ruins of Arthur's torture. Yet, he's not there. For the first time in weeks, my mind is clear; my mind is free. "He hasn't scarred me here," I say.

"How had he scarred you before?"

"He got into my head somehow. He gave me nightmares. . .I couldn't sleep, I couldn't eat, I couldn't focus."

Tilting her head forward, she looks away before itching her eyebrow. "How can someone just do that?"

I don't know, I think. It's bothered me since the first time I heard his voice, yet I've never been able to grasp how he does what he does. Unsure what to say, my mind spews out the first thing it can. "He's not normal."

"What do you mean? He seems crazy, but I guess I just don't understand."

"It's hard to explain. I think he's been following us."

"Who's us?"

"Me, Elise, and Abby. Arthur caught Elise in the city once and trapped her here. He also cut her once outside of the city. He's been attached to her, but he's never truly visible. I think once he saw that she had me and Abby, he latched onto me," I say. Looking off to the opposite side of the room, I faintly speak again. "He wanted something more than just Elise. He wanted to break down her mind, wear her out enough that he can finally get her. But, in order to do that. . .he has to have me." He has to have a fourteen-year-old fear for his life. He has to have me—a once-cocky kid now clinging to a vanishing hope of survival.

"Hadn't he worn her down already when he had her here in the city?"

"Maybe, but I think once she found my brother, he helped her regain her strength. He helped protect her from Arthur."

"So you're just bait in some big scheme to make up for his miscues?"

"That's what it seems like."

188

Confused, Ann looks around the room as she tries to gather her thoughts. "Why didn't you just leave her then? Wouldn't you be safer if you weren't with her? Then, she wouldn't have a reason to grow attached to you and you could do what you please."

"I don't think I'm equipped to survive on my own. She helped me. If leaving her meant I wouldn't be here, I still wouldn't do it. I'm alive because of her."

"You also could be dead because of her."

"I also could be dead on my own."

"I guess it makes sense. I feel safer in a group too, so I can't blame you, but we're not in groups now. It's just us and we have nowhere to go."

As I open my mouth to respond, a stifled scream reverberates outside the door. "I wonder if they're bringing in more people," I say.

"Maybe, or maybe someone tried to escape and was caught. It could be anything."

Suddenly, the hatch on the door swings open as the grimy, yellow teeth of a Lurker peek through. "Drink up. I can't throw anotha' one of yous in there if there's two of ya still alive."

"Why don't you come drink it then?" I laugh.

"Good one," he says. "Drink now or Arthur will be on 'is way."

"Bring him down. That way, he can drink it himself," I stammer back. *Whoa. Where'd that come from?* It's as if the quiet of this infested room has given me an aptitude for sarcasm—something I haven't had out here—and it's strangely satisfying.

"He's gon' like that when I tell 'im," replies the guard as a muffled screech fades as he closes the hatch behind him.

"Why did you do that?" asks Ann furiously.

"I really don't know," I say. My stomach moves around like it's mad at me. Timid glances toward the door meshed with the ongoing movement in the pit of my stomach cause me to look away from Ann. Yet, she moves closer.

"Do you think he's actually going to bring Arthur here?"

A few days ago, the presence of him would've driven me insane, but it's as if that nagging pressure, that fear, of him is gone. It's gotten to the point that I'm ready to see him. I want to see who's been tormenting me for so long. I want to see the man who's been trying to kill us. "I hope so," I say.

"What if he hurts us? What if him coming down here means he's going to kill one of us?" she says as her body twitches. "What if he kills both of us?"

"He won't," I say.

"How do you know that? You don't know him!" she screams. "For all I know, you could've just lured him here to get what you want without thinking about the safety of others." Thrusting her hands into the ground, she quickly stands up. Frantically pacing around the room, she walks in circles. "What if he tortures us? We're in a damn dungeon, Sam. He could do anything."

"You're not the one in chains," I say. "If he's going to hurt anyone, it's going to be me."

Stopping in her tracks, she gazes back at me. "Do you want that?"

"I don't know," I mumble. Incapable of producing any sort of positivity, my hands start to vibrate against my legs. "I don't know," I say again. My stomach spins.

"Then what do you want?"

"I want to see him. I want to see who's trying to kill me and I want to kill him."

"And how are you going to do that? You haven't thought any of this through!" she yells.

She's right. I know that any move, any gesture I make toward Arthur would just lead to pain. The more I think about wrapping my chains around his neck, the more my hands start to shake.

"You can't escape him now, Sam," she says. "He has you right where he wants you."

"She's right," comes a hoarse voice from behind the door. "I have you right where I want you, Sam."

Mesmerized by the handle on the door, I watch as the slight glint of gold clicks and the steel is pushed toward us. For a moment, the once-strong sense of invulnerability disappears into thin air. It fades into the room as the shadow steps in.

"I've waited quite a while to see you," he says as the darkness covers his face. "It's a shame that we had to bring you here this way. . .that I had to take you from my sister like that. She was growing so fond of you."

190

With every syllable that slips past his invisible lips, I want to stand up and beat him. I want to break these chains and wrap them around him. I want to kill him to protect Abby.

"Speaking of Abby, I have this strange feeling they're on their way to see you. . .or should I say, to see me. Too bad you won't be alive to see them," he says as his worn black shoes grace the light near my feet.

"Why's that?" I say.

"Because you're growing weaker, Sam. I gave you a way out and you haven't taken it yet. Why's that?"

"Why don't you take it?" I joke as Ann scoots closer to me.

". . .don't," she whispers.

"Don't what?" I mutter back.

"Don't look—" she spits out just as a guard grabs her arm and pulls her into the shadows.

"Don't look at me?!" screams Arthur as his head pokes out of the darkness. His greasy skin carves the path for his heightened cheekbones while a straight-line scar runs up the entirety of his right cheek. His dark black hair sits behind his ears as his forehead protrudes over his large, grayish eyes. "Why wouldn't you look at me?" he shouts as he inches closer to me.

The closer he gets, the more noticeable it becomes. His nose is crooked as if it was recently broken. He covers a sniffle with a cough as he wipes the blood from his face before nearing my line of sight once more.

"What are you so afraid of?" he asks with a scowl as he turns around.

"N-nothing," cries Ann.

"What about you, Sam? Do I frighten you?"

"No," I mutter.

"But I know everything about you, Sam. I've been following you since you got out here. I could've killed you numerous times, but I haven't."

"Why not?" I ask, uncertain if I want to know the answer.

Turning back toward me, he kneels down and places a hand on my ankle—a faded gray band around his wrist shakes. Clutching at my leg with his bony fingers, he tries to rouse me as he stares at me; his pupils glower as his cheek twitches. "Because I thought I could save you," he finally spits out.

Liar. "Save me from what?"

"From Nimbus."

"What do you mean?" I say.

"Don't listen to him, Sam!" cries Ann before silence enshrouds the shadows behind Arthur.

"Nobody should have to go back to Nimbus. The outside is the world we should live in; the shadows are where we should thrive. Nimbus is as corrupt as the world before it and I. . .I can offer you a sanctuary. I can offer you light, or so I thought."

Or so you thought? I think. *Could you ever offer me an escape? Could you ever give me a reason to join you when you're just as bad as MacMillan? Do you even want me alive or are these words just meaningless?*

"Escaping into the shadows isn't light. That's cowardice," I retort, foregoing the questions running through my mind—questions I know the answers to, but don't care to say aloud.

"Isn't hiding behind a wall the same thing?" he laughs, his grip on my ankle growing tighter.

"I'm not behind it," I quip. *And I don't care to ever be.*

"But you could be. Out here, you're free. You can live in darkness or light," he chuckles, "without being told what to do. In Nimbus, you can't kill without punishment; you can't even be out when the sun goes down. Out here, you can kill whomever you want, whenever you want, and nobody cares. You can thrive in the shadows without the Elites telling you what to do. You can be anybody you want out here," he says, releasing my ankle.

"Why would I want to kill? Why would I want to be someone else?"

Growing angry, he clenches his teeth and gnaws at his tongue. "Because you can, Sam. Rules are for the weak. The hollows of night can offer you solace; they can offer you freedom! Join me, Sam. Together, we can overrun Nimbus. Together, we can create the world you drew up. We can make a world without walls."

How do you know that? I think.

"I just do," he says as if I had spoken aloud.

"Why would you give me an escape and then say you need me? You're as deluded as anyone who follows you."

"But," he says, holding his finger into the air, "I'm not as crazy as those who don't." Pointing his finger at my nose, he smiles.

192

Without response, I stare at his elongated fingernail nearing the tip of my nose. My teeth clatter behind my lips. My eyebrows run toward each other. *Don't*, I think, but it's too late. My body reacts before my mind and before I know it, my fist is smashing into his scar. My pinky is aching as the force reverberates to my wrist.

The next thing I know, everything is black and the hopelessness I once had stings like an unending nightmare—one I'm unable to flee.

26 January 2192

Sean

We're here. We've finally made it to the city. It's just as I remember, still holding onto a darkened aura of despair. An aura so strong it's frightening, yet strangely enticing at the same time. Everything about this place is unkempt and broken-down. The city's a mess. A gigantic mess.

"I don't like this place. Every step makes my head ache more and more," says Elise.

"Yea, I don't like it either," says Abby. "I don't feel welcome."

"You're not supposed to," I say.

"I get that. This place looks dead," Abby says. "Where could Sam be if it doesn't even look like anyone is here to begin with?"

"I know where he is," replies Elise as she takes a drink from the canteen. "He's about a mile down this road."

As she points forward, I arch my neck to stare over the dusted cars. The street is completely deserted to the point that weeds have grown so high in cracks of cement that it looks as if they've formed their own communities. "How far do you think you can go?"

"Not much farther. Is there a building we can step into so I can sit for a bit?" responds Elise.

"We can go anywhere," I say. Looking around the area, I spin in a crooked circle as I try to find a place to get away. The more I look, the less I see. The more I spin, the more this jungle becomes just that: a jungle, not a city. "I don't see anything that's not overrun with vines."

"That's because this place is a nightmare," mumbles Elise as she takes another drink.

"Over there!" shouts Abby as she points ahead. "I see a broken door over there to the right."

A snakelike puddle leads the way toward a stretch of broken glass littered about. Just behind the shattered fragments, a fallen door sits perched against the ruptured steel of its former bearings. The building can't be more than a few stories high, but the once-tan bricks outlining its structure have chipped off to the point that it looks as if the cement pillars within are the only things holding it up.

As we follow the curved puddle toward the building, the remnants of what it used to be start to become clearer: it's a bank, or at least it was. A collapsed lamppost lies in a broken windowsill as if it were thrown into the building, while every window, door, and sign is in shambles.

"I wonder what happened here," says Elise as she steps through a broken window.

"It was probably the Lurkers. What else do they have to do out here?" I respond.

"Probably. This place is disgusting. There are puddles everywhere."

The farther we get into the place, the more the bottom floor looks as if it once staged some sort of event. All the desks are smashed and pushed against the walls while the chairs are stacked atop each other against the back wall. Lush patches of ivy cling to the damp ceiling, while the middle of the room sits nearly empty aside from sporadic puddles. There aren't any cash registers, computers, or even so much as a nickel in sight. Whatever happened here was violent, steadfast in its destruction.

"Sean, come here," says Elise from the front of the room. Standing amidst a pile of broken chairs, she looks toward the debris.

"What is it?"

"Do you see this?"

"See what?"

"This." Her finger trails along red smudges across the legs of the desks until she's pointing at a bolted, silver door at the back of the room.

"Is that blood?" asks Abby as she nears us.

"I think so," replies Elise. "What's behind that door?"

"Could Sam be back there?" Abby wonders aloud as she lingers toward the door.

Quickly peering back at the desks, I crouch and follow the red. Squinting closely, I brush my finger along the cold, silver legs; the slimy texture liquefies in my hands. "It's fresh," I say.

"What's behind that door?!" cries Abby.

Hushing her, Elise covers Abby's mouth with her palm as she kneels beside her.

My hands start to shiver. My eyes blur this door with the one in Nimbus, creating an image I don't care to see—one in which the thing on the other end isn't pretty. I inch closer with my hand on the bow.

"Open it," whispers Elise as Abby holds onto her waist.

Gently grabbing the door's handle, my fingertips encounter a similar moisture as I pull it open. A faint silhouette of light flashes against the back wall; the reddened trail fades and a rotting stench sullies the air. Nothing jumps out. Nothing tries to pull me in. It looks empty.

"What is it?" asks Elise as she moves her hands over Abby's eyes. "What do you see?"

"Nothing," I say.

I scour the dimly lit room in search of something. . .anything, really. The skylight isn't providing enough light into the vault as I would have liked and it's making me nervous. *Focus.* I think. *You're not afraid.* But a part of me is. A part of me is afraid that the smell is a corpse. . .that it could be Sam. I'm afraid that this could be it.

"Are you sure?"

"Give me a minute," I say as I turn around and quickly grab a desk to slide in front of the door. "Stay here. I'm just going to take a few steps in and see if I can find anything." Pausing to take a breath, I glance back outside before I follow what little light I have into the vault. Elise continues to hold her hand over Abby's eyes while her stare latches onto me.

"See anything?"

"Nothing but a few bills on the floor," I reply. I take a deep breath to slow my nerves as the shadows start to encase me. The drying blood that had tarnished the desks seems nonexistent, as if it led into here for no reason. I don't see anything. I open my mouth to whisper, but nothing comes out.

The longer I'm in here, the more the darkness starts to disorient my vision. I take a step over the line between the light and the shadows just as the door forces the desk toward the inside of the vault, causing the light to flee. The line between clarity and the opaque fades. I can't see anything.

"Find anything yet?"

"Noth—," I say as the icy grip of a callused hand grabs onto my ankle.

"Sean?" asks Elise.

". . .he. . .he's. . .comin' back," comes a whisper from beneath me.

I look down. I can barely see the outline of a man. His hand remains tight on my leg, but even that I can't see. I just feel the nagging pressure of his rigid palm pulsing on my ankle. *He's dying.*

"Who?" I ask.

"Arthur!" he shouts as loud as his weakened body will allow him to.

"What did he do to you?"

Loosening his grip on my leg, the man crawls toward the light. His face is drained of color and laced with cuts. Dried blood hovers around his saggy eyelids as he looks half asleep. "He left me to die," he tells me.

"Who's in there?" asks Elise as she steps into the vault.

"What's your name?" I ask. The man's pupils grow large as the vessels in his eyes climb toward his irises. His hand slips off my ankle as his body grows limp and blood drips from his mouth.

Screaming, Elise jumps out into the main room. Abby screams in confusion alongside Elise as she turns away from the vault. "What happened, Sean?!"

"I don't know, Elise. He said Arthur put him there and that he's coming back. That's all I know."

"But why here? How did he know we were going to come here?" a befuddled Elise mutters, her cheeks growing flushed with white.

"I brought us here," mumbles Abby. "I knew it was too good to be true."

"You didn't know. It was just a coincidence," I say knowing that it won't matter. Even if I tried to force those words back into my mouth, it wouldn't change how Elise feels. She knows that Arthur has a way about him that could allow him to know we would come here even if she won't admit it.

"We have to get out of here, Sean. We have to go back."

"Go back where, Elise? We have to keep moving!"

"How can we go forward when he's always one step ahead of us?!" she yells.

"Then we go backward," I say as the words fall out of my mouth. "If we go backward, he can't be ahead of us."

"We can't go backward! That will take us away from here and away from Sam!" shouts Abby as her eyes remain fixed on the ground.

Unable to express the idea running rampant in my mind, I look around the room hoping for a bright spot in my incomplete thought. Yet, the sky's growing darker by the second as a looming gray overruns the streets. "He knows where we are," I say. "He knows where we want to go."

"What do you mean, Sean? He knows we're trying to find Sam. He obviously knows that," responds Elise.

"I know, but if we take an alternate path, he won't know where we are. He led us to this bank. The open door was the only thing visible where we were. There wasn't another place we could've entered without making noise," I spit out as my mind continues to run in circles scrounging up any words it can find. "If we go around the city and come at a different angle, he won't know when to expect us."

"If he doesn't see us for a day, won't he expect something like that?" asks Abby.

"I don't know what he will expect. There's just no way he's thinking that right now."

"He knows everything, Sean. He's always been one step ahead and he always will be. There's only one way we can outsmart him," mutters Elise as she stands up.

"What do you think we should do?" I ask.

"We have to split up," she says as her arms shake and her eyes well up.

The instant she lifts her hands to wipe her eyes, I thrust my hands toward her wrists. "We can't do that," I whisper. "We absolutely can't do that, Elise."

"You and I both know it's the only way, Sean. It's the only thing we can do to confuse him."

I press my thumbs into her palms as I start to shiver. "We. . .we can't do that, Elise," I mutter. "I can't leave you again. I can't leave you out here."

"You can't go, Elise," mumbles Abby. "You can't leave me!"

"You'll be with Sean," she sniffles. "He'll take care of you."

I'm taken aback; I'm speechless. I want to keep saying no, I want to scream and beg and plead for her to stay, but I can't. She's right. I nod at Abby as my lips tremble and remain void of speech.

"I don't want you to be alone, Elise," says Abby. "I don't want to be without you. I don't want him to hurt you," she cries.

"He can't hurt her," I say. "He's not strong enough."

Wrapping her arms around me, she digs her nails into my shoulder blades. "I can do this," she whispers.

Nodding my head against hers, I wrap my arms around her lower back and squeeze. "I love you," I quietly say.

"I love you, too."

"Don't go," whispers Abby as she wraps her arms around Elise's waist. "Don't go."

"I have to," she says as her fingers slip off my spine. "I'll be okay."

"Will you, though? What if he gets into your head like he did to Sam?"

As Abby continues to ask Elise a flurry of questions, I turn around and walk toward the fallen lamppost protruding into the building. The condensation clinging to the rusted steel continues to slowly drip into its own puddle as a crack of light wisps through the sky—forcing me to step away from the post.

Almost instantaneously, a slight trickle of rain starts to slide down the broken glass as I turn back toward them. "One more night," I say.

27 January 2192

Elise

Stepping out into the ruins of the city, my fingers brush against Sean's as he hands me the bow. I smile and move farther down the street while the two of them head out of the city behind me. Sean glances back; Abby doesn't. *It's just me*, I think.

It's been months since I've been on my own, months since I've endured the struggle of fighting for my own life, but I think I'm ready. I'm ready to plunge into the depths of this forgotten place and pull Sam out of the rubble. I'm ready to put an end to Arthur's merciless ways. *At least, I think I am.*

My feet land in a puddle as I round the corner from the bank. Angrily, I kick my shoes out of the water and jump onto a pile of bricks—the rain slowly seeping into my socks. *Damn it.* The last thing I wanted was to run around town with cold, wet feet.

Gently hopping down from the heap of broken bricks, I look around the city. A mixture of fallen streetlights, broken-down cars, and empty crevices run around the town. Each step I take is either into an almost lake-sized puddle or over shattered glass. The only positive is that I don't see *him.*

The thought of Arthur running around the city in hopes of finding an innocent kid to maim or to lure into the shadows frustrates me. Like the pillars holding onto a decrepit building, he knows everyone is weak. If he just prods at them for a while, they're bound to fall, bound to break into the emptiness of this nightmare where he can feed. . .where he can win.

Stop it, I tell myself. *Stop thinking about him.* Yet, the deeper I get into the city, the farther my mind gets from my control and the easier it is for him to break me.

"I need to keep walking," I mumble aloud.

I pass various crippled signs as I meander about—various signs that mean nothing in this place anymore. The once-black street names have washed out of their white plates to the point that many streets are nameless. Only those who used to live here might know their history or their purpose. Now, everything is devoid of color. Instead, the town is an almost-blank canvas smeared with the disgrace of a failed artist.

As I jump over a decaying light post, my foot catches the broken glass atop the pole. "Aaghh," I shout as I tumble toward a small pool. The city streets blur around me as the area quickly fades to black.

*** *** ***

As if the sun disappeared into nothingness, a mass of shadows have overcome the atmosphere. I rub my eyes. A small light flicks on in the distance. Then another. And another. Encircled in a bright white of bulbs, the air around me starts to cool as a breeze juts into my spine. Instantly, a man grabs me by the waist and tosses me into the air. I flail my arms as I try to find something to grab onto, but there's nothing.

Suddenly, another man grabs my hands and pulls me upward. "Go!" he yells the moment my feet step onto the platform. Unsure of what to do, I stare blankly at the shadows eclipsing the lights below me. "Go!" he yells again as his hands push into my waist.

Falling into the abyss, I close my eyes and scream—the echoes of my despair barely noticeable to those around me, let alone myself. Right away, my back slams into a net and I'm thrust back into the air. Fearing the circus nightmare again, I force my eyes shut.

"Go!" yells the man's voice once more. Writhing in agony as my ankles become caught in the net, the black ropes manage to slide around my wrists. I try to scream, but nothing comes out. The ropes continue to slither across my body until I'm shadowed in a cocoon. Trapped in a mess of darkness with no light to escape into, the ropes grow wet.

I try to yell once more, but nothing happens. No sound escapes my throat as the water comes pouring in. Closing my eyes, I shake from side to side. Yet, the rope never breaks, the net ceases to disappear. In an attempt to soothe my fate, I remain still. *Wake up*, I whisper to myself. *Wake up!*

***

I open my eyes as the sky erupts above. The light has broken into the shadows. The incandescent bulbs once shining around me are gone. The city's all I see as I stand up from the puddle.

Wiping the water from my eyes, I look around for an escape from the sudden downpour—a hideout to get away from the grips of my nightmares. Though, nothing but dark, rundown buildings surround me. And even if I wanted to go into one, it would just slow me down.

Taking a deep breath, I turn around and face the depths of the fallen city as something catches my eye. Pointing toward the eye of the storm, an unblemished sign stands upright. It reads: 'One Way.'

Sam

The pulsing in my hand has made its way to my forehead, causing nearly every inch of me to ache. Forced onto my back atop the jagged concrete, my body winces in pain. *He barely hit me,* I think. Yet, he must have done it with enough force to keep me in the dark for more than twenty-four hours. Everything feels different to the point that I no longer feel safe. I fear what this room could do to me.

Rolling onto my side, I call for her. "Ann," I say into the shadows. "Ann."

I hear nothing.

Using what strength I have left, I stand up. As I look around the room, the empty vials catch my gaze. No longer is there a strange colored liquid waiting to be consumed; now it's empty, holding nothing deadly. Quickly turning from side to side, I survey the room. I see nothing.

"ANN!" I scream.

Greeted by silence, my eyes turn toward the door as my anger is thrown at the guard.

"Where is she?!" I yell.

"Read the note," responds the guard irritably.

"What note?"

"Right next to you."

Jolting my stare down, I notice a small, folded sheet of paper atop the journal. As I bend down to pick it up, the guard opens the hatch. Fixating my eyes on the note, I open it. It reads: "For each one I take away, you get one more day."

"What?" I say as the guard throws berries at me.

"Eat up."

"Why are you keeping me alive?"

"The boss says he needs you alive for when the girl gets here."

203

"But why? He said I wouldn't be alive when Elise got here! Why can't he just kill me like he killed Ann?!"

Void of a response, the guard closes the hatch.

"Answer me!" I scream as the muscles in my cheeks quiver and the words come spewing out. "Where is she?!"

"Shut up!" yells the guard from behind the door. "Shut up or I'll come in there and send you to the same place she is."

"Is she alive?"

"Why don't you figure that out yourself," he laughs.

Reaching for the food, I begrudgingly force the blueish berries down my throat. I've starved too long to let Ann's disappearance kill me. *I barely knew her*, I think as I stuff my face. *I barely knew her.*

She could be dead because of me. She could be getting tortured because of me. Wherever she is, it's entirely my fault and there's nothing I can do. I release a guttural yell as I smash the fruit into the ground.

"I said shut up!" shouts the guard.

Every word that comes howling from the other side of the door drives me crazy. I can't change what happened to Ann; I can't reverse my indispensable hatred for Arthur. No matter what I wish I could do, I can't. I can't escape to the world I want to because it doesn't exist. A world without walls is impossible. A world without walls creates the chaos that has enraged every fiber of me since day one on the outside. It's just another nightmare and I don't want to be a part of it.

It's as misleading as Separation class. They told us the outside wouldn't be this bad; they told us we could survive if we tried hard enough. What was never told was that you would have to escape misery with each passing day. You can't just 'try' to get past suffering; you have to sacrifice yourself to move past it. It's almost as if our teachers were never out here. It feels like we'd get a better heads up than that, but them not being out here, that's impossible. Separation has existed for over eighty years. Everyone has to suffer.

"But. . .what if. . ." I think aloud as I grab the journal.

Probing the floor for a pencil to jot my wandering thoughts, I look around the room. Sitting idly in the center of a paltry puddle beside me, I pull the small, broken pencil out. Thankfully, it has enough lead for a few paragraphs.

204

Pressing the chipped lead into the paper, I write:

Nimbus is a lie. Everything they taught us was a lie. Not everyone gets separated. The higher classes (the families with founders' names) don't get separated. MacMillan's the eldest surviving member of the founders and he was never sent outside. His father kept him by his side when he created Separation and MacMillan grew old with a thirst for murder just as his father did once he escaped the decaying world before us. MacMillan continues the game because he can. He even sent his own son out!

Unsure if I'm writing the truth or just scribbling nonsense, I continue to write:

Every teacher in school had a founder's last name. MacMillan, Hawkins, Chambers, Montgomery, and Fletcher. There were no discrepancies; those were the only families allowed to teach. If they agreed to teach they wouldn't be sent outside. Instead, they would be secretly educated and automatically forced into the school once they turned 25. That way, everyone would assume they had just returned from their separation. That's why that class is worthless. MacMillan insures that we're taught very little to keep the Elite numbers low. If we're not taught how to survive properly, we become automatic targets on the outside for those who have the same thirst for blood as him. We're sent out here for slaughter.

The more I write, the more sound my argument becomes. I quickly try to gather my thoughts to further my entry, but as I press the pencil down, the lead snaps—forcing me to scrawl an illegible line.

"Damn," I mumble.

Quickly picking up the splintered wood, I grab the broken half with the slight lead protrusion. Wedging it between my thumb and pointer, I press the small fragment into the journal, hoping it doesn't break again.

And no one knows of this. Nobody knows the true Elite ways except for them. They live in peace and harmony in their perfect society while the rest of us suffer. We suffer for them, so they can live in happiness. They put our lives at risk for their own sickness, for their own immaturity. We're the sheep following the herd. Herded out one by one, we follow those in front of us without knowing who really guides us—who the shepherd is. We simply follow history until we become just another name or until we become the shepherd. We're all a part of an endangered flock.

As the pencil starts to crack, I throw it across the room. The ill-natured history of Nimbus can't be as true as the jumbled thoughts of my rotting mind. It's just not possible—even if everything points to it being right. Elise said Nimbus was corrupt, but for there to be Elites behind the wall who have never experienced this torment. . .that's just too unsettling to believe.

"Let me out!" I scream as the frustration starts to fume inside of me. "Let me out!"

"You're going to die in there," whispers the guard as he holds the hatch slightly open. "You're going to die."

Sean

It's been hours since we last saw Elise. My chest tightens with each step as the storm seems to grow stronger while the clouds remain still. Hurrying past a rock-laden railroad, we jump behind a patch of trees.

"I'm cold," mumbles Abby.

"We'll find somewhere to escape the storm once we get closer to going back into the city," I say.

"How far do we have to go?"

Looking at the rails, my eyes follow the route. "About half a mile."

Shrugging her shoulders, she pulls her scarf above her nose as she droops her head. "Okay," she sniffles.

The more we walk, the quicker the storm reduces itself to nothing more than a light misting. "I hope she's okay," I mutter. *I hope she's alive.*

"Me too. She's strong, though. As weak as she might think she's getting, she's not. Without her, Sam and I wouldn't be alive," says Abby as she kicks a rock in her path. "Arthur can't get her."

I nod.

In the past, Elise would show some fear, but she wouldn't announce it. I could see it in her eyes, her cheeks, her lips, but I never heard it. Nearly every time we encountered vagrants in our time together, she'd glance at me before firing a shot. Each time we were starving, on the verge of collapsing from dehydration, she would tremble, but never speak. Her gestures were enough to push that fear into me, but not enough to let us die from it. *It made me stronger*, I think.

Gently wiping the moisture collecting on my forehead, I pull out the blade Elise gave me.

"He's going to die by that," mutters Abby.

"Yea, he is," I smile. "And it's going to be gre—" I say as I turn the weapon in my hand and my foot catches a rock. Stumbling forward, I reach out in an attempt to catch myself, but I can't. My body slams into the muck as the knife buries itself beside me.

"Don't roll over," whispers Abby as she reaches her hands out.

"Why?" I ask, shaking my head. Lying still, I reach for the blade; a nagging pain starts to dig itself into my skull making it feel like I've had another click, but that's impossible. *I don't have a chip.* "What's behind me, Abby?"

"A. . .a body," she mumbles before releasing a muffled screech behind her scarf.

Quickly jumping to my feet, I shove the knife in my pocket and look over at Abby. She's shaking to the point that I can't tell if it's fear or the weather. "Let's just keep moving."

Slowly stepping past the body, I wipe the mud from my shoulder as my eyes catch a glimpse of the corpse. The boy never had a chance. His lifeless, blank eyes gaze into the empty sky; his swollen cheeks are more or less blue; his mouth hangs agape with dried blood spattered upon his lips. Leaning closer, the marks become more visible. His neck is a dark shade of purple surrounded by cuts to his upper torso and chin. "He was choked," I say.

"What?"

"That kid suffocated. Someone choked him to death."

"What? Why?"

"That's how it is out here. You can't trust anyone."

"Who killed him?"

"Maybe a Lurker. Maybe not," I say. "I know as much as you do, but we have to keep moving."

Cringing as she tries to look away, Abby sniffles once more. "I hate it out here," she cries. "I want to leave."

"We all do, but it's not that easy."

Sometimes I wish we could just turn around and run home, but the moment we venture back into the forest, Arthur will kill Elise and Sam. If that doesn't happen, the second we step within eyesight of one of those snipers on the wall, we're dead. And even if we get past all that, MacMillan will be sitting back, waiting. He enjoys nothing more than killing someone he doesn't deem worthy of living in Nimbus—which is, frankly, everyone.

208

Then again, if Nimbus were a utopia, the outside wouldn't be. Even if we weren't sent out, those like Arthur would still exist. Anyone excluded from protection would seek retaliation; anyone not worthy of a home would desire a roof to the point that they would seek it through any means necessary. Without MacMillan or Arthur, vagrants would still find a way to demonize those different from them.

No matter which reality we seek—one without MacMillan and Arthur, or one with both—we'll still struggle. The point of life now is to survive. Nothing more. Nothing less. Regardless of everything trying to eat at us, we have to keep moving. If we don't, Arthur will shatter our minds like glass dropped from the top of a skyscraper and if that doesn't deter us, MacMillan will have us hung.

There's no way around Separation. We just have to go through it. Sometimes twice.

As I look upon the railway next to us, the pulsing in my head starts to fade.

"We've gone over half a mile," says Abby. "When can we go back toward the city?"

"Now," I say as the mist dissipates and the clouds start to break. We've strayed away long enough. If Arthur was following us, we'd know it by now. At least I like to think we would. I mean, after all, we've only been about a hundred yards from any remnant of the city to begin with.

Taking a quick sip from the canteen, Abby looks over at me. "Want any?"

I grab the bottle and take a small drink. Flicking off the last piece of mud clinging to my bicep, I stare into the shambled city uncertain where exactly to go next.

Minutes pass as we stand still, facing an empty street.

"Which way do we go?" asks Abby, her eyes jumping from building to building.

Unable to respond, I rapidly blink as I try to process the area we're in, but I can't. Nothing looks familiar; everything looks undisturbed. It's as if this part of town never disappeared. There's no broken glass littered in the streets, no dilapidated cars collecting dust in the middle of the road, no unkempt buildings swathed in ivy; this place almost looks new.

"Where are we?" asks Abby as her eyes gaze upon the preserved buildings void of wear.

"I don't know," I reply. "How is this possible?"

It's as if the buildings are vestiges of an era that never truly subsided into nothing. They're unaltered to the point that the once-bustling city could still function if there were people here to do just that. It's unbelievable.

"Someone has to be here," she says. "How could a place like this stay so perfect without someone doing something?"

"I don't know. I don't think it's possible, but where is everyone?"

Shrugging her shoulders, she doesn't respond.

"They're probably in one of these buildings," I say as I scan our surroundings.

"Probably, but which one, and do we want to go in any of them? We don't know if there are people in them or if they're good, for that matter."

"It's worth a shot. Who else would revitalize a dying city like this?"

Grinning, she says, "Someone with too much time on their hands."

I nod before I start to walk on the wet pavement toward the most unblemished building nearby. Not more than a few stories high, it looks as if it could have been a library in the past. The outside of the building is supported by dark brown brick, while in between the miniature pillars sit three immaculately clean windows. Even if the storm cleaned them in some way, it makes the building look surreal. "How is this possible? It looks untouched," I say.

"I wish I knew."

"Should we go in?"

Taking a quick step up the curb toward the building, Abby reaches out for a metal slab clinging to the brick beside the glass door. "The words are crossed off," she says as she inches closer. "I can't even read what may have been here before."

As I step up next to her, I reach for the silver handle protruding from the glass door. It opens effortlessly. "Go ahead," I say.

210

Lightly treading across the small puddle next to the door, Abby hops into the building. Following her in, I let go of the handle as the door quietly shuts behind us.

"It's beautiful," she says, taking another step in.

From dozens of feet above us to our sides, the building is covered with books neatly tucked away on oak shelves. In a sea of literature, we stand still, mesmerized in the preserved history of the world before us. "I've never seen anything like this," I mutter as I near one of the shelves neatly packed with biographies from the 1950s—none of which show any signs of wear and tear.

"Me either."

"It's the last of its kind," comes a man's voice from above.

"Hello?" I ask, not expecting a response, just a visual.

"Hello. I see you two have found my library."

Glancing from left to right, from bottom to top, I can't find the auditory source. Everywhere I look, nothing but more books jump out at me. Unable to find the man either, Abby steps behind me and shifts her focus to the ground.

"Every book in here represents what this world once stood for. Every speck of literature that ever existed in this city stands here before you as well-conditioned as we could keep it."   "It's incredible," I say, as if my mind's faltered too much in its ability to find a better adjective.

"It really is marvelous," he softly laughs before abruptly changing his tone. Deepening his voice as hands clench onto my wrists, he speaks again. "Now, what are you two doing here?"

"Let go of me!" screams Abby.

Keeping composed, I say, "We're just looking for a place to stay warm right now."

"How do I know you're not one of them?" he asks.

"Because they don't have an appreciation for anything that was once a bright part of this world and we do."

"Good answer," he replies without so much as a follow-up question regarding our visit. "What's your name?"

"Sean," I say.

"And her?"

Quietly responding, Abby whispers her name.

"It's Abby," I say. "Can you let us go?"

Snapping his fingers, the man appears in front of us as the hands slip off our wrists. His dark skin makes way toward his lustrous blue eyes while his face remains full, as if he hasn't starved a day in his life. He appears to be one of the few people I've ever seen who knows how to handle being out here: a symbol of hope that sanity does still exist outside Nimbus.

"I'm Marcus," he says. "The people behind you are Collin and Rosie."

"How many of you are here?"

"There are quite a few of us. I believe our count is thirty-eight right now."

"And where are the rest of them?"

"Different floors," he says. "But that doesn't matter. How can I trust you, Sean?"

"Because I'm a man of my word. This isn't my first time out here."

"Is that so? How is that possible?"

"I was in the Elite Guard, but I got kicked out by MacMillan for not obeying his orders. I refused to kill innocent outsiders."

Smirking, Marcus steps closer toward us. "Sounds like you're just the person I need around here."

"What do you mean?"

"I've been looking for more people to help guard this library from the Lurkers. They rarely stumble into this part of town, but when they do, they're always trying to burn it down. They're obsessed with fire to the point that it's unsettling. If this place were to ever burn to the ground, I don't think I could handle it."

"How close have they come to burning it before?"

Sighing, he looks away before replying. "Close enough. They managed to kill one of the guards last week."

"Sounds like you guys loathe them as much as we do," I say.
"Oh yea?"

"Yea," I say as I dive into explaining our reasons for being out there. Hours pass as we discuss the Lurkers, the library, and Nimbus. It's gotten to the point that the sky has become dark. Moving to a table in the middle of the place, Rosie lights a few candles as Collin sets a plate of meat in front of us.

"Dig in," smiles Marcus.

"Thanks," I say as I stuff the food down my throat.

212

"So, you're saying your brother has been captured by the Lurkers and you need our help?"

"Yea. My girlfriend, Elise, is on her way through the city to get him and we're running around the outside to confuse Arthur."

"And Arthur's the leader of the Lurkers, you say?" asks Marcus as he takes a bite of his food.

"Yea and he's my brother, we think," says Abby.

Aghast, Marcus takes a quick gulp of water. "Sounds like there are a lot of problems out here. What would you like us to do and what do I get in return?"

"We need your help in case something happens to us on our way to Elise and Sam. We need you to stay hidden and help us if we're attacked. In return, we'll ensure this place stays preserved forever."

"And how are you going to do that?" he asks while cutting another chunk of meat.

"By bringing down Nimbus."

Smiling, he sets his silverware down as he presses his elbows into the table. "Sounds like you're a man with a lot of big ideas, Sean."

"I am. We both know Nimbus is corrupt. We both know the Lurkers are demonizing the outside. With you helping us save my brother and Elise, we can kill the leader of the shadows, which will end the torment out here. After that, we can recruit more kids who, like us, hate being on the outside. With larger numbers, we can take the fight back home."

Looking around the library as if he's taking in everything he's watched over the years, Marcus smiles and looks back at me.

"I'm in."

28 January 2192

Sam

I'm not going to die here. I'm not going to die on the outside, I think to myself as I look around the room. *I'm not going to die behind the wall, either.*

"I gotta get out of here," I mumble to myself. Eyeing the room for something to break these chains, I stop and rub my arms. I haven't seen anything in the past and if I do see something against the opposite wall, it's not like I can go get it. I look beside me. The journal is worthless. The pencil, broken. The vials are covered in dust. The board that was once below the vials is gone. There isn't a tangible object around me that can saw through these chains. It's as if Elise's escape made them rethink their lackluster security. Then again, this isn't a prison: it's a dungeon.

And it makes me feel like I'm in school again chained to a desk without gaining any knowledge about my surroundings. Day after day, we sat there, learning unnecessary tidbits about our founders, running small obstacle courses, and learning less than we did in every class prior to turning thirteen. They teach you when you're young, but thirteen is when nothing matters. Being a teenager must be the perfect age for your value to diminish, for your worth to be less than that of an eighty-something-year-old monster. *I wish I learned how to escape the shadows.*

I furiously start rattling the chains against the cement. Back and forth, left and right, I drag the chains up and down in hope that they'll magically disappear into the shadows like everything else around here; as if they'll swing into the air and force themselves around the necks of the guards outside my door.

214

The more I swing, the less desirable my plan becomes. Shadowed in misery by the impossibility of an exit, I scream.

"Shut up in there," yells the Lurker outside the door.

I angrily clench my teeth and close my eyes. I quickly re-open them and grab the journal in search of an escape in the gibberish I recently wrote. *We're not taught how to survive properly,* I read to myself. *We're sent out here for slaughter. We suffer for them, so they can live in happiness.* My face starts to warm while my body remains cold. I throw the journal across the room and try to scream, but nothing comes out.

Reaching for the vials by my feet, I pick up the glasses and think about the poison that once resided in them, certain that whatever it was, it was given to Ann against her will. They probably poisoned her after they knocked me out. Either that or they emptied it thinking they could prolong my death by taking away my only real escape, by yanking the actual exit out from underneath me.

"I gotta get out of here," I mumble again.

Smashing the vial against the cement, I watch the glass scatter across the floor. Grabbing the second one, I do the same.

"What was that?" asks the guard as he rips open the hatch.

"Nothing," I carelessly respond.

"It better be nothin' or I'll come in there an' turn you into nothin'," chides the man.

I want to reply with a snide comment, but I stray away from provoking someone who I can't defend myself against. Instead, I turn around while the light continues to flicker above me. As if it's going to dim to the point of darkness, it fades in and out like someone's toying with the switch.

Throwing my hands behind me, my fingers graze an insect. Instinctively pulling my hand away, my knuckles brush against the brick and scare the bug. Scooting back toward my feet and the glass, I watch as the cockroach scurries back into the shadows. Its miniature legs sprint across the cement, echoing around the room.

I bite my cheek and close my eyes. The shifting of the bug's feet soon disappears and nothing but the click of the bulb rings throughout. *Where'd it go?* I think. With seemingly no escape for me, it's bothersome that an insect can disappear like it was never here. I turn around and face the wall—hoping to see what the bug saw, where it saw an escape.

"That's it," I say aloud to myself. *A shard.* Scavenging the floor for any fragmented brick, nothing catches my eye. I try pounding against the wall until something falls down, but nothing does. It just manages to irritate my wounded hand.

I reach for a piece of broken glass and throw it at the wall in frustration.

"Why?!" I whisper loudly.

For a second, time freezes as the glass breaks upon the wall, expelling a sliver of brick from behind it.

How?

I quickly place my ankles around the glass and throw the chains and shackles into separate puddles. With the three-inch piece of rock held firmly in my hand, I press it into the rust, causing soft waves to flow across the water. The grinding of the chains against the rock pierces my eardrums, but the guard seems oblivious. *Maybe he left.*

Seconds turn into minutes as minutes start to feel like hours before the first shackle around my ankle nearly breaks. My arms ache as I slide the piece back and forth, but I refuse to slow myself. *I have to get out. I have to see them again.* Eventually, the chain cracks. I lift my foot from the water and slam it into the ground—the shackle breaks in two, sending small pieces of itself across the room.

My prison stays silent; the light's rhythm has become a quick cadence of light and dark—mainly dark. I start digging into the second shackle. Back and forth I glide the shard when the steel snaps in the liquid quicker than the first. I unravel the cold from my ankles and try to stand up. My legs wobble and I trip. With blood sliding down my knees, I slowly get to my feet and head toward the door without any idea of what I want to do.

Elise

The dark clouds hold onto the sky as the rain slows to nothing more than a light mist. With each passing second, my eyes jump around corners hoping to find the fire that once took me away from here—that pulled me into *his* world. Yet, the farther I get, the smaller the landscape becomes and the less I know where I am. *This can't be right*, I think as I turn around and step into a tight alleyway.

Forcing myself through a short slit between two fair-heighted buildings, I jump out into a new street—one lined with nothing but skyscrapers. Some sit still in the clouds while others look as if the storms have destroyed them. Whether the building is leaking water like a man-made cascade or it's spitting out glass from each gust of wind, everything within eyesight looks lifeless. Though, the farther I look down the street, the clearer my path becomes.

"That's it," I mumble aloud. "The alleyway."

I quickly jump over a crooked fire hydrant and sprint toward the alleyway. Illuminated with red, a fire highlights the darkened brick where *he* kept me—where he's keeping Sam.

The closer I get, the farther away I want to be. But I can't run—I can't turn around when I've come so far, when I've conquered everything that almost killed me in the past. No matter how much my head throbs while the flames grow bright, I have to keep moving. I pull an arrow from my quiver and steady my bow against my shoulder.

Nothing but the caws of stray crows fill the street around me. Preparing to feast on the deceased, they perch on lampposts as their beady eyes gaze around.

Slowly nearing the alley, I tug on the string. *Don't be afraid,* I think.

As I tiptoe toward the passageway, I lower my bow and huddle behind a faded blue car. Gently gliding my fingers across the washed paint, I lift my eyes over the door. I see nothing. Stepping out onto the street, the mist turns into a modest rain. I slightly pull the string back once more.

Without hesitating, I lock the arrow back and point it into the alley. Still, no one stands outside; no one's calling my name like they were several years ago. It's as if he doesn't know I'm here, and that's what bothers me. Arthur has always known where I am. He's always found a way to get what he wants. Yet, right now, I have no clue what's going on. I just have to keep going and believe that we'll get through this. We always do.

Slowly striding across the sidewalk, I step into the alley. Approaching the steel door, I turn back. The fire dissipates as the rain continually drowns the ashes. Draping my bow over my shoulder, I draw my knife from my pocket and quietly pull open the door.

Nothing but a few torches highlight the main hallway—not enough to discern my surroundings from the dark walls. I shut the door behind me. The sudden click of the latch sends echoes throughout the corridor just as my head starts to throb and yells reverberate off the walls. I anxiously try to shake off the pain as I dig my forefingers into my forehead.

"Hey you!" comes a voice from ahead of me.

I hold the knife at my side and look for the source of the sound, but, no one appears in front of me.

"Hey you, dumb ass," says the voice again.

What is going on? I think. Drifting toward the voice, I wait for it to yell once more.

"You shut up or I'll come in there and beat you with your own weapon," says another man's voice.

It's gotten to the point that it's clear the conversation isn't directed at me. I weave around a steel beam. The voices become louder.

"Do it," comes the faded voice.

"I told you to shut up," says the nearest one.

A brief silence consumes the hallway. I halt my breath.

"This will be fun," he whispers to himself. Suddenly, the grinding sound of a door opens ahead of me—a flickering light shines against the wall.

Feet start to scatter; metal clinks against the ground. I try to hide my eyes from the light, but can't. The irritating beam won't

218

stop shaking up and down just ahead of me. Without a second thought, I head toward it. Holding my knife outward, the handle clams up in my palm.

I quickly approach the door and lean against the wall. I slowly turn into the room where I see a tall, black-haired man holding up a hatchet. Without delay, I spring toward him and jam my knife into his neck. I pull it out and thrust it into his spine. He falls to the ground; in turn, showing a weakened kid in front of him. The kid looks up and musters a gentle, "Eleee."

"S-Sam," I mumble.

"Elise," he cries. "You found me."

Stricken with happiness and fear, my body crumbles to the floor as he rushes toward me and wraps his arms around my back. I can feel his bony arms press against my spine as his body shakes in my grasp. "Sam," I cry. "I can't believe you're alive."

"I can't believe you found me," he sobs.

"We-we have to get out of here," I say.

Sam slowly lets go of my shoulders and helps me up. "I know, but where? Where's Abby?"

"She's with your brother."

"S-Sean's h-here?" he stutters.

"I'll explain later, we have to go."

With tears streaming down his cheeks, he picks up the hatchet from the guard as he wipes his face. "We have to let the others out, too," he says.

"What others?"

"The Lurkers captured dozens more after they brought me in. We have to set them free."

Reaching for the keys clinging to the guard's belt, I unclip them before we rush out of the room.

"Where are the other cells?" I ask.

"I don't know. I've been in there the whole time. They're probably around here somewhere. . .I-I can always hear the screaming," Sam says, wide-eyed and slight of breath. As a look of nausea rushes over his face, he grabs onto my hand. "We have to find Ann."

"Who?"

"She was in my room with me for a while, but then they took her away."

"Why did they take her?"

"Because I talk too much," he mumbles as he catches his breath.

"Not possible," I say as I pull him around one of the beams. "Not possible. . ."

His ill-colored face continues to fluctuate as he stays behind me—the hatchet slowly slipping from his grasp.

"Hello," I whisper rounding a corner toward a narrow hallway. With walls illuminated by nothing more than dying embers buried at the bottom of blackened barrels, it looks like a nightmare. One that only Arthur could conjure.

"Help!" comes a scream down the hall. "Help us!"

Rushing toward the cries, I keep my knife at my side as the keys rattle in my left hand. "Where are you?" I ask.

"Down here. There are six of us," replies the man.

Following the voice, I look around the shadows. Still, I see nothing.

"Where? I can't see anything."

"Here," says the man as the clack of a rock reverberates around us.

"Sam," I say. "Can you see anything?"

"Not really. Just feel the walls. The closer you get to the embers the more you can see."

"Okay," I nod as I step past a barrel.

"If you believe in the shadows, your eyes will see fine," mutters Sam. Grabbing the keys from my hand, he steps ahead of me.

"What?

As if he didn't hear me, Sam rushes down the hallway and out of sight. *If you believe in the shadows, your eyes will see fine? What does that even mean?* It feels like Sam's becoming one of them, that his time with the Lurkers has made him trust their illogical, bogus lore. That can't be it. I shake my head as I waltz down the hall, my hand shaking in the shadows.

"I found them," exclaims Sam. Quickly turning the key, the door opens. The click rings throughout the hallway.

"Thank you," says the man from ahead. "Where do we go?"

"This way," I say unsure if they can see me.

220

Bustling past me, I hear the door to the alleyway slam behind me. It's like I'm a ghost. That, or for some reason I'm the only one who can't see in this crazy nightmare.

"Sam," I whisper.

"She's down here, I can feel it," he says.

Suddenly, the cold brush of his frail fingers grab against my palm and I'm dragged along. Through the darkness we go in search of Ann—someone we don't know to be alive or even around here. I succumb to his weary spirit as he jams the keys in another door.

"She's in here."

As he pushes open the door, the dying light of a torch brings back my vision. "Finally," I mutter while Sam let's go of my fingers. At first glance, the room looks familiar. The torch sits against the furthest wall amidst of a flurry of webs and insects while the floor bathes in the shallow depths of murky rainwater. "No," I whisper to myself. "No."

"Elise," cries Sam from beside me.

I grit my teeth while my arms shake and my knife falls to the floor. There, against the wall, she sits chained and bloodied. Lacerations run through her arms and up to her face while her hair covers her bruised chest.

"We have to go," I say, viciously grabbing ahold of Sam's arm—his bony biceps digging into my thumb. "We have to go!"

"We can't just leave her!" he screams.

"Can't you see?! She's dead! We have to go!"

"NO! This is my fault! She's not going to stay here!"

Clenching my teeth, I jam my other hand into his other arm. "I can't be here again," I say as my undulated voice cracks. Tears slide down my face; my eyes start to burn. "I can't be here."

"Neither can I. Neither can she. We can't leave her here. What if she's alive?"

I try to muster up the strength to check her pulse, but my body aches. My legs feel like they've been tossed into a blender and turned into mush. The searing pain of the words, 'Shadow Lurkers' written on the wall across from us are ingrained into my feeble body and I can't budge.

"Check her pulse," I utter.

He quickly stands up, his pale skin glistening in the light as he approaches her. Before reaching for her wrist, he parts her bangs and shakes her reddened shoulders. Suddenly, the melancholy of this place forces him to shout, to erupt the sorrows that have burdened him since his first day out here. Plagued by constant fear, he screams. . .and screams.

I sit idly by as I try to regain my strength, but I can't. This prison is tearing me apart. This room is recreating the torment from years ago.

"Sam. We have to leave."

"Why?!" he yells. "So we can go outside and deal with the same fear that we've dealt with in here? Don't you get it, Elise? There's no escape. Every place we go, he's there. Every escape we think we have is just another piece to his never-ending puzzle. No matter what we do, no matter where we go, he wins. He has us. There's nothing else we can do."

"There's always something we can do, Sam. We can't give up. We can't stay here. We have help out there. We have Sean. We have Abby. We have each other. We have more than he'll ever have. This—this game he's playing isn't one he can win. He thinks he can tear us apart one by one. He thinks he can get into all of our heads and break us apart, but he can't. He can't beat what we have. He can't fathom the strength we have in our hearts because unlike him we don't have a black sludge pulsing through our veins. We're not weak and crippled by the delusional thoughts of the abyss. We're stronger than that. We're not him! Don't you understand?!" I scream, the thoughts angrily spewing from my mouth.

He's not a ubiquitous being. He's just some nut who takes those who have broken down just as easily as he has and shows them the "light."

"There are more than just him, Elise. Four of us can't bring down fifty, maybe a hundred of them. There's nothing we can do but run, and I'm tired of running. I'm tired of hiding, of being scared. I just want everything to stop."

"That won't happen, Sam. The outside doesn't stop."

"Then maybe we should just let him take us away from here. At least the vials offered an escape."

Worried by his reckless thoughts, I exhale. "Then he still wins. Death is not an escape, Sam. It's a coward's route to self-righteous desertion. It's wrong."

222

"I don't even care anymore," he sighs as he wipes his face. "I can't do this."

"You can. I've been there. We can escape. We can beat him," I say as my head throbs and my muscles tighten. "We can do this, but we have to get out of here first."

Reluctant to leave her body, Sam rests his back against the wall. "Go without me."

"I'm not going to do that," I say. As I try to stand up, my thighs shake beneath my attempted gait. Slowly regaining my strength, I grab my knife from the floor and hobble toward Sam.

"Just go!" he shouts.

"I'm not going to do that," I reply as I jam the butt of the knife's handle into the side of his head—catching him as he falls to the side. Rather than arguing with his rattled mind, the process of knocking him out seemed simpler.

Crouching, I grab onto his waist and toss his meager body over my shoulder as if he's just a flimsy sack of flour. Hurrying out of the building and into the rain, I start to look for shelter as the skies continue to spit.

29 January 2192

Sean

I roll onto my side as the sunlight pierces my eyes—instantly forcing me to roll back onto my stomach. Shoving my head into the pillow, I lift the sides up and around my ears—cocooning my head in its soft, luscious silk.

"Wake up, Sean, today's the day," says Marcus.

I slowly unwrap the pillow from my temple before pushing my palms into the ground and standing up.

"I haven't had a night's sleep like that in years," I say. Behind the wall I had a bed and a warm place to sleep, but I was plagued with nightmares from my time outside, from the nights spent hiding in corners hoping Arthur wasn't coming. Countless sunsets and sunrises came without so much as a blink. When you're afraid of someone taking who you love away from you, you can't do anything more than fight. You can't think. You can't even speak at times. All you can do is fight. It's comforting knowing I don't have to do the watching anymore.

"I find peace knowing that everyone here believes in the same things I do, so I can't remember the last time I had a bad night's sleep," chuckles Marcus.

"You're lucky," I say with a half-smile. "Out there," I point, "More than two hours is considered a successful night of sleep."

"We're lucky to be here," smiles Marcus. "I can't imagine the real pain of being trapped in the forest."

"It's not pleasant."

Marcus doesn't respond. He cranes his neck toward the window, shifting his eyes around the unblemished remnants of what he's saved.

I stand up and throw on my shirt and sweatshirt. Marcus smiles before heading downstairs—Abby jumps in the moment he steps out. Holding a small, white box with a red piece of silk wrapped around it, she lifts it toward me.

"What is it?"

"Marcus just told me to give it to you," she says.

"I wonder why he couldn't give it to me."

"I don't know," she quickly responds. "Just open it."

Taking the gift from her hand, I untie the string and remove the lid. There, sitting at the bottom of the box, lays a pistol with three bullets beside it.

"Why only three bullets?" asks Abby.

"I don't know," I say as I load the gun, check the safety, and wedge it in my belt.

"We should go ask him."

"We should," I grin. Stepping out the door, I move toward the spiral staircase as Abby follows. Grabbing onto the lightly chipped black paint of the railing, I hustle down the steps while nothing but swirls of books grasp ahold of my sight.

"Marcus, where did this come from?" I ask, upon reaching the bottom of the staircase, as he pulls a book from a nearby shelf.

"From an old police station," he replies—his focus remaining on that of the book. "One of my men found it a few days ago while he was scavenging for supplies. He said it was the only one he could find and those three bullets were all that were available, so I figured you could put more use to it than I could."

"Thanks. I appreciate it. I'll be sure to use it on Arthur."

"That's what I was hoping you would do," he says as he opens the book.

Smiling, I pull out a chair behind him as Abby does the same. "Hey, Marcus."

"Yea?" he mumbles.

"I was wondering. . .how have you managed to keep this library so pristine? Who's been protecting it for you?"

Stepping around us, Marcus closes the book and places it on the table. "Malcolm, Collin, Ella, Rosie, and Miles have been. After losing Shane last week to the Lurkers, they've all stepped up to ensure that doesn't happen again. Without them—without everyone who's helped preserve this place—we'd be struggling to survive just like everyone out there. We would be just as lost and maybe just as mad as the Lurkers."

"I don't think it's possible to be that insane," smirks Abby. "They're more than just insane; they're. . .I don't know. . .psychotic, delusional, irrational maniacs."

"That's a good way to put it," I say. "And Arthur is the all-powerful leader of a pack of worthless lunatics."

Marcus laughs. He opens the book in front of him and appears to read it. "A shark will weaken if you puncture its gills," he says before looking up at me. "The more of his men we can remove from this world, the easier we can take him out."

"And that's what we're going to do," I say. "Unless, of course, we can get to him first."

"We'll see," replies Marcus as he picks up his book and leans back in his chair. "Now, you two run along. My men and I will follow you here shortly."

"Will do. Just make sure to stay low and out of sight," I say.

"We will."

With the sun hanging high in the sky, I glance back at Abby as she stands, holding the blade in her hands.

"Are you ready?" I ask.

"Yes," she answers.

I take a deep breath as I walk toward the front door, toward the one thing between the city and us. Pausing, I exhale.

They're both alive. They're both alive, I think to myself.

I reach for the silver handle and push it outward. The surprisingly warm air spreads across my cheeks. I close my eyes and inhale as the door shuts behind us.

"Where do we go from here?" asks Abby.

I open my eyes. "Toward the part of the city that looks dead."

"That's the whole city," she laughs.

I don't reply; instead, focused on locating the tallest building—the one skyscraper truly above everyone and everything beyond the walls of Nimbus. It's the one place Elise would know to hide, the one spot she knows I would run.

226

During my first year outside, I was just as terrified as those around me. Two others were separated with me, but I didn't dare pair up with them—Harris Bigelow and Tommy Martelli—because of how immature they were. Always picking on others in school, never paying attention in class, they simply didn't seem to care about the next eleven years of their lives. The moment the doors opened, I ran. They didn't chase me. They just stumbled out, aloof and distraught, unprepared for the rigors of Separation.

So, I kept running. I saw bodies, I saw flames, I saw the pain besetting this world, so I kept going—only letting up for light naps and berries. Eventually, I ended up where all those who run end up: the city.

No Lurkers came after me. No others passed by. I was, oddly enough, alone. My legs were weary, my eyes were tired, my body was defeated, but I was alone. In school, we were taught to always keep our guard up for unsuspecting vagrants desiring to hurt us, but at that point, mine didn't exist. I had nothing left to hide from.

I just needed sleep. Being the frightened kid I was, I searched for shelter—shelter above the forest because I couldn't run anymore. And that's when I ended up in an unnamed financial building in the heart of the city. It stood taller than all of those nearby—unafraid of being pulled down into nothingness like everything around it. It helped me realize I couldn't just keep running away, I had to be bigger than everything around me or I wouldn't survive.

As we step past looted cars and lifeless buildings, flashbacks of being fourteen jolt into my mind. The darkness coupled with warm nights on cold tiles; the constant desire to run away from stress; the unyielding tears from the adolescent torture of Separation; the uneasiness of being alone. Every last thing played a part in my suffering and every part of it helped me wake up. I take a deep breath and try to push away the memories of who I used to be.

Rounding a corner onto an unnamed street, Abby looks up at me. "Have you ever been this far into the city?"

"Yes," I reply.

"When?"

"When I was fourteen."

She doesn't pry. She just looks around the city in awe—her steps slowing as she gazes in wonderment.

"Keep up," I say.

With my focus on wandering toward the tallest building, I think not of what this place currently is, but what it was when I first came. There was nothing to be afraid of, nothing but the nightmares created in my own mind—and even those could be avoided.

But now, the mere thought of turning a corner and seeing *his* face sends shivers down my spine and into my legs. It provokes an irrational fear in my mind that he could have killed both of them, that he could have staggered from the burrows of his unholy darkness to bring me their corpses. But, that's not possible. He needs to kill me too if he wants to be satisfied. He needs to make me afraid of this place again. After all, I'm the one who scarred him and I'm the one he should fear.

Jumping over a small chasm in the earth, we round another corner as heightened buildings start to appear. One by one, the skyscrapers jut farther into the sky as if they're each trying to beat the other in some sort of game, as if superiority is present at the highest peak.

"Where could they be?" asks Abby.

"They're in the tallest building or they're with him," I say delicately.

"Why the tallest one?" she asks as she stares straight up.

"It's where I ran when I was by myself. It's where I felt safe."

"Does Elise know that?"

I stop in place and nod. "It's this one."

Covered in the brown roots of dead ivy, the front door looks as if it's making way for a forest rather than a financial institution.

"This stuff is everywhere," I say as I duck under it and into the building. Reaching back for Abby's hand, I lightly pull her onto the main floor.

With the sun shining through to provide us light, the glistening appeal of the water fountain seems nonexistent. The marble's been cracked and covered in graffiti while the water's all but evaporated. *Same as last time*, I think. Behind the fountain sits an escalator. With a few rotting newspapers and a broken office chair sitting on the descending one, they don't appear in as bad of shape as the rest of the floor. At least they're usable, unlike the elevators.

228

"How far up should we go? We don't even know if they're in here," says Abby.

"I don't really know. Just keep your knife ready, I'm going to yell for them."

Taking a deep breath, I shout, "Sam! Elise! Are you here?!"

As the wind echoes against the glass, I hear nothing. Taking another breath, I try again. "Sam! Elise! Abby and I are here!"

Once again, no response. The building's as empty I remember it.

"Maybe we should go up a little farther just in case," says Abby as she starts walking toward the escalators.

"Probably."

As we step up the broken stairway, the first thing that catches my sight is a spray-painted flag loosely hanging in the middle of a wall of screens. Five across, five down, and back around, the screens are broken with wires hanging out the backs. But, it's the flag that differs. The words are illegible, but they're in black. I step closer.

"What does it say?" asks Abby.

"I'm not sure," I reply. Stepping onto a desk, I reach up for the flag and pull it down—a black mass of what I thought was paint poofs into the air. "Is that ash?" I cough.

"It must be."

Wiping the fog of black away, I turn around. "Why would someone write in ash?"

"It's probably *them*," Abby softly replies.

"We need to keep moving."

I wipe my eyes and shake the dirt from my hair. Behind us sits a room scattered with desks. Most have miniature lamps and are covered in various decaying papers while a few closer to the monstrous glass windows are entirely empty except for one with a broken computer screen. There are no other indications that someone else was here. No illegible phrasing. No bodies. Nothing.

"Look for the stairwell," I say.

Swiftly bypassing the desks, we continue to look around and examine what once occupied the entirety of this building.

"This place must've been beautiful decades ago," says Abby while she points ahead toward an empty hallway with glass elevators on each side.

"Yea, it was probably pretty unbelievable," I respond as we step into the hallway. I look past a cluster of empty elevator shafts toward a sign at the end. Next to a water fountain with scratched-off letters, the sign reads, 'air.' "The stairs are over there," I say before heading toward the unbolted door.

I move it to the side. We head into the darkened stairwell.

"You wouldn't happen to have a lighter or some matches?" asks Abby.

"Nope, I gave my lighter to Elise when I was last out here, so we'll just have to walk through the dark."

Reaching for my hand, Abby squeezes tightly and stays close. I grab the first railing, allowing the cold steel to guide me through the dark.

"It'll be okay, Abby," I say as her grip grows tighter with each step. As we approach the second floor, I feel around for a door handle. After many misses, I eventually grab hold of one. I push down. The handle doesn't budge. "Looks like we have to try the third floor."

"Okay," she mumbles.

Turning around, I blindly reach for the railing once more. Quickly grabbing ahold of it, I try to focus on the next set of invisible stairs. Gently hovering my right foot above what I believe to be the first step, I place it down. . .and miss. Abby's grip tightens as she pushes me back up with her other hand. I slowly try again before moving up the rest, hoping not to send us both back down.

As the third floor arrives, I calmly feel around for the handle again. After a few misses, I nick it and it clicks open.

Eagerly stepping into the open area, I open my mouth and yell for them again. "Sam! Elise! Are you here?!"

"SAM!" cries Abby from next to me, but still, we receive no response.

"Maybe they're not here," I say.

"I think we should at least try the first ten floors," replies Abby.

"Why ten and not eleven?"

"Eleven sounds good. Let's just do that and if we don't hear from them then they're probably not here."

They have to be here, I think. I think back to the ash-ridden flag on the first floor. Even though the Lurkers may have been here,

I've never actually seen anyone in this building. *There's nowhere I feel safer.*

Nodding in agreement, I grab her hand as we turn back toward the stairwell. With the door held open behind me, I latch onto the steel as I guide us up to the fourth floor. Quickly opening the door, I yell. Once again, silence consumes the area. The next five floors garner the same results, leaving us doubtful that they were ever even here.

"Two more floors," whispers Abby as she clenches my hand.

"Fingers crossed," I mutter back as I round the steps up to the tenth floor. With nothing but darkness muddling my vision, I hop up the final step and release the railing. I feel around for the door. "I can't find the handle anywhere."

"Let me try," gulps Abby. She lets go of my hand. After seconds of silence, she exhales in front of me as the slight click of the handle reverberates off the walls. "It's really hard to open."

"Grab my hand and guide it to the handle," I say as she does accordingly.

With the grip in my hand, I click it downward and pull. Yet, the door won't budge. It feels as if something is pulling it back like someone or something doesn't want us in.

"It feels locked or like someone is yanking it in the opposite direction," I say.

"SAM!" yells Abby. "Sam, is that you?!"

Still, the more she yells, the quieter it becomes.

"Must be another broken door," I say. "Let's go up to the eleventh."

"Okay," she faintly replies.

Slowly extending my hand backward into the dark, Abby grabs hold of it as I guide us up the last set of steps we desire to climb. *They have to be near,* I think. After all, eleven is Nimbus's lucky number.

"This is it," I say as we approach the final doorway. Thrusting my hand into the darkness, my fingers nick the edge of the handle almost instantly. As I push it down, the click rings loudly while I pull the steel toward us once again. Without hesitation Abby yells for them. Unfazed by the sun shining heavily through the ten-foot windows, she steps into the office and shouts again.

"Sam! Elise! Are you here?!"

Enshrouded in silence, I step farther into the room. All the while, Abby is running around the desks searching for the unknown. "Sam! Elise! We're here! Come out!"

"Elise!" I yell as I walk toward the windows.

"They're here!" cries Abby.

"Sean!" yells a familiar voice from behind me. "Sean!"

I quickly turn around to see a blur as Sam jams his hands into my gut. "I can't believe you're here," I say as I wrap my arms around his shoulders.

"I can't believe you're h-here," he mumbles into my shirt.

"Me either," I smile as I tighten my grip around his back. "It's just like back in Nimbus when it was your Separation Day. I told you I'd always be there when you needed me."

"Y-yea, you did," he sobs, burrowing his head into my chest.

Several minutes pass as Sam refuses to let go of my back while Abby clings to him.

"I think you can let go now, bud," I laugh as Elise smiles in front of me.

"I'm glad you found us. I wasn't sure if this was the hiding spot you had in mind," she says.

"It felt right. I'm glad you remembered this place."

Turning to her side as she stares out the window, Elise exhales. "The higher up you get, the closer to the light you can be and for Arthur, that's not a good thing."

I smile. "How did you guys escape? Where was Sam?"

"They kept him at the same place they had me, but he was in a different room. The whole area seemed deserted aside from the prisoners. There was only one guard by Sam's cell and he was easy to take down. Something just felt off. . .it wasn't supposed to be that easy."

"Yea, that doesn't seem right," I say as I turn to Sam. "Are you okay?"

Nodding, he smiles. He appears as if he hasn't eaten in weeks, so I pull some bread from my bag and hand it to each of them. As they eat, we sit atop a row of desks watching the clouds descend into the once-clear sky. "I-I'm just defeated," he sighs while rubbing the side of his head.

"What happened there?" I ask.

"Elise."

"What about her?"

Chiming in, Elise swallows as she speaks. "He was going to give up and die there, so I had to do what I could to get him out. I didn't know if the Lurkers were going to come back or what was going to happen, but I couldn't argue with him, so I knocked him out and carried him up here."

Unsure of what to say, I rip off a piece of bread.

"Why do you think it was so easy to get out?" asks Abby as she inches closer to Sam.

"I think it was all a part of his plan," replies Sam.

"It probably means the worst is coming," says Elise as the windows become overrun with a thick, gray fog.

"Then, we should probably get going," I say, swallowing my last chunk of bread. "We know how to get out."

"But where to?" asks Elise.

"We have people that can help us."

"Who?"

"We found a group of survivors in an abandoned library. They're led by a man named Marcus and he has a few of his people around us to ensure we get back to them safely."

"And how can you trust them, Sean? Nobody out here can be trusted," she firmly says.

"Because he's not like anyone I've met out here before. He's like us."

Sam

While I hold the lighter in my outstretched arm as we wander down the empty stairwell, my mind strays toward the tiny fire guiding us through the darkness. It reminds me of that prison. Every page of that journal was covered in phrases about the fire guiding you and the shadows consuming you. It's as if this small, fire-wielding device in my hand guides everything they believe in, as if the slight glow of red fuels them. It's something I'll never understand. If they believe the soul needs the black to survive, the vibrant reds, oranges, and yellows of fire should be the furthest thing from their idea of salvation. After all, it's light. It's a strange thing.

Just trying to fathom the rationality behind their deranged minds is difficult. Even after spending weeks around them, I still don't get why so many people follow *him*, why so many kids think he's the epitome of survival. He does nothing but torture those different than him. I don't get why he does it; I don't understand anything about this world and its obscured vision. None of it makes sense and I don't know if it ever will.

"Sam," says Sean from behind me. "Can you grab the door?"

"Yea," I reply as I reach for the door to the first floor.

I quickly cap the lighter before Elise takes it from my hand. "Where to now?" she asks.

"Just follow me," replies Sean as he heads toward the front atrium.

I step down the escalators behind Sean and toward the unknown. The fog continues to accumulate. Further pressing itself into the windows, it's to the point that it's hard to see anything. Like a thick mass of clouds hovering in front of the sun, the fog takes over, leaving no room for clarity. I'm afraid to step into it. I'm afraid to get lost.

"Should we really go out there?" I ask as a slight shiver awakens my body—forcing me to press my lips together.

234

"We have to," says Sean.

"Why can't we wait until the fog disappears?"

"The fog is our guide, Sam. Arthur can't find us when he can't see us."

"But he can't see us in here either," chimes in Abby as she reaches the bottom of the steps.

"Would you rather wait here and risk him finding us, or go out there and rejoin Marcus where we know we're safe?" replies Sean angrily, as if he's mad at me for suggesting an alternative.

"Let's go then," I say. Glancing over at Abby, I bite my lip before shifting my stare toward the tile. She shrugs her shoulders and turns toward Sean.

"Good," he says as he crouches under the brown ivy blocking the glass doors while motioning for Abby and Elise to follow.

As they promptly step underneath the blockade, my mind spins into a frenzy—one that I can surprisingly control for once. Tattered moments from that cell hang loosely onto my mind as I shrug off the evil that wanted to keep me chained up, from the lunacy that wanted me to stay without a reason. Yet, the more I think about leaving this building, the more my mind wants to keep me here. It feels as if isolation is the only thing that can keep me safe.

"Stop it," I say aloud to myself while I crouch beneath the ivy.

"Are you okay, Sam?" asks Abby as she helps me up.

"I'm fine," I reply.

Gritting her teeth, she lets out a half-hearted, "Okay. I just wanted to help."

"There's nothing to help," I reply.

Abby steps ahead of me and grabs onto Elise's arm. I run my fingers through my hair, exhaling into the cold. *We shouldn't be out here.*

I can barely see anything. The fog is like a thick mist of ash consuming every inch of air around us. It's nearly impossible to see anything outside of the four of us. It's terrifying.

"Elise, grab ahold of my hand. Abby grab Elise's and Sam grab Abby's. We have to stay close," directs Sean as he intertwines his fingers in Elise's.

Why do I have to be at the back? I think to myself as I grab onto Abby's hand.

As if he heard me, Sean turns around. "Sorry for putting you at the end, Sam. I just felt you could handle it."

"It's okay."

"Now, everyone be on alert. If you see or hear anything, let everyone else know. We should be safe out here, but you never know what to expect in the city."

And he said we'd be safe out here.

Stepping onto a light pole submerged in a puddle, Sean slowly walks across the back while we all follow seconds after the person before us starts to move. Cautiously walking along the slick steel, we stay close as the building fades into the gray behind us.

The farther we walk, the more the nagging chills of fear bite away at the nape of my neck.

"This isn't right," I mumble under my breath.

Abby slightly cranes her neck backward indicating she heard me, but she waves it off as she turns her head back toward Elise's hand.

This can't be right. We shouldn't be out here. "This isn't right," I say again. This time aloud.

"What isn't?" questions Abby.

"Being out here. This doesn't feel right."

"It's a little frightening, but Sean knows what he's doing."

"I'm not saying I don't trust Sean, but this seems to be what Arthur would want. This fog feels like a trap. It's nature's way of claiming us for him."

"What do you mean?" says Elise.

"To us, the fog seemed like an escape, but to Arthur, fog is his best chance to break us."

"Why's that, Sam?" asks Sean as he stops in his tracks.

"He wasn't in the prison when Elise and I got out. In fact, no guards were. He must've known you were coming through a different way than Elise, so he backed out of the one place he knows Elise would go because he doesn't want to kill us separately. He wants us all together. Right now, we're as close as we could ever be."

"He couldn't have predicted the fog, Sam," says Elise as she tries to look around the misted street.

"I know, but he's always been a step ahead. You guys figured splitting up was for the best, but maybe he knew you'd do

236

that. I don't know. I just don't feel right out here anymore," I say with exasperation.

"We can't go back, Sam. We have to keep moving," says Sean firmly as he pulls Elise forward, in turn pulling Abby and I.

As much as I want to prove my point, I don't want to argue. Sitting still is the last thing we should do in this situation. If we hovered aimlessly in the streets arguing about the appropriate way to get to Marcus, we'd never make it.

My grasp on Abby's hand grows tighter as Sean's pace increases. Unsure of where we are, I try to look around my surroundings without looking forward—causing myself to trip in the process.

"I'm okay," I say as I stand up with a slight tear in my pants.

"Watch your step, Sam," grins Abby with a sarcastic perk in her cheeks.

"Sorry," I whisper, unable to appreciate her light-hearted humor due to my fear.

With each passing second, I try to fixate my eyes on the ground and not the abundance of fog around us. I stumble a few times in the process, but I don't fall.

I don't want to be here, I think as I close my eyes. Cloaked in the darkness behind my eyelids, a dim burst of light erupts in the distance. As I force my eyelids further into the tops of my cheekbones, the light grows brighter. Unsure of what it is, I tighten my closure, but as I do the light disappears.

I open my eyes hoping to see what was glowing in my head, but instead am pained when a piece of metal catches onto my pant leg and forces its way into my shin.

"Ahh!" I shriek as my hand slips out of Abby's.

"Are you okay?!" exhales Abby.

"Sit still," says Elise as she turns around and crouches beside me.

"Get it out of me!" I yell. Blood runs down my leg while the end of the shard is invisible. Unable to drop to my knees, I clench my teeth. "Get it out of me!"

I try to compose myself, but I can't. The piece has clawed its way into my shin like the light forced its way behind my eyelids. Reaching for Abby's hand, I squeeze tightly. She clenches back.

Despite not moving, the pain feels unending; it feels like the metal is digging through my entire leg. I tilt my neck back and yell.

"Be quiet, Sam!" shouts Sean as he places his hand over my mouth.

In the midst of my agony, my scream muffles in Sean's palm. I try to hide my pain, but I can't. Every second is another moment of doubt burrowing itself in my head. Every pull spills more blood down my leg as Elise tries to pull my leg out of the metal without tearing every ligament in my calf. I'm starting to feel light-headed.

"He's losing a lot of blood!" shouts Elise as Sean's hand moves away, only to be replaced by Abby's.

At this point, I want to try and yell once more, but I can't. I feel weak; with the only sensation being the tightening of pressure below my knee, I look down. My leg is free, but red. I'm unsure how I'm still standing.

"You're going to be okay," says Abby as her watery eyes drip beside me.

With each second growing longer, the fog thickens as a mass of black spots appears in the distance. I can't tell if I'm hallucinating or not, but the more I squint, the closer the dots get.

"Don't look. . ." I say as the fog obscures my vision and the pain disappears.

Elise

"Sam!" I yell as the pounding in my chest beats faster and faster. "Sam!"

"Quiet!" hushes Sean as he tightens the wrap around Sam's lacerated shin. "They're coming."

"I don't see a way out!" screams Abby as the once-distant spots of black inch closer.

"Run!" shouts Sean. Throwing Sam over his shoulder, he sprints ahead, barely slowed by Sam's weight upon his shoulder.

I quickly grab ahold of Abby's hand as we sprint behind Sean. Yet, the more we run, the more shadows we see. Each stride is another stepping-stone toward *them*. Each turn is another blackened corner of misery.

"There's no way out!" I cry. Forced to stop in our tracks, I tightly clench Abby's fingers.

"There has to be. There can't be that many of them!" shouts Sean, Sam's legs flailing behind his head.

"There are," comes a daunting voice from the fog.

"Leave us alone, you bastard!" I yell. Releasing Abby's hand, I pull my bow from my back and aimlessly point it into the gray.

"I'm afraid I can't do that," replies Arthur.

"And why is that?" asks Sean as he reaches for my hip.

"Because I've waited a long time for this moment," he says while remaining hidden amidst the endless fog. "I never thought I'd get all four of you at once, but I'm glad I did."

"Why do you think you need to kill us? Why do you have to torture us?"

"Why does MacMillan have to send us out here? Everyone has their reasons, but some are more justifiable than others. For example," he says as his voice grows louder, but his whereabouts remain hidden. "I tortured Sam's friend because she was a coward. . .

239

.and we all know cowards don't survive out here, so I made it easy for her."

Baffled, I turn left and then right trying to follow his haunting voice.

"How does killing someone solve their fear? Everyone is scared out here. You just make it worse by preying on it," I say.

"I wouldn't say I make it worse, Elise."

The moment my name slips from his mouth, I fire my bow.

"I wouldn't have done that if I were you," he says as the sound of a body falling into a puddle echoes around us.

"Why not? If you're going to kill us anyways, shouldn't we at least go down with a fight?"

"I mean, I suppose you could, but where's the fun in that? I don't plan on killing you right here. I just want to hurt you. . ." he trails off. "Just a bit, for old time's sake. I think it's only fair if I give Sean a nice scar on his face, too. Then, when he's out of the picture, I can take you right back to that cell you're so fond of, Elise. Doesn't that sound great?" he asks with a momentary chuckle.

As if every second of agony and displeasure is a second of bliss for him, he continues to ramble.

"I know how much you liked that place. I know how much you like the pain. I know you like it as much as I do."

"Nobody likes it," I mumble. "Nobody likes to suffer. Eleven years of pain and torment are enough, but it's only worse when someone like you actually thrives in it; you shouldn't have been sent out here in the first place."

Laughing, he steps out of the fog and into our sight. With a knife held at his side, his bony fingers flip the blade in circles. "But aren't you glad I was? Without me, this world wouldn't be as fun."

"Without you, this world would be habitable," says Abby. "Without you, I would've enjoyed my childhood. Without you, Aden, I wouldn't be afraid of the shadows. . .and even with you here, I'm not afraid. I'm not afraid of who you are and what you've become; I'm not afraid of you anymore."

"Oh sweet Abby, I never wanted you to be afraid of me. I wanted you to envy me."

"Why would anyone envy you? You're a murderer!" she cries as she rips the knife from her pocket and steps toward Arthur.

Drawing his weapon in retaliation, Arthur holds his knife toward Abby's as they glare at each other.

"Put that away, Abby. You'll hurt yourself. It's not safe to play with something you know nothing about."

"I know this is your knife and I know I'm going to kill you with it."

"So you found my knife? That was very kind of you, but you can't kill me. We outnumber you," he says as dozens of Lurkers step into the circle—each with a burnt 'S' and 'L' on their right cheek.

"You're wrong," states Sean as he snaps his fingers and screams begin to echo around us.

Suddenly, the Lurkers start to disappear into the mist as others I've never seen, but assume are from the library, step into sight.

With one last glance, Arthur takes a step forward and smirks before fleeing. "This isn't the end. I'll see you again soon."

Sean

"Sean, come this way!" shouts Marcus from behind us.

"Where are you?!" I yell, the fog blinding my line of sight. No matter where I turn, I can't see him. I can't see anything. The endless stretch of gray refuses to dissipate as the screams echo behind us.

"Follow my voice!"

"I'm trying!" I shout as I reposition Sam over my shoulder. Elise's nails dig into my palm as my body starts to shiver, fearing that something will obstruct our escape.

"Keep following me, Sean. There's nothing but road ahead of you."

I try to focus on Marcus's voice as the screams in the distance start to vanish, but the constant fear that something's going to pull me into the abyss hangs onto my body. I try to shake off the burden, but the nagging panic keeps creeping up. It's not a feeling I've felt much in the past, but it's one I imagine Sam's had since his first day out here. A feeling so terrifying that no matter how much you run from it, it's always there; it's always trying to pull you back in.

"We need to hurry!" yells Elise. "We need to get out of this fog!"

"Just stay with me. We're almost back," calmly states Marcus.

"What about them?" I ask. "What about the people you brought to help us?"

"They'll be okay. They know where to go and how to fight."

"What about Arthur?" asks Abby from behind.

"Let's not worry about that now," replies Marcus as his figure starts to appear ahead of us. "We're almost there."

"What if he's near us now?" she shrieks.

242

"He's not. I saw him run off." Reaching back for Abby's hand, Marcus leads her in front of us as he points in the distance. "We're just about there. Rosie's up ahead."

I squint as the fog starts to disperse and the library becomes apparent. Rosie waves her hands back in forth as she whistles.

"Go ahead, Sean. I'll make sure there's no one behind us."

"Thanks," I reply.

"This way, this way," says Rosie as she hurries us through the door. Quickly shutting it behind us, she calls for Collin, who rushes down the spiral staircase holding a first aid kit. Motioning toward a table near a cart of books, she looks at Sam. "Set him here."

Slowly lifting him off my shoulder, I rest him atop the wood. With blood from his tourniquet spattered across my shirt, I exhale and close my eyes. *Please be okay*, I think.

"We'll get whatever's left out of him and stitch his leg up, but he's going to need to rest. You guys are, too. Feel free to go upstairs and do so."

"Thank you," I mutter.

As I start to walk toward the staircase, Collin grabs ahold of my shoulder. "Could you go check to see if Marcus is still out there?"

"Yea, sure."

"Thanks," he says before turning his attention back to Sam.

"You guys go upstairs. Abby can show you where we're staying," I say short of breath. Elise bites her bottom lip before pressing her lips into my cheek.

"I love you," she whispers.

"I love you, too," I say as the sound of screams from the streets force their way into the library.

"Help!" I hear.

"Stay here!" I yell as I sprint toward the door. Violently pulling it open, I run onto the street in search of the cry.

The second I get out the door, I see Marcus's limp body being dragged across the street by two people.

"Marcus is hurt. Help us carry him into the library," says a man whose face is covered in ash while blood stains his neck.

"What happened?"

"He went back for us and someone came out of nowhere and knocked him unconscious. We need to get him inside now!"

Grabbing ahold of his left arm, I lift him up as the girl runs for the door.

"Where are the rest of you? Did you scare off the Lurkers?" I ask.

"I don't know. I don't know what happened back there; it's all a blur. It was hard to see, hard to focus on anything," he says as his teeth clench while we lift Marcus up the curb. "I got one of them as they were fleeing, but that's it. I think Ella said she saw someone take down another one."

As we pull him through the door, Ella yells for Collin. "Marcus is unconscious!"

"Get him here now!" replies Collin while he tends to Sam.

"We're trying," says the man helping me.

"I got him," says Collin as he turns around and grabs ahold of Marcus's arm as we lift him onto a separate table next to Sam. Turning toward us, he glares at the dark-haired man next to me. "Ted, go downstairs and get me some water." Ted obliges and shakes the ash from his head as he steps out of sight. Collins shifts his wide-eyed stare to Ella. "Ella, were there any other survivors?"

"I don't know," mumbles Ella as she wipes her golden brown hair from her eyes. "I really don't know."

"How many did Marcus bring with?" I ask.

"He brought eight including himself. He didn't want our number to decrease to anything under thirty," she exhales as she pulls out a chair.

"And you didn't see anyone else leave with you guys?"

"We couldn't see anything, just like you. That fog is miserable."

"It was something else," says Ted as he hands a canteen to Collin. "We're lucky to still be here. Especially with their strange fighting methods."

"What do you mean?"

"Can't you see? One of them threw ash at me," he smirks while wiping his face.

"Yea, they're definitely different," I say as three more people burst through the glass door covered in a mixture of ash and blood.

"Phew!" sighs one of the men before he wipes the soot out of his blond hair. "That was ridiculous."

"Who are we missing?" asks Ted as he looks at the three new arrivals.

"Sandra and Hector didn't make it," replies the man. "The Lurkers got to them."

"Damn it," Ted exhales. "I thought we weren't going to lose anyone."

"We tried to save them, but it was too late. The fog wouldn't let up and we couldn't reach them in time. We killed about four Lurkers before they got away, though."

"Good job," I comment as the men head toward Marcus.

"Thanks. What happened to Marcus?" questions the blond-haired man.

"He got hit by someone, but we don't know who," answers Ella. "Collin says he'll be alright, though."

"That's good," smiles the man. Looking over at Marcus once more, he nods at me before heading upstairs.

"Yea, it is," says Ted. "I'm going to go clean up."

"Me too," says Ella. The two of them disappear upstairs.

I take a seat beside Sam. Stretching out my legs, I close my eyes and lean back in the chair.

"You should go rest upstairs, Sean. Those chairs will just make you feel worse later," laughs Collin.

"That's probably a good idea. Thanks again," I say before walking toward the steps as my eyelids grow heavy.

"No problem. Your brother's going to be just fine. Come back and check in in a few hours; he should be awake by then."

30 January 2192

Sam

Where am I? I wonder as the soft glow of candlelight bounces beside me. *What is this place?* I flutter my eyelids and try to focus on my surroundings, but everything is blurry. I rapidly blink at the ceiling until clarity arrives. "Where am I?" I mumble to myself as I try to sit up.

"The library," responds a familiar voice.

"Abby?"

Slowly working my way up, I turn to my side to see Abby with a book in her lap as she pushes her bangs out of her eyes. "How are you feeling?" she asks.

"What do you mean?"

"How's your leg?"

My leg? I don't know what she's talking about. I noticed a stiffness when I sat up, but that was it. "What happened to my leg?" I ask as I lift the blanket.

"A shard of metal or something jammed into it back in the city. Don't you remember?"

Gently tossing the blanket to the side, I press my index finger and thumb onto the ridge of my nose before I look back at her. "No," I whisper. "I don't remember anything. I just remember the black."

"Those were the Lurkers. Everyone's okay though."

Looking back at my leg, I notice a patch of gauze with slight splotches of red. "How bad was the cut?"

"Collin said you're lucky it didn't go any farther, otherwise you might not have been able to walk on it for a while. He said once you woke up, you were free to see how it felt." Standing up, she

246

walks toward me and places her hand on my shoulder. "I'm just glad you're okay," she whispers.

Collin?

I smile and place my hand atop hers. "Where's Sean? Did you see Arthur?"

"You sure do have a lot questions," she laughs.

"I just want to know what happened. Is he dead?"

"No. He got away," she sighs. "I was going to kill him, but Sean and Elise stopped me. If I had gone after him we might all be dead."

"I guess it's a good thing you didn't, then." Swinging my legs over the edge of the couch, I wince as the subtle move irritates the wound.

"But he's still out there. He's still alive."

"He won't get away next time."

"If there is a next time," she murmurs.

"There will be. There always is with him."

"I guess so. Anyways, you never answered. How does your leg feel? It looked really bad back in the city."

"Sore," I reply, pulling the blanket off from around my ankles.

"I figured. Do you want to go talk to Sean and the others?"

I nod. Abby steps in front of me and holds her hands out. I grab onto her palms and press my foot into the carpet. Instantly, a stinging sensation courses through my leg—sending me back onto the couch.

"Are you okay?" she asks.

"It just stings," I say as she helps me stand upright. With her arm around my back, Abby guides me toward the spiral staircase. Upon reaching the railing, I peer over and smile. Sean waves from the floor below.

"Sam!" he yells.

I wave back before eagerly limping toward the staircase. Feeling impervious to the pain, I run down the spiral as fast as I can.

"Sean!" I shout.

With his arms wide open, he speeds toward me. "How are you feeling?" he asks as he wraps his arms around my back.

"Better," I say.

"That's good. I want to introduce you to someone," he says as he gestures toward a man with a bandage around his head. "This is Marcus."

"Nice to meet you," I say, extending my hand.

He shakes my hand firmly and smiles. "It's nice to meet you too, Sam. I've heard a lot about you."

Unsure of how to answer, I manage a half-smile. Rather than forging up a bogus response, I gaze around the room. Nothing in Nimbus ever looked this perfect. Down to the table we're sitting at, everything is impeccable. I could get lost in the words of others here. I could stop the chaos in my mind from the darkness trying to control it. I could escape. I could actually escape.

"Marcus and I were just talking about how to take down MacMillan," says Sean.

I don't reply. Entranced in the perfection of this room, in the beauty of this place, I can't help but fall in love with what this library holds. I itch my face just below my eyes. "Why is this place so perfect?" I ask.

Laughing, Marcus replies, "Some things are worth saving."

"How have you kept it this perfect?"

"Hard work. I came out here when I got separated and a man named Kyle Bishop found me and brought me here. He was in charge and he had about ten others with him. He taught me the importance in preserving what little civilization still existed out here, so I obliged and I found more people who needed help. Over time, we've strived to rebuild this library in its entirety while also managing a structured society. Unlike Nimbus, this place isn't corrupt. It's beautiful no matter how you look at it."

"What happened to Kyle?"

"He got taken for his re-entrance exam."

"Did he pass it?"

"We don't know," exhales Marcus. "We just know that his message will always be here and that we'll never stop trying to salvage what's left."

"What happens when you have to take you re-entrance exam?" asks Elise.

Gingerly scratching his bandage, Marcus says, "I hadn't thought that far ahead. I'm only twenty."

"Plus, he's not going to have to. We're gonna take down Nimbus," says Sean.

"Exactly. The library will be here waiting when we get back and it will always be my home."

"What about your family?" questions Abby.

"They'll come with me. Together, with all of us, we can rebuild this city. We can construct a new world. . .a world without walls."

A world without walls is just another nightmare. It's one that we're living in every day. *At least a wall limits our scope of fear,* I think, scrunching my forehead in the process. It's gotten to the point that there's no world I could feel safe in and I only have two choices.

"That's not possible," musters Abby as she stares at me. As if she managed to dig into my mind and pull out my thoughts, she continues to speak. "A world like that would be just as dangerous as the world we're in now. People like the Lurkers are lunatics. Every world without walls would have people like that."

"I guess so, but behind the wall, the only disillusioned people are those who follow MacMillan and that's not necessarily their fault. The wall offers a sanctuary—an escape from this," replies Marcus as he motions toward the windows.

"That's true, but what if there are others?" I ask.

"Others where?" asks Marcus as he furrows his brows.

"Others outside our world. Others that escaped when the city fell apart. Others who didn't run to Nimbus."

"There aren't any others. Those who survived live in Nimbus."

"Wait a second," says Elise as she looks around the room—trying to find her words. "What if that's why there's the 'pop point?' What if the barrier was set to prevent us from finding other survivors hundreds of miles from Nimbus?"

"Then why haven't we seen elders around here?" replies Sean. "Wouldn't someone else have found a way into our world? Wouldn't someone else still exist in the city?"

"Not if they were killed," I say.

"All of this is just a hypothetical," says Marcus. "None of us have ever seen or heard of any others, so isn't it just safe to assume that maybe the teachings behind the wall were correct: that we're the last survivors in this world?"

"They taught us a lot of lies," I sneer. "But that might be the only truth."

"Anyways, we've run off course," says Marcus. "We need to figure out how to get into Nimbus, not whether there are others out here. We'll cross that bridge when we come to it."

"I guess so," I quietly reply.

"He's got a point, Sam. We really don't know if that's even possible. Our main priority needs to be reaching MacMillan and saving future generations from his terror," says Sean.

I guess so, I think as a brief shiver runs through my shoulders and down to my legs. Lightly pressing my forefingers into the gauze atop my gash, I massage up and down. Abby cocks her head to the side; her eyes ask if I'm okay. I smile.

Looking over at Sean, Elise itches her forehead. "So how do you think we do that?"

Sitting with his hands clenched into fists on the table, he fidgets his thumbs. "I don't know. I really don't know. This isn't how I had it envisioned."

"How did you have it envisioned?" asks Marcus.

"It's a long story, but it only worked if I started on the inside."

Standing up, Marcus looks out the window. "You used to work for the Guard, right?"

"Yea."

"Were there any secret doors into Nimbus that you might know about?"

"There weren't any. The only way in was the same way we got thrown out."

"Looks like that's our way in, then," laughs Marcus heartily. "It's going to be tough, but there's always a way. We just have to wait until someone gets separated or until someone around here has to take their re-entrance exam."

"Is anyone around here twenty-four?" asks Sean.

"I am," replies Elise.

"But your birthday isn't until August."

"I know, but I might be your best chance."

"It's still winter," mentions Marcus. Leaning against the glass, he waves his fingers in the air. In an instant, a tall, lanky

250

blond-haired man comes toward him. Fidgeting with a book in his palm, the man slowly nods.

"What do you need, Marcus?" he asks.

"Can you see if you can find anyone who turns twenty-five in the upcoming months?"

"Will do."

"Okay, Malcolm is going to see if anyone around here is close. Until then, do you suppose that that's our only real entrance, Sean?"

"I believe so."

"He's right. The way out is the only way in," I say. I remember running around Nimbus after class in search of an exit, in search of a way to see what the world looked like outside of our city, but I never found it. The steel was rooted into the dirt to the point that even if you dug, you couldn't find the bottom. Now, I'm glad I never found anything because any extra seconds out here wouldn't have been worth it.

"And how do you know that, Sam?" asks Marcus.

"Didn't you ever run around Nimbus growing up?"

"Yea, but what's your point?"

"Did you ever see another door?"

"I guess I never really looked," he says as his eyes wander around the room, bouncing from door to door along the way.

"Well, I looked and I never saw anything. MacMillan wouldn't want any outsiders finding a way in, anyways," I say.

"That's true. He always kept a lot of men on the top of the wall near the exit and not so many around the rest of the wall," says Sean.

"I guess we'll just have to keep that entrance as our primary focus then," replies Marcus.

"Marcus," says Malcolm as he appears at the end of the table.
"Yes?"

"Nobody here is twenty-four. The eldest is only twenty-two and that's Marie."

"Okay, thank you, Malcolm."

"Now what?" asks Abby.

"Looks like we'll have to find a time to head back to Nimbus and wait out a separation," says Marcus as he turns around and gazes out the window. "Unless you have another idea, Sean."

251

"I don't. I think it's best to head back and wait for a chance to sneak in rather than risk Elise's life by waiting until August," says Sean as he stands up and moves toward Marcus. "I can't risk her getting hurt just because I have unresolved tension with MacMillan."

"I think we all have that in some way," says Marcus bluntly.

I slowly stand up; the pressure in my leg aches. "I'm okay," I mutter toward Abby's outstretched hand. "Sean," I mumble as I gradually near him.

"Yea?"

"What about Arthur?"

"What about him, Sam?"

"Isn't he still alive?"

"I'm afraid he is," exhales Marcus as he itches his scalp. "And I fear that that wasn't the last time we'll see him. He thought he was going to get you guys then. You could see it in his eyes."

"So what do we do about him?" I ask.

"As hard as it may be, we just have to forget about him," answers Sean. "We have to move past him regardless of how much we want to kill him. If we get out of the city, there's less of a chance we'll see him again."

"But we can't just let him live," asserts Elise from behind us. "He's caused too much torment to so many of us here. He shouldn't be allowed to live."

"So what can we do, Elise? Should we just go after the man who's been stalking you for so long? We can't risk more lives just to find someone that we've never found."

"But he shouldn't be allowed to live," she reaffirms. "We can't build a new world with him still around."

"You have to realize that he's always managed to find you," says Marcus, his gaze still aimed out the window. Turning toward the table, he lifts up his chin before pushing his fists into the table. Looking around at each of us, he speaks. "From what I've heard and from what I've seen, Arthur moves like the cold, grievous hand of death. He's either there to take you away when you least expect it or he's nowhere to be found. And I personally believe you shouldn't go chasing something you're not sure exists."

"What do you mean?" I ask.

"You know Arthur's real, Sam, but have you ever tried to find him?"

"No," I say. "Why would I want to find someone that's tried to kill me?"

"Exactly. Why would you go after someone who just wants your head?"

"Because of what he could do to others," says Elise with a sense of urgency in her voice. "Because of what he's done to us." Taking a breath, she stands up and glares at Marcus. "Arthur has tried to kill all of us at one point or another, so why should we let him live? Why should some sick, cruel, demonizing human being like him be allowed to live? Answer me that."

"I'm not saying he should, but I'm saying that there's a better chance that he comes to us before we can get to him."

"That's true. We never know where he is," says Sean. "He wasn't even at the prison when you went there, Elise."

Sighing, Elise sits back down and presses her palms into her cheeks. Muffled, she says, "I can't go on knowing he's still out there."

Neither can I, I think, but Marcus has a point. Arthur always comes to us. I would never intentionally seek out the nightmares that have scarred my mind even if it meant they would end, because I could never be certain what I might find along the way. Even if we think we're closing in on him, he could disappear and find another way to torture us.

"Then we'll wait here for a few days," says Sean. "If Arthur truly wants to find us, he'll find a way. He doesn't know of our plan to head back to Nimbus. There's no way he could, so we'll stay here for a while. It'll give us time to devise an exact plan anyways."

"He always knows," says Elise as she buries her head further into her arms.

"It's true," I say. "He knew where we were when we headed out into the fog. He knew where we were at the shack and at the farm. He always knows where we are and what we want to do. He's everywhere."

"Then let's get one step ahead of him," says Marcus.

"It's not that easy," I say.

"Why's that?"

"It's just not. I'll tell you this though," I say as my mind wanders back into the empty cell. "Whenever *he's* near, my

nightmares don't exist. Whenever he's close, I feel safe. . .and right
now. . .I feel safe."

Elise

A slight pulsing runs across my head like a mouse racing through a maze. The mouse is trying and trying to find the cheese, but no matter where it turns there's another wall: a wall blocking any and every entrance to the prize. Yet, it keeps running around in hopes of finding what it's searching for, but it's impossible. The cheese sits outside the maze.

It's dumb to think these headaches will ever subside. As long as *he's* alive, the mouse will never escape.

"I can't guarantee going straight through that door without ideal weaponry is our best idea," says Sean as I stand up, waving off his futile attempt to keep me interested. "Where are you going?" he mumbles.

"Upstairs," I say.

I need to get away from this discussion. I can't stand thinking about *him* and talking about a return to Nimbus. I just want to lie down and forget about leaving. Nothing seems safer than this place.

They say that killing everyone who stands against us is the only way to save this world, but they don't consider that the only person we need to kill is *him*. The only person who's caused us any harm is *him*. If we don't go back to Nimbus, we could thrive out here. We could wait for the Elites to come find me and we could kill them. We could find a way to dismantle the chips in our heads; we could do it.

Except we can't. We're not equipped to live out here forever. Everyone's as useless as a mouse lost in a maze without an exit. No matter how far we run or how hard we try, we're not strong enough to bring down the Elites. Some of us aren't even mentally prepared for all-out war with anyone. I know I'm not.

"Elise," says Abby.

"Yea?" I say as I step onto the balcony.

"What's going on down there?"

255

"Just crap I don't care to talk about. Where's Sam?"

"He's lying down. We were going to nap."

"That sounds like a good idea," I say as I follow her into the room.

Lying stiff on the couch with his leg propped up on a pillow, Sam gives me a crooked smile before closing his eyes. "What're they talking about now?" he asks.

"Nothing important," I respond. Sitting down on a twin mattress next to Abby, I slow my breath. A maroon blanket lays folded at the edge of the bed; I grab it before lying down. "The only thing that matters is you-know-who."

"I know," replies Sam. "Sean knows *he* needs to be out of the equation before we go back to Nimbus, but he doesn't seem to care."

"He just thinks we're blinded by vengeance, Sam."

"But we're not, right?" he asks as he sits up and slouches over his leg.

"I don't know," I say. "At this point, I just don't know."

"You kind of are, but it makes sense. He's tortured more people than just you two. It's more of a vengeance for the common good," says Abby as she unravels her scarf before folding it over and placing it over her eyes. "But it's still technically vengeance."

"But like you said, it's revenge for the common good, so really, we have the right idea," says Sam.

"I guess so," I mutter as I pull the blanket over my chest. "I'm still afraid that he's going to get to us before we get to him."

"Me too," mumbles Sam before laying back onto the couch. "I don't think he's that far from us now."

"Neither do I."

It feels like he's just outside, holding out a plate of cheese, waiting for us to be tempted by such a prize. Unaware that the prize is himself, he stands there, waiting still as the ploy to draw in its victim runs its course.

"It's kind of frightening," says Abby. "He could be anywhere right now."

"He's always been everywhere," says Sam.

"It's true," I mutter as I roll onto my side. "He always seems to have the advantage, but his luck is bound to run out."

"I hope so."

"You don't think he'll find us here, do you?" I ask.

"I hope not," says Sam, perching his leg back up in the process. "We have a lot more people here looking out for us than we did when we were out on our own."

"I think we'll be safe here for as long as they allow us to be," says Abby.

"What do you mean?" I ask.

"I guess it's not really our choice."

"Why's that?"

"Like you said, he always has the advantage. We may have them outnumbered, but our fate's really been in his hands the whole time."

Unsure if it will ever escape, the mouse continues to run into the wall. Maybe, just maybe, if it tries hard enough, the barrier will break before it does.

1 February 2192

Sean

We've spent the last few days outlining a route and a plan to attack Nimbus, but so far every time we speak about it, I get uneasy. I mean, I feel safe here. I've never felt this way on the outside and I don't want to run from it. I'd like to plant my feet here and stay forever, but we can't. We have to stop MacMillan.

Regardless of what feels more comfortable, we have to toss any feeling of complacency to the side; we have to do what is right. We have to save humanity from unwillingly succumbing to the reign of a lunatic hungry for power. We have to change the way Nimbus works. If we don't, every death out here will become less and less important.

And the only way to fix Nimbus is by the plan Marcus and I agreed upon.

With the back of his chair resting against the wall, Marcus closes his book before looking up at me. "When do we want to head out, Sean?"

"Once everyone is ready. Once they know what we intend to do when we get there," I say.

"I briefed Collin, Rosie, and Malcolm on it this morning and they were to inform the others."

"I told Elise, and she was going to tell Sam and Abby."

"Then perhaps we should leave shortly, Sean. Is that alright? You seem a little uneasy," says Marcus as the legs of his chair fall onto the floor.

"I'm fine," I mumble. *Just fine*, I think.

"If you insist. I know it's going to be tough, but I'm leaving behind three people to help protect this library while we're away. As long as this place is safe, we'll always have a home to come back to."

"If we come back."

"We'll come back. You know that."

"I know. I guess I'm just nervous."

"We all are," he says as he stands up and walks toward me. "Nervousness is just a state of mind; fear is a state of being. If I had to choose which one I'd rather be, I'd be nervous every time."

I manage a quick smirk as he walks past.

"Sean," says Elise as she lays her hand on my shoulder.

"Yea?"

"I just told Sam and Abby. They think it's a solid plan. As long as we stay out of sight, we should be able to get past that door."

"I think so," I say as I wrap my arms around her waist.

"I know so," she smiles as her fingers run up my spine.

As she gently presses her lips into mine, her hands start to run up my shoulders, sending a frenzy of jitters down my cheeks as our lips join. Her love makes my nerves cease to exist and the tighter she pulls my body toward hers, the looser my mind becomes; the freer I feel.   "Gross!" shouts Abby. "Get a room, you two."

As Elise's lips pull away from mine, she turns around and sticks her tongue out. "Nah, I like to kiss him right here," she says.

"Whatever, you two are weird," smiles Abby as she turns around and heads back into the room.

Turning back around, Elise smiles at me. "And there's nothing wrong with that."

"Nothing at all," I whisper as I smile at her.

"So when will you be ready to go?" she asks.

"Soon. I just gotta go pack up."

"Okay, take your time. Marcus set a bag up in the room for you."

I muster a soft "okay" as I turn around and walk toward the steps.

With each step, the ping of the steel vibrates through the air like an echo bouncing its way through an auditorium. It's almost as if the books are pushing the sound back at me, like they don't want the noise either. I feel trapped. I feel like everything is weighing on me; that every decision we make falls back on me. If anyone gets hurt, it's because of me. I manage to trip up the last stair as my nerves get the best of me.

"You alright?" asks Sam.

"Yea, my foot just got caught," I say.

"I packed most of your stuff into your bag. I put some food and water in the front pocket, too. Marcus came by and gave us a fresh set of clothes as well. Yours are sitting on the couch."

"Thanks."

"No problem. I'm ready to get going."

"How's your leg?"

"It's getting better. Still a bit stiff at times, but I'm not hobbling as much as I was," he responds with a smile.

"That's good. I'll meet you down there in a little bit. I'm just going to grab my things," I say.

I step into the room. Abby's resting on the mattress with a small red book held above her head. She flips the page as I try to get a glimpse of what she's reading. The title appears scratched and illegible, while the picture on the front is everything but peeled off.

"What are you reading?" I ask.

"I don't really know. I just picked it up down there a bit ago."

"Okay," I laugh. "Let me know if it's any good."

"Okay," she replies with a smile as she sits up. "Should I leave so you can change, or are you just going to pack those clothes for later?"

"I think I'm just going to pack them."

"That's what I did with mine, too. They may be new, but they aren't the prettiest," she says, her cheeks perking up when she looks over at her bag.

"We don't want to scare anyone off with our dashing good looks," I say as I hold up the shirt and jeans Marcus left for me. "I hope these are my size."

"Who cares, they're free," she says. Rolling over, she gets up and places the book in her bag.

"That's true."

"Do you have everything you need now?" she asks.

"I think so."

"Still have the gun?"

"Yea, it's in my belt. I still have three shots."

"Good, hopefully you don't have to use them, but if we see him again, use them," she says firmly without so much as a break in her speech.

"I will."

"Are you two ready up there?" comes Marcus's voice from below.

"We're coming," replies Abby. Turning toward me, she throws on her backpack before gently wrapping her arms around my back.

"What's this for?"

"For everything. Thank you for protecting us. . .for keeping us alive."

I drape my arms over her shoulders as the nerves that once encompassed every fiber of my mind start to dissipate more and more. "Thank you for keeping Sam and Elise safe while I was still behind the wall, Abby. I think I owe you more than you owe me."

"Not possible," she says, letting go.

I smile as she heads out the door. Quickly turning around, I shove the clothes into the bag.

"C'mon," she says from the hallway.

"I'm coming. Hold on."

Pressing the clothes into the back of the bag, I pull the flap over just as a small cracking sound echoes outside.

"Did you hear that?" asks Abby as she steps back into the room.

"Yea, what was it? It sounded like breaking glass."

"I don't know. It looks like Marcus is sending Malcolm and a few others outside to see if they can spot where it came from."

I swiftly throw my bag around my shoulders as I hurry Abby downstairs.

"What was that sound?" I ask breathlessly.

"I don't know," responds Marcus. "It sort of sounded like someone broke a window or something."

"That's what I heard, too," says Elise.

"You don't think it's them? Do you?" asks Abby.

"I hope not," Sam says quietly.

With widened eyes, Marcus's expression becomes that of dread as he looks over at me. "They're here."

Time stops. A brief moment of silence is broken when Malcolm rips open the front door and screams, "Lurkers!"

"Everyone stay quiet!" shouts Marcus.

"We have to get out of here," replies Sam. "They'll kill us if we stay in here."

"They can't get in here. They don't have the weapons to get in here without getting past us," says Marcus as he turns back toward Malcolm who's holding his hand outward.

"M-M-Marcus," he stutters.

"What? What?"

"L-look," he mumbles as the sound of shattered glass rings loudly throughout the library.

"Everybody get outside!" I yell as irradiated beams of orange fall through the windows like cascades of light casting themselves upon a waterfall.

"Everybody go!" cries Marcus before he sprints to the back of the library.

"Elise, Sam, Abby!" I yell. "Go out front with Malcolm. I'll help Marcus get the others out of here."

Instantly, more windows around the library start to collapse as a mass of molotovs fly throughout the area igniting every shelf in sight. The flames quickly climb high into the building, enveloping everything they touch.

Signaling for them to get out, Elise grabs ahold of Sam and Abby as they hustle out through one of the broken windows alongside Ella and Malcolm.

"Marcus!" I shout as shelves start collapsing into the fiery mist around us. "Marcus!"

"Sean!" he yells back. "I can't just let this place burn," he cries as he empties the contents of his bag while attempting to fill it with books. "I can't let them take this away from me."

"We have to get out of here," I say as the flames grow taller; soaring to peaks, the fire climbs higher and higher until it seems it's going to spill onto the surface like a wave crashing into the sand. And each second we waste, the weaker everything around us becomes.

"We can't leave everything," he cries as the blaze shines upon his cheeks.

"We have to! Don't be crippled by fear!" I say, knowing the words hold no value. "We have to go now!" I grab his arm.

"NO!" he retaliates. "This place is why I'm still alive. This place. . .is my home."

"And if you stay in it any longer you'll get us both killed," I shout as I pull harder. Screams reverberate off the walls as the wood around us starts to burn into nothingness. "We have to go, Marcus! I'm not leaving without you!"

"Okay, okay!" he exhales as he grabs his nearly empty bag— kicking away a burning book in the process.

Clinging to his wrist, I turn around. "How do we get out of here?!" I yell.

"That way!" says Marcus, pointing to the stairwell. "We have to go up and out."

Hurrying up the steps, the room becomes more and more engulfed in flames. I catch a glance out of the side of my eye only to see a vast orange consuming the floor like lava. My chest tightens. The loud cracks of falling shelves make my hands shake.

"This way!" shouts Marcus. Effortlessly breaking a window with a chair, he looks back at me. "We're gonna have to jump."

Without hesitation, he jumps onto the street below.

I violently rip off my bag and throw it down to him. With one look back, the roaring flames ignite the door behind me as the smoke grips onto the ceiling.

"Jump!" shouts Marcus. "Jump!"

GO! I think as I close one eye and jump.

"They're all around us," shouts Elise as she hands me a knife while I steady myself. "We have to head toward the forest. It's our only hope right now."

"Good luck with that," says a heinous voice. "You're not getting away from me twice."

"Don't you mean you're not going to get away from us again, Arthur?" says Elise as she wraps her arms around mine and Abby's while Abby grabs Sam and Sam grabs Marcus.

With our backs pressed together, I reach back for the gun.

"I wouldn't grab that if I were you," sneers Arthur as he flashes his yellow teeth. "The moment you fire one shot, that's the moment I kill your brother. . .or perhaps Elise."

"How can you kill anyone if I kill you first?" I ask.

"Look around you, Sean. We outnumber you."

I remain focused on Arthur as shadowed figures start to step into my peripherals. "I'm not afraid of you. . .or them."

"But aren't you? Aren't you all afraid of me just a little?"

"No," mumbles Sam. "None of us are. You're just crazy."

"Crazy? Maybe just a little bit. Demented? Yea, for sure. But really, I'm just what I need to be out here. I'm what everyone should be out here. I'm free. . .more or less," says Arthur as he steps closer while still remaining several feet from our circle.

More or less? I think. *What does that mean?*

I take a half step forward. Arthur scowls.

"We're all free," says Marcus as he glares at Arthur. "We're all free from that place that sent us out here, from the society that didn't think we were good enough when we turned fourteen."

"But we all have to go back, don't we?"

"Not if we choose to do otherwise," mutters Marcus.

"What else could you do?"

". . .this," whispers Marcus, as he breaks free from the circle and charges at Arthur. With his knife held up, he swings, but misses. Arthur ducks the attempt and thrusts his fists in Marcus's stomach. As he's tumbling back, Arthur swipes at his legs and forces him into the ground.

"That wasn't very smart, now was it?" he says while kneeling over Marcus's writhing body. "If you didn't want me to burn down that place, maybe you should've come outside a little sooner, so we could've talked."

Spattered in blood, Marcus rolls over and spits onto the cement. Cocking his head to the side, he looks at Arthur. "Go to hell."

"It's not my turn," replies Arthur before he buries the bottom of his shoe into Marcus's face. Screams from Rosie, Malcolm, and others from the library enshroud the street. "Shut up!" shouts Arthur before turning his attention back to me. "See what I did there, Sean? I don't need help to take down one of your men, but like I said, I have plenty of it."

"What do you want from us?!" shouts Abby.

"Oh you know what I want," he says as his attention turns to Elise.

"You can't have me," says Elise. "You can't have any of us."

"That's not fair. See, I get to have what I want because I'm in charge, because I choose who suffers and who doesn't."

"Why does anyone have to suffer?" I ask.

"Because you need to feel my pain. Everyone needs to feel my pain. Everyone needs to feel the rage that I've felt each and every day of my life. That's why. Plus, this is what I was told to do."

By who?

My fingers grab hold of the gun, but I don't ask anything. Arthur continues to spew nonsense.

". . .and if no one suffers like I do, then what's the point in living, huh? What's the point of being outside of Nimbus if you can't go," he pauses, "a little crazy? If you can't let your true self show? Personally, I don't see the point."

"You can try to survive; try to find a way to get back at those bastards for putting you out here," I say. "There's a lot you can do in eleven years."

"There really is," laughs Arthur. "Don't you know how many people I can prevent from going back to Nimbus in that time frame? I'll give you a hint—it's a lot."

"But why? Why do you have to do this?"

"I already told you. Weren't you listening?" he asks as he takes another step forward—my grip growing tighter. "This is what I'm supposed to do. We all have a purpose and mine is to prevent yours."

"So what's my purpose?"

"To bring down Nimbus; to prevent me from having such a good time out here."

"And why do you think it's that?"

"Because that's why he doesn't like you."

"Who?"

"Oh, did I say he? I think you know what I meant. That's really why nobody likes you. You're trying too hard, Sean. Just be yourself; be a little. . .crazy," smiles Arthur as he parts his hair from his eyes.

"What are you talking about?" asks Sam.

"Oh, Sam. You know perfectly well. After all, you wrote about it. You know what's really going on back in Nimbus."

"Sam, what is he talking about?" asks Elise.

"Go on, Sam. Tell them that you know the founding families aren't sent out here. If they didn't know that already, then I'd say they haven't been very observant in the first place."

"What does that have to do with any of this?" I ask.

"Don't you see? Don't any of you see the connection?"

I try to gather my thoughts as Arthur's delusion sends my mind sputtering about. "What are you talking about?"

"Oh c'mon, guys. Not everyone has to deal with this world; not everyone is forced out here because. . .?" He leans forward—his eyes practically protruding from his skull. "Can anyone guess?"

"Because the Elites want to keep their numbers low," I say.

"Yes! There we go. Because they want to keep their numbers low. And what's the easiest way to do that? I'll get this one for you. It's by keeping some people on the inside and sending others—like me—out here to ensure not many get to take their test."

MacMillan personally sent Arthur out here? He was sent away to do nothing more than kill those out of sight of the wall? My mind spins with questions and not answers. I don't speak.

"What do you mean, others like you?" asks Sam.

"Look around you, Sam. I'm not the only delusional one out here."

"I still don't get it," I say.

"Because you're not focusing on the right parts!" shouts Arthur. "Anyways, this is taking longer than I wanted. Say your goodbyes now."

"NO!" I yell. Tightly clasping onto the pistol, I pull it out and fire.

The first shot clips Arthur's shoulder—forcing him to charge at me as the black mass around us tightens. I fire again. This time, the bullet flies through his chest.

"NO!" he screams as Elise draws her bow.

"Say your goodbyes, bitch," grits Elise as she pulls back an arrow.

"This. . .this. . .was not supposed to ha-happen," he says while blood drips from his mouth onto the concrete.

"And aren't you glad it did?" smiles Elise as she releases the string—sending an arrow straight between his eyes.

Instantly, the black mass dissipates further into the streets as those who survived the fire in the library try to snag any Lurkers

266

they can, all while the building burns brightly beside us. I turn around. Malcolm and Ella have a Lurker pinned while several others are throwing bricks, chunks of concrete or whatever pieces of metal they can find at the scrambling Lurkers.

"Over here!" screams Malcolm.

"Elise, check on Marcus. Sam, Abby, come with me," I shout before sprinting toward Malcolm as he thrusts his knee into the back of one of the Lurkers.

"Let me go!" screams the man. Angrily shaking underneath the pressure of Malcolm's knee, Malcolm jams his other knee into the man's spine. The Lurker doesn't move. Silent and immobile, he spits a dark red onto the street.

"Never," says Ella angrily as she kneels beside Malcolm and grimaces at the man. "You're not getting away like the rest of those cowards."

"Where'd the rest of them run to?" I ask.

He doesn't respond.

I crouch down next to Ella while the man's face is further pressed into the asphalt as he starts to mumble nonsense, or what sound like incoherent rhymes. He spits more blood.

"Where did the rest go?" I ask again.

"It doesn't matter," he whispers.

"Why not?"

"Because you'll never catch us."

"We caught you," laughs Ella.

"And it wasn't that hard," says Malcolm.

"You'll never catch all of us. Once the darkness takes over, we'll be gone."

"Except you," I say. "The others left without you. They don't seem to care what we do to you. And without a leader, what would you even do?"

"We don't need him. We have another leader," gibes the man. "One much greater than Arthur. One you can't kill."

"Are you sure about that?"

Laughing, the man tilts his head to the side. His gray eyes waver as his lips fidget. "Of course, Sean. He's always watching you."

"Who is he?"

"Let me go and I'll tell you."

"It's not that simple," I say.

"Then I guess you'll never know," smiles the man.

"Should we just let him go, Sean? What's he going to do to us now that he doesn't have anyone with him?" asks Malcolm.

"True," I say. He won't last a day by himself. "Let go."

Slowly pulling his knees out from the man's back, Malcolm pulls him up by his wrists.

"Who's he?" I ask again.

"Who do you think?" he says as he shakes free from Malcolm's grip—causing Malcolm to mumble a cuss.

Reaching back for the pistol, I watch as he continues to run down the street. Sprinting as if he's being misguided by a foolish belief of freedom, he looks back.

With a smug expression strewn across his cheeks, he stumbles as I fire.

"Nice shot," says Malcolm.

"I wasn't ever planning on letting him escape. I just figured he might tell us if we let him stand up, but I guess he got what he deserved," I say.

"That he did," smiles Ella. Pushing her auburn hair from her eyes, she looks over at me. "Those guys are really strange. Do you think the others will come back?"

"I hope not," says Abby.

"Me too," mumbles Sam. "My head is finally starting to clear up."

"Mine too," says Elise as she steps in with Marcus's arm draped around her shoulder, his head drooping forward as blood drips from his mouth.

"Marcus?" I say.

"I'm okay," he says as he looks up. Gently wiping the blood from his lip, he smirks. "I probably shouldn't have gone at him like that. I didn't really think he'd be that strong. He seemed sort of scrawny."

"He was," says Elise. "I don't know where he could've learned that. The rest of them ran away in fear after we killed him."

"It doesn't make much sense," says Marcus as Malcolm and Ella help lift him off of Elise's shoulder. "Where do you think the rest fled to?"

268

"I really don't know, but I think they're the last of our concerns now that *he's* out of the picture," I say as the heat from the flames start to warm the air—slightly scalding our cheeks in the process.

"We should probably get away from this place," comments Elise as the smoke from the building wafts higher into the sky.

"Where should we go?"

"To the forest? Toward Nimbus?"

"Why don't we stay in the city where we at least can have a roof?" asks Sam.

"He's got a point. We know what can happen to innocents in the forest. Those Lurkers have raided camps before and if they're still out there, they'll be looking for anything to keep surviving," says Marcus.

"True," I say.

"Where to, though?" asks Elise.

"Just away from here."

"Back to the skyscraper we were in before?"

"Anywhere on higher ground seems ideal to me," says Marcus as he sits down. "But first, how many survivors are there?"

"Maybe twenty," grins Malcolm.

"Are Collin and Rosie alive?"

"Rosie is, but I haven't seen Collin," says Ella. "Rosie's over there with a few of the others," she says as she points just north of the burning library.

"Can you get the others?" asks Marcus as he lays back. "I need to rest just a bit and I'll be good to go."

"Sure thing," replies Ella.

As Malcolm and Ella head toward the others, I turn around and sit next to Marcus. With his head buried beneath his forearms, he speaks. "I still can't believe it."

"Me either."

"That was our home. That was our future. . .and. . .and just like that, it's gone. Everything we worked so hard to preserve just disappeared into thin air like the world before us. It's unbelievable."

"It's unstoppable," mumbles Elise. "No matter what we do to hold onto the little things that keep us sane, they'll be taken from us. That's how this world works and you can either accept it and fight or you can keep running."

"I don't want to run," grimaces Marcus as he stretches his back. "I want to fight."

3 February 2192

Sam

"This world can turn even the nicest of people into savages. Survival isn't for the faint of heart; if you don't want it, you don't get it. You have to earn the right to breathe out here," says Elise as she sits up with her back pressed against the leather couch.

"And I think we've earned that. *He* didn't deserve it, but he also didn't deserve a lot of things," says Abby. Fumbling with the blade in between her forefingers, she looks around the office.

I watch as her chestnut-colored eyes remain fixed on the view: the waning sun setting in the distance across a landscape of buildings. As if they're a stairway to the sky, the buildings stack up into the fog—only coming back down a half mile away. I can't see how far the street extends, but no matter where it goes, it's clear whoever used to live here never ceased their desire to be at the top. But, something had to bring an end to the competition—something had to stop the city from expanding. As if corruption and war weren't enough, something else had to drive these men and women mad.

Maybe ambition faded. Maybe desire to create disappeared. When everything's the same, it's hard to see something better. Instead, you just get used to it until something new comes along and frightens you. Maybe change brought down this world. Maybe that fear pushed everyone out. No matter the reason for its downfall, the city now thrives in its ugliness. Now I know why Arthur reveled in it, why he thought this was utopia.

I look left. Each building is as black as the one next to it, as if the Lurkers spent countless nights shading the skyline in shadows.

Some buildings have gaping holes on random floors, while others have shattered glass and contorted lines of ivy clinging to them. A desk hangs out one window. A chair leans into broken glass in another. A ripped shirt ruffles in the wind atop a third. No matter the issue, each one is different than what it used to be. Each one is a new design sculpted by the destruction of man.

"He definitely didn't deserve to have a sister like you," I say. "He didn't deserve any love."

"He never got any from me anyways," she says as she turns back toward us. "He was always unusual. It was like the world didn't make sense to him. He never fully grasped compassion, even when we were young. We never ran around and played outside together. We never hung out and played board games or did anything. He always preferred to be alone, trying to figure out what he should do next, but he never really knew. He would just sit there and blankly stare a lot. Sometimes it seemed like someone else had control of him."

As Abby speaks, my heart starts to pound against my chest. A part of me wishes I had known her pain while back at Nimbus, so I could have befriended her earlier and given her the childhood I had. I didn't have Sean most of my life, but I also didn't have a nagging fear that when he was around, something bad was going to happen. It pains me that we weren't closer at school; it irks me that we only spoke in passing.

I inch closer to Abby and put my hand on her knee.

"You did say he always had another side to him," says Elise as she folds her knees into her chest. "Do you think that was what he was always at war with?"

Nodding, Abby clasps her fingers together—her thumbs pressing against each other before spinning around the other. "I do. He was so torn between being Aden and being Art that he would just be both," she pauses. "Which is why he seemed so confused. When it came closer to his separation, he became more distracted by violence and that's when I knew I never wanted to see him again. I don't want to sound cold-hearted, but I was kind of hoping he had already died when we got out here. I didn't want to run into him and have him torture me. Art seemed to have a stronger grip on him than he had on himself at times."

"And Arthur had a strong grip on us," I say as I look over at Elise.

"Yea, I'll never understand that either. I mean, my head feels clear now, but what he was able to do. . .was unnatural."

"I don't get it either and I don't get why he didn't do it to me. He sort of just avoided me," muses Abby as she turns her attention back to the setting sun. "I mean, he did that growing up, too."

"Maybe he always liked you and he just didn't want you to suffer like he was," I say.

"So why would he make the people close to me suffer?" she says.

"Because he had no sympathy for anyone," says Elise. "You were family, Abby. I know that even if I hated my brother with everything inside of me, I would never be crazy enough to kill him or hurt him. Family's family and regardless of how you feel about them, you don't hurt them."

"I guess so," she quietly replies. "I still don't understand him and now I never will."

I fold my lips together and itch my ear. "He was just lost in all the chaos," I say, my focus on my hand rather than on Abby.

"More so than anyone else. But he's dead now, so everything will be okay out here, right?" she asks, turning her attention to Elise.

"I don't think it's possible for everything to be okay out here. Granted, it will always be better than being stuck behind a wall forever," responds Elise.

"Anything would be better than going back there for the rest of our lives," I say while fidgeting with the dirty bandage around my finger.

"Which is why we won't be doing that."

"But it won't be that easy. We still don't know if the Lurkers are going to be coming after us anymore."

"True, but without Arthur, who's in charge? Who's going to tell them what to do now?"

"The Lurker who Sean killed mentioned that there was someone in charge who was bigger than Arthur, who had more power than him. Who do you think that is?" I ask.

"I really don't know. I didn't think there was anyone else out here as insane as him."

"In every game of chess, there's always someone controlling the pawns. Maybe Arthur was the first one out. There could still be a king or queen guiding those around it, willingly sacrificing everyone at its disposal to get to where it wants to be, to corner its opposition," says Marcus as he and Sean pull up a couple office chairs next to us.

"I think Arthur was more than just one small pawn. I don't think someone with so little power could do so much damage," says Elise as she pulls her bangs out of her eyes. Tying up her hair, she moves closer to Sean.

"You never know until you play. Sometimes it's the smallest pieces that are the most effective, whether you see it or not," he replies as he leans forward. "Maybe the one in charge is just an expert at the game."

"So you're saying someone was guiding Arthur's every move? Someone was helping him torture us?" I ask.

Sean bites his bottom lip like he wants to speak, but doesn't know what to say.

"Essentially, yea. Do you really think one man with a bunch of naïve followers could do everything he did by himself? It just doesn't make sense to me."

"It doesn't make the slightest bit of sense. Someone from afar had to have been helping him. I mean, how else could he have always been one step ahead of us?" asks Sean. "He had to have had eyes everywhere."

"But he had a bunch of followers. They could've been helping him stay on our trail," I say as I unwrap the bandage to rewrap it tighter.

Staring at my hand as I mess with the wrappings, the last glint of light fades in the distance, making it hard for me to see what I'm doing. Immediately, others start to burn candles around the office.

Abby huffs. "Why would he need to be on our trail? Why did he have to follow us? Why us? We didn't do anything to him!"

"I don't get that either," I frown.

"It all started when I went into the city. I put this evil on us. I was young and foolish. I didn't listen to his warning to not go into the city. He told me not to go, as if he didn't want to do what he did next," says Elise as she scratches her forehead. "It's as if some part of him still had empathy. He only went after us because he could get

274

more of us at once, because he didn't feel pain if many suffered. It must've only bothered him if just one did, but I don't know why."

"Because he suffered alone when he was young," whispers Abby. Raising her pitch, she looks around. "Because he knew what it was like to be tortured without an escape."

The room goes quiet. Eyes drift away from our crooked circle.

I open my mouth to speak, but close it before I mutter something useless.

"That's why when he had Sam and I, he left us alone. He wanted us to feel his pain even though he wouldn't dare watch it himself. He was a coward," stammers Elise. "He deserved no sympathy."

Abby clenches her jaw. Her eyes widen. She looks away. "You're right."

"I know what he was hurts, Abby, but there was nothing anybody could do. He was a lost cause."

"I know."

Sean interjects—changing the focus. "MacMillan always said the vagrants were the strongest on the outside. If you could ward off one of them, you were going to survive and I think being here proves we all did just that."

"Because I couldn't do it myself," mumbles Elise. "I was weaker than the man I just called a coward."

"But you're not now," says Abby. "We're stronger because of you."

"But we will always be weak in some form. We chopped the head off the snake, but that doesn't mean its body doesn't want to coil around us until we break. Like Marcus said, Arthur could have just been a measly pawn in a larger ploy. . .and if it's a mental game, Sam and I will be the first to go. He had us cornered."

"Who else can get into your head at this point? You both said your headaches were gone."

"I don't know, but if there's someone else out there, someone stronger than him. . .well, then we're basically dead already."

"But we're not," I say. "There's nothing else out there that can break us. You know that, Elise. I don't get why you're acting like you don't."

"Because you haven't been out here as long as us, Sam. You haven't seen the entirety of this world. You haven't experienced all the torment, all the torture, all the pain of what the outside has to offer. This place is a living hell," she says as she wipes her cheek. "Yea, we have a plan to bring down Nimbus, but will that resolve our sanity? Will that make everything normal again?"

"Nothing will ever be normal," mumbles Abby. "That doesn't exist anymore."

"Exactly," replies Elise. "Normal isn't real."

Standing up, I walk toward the window as the flashing light of the candles burns halos of light around the glass. "You only get one life," I cough. "You can't waste it always being afraid of what's next, of what lies ahead or what sits behind us. Who cares if normalcy isn't real anymore? If you sit in constant fear of the future or of figuring out what to justify as normal again, you'll never get anywhere. I know you don't want that, Elise. I don't want that either. I want to be someone who's not always afraid of what's ahead of me or what's behind me. I know that deep down inside of you, you're stronger than you feel right now. And if I've learned anything since I've been out here, it's that nothing—absolutely nothing—can break you."

Stepping back into the circle, I smile at Abby. Her cheeks rise toward the sky, toward a limitless expanse greater than this circle of hope. Just the way she looks at me makes me feel that everything will work out. Her bright smile helps me escape the darkness that once consumed me.   "Well said, Sam. We can't sit here and think about the harshness of our situation. We have to focus on the positives and what we can do to better it," says Marcus. "Nothing is given out here. We need to earn our spot in history. We need to prove that our will to live is more important than the Lurkers' need to break us apart."

"And how do we do that?" asks Elise.

"By following our plan to attack Nimbus."

"But we only have twenty-some of us. We can't beat an army of Elites with that many people."

"Sure we can," says Sean. "Just trust in the plan. It will work."

"And what's the plan, again?" I ask unsurely.

"First off, we have to wait for a separation. Since there tends to be one every day or at least every other, it shouldn't matter when we get back. The only thing that matters is that everyone is on the same page," replies Sean as he sits up in his chair. "When we near the wall, we'll climb into the trees about a hundred yards from the wall."

"Won't the guards atop the wall see us from there?" I ask.

"Not if we stay invisible. We have to be cautious, alert, and, of course, slathered in a bit of mud," smirks Sean as he slides his fingers across his cheeks.

"But then what do we do next?" asks Abby.

"When the sun rises, Marcus will lead a few others out of the trees and around the wall, making as much noise as possible. This will create a distraction while Elise, Malcolm, and Ella sit in the trees and fire arrows at the guards atop the wall. At the same time, we'll attack the guards bringing out the kids."

"And what if they close the door as we're attacking them?"

"A few others will prevent that from happening by sprinting in and killing the men behind it. There are only two men who sit behind the door. And while that's going on, you and Sam will run inside and find our parents. They'll alert the others that it's time to fight and that's when it will begin," replies Sean.

I look around the office; a shiver runs down my spine. The thought of going back *home* was once a sought-after feeling I thought would cure my fear. Now, the idea of going back frightens me. Just thinking about the power MacMillan wields makes my body twitch; it makes my finger throb.

I try to shake off the pain, but it refuses to subside.

"Are you okay, Sam?" asks Sean.

"I'm fine," I mumble.

"We won't leave for another day or two. It should give you time to settle your emotions."

"I'm just a little rattled," I say. "I'm afraid of losing anyone else."

"You're not going to lose anyone else. We're never going to leave you again. We're all family now, and we'll fight as a family and we'll die as a family."

"Is saving Nimbus worth dying over?" I hesitantly ask without looking up.

Clenching his teeth, Sean looks over at Elise as she brings her gaze down to the floor. "Why wouldn't it be? Our parents are still there."

"I know, but what if they're not?"

"They are. There's no way out once you've been re-admitted."

"Except the way you got out," mutters Abby.

"That's different," retorts Sean. "Not everyone got the chance I did to draw blood from our fearless leader," he laughs.

"I guess so," I mumble. "I just don't know if I want to leave here." As much as it hurts me to say it, it's true. The reality of this world is that no matter where you go, fear will follow you, so maybe by sitting still it won't bother us.

"We have to leave. If we sit here forever we'll die. We can't go beyond the city, either. The only solution is to go back, kill MacMillan, and shut down the grid. That way, the chips will deactivate and we can go wherever we want. We can find a new world. . .if it exists," says Sean. "Wouldn't you rather live in solace than die in darkness?"

I mutter a simple, "yes" as I sit down on a desk. Avoiding eye contact with the rest of the circle, I turn toward the window. Abby sits beside me.

"He's right, Sam. A new world is out there and we're going to find it, but first we have to bring down what we know to be the false world—a corrupt reality thrust onto a barren planet," says Marcus as he stands up. With his head held up, he walks toward me. Setting his hand on my shoulder, he looks around the office. "We need to fight for that world. We need to prove that our generation is the next generation. We need to ensure that the future of mankind is in the hands of survivors—survivors who relish in the simplicity of an undying bond to help one another. Not those who bury themselves in malicious acts of deceit, but those who find strength in their hearts to stick together. For those are the ones who can foster a new generation; those are the ones who can be the pillars of a new society. And if I know one thing, it's that we're going to be those pillars. We're going to become everything Nimbus couldn't be, everything the world before us couldn't be. We're the future," he says as he wipes his eyes. "And nothing can hold us back from our destiny. We're a family now, and nothing can break us."

278

4 February 2192

Elise

I roll my chair across the hallway through a pairing of desks and past a fallen glass door. The farther I allow myself to freely ride on the rickety wheels of this chair, the farther my mind wanders from our return to Nimbus—the farther I get from returning to a place I once called home.

I weave through a few more desks, gliding past broken shelves and shattered computer screens until I near the endless wall of glass. Like a seamless line above the world, the windows are spread across the entire level. No matter where I go, it feels as if I'm flying—not into oblivion or the circus, but into bliss. It's incredible.

The wheels shake as they nick cracked tiling, but the moment never ceases. The solace of the spinning world latches onto me like a bee landing itself on the petals of a blossoming sunflower. As it sits, absorbing the nectar of the flower, it collects everything it needs while the world around it continues to move. It's as if time has stopped while I hold onto the one thing I need to survive.

I need this, I think as I continue to roll around aimlessly like a child. *I need this.*

Whether it is the simplicity of meandering around a run-down floor or the freedom of a clear head, this is what I've needed. I need to forget the irrationalities of my fear and self-despair that have riddled my mind since my first year out here. I'm still alive. I've survived brushes with death. I've survived the chaos that conceals itself in the darkness. I've survived everything. If I keep thinking that my weaknesses can't become my strengths, then I'll become just as worthless as those who have died out here before me, and I can't have that.

I roll past Sam and Sean while they sit at an elongated wooden table discussing who knows what. They smile as I wheel myself around the corner toward a stockpile of broken chair legs—mostly burnt ones at that. I thrust my feet into the wall before pushing myself past the heap and toward a few people hanging out on sleeping bags playing various card games. I smile as I glide past them.

I know I'm not always afraid and I know that I rarely succumb to the lethargy of my weary mind when faced with death, but something about being helpless has always nagged me. The fear of being unable to save someone or being unable to save myself terrifies me. When you grow up protected by a giant barrier, you feel invincible. Yet, the moment you get past it, the metaphorical shield protecting you disintegrates into dust before you even get a chance to hold it. It's unfair.

Everything out here is unfair, but that's life. The world before us might not have been this difficult, but they were consumed by the futility of false hope. Naturally, so were we. Slaying the invisible beast that haunts your reality will always be tough, but that doesn't mean it's impossible. Everyone has a demon whether they want to admit it or not. But, nobody has one that can't be killed.

I feel unstoppable as I spin past Sean again—this time he winks. My smile grows. I feel like the burden of Arthur's unbearable suffering has been lifted, like the world has fallen off Atlas's shoulders into capable hands of someone else. I've never felt this free.

I wish I could feel like this forever. If only fear could die out and be replaced by tranquility. If only my anxiety could have died in that fire.

"Elise?" comes a voice from behind me.

"Yes?" I reply.

"How long are you going to ride around the office?" asks Sean.

"I really don't know," I say. "It's freeing."

"Okay," he smiles. "Take your time, but when you're ready to be done, come sit with us."

I nod as I push off the table and glide back toward the windows. The sun sits still in the sky as clouds run sparingly across the blue.

As my chair hops over another bump, I place my feet on the ground. Shoving the broken soles of my shoes into the tile, I start to run while remaining seated. I run and run until the sky becomes a blur, until the room around me swirls into a mix of colors. *Too fast*, I think as I recklessly swivel past the pile of legs and come bustling toward a few people. Thrusting my feet into the ground, I let out a soft, 'whoops' as I try to slow my pace.

The rush of going that fast was enticing, but the fear of crashing into someone or something was just too much. It felt like the fear of being trapped. It was as if the colors blurred into that prison cell again—into a darkness that I thought I had escaped.

"You're okay," I mumble to myself as I stop my chair. "You're okay." I just need to remember that the world's only a nightmare if I make it that way. Those who hide in darkness can't beat me; those who once thought they could kill me can't anymore. Nothing can break me. Especially not myself.

No matter what's thrown at me, I'll win. I choose not to hide behind the veil of shadows, but to embrace the future of this world whether it's ready for me or not.

5 February 2192

Sean

The sun perches itself atop a fatigued building in the distance as it sends a wave of light through the glass and into my eyes. I roll over toward Elise.

"That's bright," she whispers as she rubs her eyes.

"And beautiful," I say.

"But mainly bright," she laughs. "Can't it just go away for another hour or two?"

"That would be great," I laugh.

Wrapping my arm around her waist, I pull myself closer as she nuzzles her head into my chest. *I can't lose this*, I think. *I can't lose her*.

Amidst the chaos of the outside, the one thing that's allowed me to feel safe has been her. Despite her fears, it's her strength and everything she embodies that's kept me from floating adrift. Without her, I'd be worthless. Without her, I could be dead.

I sit up and look out into the sunlight. Marcus walks over. "You ready to head back?" he asks.

"Can we get some time to wake up?" I grin.

"I guess so," he laughs. "I've just always been an early bird out here. I can't ever really sleep no matter how comfortable I am."

"I know what you mean," smirks Elise as she sits up. "You just can't let the fear in, and you'll sleep like a baby. I mean, for once, I just had a great night's sleep."

"Me too," smiles Sam as he throws his shirt on and takes a seat next to Marcus.

I slowly stand up—an ache coursing through my back and into my legs—and make my way toward Malcolm. Happily smiling, he hands out morning food rations to everyone. Meager as it may be, a handful of berries and a bottle of water are more than enough for me right now. I nod and take my keep before walking back toward Elise.

Picking off the blueberries from the stem, I take a seat next to Marcus.

"How are you feeling this morning?" he asks, taking a sip of water.

"Tired, but ready," I mumble as a small piece of stem catches on my back teeth. Picking it out, I take a drink and rub my eyes. "It's going to be a long walk."

"Definitely. I'm not entirely sure if I even remember the route."

"I think I have a general idea," I say.

Marcus's lips move like he's going to speak, but nothing comes out. After a few seconds, he forms a crooked smile and bites into his drying lips. "I'm glad I'll never have to take that re-entrance test."

"I'm glad none of you will ever have to take it," I smile.

There's nothing more frightening than the moment you're abruptly grabbed from the outside to take your test. The second the Elites show up, your heart stops. I tried not to worry about it, but it was impossible. No amount of preparation can make you ready for those questions. Even if you think you're sane, they could say you're not and next thing you know. . .you're dead. It's a grim fate this world has thrown at us.

"What was it like?" he mutters.

"I can imagine it felt like walking toward the noose before being hanged. Your body sort of clams up and shuts down while your mind runs rampant. You don't know if your words can free you, but you have to believe you've proved yourself on the outside. It's very unpleasant," I say as the sweat runs down my wrists. "I feel sick just thinking about it."

I shake my head and wipe my hands on my pants. Elise places her hand on my shoulder.

"What were the questions?" asks Marcus.

"There were three questions. Simple ones, really. First, they ask you your name. Sounds easy enough, but they have a board behind the guard who asks you the questions. The board has numbers, one, two, and three on it. Each number has a certain amount of exes next to it referencing where previous kids failed." I take a drink of water. "You'd be surprised how many there were beside question one."

"What were the other two?" pries Marcus.

"The next one was the same thing you recite in school every day. 'Are you prepared to work, think, act and do as an Elite would do?' Even if you don't mean it, you have to answer 'yes' quickly." I take a breath and look over at Marcus. "The final question was, 'Are you here to revolt against Nimbus?'"

"How did you answer that one?"

"As quick as I could, I said I wasn't."

"I'm glad they couldn't see through your lie," he smiles.

"Yea, but I won't forget that experience. They hold a gun to your head the whole time."

"How do they expect you to act normal when fear is running down your neck?"

"I really don't know. That 10 percent return rate isn't a joke. I'm sure a lot of kids see the gun, get scared, and try to flee. You just have to calm yourself and hope you'll get through," I pause, "because fear doesn't give you a second chance in Nimbus."

"Well, I'm glad you made it. I mean, your situation behind the wall didn't sound too gratifying, but at least now you get a chance to kill that bastard," smiles Marcus.

"And I won't miss it."

I stand up. The warm glow of the sun spreads across my neck. I scratch the side of my head as my mind envisions the cold steel pressed into my skull. Shaking it off, I turn toward Elise as she stuffs a few berries into her mouth.

"When ar' 'e headin' out?" she asks while swallowing her food.

"Once everyone is ready," I reply.

"We're ready," says Abby as she rolls up her sleeves and rests her head on Sam's shoulder.

"Yup," he casually mutters while fidgeting with his fingers.

"Soon," I smile.

I look around as everyone shoves berries down their gullet. One by one, each person consumes his or her morning rations like they'll get more for eating quicker. But that's not the case. Food won't last as long for this many of us.

I inhale.

The empty skyline dips into my peripherals. I turn my head and watch as the sun hides itself behind a blanket of clouds, slowly fading from its peak to become nothing more than an all-too-familiar gray.

I exhale.

I grab my backpack and walk toward Marcus. I nod as I approach him.

He takes a breath and addresses the room. "Is everyone ready?"

With separated nods and mumbles, everyone seems ready. Though no one wants to admit it aloud, none of us really are. Too many of these kids haven't experienced the true horrors of what lies out there. They may have survived a night or two when they were fourteen, but that was it. There's no protection out there. There's no library to hide in.

Maneuvering past each other toward the door, we start to form a staggered line. Once everyone lines up, we slowly head into the stairwell.

I grab ahold of Elise's hand and flick the back of the lighter with the other. With my arm extended, I hold out the flame and guide the group down the abandoned stairwell. Each step loudly echoes throughout the hall as the twenty-some of us trudge down the remaining floors back into the front atrium.

Quickly managing our way down and out of the area, we step into the main hall of the building. The endless windows remain unscathed by decay; the wind gently tossing broken twigs and leaves against them. Hurrying down the broken escalators toward the ivy-ridden entryway, I turn my focus toward the exit.

"This is it," I exhale. Lifting up the lifeless vines, I hold them against the glass as everyone crouches under and into the open air. I step out last. The limp ivy drops behind me; I wipe the dirt from my shoulders.

"Why don't you take charge, Sean," motions Marcus from the front of the pack.

"Yea, just hold on," I say as I near Elise.

"Do you want us up there with you?" she asks.

"Yea. You might know the way back better than me since you had to go back to find Sam in the first place."

"I have a slight idea, but I don't know for sure."

"Any idea will help," I half-smile as I grab her hand.

Lazily walking our way toward the front of the group, a slight gust brushes against my chest. I pull my sleeves down. Leaves rustle against the curb.

"I've always wondered what this place used to look like," says Marcus, slowing his strides beside us as he takes in the overcast landscape.

"I can imagine it wasn't as dark," I say.

"Definitely. I bet, in a way, it was very ostentatious. I can just see all the lights, all the people, all the traffic, everything. The city probably never stopped moving," he says while slowly spinning around, aimlessly staring at the now-shoddy city.

"I bet it was beautiful," smiles Elise. "If we were here a hundred years ago, I bet we'd love it. And now. . .now, it's just a dreary dump."

"Maybe someday it'll come alive again," voices Marcus as he turns back toward us. "Maybe someday, we'll be back to rebuild."

"Someday," I say as a soft crack of thunder breaks across the skyline.

As much as a return here seems ideal, there will always be a nagging fear that we might never come back. This city's been a nightmare and a salvation all in one; it's disorienting. The inherent burden of death will always sit in this city. The idea that once you get in, you can't get out, will always be a part of this place.

Even though Arthur's dead, there's something more. There's something we haven't seen before. And I just have this feeling that whatever or whoever was guiding him, is something or someone whose death might not save us. No matter where we run or what we do, we can't kill that fear. All we can do is try to hide it.

"I hope so," mumbles Marcus.

"Me too," says Elise. "Anywhere is better than Nimbus as long as the Elites and the Lurkers aren't apart of it."

"Not everywhere," I mutter.

"What do you mean?" asks Elise.

"I don't know. We've talked about it in the past, but there's always the chance that there are others out here. . .and. . .and we don't know if they're dangerous or not," I say, trying to piece together the jumbled thoughts running around my mind.

"And what if there are others? And what if they're just like us?" questions Marcus.

"Then I guess we have nothing to worry about, but there's always the chance that there's more to this world than what we've discovered," I reply.

"That's right, but we've never seen any outsiders. We've never run into anything different."

"I know, I know," I mutter. "I'm just saying that maybe somewhere better doesn't exist. Maybe the best the world will ever be is the brief moments of victory after we kill MacMillan. Maybe then, maybe after the chaos calms and the dust settles, we'll experience something better, but how long will that last? How long can anything last in a world built upon survival of the fittest?" I ask as my stomach tenses. "Everything good always comes to an end."

"But it doesn't have to if it's *our* world," retorts Marcus. "We have the ability to build something the world's never seen. We have the chance to start from scratch, to establish an orderly world structured on the foundations of integrity, honesty, and justice."

"I know, Marcus. I'm just saying, no world is perfect. No matter how you draw it up, is there truly an escape from the unknowable? Is there ever a way past self-destruction to discover the unknown?"

"Yea, if we discover it ourselves," says Elise. "If we take the chance to see what this world's truly made of; then, we can achieve a better world. We just have to keep our heads up and believe what we're doing is right. If it's wrong, we learn. If it's right, we keep going."

"I guess," I shrug.

"She makes a point," states Marcus. "I guess the only way for a better world to exist is if we find it ourselves."

"Well, maybe someday we'll do just that," I say, jumping over a small chasm in the street.

"Maybe we will," smiles Elise.

I don't reply. We round a corner toward the library; or what's left of it.

The blackened walls hang loosely against the beams that once supported them as a plethora of books lie scattered in the streets. Some sit face-down in puddles, while others sporadically lie split in half and covered in ash around the street. The once-tall, pristine windows in the entryway have become nothing more than empty rectangles held together by crooked steel bars. Beyond the non-existent windows sits a mound of ash with half-burnt shelves poking out. But none of that is as troubling as the spiral staircase. As if the flames avoided it, the staircase remains intact, but pointless. It leads to nothing.

Marcus diverts his eyes toward the end of the street, but I can't look away. I have to see what a future out here can do even if I've seen it a million times before. I've felt what it can do, I've seen what it can do to others, but I've never felt this. I've never wanted so much for so many, but been this afraid to do something. At this point, all I can do is believe in every reason that's kept me alive thus far—in everything that's kept this group alive.

I turn toward Marcus. "Are you okay?" I ask as I place my hand on his shoulder.

"I'll be fine. It's just tough," he says with a slight sniffle. "That was our home."

"And we'll find a new one soon enough. Let's just keep moving."

"Yea, it's probably for the best. I don't want my mind to run back into the fire."

I nod and glance back at the building as the wind sends ash into the air behind us. It glides through the sky like leaves blowing on an autumn morning—searching for a place to sit, a place to collect itself, but it finds nothing. Instead, it aimlessly blows farther into the city, eventually hiding itself under a canopy of collapsed brick.

As we near the edge of the city, the trees jump into our line of sight. "Finally," I mumble. "It's not like we really had to walk that far," laughs Elise.

"But still," I say. "It feels nice to see something other than this place."

"I know what you mean," she smiles.

"I haven't been in the forest in years," says Marcus. "I'm excited and afraid."

"There's nothing to fear," I say. *There's nothing to fear.* Nearing the crooked railroad nestled in a body of trees at the end of the road, I look around. "We're past the point of being afraid."

Nodding, he tightens his grip on his backpack as he continues to move forward.

The closer we get to the tracks, the more I can see the body of that choked boy buried in the mud. My mind quickly wanders into the woods, into the trees where I killed to survive, where Elise and I fought off vagrants to earn another night. Back to where I almost died in the dead of winter alone. *I want to run*, I think. But I can't. I can't let my inner sorrows overpower my exterior strength. I can't let anyone see my struggles. *I have to lead.*

As we step over the tracks behind the trees, I glance back once more. "Say goodbye to the city."

"There's no need for that, Sean. We'll be coming back," says Marcus.

"Maybe."

"We will," smiles Elise as her thumb rubs against the back of my hand. "It's a good place to start."

Her fingers gently graze the drying skin around my knuckles as my palms start to grow moist. I keep thinking about every run-in with fear, every encounter with vagrants that Elise and I had, and I'm just hoping that doesn't happen again. I almost want the forest to be dead just so we don't have to deal with other people.

"Which way should we go? Should we just keep moving forward?" I ask.

"I think so," says Elise. "Maybe just keep walking until we see an empty field or the farmhouse."

"O-okay," I stutter as I pull my hands out from her grip and wipe them on my sweatshirt. The moisture fades for a brief second only to instantly return the moment I remove them from the cotton. *Damn it.*

We traipse past discolored, leafless trees as their branches wave in the wind. Various insects crawl along giant mud-ridden patches ahead of us. Seemingly forced out by a storm that didn't hit the city, the bugs flee from our path as the clouds open back up.

With each step through the muck, our footprints mark themselves behind us. They create a way back—a way I don't know if I'll ever decide to follow, but it's good to know it exists. No matter

289

how unbearable it is to deal with constantly soaked feet, it comes with the territory. Every step through the mud is another step toward the inside, another stride toward ridding the agony that comes with this game.

Tugging on the back of my sweater, Abby stops us. "What should we do about the rain?"

"We can't do anything," I say.

"I know, but should we find a place to camp until it ends?"

"What do you think, Marcus?"

"I say we keep walking until it gets too bad. If it becomes a nightmare, we'll huddle together until it ends because that's about all we can do."

"He's got a point," says Elise. "Let's just keep going."

I grab her hand. She smiles as we continue to wander through the forest in search of any sign that could guide us back *home*.

Every second we're out here feels like a minute, while every minute starts to feel like an hour. The rain ceases to stop as each step opens up the forest; the clouds grow darker, but the path clears. I can't see everything ahead of me, but I know I won't run into a tree.

"We should probably find a place to camp," says Sam.

"I agree," mumbles Abby. "I'm getting tired of walking."

"We all are," shouts Ella from behind. "Let's settle here."

"Alright, everyone, try to find somewhere dry, under a tree preferably," says Marcus while turning to address everyone. "If you can get a fire going, keep it small. We don't want to attract any unwanted attention."

"And if you hear or see anything that isn't one of us, let everyone know immediately. These woods are dangerous. Just because one man is dead doesn't mean we're in the clear," I say firmly.

"Where should we sleep?" asks Elise. Spreading her wet bangs across her forehead, she looks into my eyes. "I have no preference because all ground is the same."

"You pick. I'll probably stay awake for a few more hours and keep watch anyways."

"Okay," she answers as she heads toward an opening beneath two crooked trees nearly intertwined above.

I shift toward Marcus. He uneasily looks around the area, almost reluctant to even sit down. "I can't remember the last time I slept outside."

I feign a smile and look around at everyone else inefficiently trying to find a place to set up for the night. Some stand with hands on hips bemusedly searching the space while others sit atop their backpacks and lean against trees. Ella's already asleep. Malcolm's scratching his head and crookedly staring at me. I point at Ella. He smiles. "Good luck sleeping," I say to Marcus. "You won't get much."

"I think I'll just read," he replies before walking toward Malcolm, who's still aimlessly looking around.

"That's probably a good idea," I reply before moving back to Elise. Lying on her shoulder upon her sleeping bag, she smiles at me. I watch as the clouds behind her start to disperse into the sky, slipping behind the yellow of the moon. "Comfy?" I ask.

"It'll suffice."

I prop my backpack against the decaying bark beside Elise before unraveling my sleeping bag.

"I thought you were going to stay up?"

"I am. I'm just going to rest my eyes for a minute."

Drifting into the solitude of my mind, I start to relax beside Elise. I inhale. A soft flickering finds its way behind my eyelids before I have a chance to exhale. *Go away*, I think as the shining moves back and forth. I roll over. It doesn't leave. Irritated, I open my eyes as someone shrieks. Quickly jolting up, I hit my head on a small branch as she shouts once more.

"Body!" she screams.

I'm forced out my short-lived relaxation and into a state of panic. *Who's screaming?* I think.

"Over here!" shouts Marcus.

"Where?" I loudly reply as I stand up. "Where is it?" Quickly moving toward a few people standing in a semi-circle, I step through.

"Look ahead," says Marcus.

I squint, but I can't see anything. I take another step forward. Just ahead, the small frame of someone sitting perched against a tree holding onto a glass bottle pierces my sight. I can't see a face. I can just see flesh. Next to that person, another body with slashes of dried blood across its naked back lies face down. "What do you think happened?"

"One of those must be a Lurker," he says.

"Why do you say that? I don't see a scar."

"It just has to be one."

"It doesn't have to be anything," says Elise as she steps beside me. "For all we know, whatever happened, happened several days ago."

"No matter what happened or when it happened, it's not a good sign," I say. "We're lucky it's only two people and not more." Another scream echoes.

"Another body!" screams Rosie.

"Where?" I ask aloud.

"Turn around," she says.

As I do, the naked body of a woman facedown in the mud runs across my blurred vision. I avert my stare. *How did we not see these ten minutes ago?*

"What do we do?" asks Marcus, his voice cracking.

"We have to keep moving," I say. "This area isn't safe."

"Those bodies weren't there when we set up camp," mutters Malcolm, his voice shaking. "Those bodies weren't there five minutes ago."

Biting his lip, Marcus raises his hand. "You heard the man. Pack up, we have to keep moving."

292

6 February 2192

Sam

It's hard to not feel like the fateful eyes of *him* are still on
you. With what we've seen since leaving the city, it's as if the
Lurkers have gotten stronger, or at least more reckless. Their shadow
never seems to disappear. It's like Arthur was just a catalyst in
something bigger than us—something bigger than Nimbus—and it
makes my chest constrict.

"How much farther should we go?" asks Elise. "It has to be
sometime after midnight."

"Until we haven't seen a body for hours," replies Sean.

We haven't seen one for at least an hour and the last one we
saw was a woman facedown in the mud again. Malcolm went toward
the body and said that it wasn't a Lurker. He said it was just a girl
trying to survive when she came across some bad luck, which, to me,
sounds like she encountered the plight we've been trying to escape
since day one.

And if seeing another body means anything to me, it's that no
one should be out here alone. I don't know how Sean did it. I don't
know how Elise managed. I can't imagine being out here by myself
for more than a split second. At least when I was in the prison, I had
walls. I wasn't in the cold dark of night wandering. I didn't feel the
still finger of death pressed against my neck. I suffered, but I wasn't
killed. I wasn't stripped and thrown into the black.

I'm still breathing.

It would be a nightmare in this forest with nothing but hope
on your side. It's bad enough when someone's trying to kill you

even when you have others with you. Hope can't save you. It can just make the knife hurt a little less.

I turn around and look at Abby. She extends her arm. I help her over a mossy trunk. Grabbing her cold fingers, I intertwine them in mine.

"It's at least been an hour since I've seen anything," she says.

"Same here," I say.

"Let's just go a little farther," shouts Sean from behind as he guides his flashlight around the woods.

Holding onto the miniature flashlight with my thumb and index finger, I casually maneuver it around the path in front of us. Yet, the more I move it around, the clearer the area seems. "I feel safe here," I mumble.

"Me too," replies Abby as she turns her hand into a fist and buries it in my palm. "I just want to sleep. I'm exhausted and cold."

"Yea, I am too. I feel like we've spent the last twenty-four hours walking."

Slowing our pace as Sean, Elise, and Marcus pass us, Abby and I take a few steps back to the middle of the group. With a few people a dozen or so feet behind us, I step close to her and wrap my arm around her shoulders. She leans toward my chest as our pace starts to slow.

"Do you remember our first few nights out here?" she asks.

"Yea, they were rough. I try not to think about it." *Phil's humor. Being lost. Utter darkness.* I shake my head.

"We spent our whole first day just walking around. We slept next to a group of muddy branches because we thought no one would care to look," she laughs.

I chuckle as I look over at her. "It was all Phil's idea."

"Yea, I guess it was. It was great until we woke up with a few bugs crawling down our legs. That was awful," says Abby as she sticks out her tongue in a state of disgust.

"It really was. That was probably the last time anything funny really happened out here. It's been out of control ever since," I say bitterly.

"Yea," she softly replies. "That was the one of the few days we had with Phil."

Unsure of what to say, I tighten my grip on her shoulders.

Abby looks over at me. "Imagine if he was still alive. Do you think that would have changed anything that's happened to us?"

"I doubt it," I say. "Fate has a weird way of playing itself out and I think even if he survived that day, it would have found its way to him eventually. It's sort of playing a longer game with us."

"I guess so. We've been through a lot since then. You losing part of your finger, someone almost killing us at the shack, me almost getting killed at the farm, you getting captured, Arthur dying. We've been through just about every bad thing imaginable out here," she says. "I just hope it brightens up at some point."

"I'm sure it will. It hasn't even been a year yet. It has to." I say quietly.

They say every good thing comes to end, yet each time I think about it, I believe a little less that there are any good things left in this world.

"As much as I hate constantly being afraid, I'm glad that I've gotten to spend most of it with you," mutters Abby.

"Me too," I say. "I'm glad that all the distress hasn't forced us apart."

"Every day alive really makes you appreciate everything you have," she smiles.

"It really does," I say as my brain scatters, preventing me from saying anything else.

At this point, I sort of want to kiss her on the cheek, but I'm nervous. I don't want to make anything awkward. I just want her to know that I won't let anything happen to us again; that I'm not going anywhere and I won't allow myself to be a coward. I just want her to know everything will be okay and that I'll always be there for her.

"Thanks for staying with me," she says as she leans in and presses her lips against my cheek.

Instantly, my face flushes with red. I can feel a slight tingle run down my spine.

"N-n-no problem," I stutter. The word 'idiot' climbs into my brain as I awkwardly shine my flashlight at Abby while trying to pretend I was just scouring the area more. "Sorry," I mumble as she waves down the light.

She laughs and wraps her arm around my waist.

I shyly grin as I guide my light toward Sean.

"Yea?" he responds, nodding for me to aim my light elsewhere.

"Can we rest now? We haven't seen anything in a long time."

Quickly looking over at Elise, she nods her head as Sean answers. "Sure. Let's set up camp here."

I smile at Abby. "Finally."

"Where should we set up?" she asks.

Aimlessly pointing my flashlight around the woods, nothing grabs my attention. The vast emptiness—aside from the trees—of the field intrigues me, but exhaustion weighs heavier on my mind. I'm just hoping I don't see anyone or anything in the darkness. "Why not right here?" I say.

"Okay," she mumbles.

Slowly pulling the sleeping bag off the top of my backpack, I unravel it; my bandage catches itself on the zipper in the process. I try to force it out, but it won't budge. I yank and yank, but that's only tearing it. After several failed attempts to unhook the gauze, I end up ripping it out. As the padding tears, the scarring atop my finger thrusts its way into my vision. It's the first time I've really seen it and yet, it doesn't faze me. It's ugly and discolored, but it's something I have to live with.

"Are you okay?" asks Abby as she sets her sleeping bag next to mine.

"Yea," I quickly reply. "I'm fine."

"Do you want me to find Elise so she can rewrap it?"

"No, it's okay. I'll let it breathe for a night."

"If you say so. It might be sensitive, so be careful."

I muster up a quiet, "I will" as I accidentally press it into the dirt, causing a quick zipper-like sensation to course through the scar. I try to conceal my pain through an awkward smile.

Opening my backpack, I grab the gray sweatshirt Marcus gave me at the library. It's a little big, but if I fold it just right it can be the perfect pillow. As I tuck the hood under the back of the sweatshirt, I slide into my sleeping bag and try to rest my head. A cool gust pushes past us as Abby inches her sleeping bag closer to mine. I turn around and reach my arm around her shoulder while I use my other hand to click off the flashlight.

With nothing but the gloom of the night sky encompassing us, I close my eyes.

Elise

I awake to the discomfort of my makeshift pillow: also known as Sean's shoulder. Despite its lackluster abilities at soothing my aching head, I still managed to get some sleep. I roll over onto my sleeping bag; now, my head virtually rests against the dirt.

"Good morning," I mumble as Sean stretches his arm across my chest.

"Morning."

I press my palms against the ground—my fingers lightly sink into the mud. I push out my bottom lip and let out a slight, "ugh." The sun slowly crawls above the trees as if it, too, is exhausted. I lean toward Sean and stand up. My ankles pop.

Locking my hands together, I push outward. My knuckles crack. I let out a quiet sigh of relief as Sean stands up and does the same. Though, the sound of his knuckles cracking makes it seem like he cracked everything twice without a second thought.

"That's gross," I laugh.

"But it was much needed," he smiles.

Walking toward us, Marcus cracks his neck. "How did you guys sleep?"

"Crappy," I quickly reply.

"Same here. I stayed on guard for the first hour or so, but after that I couldn't get myself to fall asleep. I stared at the sky for what seemed like hours," he yawns.

"Did you see anything when you were on guard?" asks Sean.

Lightly biting the dry skin off his bottom lip, Marcus nods.

"What did you see?" I ask.

"Another body. I noticed it in the distance, but I didn't see anyone else. I just saw what looked like a face staring at me. It didn't move either, so I assume it was lifeless."

"Why didn't you alert any of us?" asks Sean.

"I didn't want to alarm anyone. I knew it was dead, so I didn't want to wake anyone up. We haven't gotten much sleep for a few days now. The least I could do was allow them some rest," Marcus stiffly replies. Turning his focus to the side, he glances around.

"That's fine then," Sean says. "Maybe we should walk toward the body to ensure that it was nothing more than that."

"By all means."

"Do you know which way it was?" I ask.

"I think that way," he says as he points to our right. "I didn't look back once I caught its eyes the first time. The blank stare of death is frightening. It latches onto your chest and tries to pull out your heart. It feels like it wants to claim you, too."

He's right. The glazed-over eyes of a corpse are a demoralizing sight, especially when you know the victim was innocent. Just as the twins were when Sean and I were hunting. *They didn't know what they were doing; they didn't know how to protect themselves*, I think as the expressionless gazes of their limp bodies jumps into my mind. Trying to stave off the memory, I shake my head. *Disappear*, I think. *Disappear*. "It's not pleasant," I mutter.

"But we still need to check to make sure that it was something," says Sean. "If your mind's playing tricks on you then we can always take more time to rest."

"I know what I saw. Something was staring back at me with unblinking eyes. Something was out there."

"I believe you," I say.

"Thanks," he says as he clips the straps from his backpack around his waist. "After you find it, we should head out," he adds before turning around and walking toward Ella.

I nod and turn toward Sean. "What's going on out here? If we can't find one safe spot to rest, then who's to say there's any comfort out here?"

"There won't be comfort out here until we get to the wall, Elise. We both know that. I know as much as you do as to why these bodies are building up and just like you, I hate it. It's sickening," says Sean. Bending over to roll up his sleeping bag, he yawns before tucking it atop his backpack. "Let's just try to focus on getting to Nimbus."

298

I mumble a half-hearted "okay" as I lean down to roll up my bed.

I'm not sure why there are so many bodies out here and I don't know if I want to know. Whether it's the Lurkers, the Elites, or some other group, someone clearly knows what we're doing. Each step closer to Nimbus guarantees someone will die. Even if it's not instantaneous, it's inevitable. Someone doesn't want us to go home. I just hope that person gets what's coming.

"Elise, are you ready to go?" yells Sam.

"Yea," I answer. I tuck my sleeping bag atop my backpack and shout, "I'll be there in a second!"

Pulling my bag over my shoulders, I take a deep breath and look around the forest. I don't recognize where we are. Though, it's hard to tell the difference when you're constantly immersed in trees.

"Let's go!" shouts Sean.

"Coming!" I yell back. Quickly moving in Sean's direction, I grab ahold of his hand. "Are we heading toward the body?"

"Yea, Marcus says it wasn't too far away."

"What if it's not there?"

"He seems pretty adamant that it's there. If it's not then maybe he's just exhausted," says Sean.

"Or maybe something else took the body?"

"What do you mean? There aren't any supernatural creatures or beings that exist out here. This isn't science fiction, Elise."

"I'm not saying it is. Just, what if the body wasn't a Lurker? What if it was someone else and it was taken away by a Lurker?"

"That could be it. If it's not there, maybe a Lurker just dragged it away. Let's just hope what he saw was real," says Sean. "I'd prefer it if he wasn't delusional."

"Even if nothing's there, I don't think he is. This world loves to play tricks on the innocent," I say. The more innocent you are, the tougher it is to live out here. If you have one second of doubt, you become a target for *them*; you become a piece of glass just waiting to be broken.

"It really does," mutters Sean.

From ahead, Marcus stops. "It was over here somewhere. Everyone look around. If you see a body, notify the rest of us."

As we come to a stop, Sean lets go of my fingers. "I'm going to look over here, you go over there," he says pointing toward a small gathering of stumps.

"Okay," I nod, rolling up my sleeves in the process.

I turn around and start to walk toward the wounded stumps. Some sit higher than others while a majority of them lie next to their fallen timber. Covered in moss beneath a canopy of crooked branches, the broken trees sit unwavering in the light breeze. As I jump onto a stump to get a better view, I notice everyone else slowly meandering around the area. It seems as if we all believe Marcus, but there's nothing to justify his claims.

I step down from the broken trunk and start to traipse around the breadth of trees. Yet, the more I wander around, the less viable this venture is becoming. I don't see anything or anyone outside of our group. "I don't see anything," I say to myself as Sean starts walking toward me.

"I didn't see anything either. I don't think there was anyone out here."

"I know what I saw," says Marcus as he starts walking toward us. "I saw eyes. I know it!"

"Your mind could be messing with you, Marcus," says Sean. "We can always stop and rest if you need."

"I'm not tired. I saw something out here, Sean. Granted, it's probably better if there isn't anything."

"True," I mumble. "Maybe we should just get going then?"

"That's probably a good idea," nods Sean.

As we turn around to signal for everyone else to follow us, I can't help but feel that being outside of the library is starting to bother Marcus. Maybe being in one place for a majority of his time out here has made him more vulnerable than us; maybe the outside is finally starting to toy with him. I can imagine it feels like being thrown outside of Nimbus all over again and if he wasn't scared the first time, maybe this time around he will be.

After a few minutes, everyone reunites from their separate searches. "Did anyone see anything?" asks Marcus aloud.

Everyone shakes his or her head in unison.

"Malcolm? Did you notice anything out of the ordinary?"

"Nothing, Marcus. I didn't see anything and neither did Ella," he replies, Ella nodding lightly next to him.

300

"Rosie?"

"Nothing," she says. "I didn't see anything out of the ordinary."

As Marcus goes around asking everyone individually despite his or her disapproving nods from the beginning, he seems to grow more and more frustrated. "I know I saw something!" he shouts.

"We've all felt like we've seen something before," I say. "This place messes with everyone in different ways. We just have to keep moving and not let this one instance get into our heads."

"Yea, we've seen a few bodies already. Not seeing another is probably a good thing," says Sam while Abby nods in agreement next to him.

"Sam's right," says Sean. "The less we see, the better. Let's just keep moving."

The more he mindlessly looks around, the more apparent Marcus's distress is becoming.

"It's just one thing. I don't get why he's getting so worked up about it," I say to Sean.

"Me either, I'll go talk to him."

"Okay," I smirk as I start to walk toward Sam and Abby.

With each step through the drying muck, I notice everyone's attention is focused on Marcus. They've known him for years to the point that seeing him thwarted by such a minimal issue must be upsetting. Especially since he's always been calm enough to the point that his peaceful behavior has imbued feelings of contentment in all of us. *I hope he's okay*, I think as I step onto something squishy.

"Elise!" shouts Sam.

"What?" I say, taken aback.

"Don't look down," he says.

"Why? What did I step on?"

"Just keep moving and don't look down," he says.

"Why not?" I ask again. "What did I step on?"

"Marcus!" yells Sam. "Come here!"

"Sam! What are you talking about?!" I shout as I remain still. "I'm moving."

I take another step off the mush toward Sam as Marcus and Sean stop beside him, out of breath.

"I told you I saw something!" shouts Marcus.

"What? What did you see?" I ask as Abby grabs ahold of me and turns me around.

"Look down," she says.

I slowly tilt my gaze downward into the mud. There, sits an eye. Not just one half-smushed one, but two half-smushed ones pressed into the ground. I immediately look away—the horrific image trying to latch itself into my mind. "That's disgusting," I say.

"Disgusting, but it's what we were looking for," says Sean.

"When I knew something was looking back at me, I didn't think this would be what it was," says Marcus. "This just means that there's something else out here that could be worse than the Lurkers."

"That, or the Lurkers are starting to lose any composure they once had," I say. "This is nasty."

"But it's what we figuratively needed to see," says Marcus. "This just means we could find a body we don't want to later on."

"Gross," exhales Abby as she shakes her head in disgust.

"Can we just get moving now?" I ask. "I don't want to be around this anymore."

Turning around, Marcus waves his arm into the sky. "Let's go!" he shouts.

Quickly grabbing ahold of Sean's hand as we step away from the unseeing eyes, I stride toward the front of the group.

"Do you know which way to go?" I ask.

"Sort of," he says. "The sun hasn't been up too long, so we just need to stay on the path we were on."

"Sounds good."

"Hey Elise," says Abby from behind us.

"Yea?"

Seemingly troubled, she asks, "Why do you think there have been so many bodies out here lately?"

"I know as much as you do and I don't like it either," I reply.

"Do you think we'll see more as we get closer to Nimbus?"

"I hope not."

"But what if we do?"

"I don't know, Abby. We just need to keep our heads up and not focus on that right now."

"Exactly," mutters Sean. "We're all mystified as to what's going on, but it's something we have to push past if we don't want to end up like them."

"Has it crossed your mind that maybe other survivors like us have been killing the Lurkers?" asks Sam.

Not really, I think. The thought of others killing the people who terrorized us for so long never stepped into my mind. "If it is other survivors, why would one go through such horrifying measures to kill someone? Gouging someone's eyes out is not normal."

"It really isn't, but what the Lurkers did wasn't either," he says.

"I guess there really isn't such a thing as normalcy or decency out here," says Sean. "Maybe we should just stop talking about it and focus on getting back to Nimbus."

"If you say so," Sam says.

"I do."

"One more thing: do you think the Lurkers are fleeing back to the wall like us?" he asks.

"It's a possibility, but they'd have no reason to return when they're the ones who like it out here," answers Sean.

I tighten my grip on his hand as we simultaneously duck underneath a branch caught between two trees.

Sam could be right, but the idea of those monsters doing what we're doing doesn't make much sense. Yes, they're cowards, but they have no reason to flee to the wall when they'd be shot on sight just as we would be without a plan. It's almost as if a lack of leadership has scrambled their brains into giant puddles of idiocy— even if they somehow weren't that way already.

"How close do you think we are?" I ask as I roll my sleeves back down.

"I don't know. Hopefully less than a day or two. I'm sure we'll start to recognize the terrain eventually," says Sean.

Hopefully.

Marcus stops.

"Marcus?" I say.

"Why'd you stop?" asks Sean.

"Come up here," he says.

Hurrying toward him with our backpacks shifting in rhythm, he holds out his arm. "Look," he says.

"Where?" I ask.

"There," he responds, pointing several feet ahead and to the left.

There, a few bodies sit slung to a tree. Each sits with its back pressed against the bark while its head droops downward. A long, black rope digs tightly into their bare chests as dried blood slathers their stomachs.

"What. . .happened. . .?" I quietly ask.

Sean and Marcus step closer to the bodies. Tilting their heads downward in unison to see if they can recognize any of the faces, they both jump backward immediately.

"N-no. . ." mumbles Marcus. "No. . ."

"It can't be," says Sean.

I try to tilt my head down to see if I can see what they're seeing, but I can't. The smear of red around the men's faces is all I notice. "What did you see?" I ask.

"They're gone," says Marcus.

"What's gone?"

"Eyes. . ." he quietly replies.

"We have to keep moving then," I say, my jaw stiffening as a shiver runs down my spine. "We can't stay here. Something is hunting them and it could be hunting us, too."

"Let's just keep going then," says Marcus. "But whatever is doing this to them might be avoiding us."

"Why?" asks Sam.

"Well, nothing has happened to us yet."

"That's because these deaths could be warning signs that we need to turn around. Maybe we're heading in the wrong direction and we're not wanted."

"That could be true, or maybe whatever was pulling them this way is also pulling us this way? Maybe we need to keep moving to see what's at the end," replies Marcus.

"Why should we keep moving after this?" asks Abby.

"Because we have to," answers Sean. "We have to keep moving because we have to put an end to this torment. These bodies are a sign of what this world is like and we can't stand for this to continue any longer. We have to keep moving or else we could end up just like them. Cowardice is for those unable to move past fear; resilience is for those who can."

304

Without responding, we continue to move forward as Marcus and Sean start walking past the bodies.

With each step, it feels like my first week out here all over again. Something could be pulling others toward the wall, just as something pulled me into the city. It almost feels that our journey was for nothing, that this is where everything ends.

7 February 2192

Sean

A dark bank of clouds blocks the sun as a light breeze rustles through the forest. Branches quiver as the clouds grow thicker amidst an empty sky. It feels like the daunting power of nature is trying to hamper our attempt to get to the wall. It's almost as if it wants us to give up.

I peer past several branches in search of the path toward Nimbus, but the more we walk, the further it hides itself from my sight.

It's been days since we left the city, days since we've seen any recognizable landmark. It's frustrating. Sometimes it seems like we're lost to the point that we might as well meander through the forest in search of nothing. If we're not doing that already, then I don't know what we're doing. Nobody knows exactly where to go because they've been away far too long. It's nearly impossible for me to be the guide when the very place that kicked me out is what we're in search of. I feel like a criminal searching for a petty crime just to get himself back behind bars, back where he has some semblance of life.

"Do you know where we are, Sean?" asks Marcus as he steps up beside me, his long, self-made walking stick jamming into a log next to us.

Unsure of what to say, I nod. "Sort of." Really, I don't. I'm just as lost as everyone else, but I won't admit it. We've come too far for me to tell them the truth; we've overcome too much for me to throw it all away. I turn my head from side to side in search of the path back toward the wall, but it remains hidden. It would be great if something would jump out at me.

"The path has to be around here somewhere," says Elise, her fingers slipping from mine as she cranes her neck forward.

"I know, but I can't see it. The clouds aren't helping," I say.

"Just keep your eyes peeled. This area looks familiar."

"Everything looks familiar," I laugh. "But so far, nothing has really proven itself."

"I guess. As much as I don't want to see that path because of what it leads to, I would rather see Nimbus than spend another night out here," replies Elise as her fingers grab ahold of mine again.

"Me too." Despite knowing what lies behind the steel blockade, I'm ready to see if our *home* still exists or if MacMillan used my punishment as a stepping stone. *I hope Mom and Dad are okay.*

With each momentary gaze farther into the woods, nothing jumps out. No bodies. No wall. No Lurkers. Nothing. I hope that means every body we saw wasn't a sign. A sign that might as well have said, 'Wrong Way.' I tighten my grip on Elise's hand.

"What are we supposed to be looking for?" asks Sam from behind me.

"A path. The same one where Elise probably found you. It's really just a straight clearing of trees."

"Do you know if we're close?" questions Abby.

"Unfortunately, no," I mutter. "We just have to keep moving."

With my eyes lingering in search of the invisible, I step into a paltry puddle. "Shit," I mumble under my breath. I can feel the water forcing its way through the soles of my rugged shoes and onto the arch of my foot. My socks instantly cling to my feet as I pull my shoe out. My whole body shakes with ire as I kick my heel atop a stump—prying the mud off the end.

My head starts to throb. I close my eyes. With a violent pulse running across my temple, I press my thumbs into my forehead.

"Are you okay, Sean?" asks Elise.

"I'm fine," I mumble.

"Should we keep going?"

"Give me a minute."

I can feel sweat trickling down my spine as I clench my teeth in frustration. *We need to find the path*, I think as I try to soothe myself. *We need to get home.* The longer we're lost, the easier it will be for me to lose it. The easier it will become for me to blame myself for our sufferings.

We have to be close. I'm not one to get this upset over something so minimal, especially when it doesn't implicate my survival. Though, the longer it takes to get to Nimbus, the longer we'll be alive.

"Okay," I say. "Let's keep moving."

As we push away from the eye of the storm, my vision grabs hold of the emptiness of this world. Even this forest isn't as plush, green, and inhabited as it used to be. Yet, with whatever it's become, we've survived. We've survived on rations, on limited fruits, on partially contaminated water, on fear; we've survived.

I step over a miniscule puddle as it stares back at me— aiming to trick me into its mud just as the other one did. The farther we walk through the misguided misery of this forest, the closer we get to realizing where we came from. With each step, the uncertainty of our future looms larger.

"I think I see something," exclaims Elise as she pulls me forward.

"What? What is it?" I ask.

". . .it's over there," she coyly replies.

"Nimbus?"

"Ye-yes."

"Finally," I say as I try to catch a better glimpse of the wall. I take a few steps forward before jumping onto a low-lying branch. As I grab ahold of the decaying bark of the tree, I dig my nails into the crumbling skin. "There it is," I mumble to myself. The sky mirrored on the wall almost makes it invisible, but the sporadically placed guards at the top make it evident. Nimbus isn't that far away.

"Should we move quicker toward it before the storm hits?" asks Marcus.

"No," I say. "The sooner we rush it, the sooner we'll get shot. They're keen marksmen with suppressed weapons. If they see so much as a leg, it gets hit. . .and nobody, I mean nobody, but the victim will notice at first."

"Then what do you suggest we do?"

"Keep at our pace until I tell us to stop. Once we get to that point, we'll offload our supplies and get into our vantage points," I say firmly. "Plus, we're not on the path yet. We need to get on that and take it for about a half-mile. Once we get to the end, we'll wait for the next Separation."

"Hopefully it's tomorrow," says Elise.

"Fingers crossed," I say as half the group storms past us to get a better look at the wall. "Slow down," I say loudly.

Yet, they don't stop. A dark-haired man pushes past the crowd and steps a few dozen feet ahead of everyone else. With his head crooked as he stares into the distance, he keeps moving forward.

"Thomas," shouts Marcus. "Stop moving."

Seemingly ignoring us, he keeps moving. We take a few steps forward, but he keeps increasing his strides. Eventually, it starts to appear as if he's running. "Thomas!" I shout, but he doesn't stop. The man keeps running toward Nimbus.

"Malcolm!" yells Marcus. "Can you catch up to him?"

"Yea," replies Malcolm as he starts after Thomas.

We remain still with our attentions fixed on Thomas. With his head hung high above his shoulders, he's starting to move at a dead sprint straight through a clearing of trees—one eerily similar to that of the path we've been searching for. With each giant stride into the opening, his speed slows while we move closer and closer to what looks like the clearing we've been looking for.

As Malcolm closes in on Thomas, Thomas falls to the ground. Simultaneously, Malcolm does, too.

Everyone jolts back in fright as they lie immobile hundreds of feet ahead of us. Ella shrieks as Marcus throws his hand over her mouth. "What was that?" he says, unnerved.

"The guards. . ." I say.

"I didn't think we were that close!" he yells as he covers his own mouth.

"Neither did I. MacMillan must have given them free range to shoot anything and everything as far as the eye can see."

"What do we do now?" asks Elise as she moves to comfort Ella.

"I-I don't know. We should probably stay here."

"Then how are we going to know when the next Separation is?" asks Marcus, clearly agitated.

"We'll have to go closer to the wall at night. Only two guards have night vision goggles and they're each on opposite sides of the wall."

"Will there be one on this side?"

"Yea, there's one by the door and he's probably the one who took those two out," I say as I scratch my forehead. "His name is Jaxon. He's the deadliest shot they have."

"How deadly?" asks Marcus as he squints at the wall.

"I'm sure if I threw my shoe out there right now, he could untie the laces in one shot."

Nodding his head in frustration, he throws off his backpack before slamming his back into a nearby tree. "So what now? You never said they would be taking us out from this far away, Sean. I wouldn't have sent Malcolm after him if I knew he was going to be killed!"

"I didn't know," I say, taken aback. I really didn't. MacMillan always had us shooting anything nearby, but he never had us shooting to kill everything we saw. It's as if he doesn't want anyone to return to Nimbus. Maybe a 10 percent return rate is too high for his unrealistic standards. "We were never given orders to kill people this far out when I was up there."

"So what do you suggest we do?"

"Wait. It's just a game to MacMillan. We need to follow our plan, but we can't do it until sunset. . .or until a storm pushes through."

"Luckily, the latter is possible," replies Marcus as he moves toward Ella, who has tears streaming down her face.

"What do we do now?" asks Sam as he comes up from behind me. Fidgeting with his bad finger, he turns to face the wall—or what he can see of it.

"We have to wait. He might think there are others heading toward the wall now," I say.

"Do you think he knows we're coming?"

"I don't know. I don't know how he could know."

Nodding, he says, "There are a lot of things we don't know about this world." Gently placing his hand on my shoulder, he smiles and walks away.

310

I lightly press my forefinger and thumb against the ridge of my nose as I let out a quieted sigh. It's almost gotten to the point that I would rather turn around and walk back to the city than trudge on any farther. We know what's ahead. We know that this day could be our last. I believe in our cause, but I'm starting to become afraid of its path.

Pulling off my backpack, I rest it against a nearby tree as I sit down and push my back into it. I look around the area as Elise, Marcus, and Ella sit in a poorly formed triangle while others sit in a crooked semi-circle around them—each with their heads slumped forward and buried in their hands. I can't help but think this is my fault.

I can't shake the fact that they're dead because of me. Even if Thomas's mind was already made up before I could pull him back, it's still frustrating. *Stop thinking about it, you'll just weaken yourself*, I think as I push the back of my skull into the tree.

"I'm sorry," I mumble in the direction of Ella as I look into the sky.

"It's not your fault," she says. "It's nobody's."

"I guess," I say with my eyes fixed on the darkening clouds heading our direction. "I should have grabbed him. . .I shouldn't have let Thomas go any farther."

"That couldn't have been prevented," says Marcus. "He never seemed content out here. We took him in because we knew he wouldn't survive on his own. He was always a little. . .different, but he was a nice kid."

"Then what about Malcolm? I should have gone after Thomas; not him," I say as I pull my head down.

"That was my choice. . .my instinct," mumbles Marcus. "Malcolm was always willing to do whatever he could to help. . .and. . .without Collin, I figured he would help in any way he could to ensure everyone made it back to Nimbus alive. I shouldn't have told him to go after him. I just didn't know that would happen," cries Marcus as he wipes his face. "This is my fault."

Scooting toward Marcus as she places her arm around his shoulders, Ella nuzzles her head against his as she wipes his face. "It's not your fault. You did the right thing and tomorrow, we'll do the right thing for him. We'll take down Nimbus and we'll kill the bastard who killed him."

Sniffling, Marcus shows a half-smile. "I'll kill him myself."

Something about those words coming from Marcus makes a slight shiver course through my body. I've never heard him sound so relentless, so invigorated by the idea of revenge. It's as if the uncertainty of our fate has made him apathetic, but in a good way. It's those words that instill a sense of hope in me.

"This will be the last night for Nimbus," says Elise as she stands up and walks toward me. "There's no way those cold-blooded murderers get more than one night alive. If Malcolm couldn't have it, neither can they."

I nod in agreement as I look back into the sky. The clouds have started to push toward Nimbus as they loom large overhead. With each passing moment, the atmosphere grows darker.

"I think we should get ready to head toward the wall," I say as I stand up.

In all my time on the outside, it's stormed hundreds of times. It's inevitable. No matter how far we move or how comfortable we get, a storm usually finds its way toward us—each one seemingly worse than the worst one before it. And each time, the storm deprives us of shelter; it takes away any comfort we thought we might have found, but this time it's different. The inclement weather is working for us as if it knows the malicious intent of Nimbus, of MacMillan. It's a paradoxical event—one we've needed.

I tilt my head back down and look around the camp. The mournful red eyes of those who were close to Malcolm capture my gaze as a light rain starts to fall—pushing the drying tears down their cheeks. I tuck my lips back and nod at Ella as she stands up. With trembling lips, she gathers her stuff before walking away toward a small grouping of others.

"I'm sorry," I mumble to myself as she turns her back away from me. Each time my eyes catch those of someone from the library, I instantly divert my focus to the ground. The pain of witnessing someone else's sadness is nearly equal to that of personal loss. I barely knew Malcolm, but through everyone else, I feel like he was a good friend of mine.

"Where should we put our bags?" asks Sam as he and Abby move toward me.

312

Shaking my head, I wipe my cheek. "Just throw them behind a tree that you'll remember, so you can find them when we come back."

"Okay."

I pull a knife from my backpack and shove it into my front pocket. I turn around. "Everyone be sure to place your stuff securely behind or up in a tree. As long as you know where it is, we should be able to salvage it. And even if you lose it, we'll have all the resources behind the wall when we prevail."

Prevail. The word's meaning is lost on me at this point. We can't win anything. All we can do is kill to erase the pain, but even that won't help. Pain is a part of life. Pain leads to vengeance. If no pain existed in the world, then, and only then could we prevail. But, really, we'd have nothing to win.

"I'm just going to put my bag on top of yours," says Elise as she steps closer to me.

"Works for me. Do you have enough arrows?"

"I whittled a few more with Rosie and Dean the other night. We should have enough."

"Good. Do you think we shou—" I say as a crack of thunder erupts overhead, scattering every bird foolish enough to be nearby. Wrapping my arm around Elise's waist, I smile. "Do you think we should start moving? Do you know who's going in the trees with you?"

"Rosie, Dean, Mitch, and I think her name was Hannah. Do you know who else is going to attack the guards bringing out the kids?"

As I start to speak, the sky starts to spew heavier rainfall. I nod as I lift my arm over my head, doing all that I can to make myself heard. "Malcolm was going to come with me, but I know Ella, Miles, and Ben will be with me. Maybe one more too. Then, Marcus has whoever's left. Sam and Abby are going into Nimbus alone."

Shielding her face from the rain with her arm, Elise wipes her forehead with her other hand. "Are you sure they'll be able to get to your parents quick enough? We can always send a few more with them."

"They'll be fine. I trust them," I say.

"I do, too. I just would rather have us be safe than sorry."

"We'll all be safe," I say as I lean in toward her lips. As I press mine into hers, the rain slides down our cheeks. My hands embrace her back. "I love you."

"I love you, too."

As our bodies let go, I turn toward Marcus. "Is everyone ready to move?"

"I think so," he replies as he waves his arm into the sky. "Everyone come here," he yells.

As everyone slowly maneuvers themselves around trees toward Marcus, Elise and I, I start to speak. "Alright, once we're ready to move, you should get near the people you'll be working with. I know some of you might be nervous, but we need everyone to stay calm and follow the plan." Granted, that's easier said than done. I wipe my face as Marcus kneels down beside me. "It's nearing nightfall and despite the storm, everyone needs to be alert and focused. We're not guaranteed a separation tomorrow, but it's inevitable that one will be here within the next day or two—" I say as Marcus stands back up with his hand held above his head.

Lowering his arm, he looks around the forest. With each fading second, he gazes into the eyes of those around him before he starts to speak. "I know some of you are afraid. I'm afraid too, but eventually this world will die out and we will weep. . .not for our losses, but for the new world that will blossom, for the new hope that will grow. A hope that will create a new home. . .a place in which we'll finally be safe from the tyranny of MacMillan. We'll be guided down the path of lights into a world of serenity, into a home that can't be killed, burned, or taken away from us. Wipe your tears, dry your eyes, and save your cries for the rebirth of this world because if you don't, he will win. . .and that's something this world's not made for." Taking a slight breath, he bobs his head lightly as if he's not done speaking.

I wrap my arm around Sam and Elise as a beam of light streaks across the sky.

"The most convincing guise evil can use is one where it makes us believe there is salvation at the end of every struggle, when in reality, the struggle ceases to end. Even if we find a moment of happiness, we have to keep moving until we find the next one. Until MacMillan is dead, permanent salvation is just a dream," says Marcus as an emphatic crash of thunder reverberates the skyline.

314

Eager and ready to move forward, everyone smiles as they bend down and start smearing mud across their cheeks before moving toward the path. Throwing my hood over my head, I bend down to dip my fingers into the muck. As a loud crack bursts above us, I smear the mud across my cheeks. Slowly turning toward Marcus as we start the walk to Nimbus, I grin, "Nimbus was our beginning. Nimbus won't be our end."

8 February 2192

Sam

The clouds march through the sky like a mass of ants retreating to their hill. The rain lessens to a drizzle, in turn slowing the clouds' walk. It's still dark enough that it's difficult to see, but the doors haven't opened—keeping me optimistic that when the light shines, I'll be ready. Then again, Sean never gave us instructions if there wasn't a separation today. He just seemed certain that it was going to happen no matter what.

I straighten my shoulders against the rigid bark as I push my legs farther up the branch. Abby remains still on the ground a few feet beneath me with her head tucked into her muddy sweatshirt. I told her she could sleep in the tree, but she insisted on slathering her clothes in mud instead, apparently.

While waiting for the clouds to dissipate, I peek around the edge of the tree. Unwavering in the wind, the wall stands firm. Towering above its surroundings like the skyscrapers in the city, the wall protecting Nimbus reins paramount out here. There's nothing to compete with it. There aren't any buildings climbing toward its height, no ivy coiling itself around it, no dents or cracks deteriorating its appearance; nothing. The wall is the only one of its kind.

Pulling my head around, I close my eyes. Eagerly, my mind travels to a world without a wall: an unfamiliar world.

The streets roar loudly with the humming of the exhaust. Cars speed past, unfocused on the vehicle sitting outside my door. I stand atop the front stairwell, watching. She steps out of the door. Her light brown eyes glance at mine. She blushes. The sun rises

316

above the skyscrapers. I feel unstoppable. I feel loved. I rush toward her.

It's too easy to get lost in a world that doesn't exist—one that couldn't exist. There's something about living in a world without any boundaries that draws me in. If only a new world could uproot this one. One where society functions without the evils of a dictator watching our every move; one where we're free to roam without having to worry about being killed or wounded with every step. Maybe someday this place could exist, but when you're trapped in a constant nightmare and a state of disarray, every dream seems unlikely—especially the happy ones.

"Sam," mumbles Abby from below.

"Yea," I answer quietly as I wipe my eyes.

"Has anyone come out yet?"

"Not that I've seen."

"Do you think it'll open soon?"

"I really don't know. We just need to stay awake," I say as I massage my forehead in order to prevent myself from dozing off.

I look around the woods. Various members of our group sit idly by as they wait for the moment. Some remain fidgety on their branches while others appear to sleep sitting upright. Though, I doubt anyone managed a good night's sleep amidst the storm and uncomfortable sleeping arrangements. Maybe the lack of comfort will ignite everyone; maybe the painful night will make them hungry for a brighter future.

Several minutes pass as Abby cozies herself back into her hood while I try to stretch out my body on this coarse bark.

"Wake me up when it's time to go," mumbles Abby from below.

"Yea, sure," I reply as I turn around. This time my feet press against the tall base of the tree as my body unwinds itself up the branch. Despite the stark reality of what I can now see clearly, I refuse to focus my attention on the wall. Instead, I close my eyes and wait for Sean's voice to wake us.

Fleeting moments of the night fade into nothingness as I hide behind my eyelids. Unable to fall back asleep or even into some sort of nap, I blankly stare at the darkness. I wish everything were over. I wish we'd already won.

"Sam," comes a voice to my right.

"Yea?" I reply, my eyes still closed.

"Climb down. I want everyone to be ready," whispers Sean.

"Already? It's still dark."

"Yea, but it's getting lighter every moment. Who knows when the separation is going to happen."

"Okay," I mutter. Sleepily opening my eyes, I learn over and swing down. Quietly landing just above Abby, I position myself behind a tree next to her. Slowly waking up, she wearily looks over.

"Why are you up?" she yawns.

"Sean wants us to be ready."

"But it's still relatively dark."

"That's what I said, but he thinks it will happen sooner rather than later."

"Okay," she says as she wipes off the mud clinging to her sweatshirt.

As Sean wakes everyone up around us, Marcus comes around with a backpack. Throwing it in front of us, he says, "Grab something." Looking into the bag, I pull out a small knife with a dark black handle. The handle has a smudged engraving at the bottom, but the blade appears sharp. Folding it and placing it in my pocket, I grab my hatchet sitting next to Abby and wrap my belt around it.

Quickly grabbing another knife for herself, Abby's eyes fixate on the serrated edge of the blade. "Will these two be enough?" she asks as she holds out the knife with the A.Y. engraving.

"Should be," I say.

With her eyes running rapidly over the knives in her hands, she puts them in her pocket and takes a deep breath.

"Are you okay?" I ask.

"I don't know," she says. "I haven't killed anyone before."

"And you still might not have to. Those are just for safety."

"I know, I just don't know if I'll be able to kill someone if I have to," she mumbles.

"I know. I haven't killed anyone either. I've come close, but I always end up getting hurt instead," I laugh. It seems neither of us are cut out to be cold-blooded murderers.

"What if I have to stab someone?" she asks dejectedly.

318

"Then you have to. If we want to survive, we're going to have to be strong. We can't just be the two newbies who are afraid of everything. We have to toughen up."

"I can do that. I can be strong," she replies.

"I know you can. You've been strong since we've been out here. You've been stronger than me," I smile. "You've kept me sane, Abby. Thanks."

Smiling, she brushes her hair from her eyes as she straightens her back against the tree.

"Now, let's take back Nimbus."

Closing my eyes, I take a deep breath and slowly bury my back into the crumbling bark. *This is it.* The moment the gate opens, everything will stop and everything outside of us will be nothing more than a memory. Once the gate opens, we fight. We fight for everything that's wronged us for years, for the society that should be rather than the one that exists. We fight for a new world.

Taking another breath, I open my eyes and turn toward Abby. With her head held upward, she stares into the empty sky. Knowing the world could end today, she takes another breath before peeking her head around to get a glimpse of the wall.

I focus on her eyes and then her lips. This could be the last time I get to truly see her. This could be the last time either of us breathes.

"Ab—" I say as I'm cut off by the sound of men yelling nonsense behind me. I turn around and focus my attention on the wall where the silver-encrusted lining in the front splits in two. Guards pour out while three kids meander around behind them.

Immediately, Sean looks over and nods. "Find Mom and Dad. I'll see you in Nimbus soon. Now, go!"

Looking back at Abby, I grab her hand. "Let's go," I say as the sound of chaos erupts ahead of us. With my hand in hers, we run toward the fight, toward the guards ruthlessly firing at Sean's group as Elise fires arrows at the men atop the wall.

Bodies fall from the wall like a deathly rain of flesh as screams echo around us. I turn around as Sean picks up a gun from a dead guard and starts firing back at the Elites.

"Keep moving, Sam!" yells Abby as she pulls me into Nimbus.

Hurriedly getting behind the open doors, I see several motionless bodies lying in the street. The guards behind the doors are nonexistent. "Where are we going first?!" I yell.

"Split up!" shouts Abby.

"No, no, no!" I reply.

"We need to get the message out so they don't die!"

Nodding against my will, I pull her close to me and press my lips into her forehead. "I'll see you soon," I say.

"In a few minutes," she smiles before sprinting down the stone street ahead of me.

Following behind her, I run as fast as I can toward the home I grew up in, toward my past. The streets remain empty and void of life as if nobody's heard the ensuing battle outside their homes. The sky continues to brighten as the harrowing cries of war ring loudly throughout Nimbus. *Where is everyone?*

Bustling through the empty street, I look for signs of life, but nothing jumps out. Nearing my house, I take a quick left up the front steps and rip open the front door. I run inside.

"Mom! Dad! It's beginning!" I yell. Yet, nobody responds. The cold air clings to the dead silence.

I run upstairs—knocking a few pictures off the wall in the process—and into my parents' bedroom. "Dad!" I yell, but no one's there. "Mom!" yields the same response.

Agitated and confused, I sprint back downstairs. *Where is everyone?* I think. Running into the front room, I shout once more, but nobody responds. Finally, I run back into the kitchen and look around for a signal, for some sign to where they might have gone. But, there's nothing. No note, no clues, no evidence as to where they might be. Taking one last gasp of air, I scream. "MOM! DAD!" My cries return nothing but empty sound.

Frantically running around the house, I start to lose focus. My head grows weary as my eyes become irritated. Distraught in the vacancy of my own home, I fall. "Mom! Dad!" I shout once more.

Growing restless in search of something that's clearly not here, I stand back up. Shaking my head, I move toward the front door before running back outside. Gunshots ring loudly above while the street remains uninhabited. "Where is everyone?!" I yell as I look down the road toward Abby's house. "Abby!" I yell. Once again, my cry goes unheard. The emptiness of Nimbus makes my heart pound against my chest—it terrifies me. I feel more alone than I've ever been.

I wipe my eyes and run to Abby's home. Sprinting through a ghost town, I shake my head and turn onto her front steps. "Abby!" I yell again.

"Sam! Help!" howls Abby. "SAM!"

Hurrying up the stairs, I yank open the front door only to see Abby tied to a chair with red marks across her face. Standing next to her, a guard towers above with a menacing grin strewn across his face. "Did you come to join in the pain too, little man?"

Enveloped with rage, I run across the room, plant my foot into the creaking hardwood and jump onto the man's back. He starts to shake from side to side as I claw my fingers into his cheeks. With each struggle, my fingers dig deeper. I cling to his bulky frame with everything left in me.

"Get off me!" he yells as he reaches for my hands. Quickly grabbing onto my wrists, he pulls me over his head and throws me across the room. My back slams into the wall behind Abby, unwedging my hatchet from my belt and onto the floor next to me. Cringing in pain, I try to reach for the hatchet, but with each extension a throbbing pain courses through my body. "You're just a child, you can't kill me," he laughs while wiping blood from his cheeks—further smearing it across his face.

Reaching once more for the handle, a searing pain runs through my back and up into my neck. I contort my face; my outstretched arm falls short of the weapon. Laughing, the man steps toward me as I reach out once more. With his gun held out, he starts shooting at the hatchet.

"You're not going to be able to use that," he laughs, blood still dripping from where I clawed into his swollen cheeks.

The non-stop aching refuses to subside. I stare at the weapon, hoping he'll look away, but he doesn't hesitate and now I'm terrified. I know that if I reach for the weapon, he'll shoot. I know that if I so much as move, I'm dead. I basically have to wait for him to come kill me. It's to the point that everything I've done seems for nothing.

"Leave him alone!" shouts Abby. "Don't kill him! Kill me!"

Taken aback by the sudden outcry, the guard turns toward Abby. "I think I'd much rather have you watch your little boyfriend die."

As the words reverberate off the walls, I reach for the knife in my pocket. Pulling out the switchblade, I take a deep breath and charge at the man. Digging my feet into the ground, I pounce onto his back like a lion taking down its prey. With the knife held outward, I shove it into his neck. Quickly pulling it out, I reach my arm over his shoulder and shove it into his chest. Struggling to fight back, the guard falls limp onto the floor.

"S-Sam. . ." mumbles Abby.

I look up from behind the fallen corpse, my face spattered with blood. "I don't know where that came from," I say as I lunge toward her, cutting the ropes from around her hands.

"Thank you," she says as she jolts up and wraps her arms around my back. Tilting her head to the side, she rests it against my chest. "Thank you."

Elise

"There are a few more coming in from the right!" shouts Hannah.

"The left is clear!" yells Mitch.

"Dean, Hannah, focus on the right! Rosie, Mitch, come with me. We're going inside to find Sam and Abby," I reply before jumping down from the tree. Wrapping my arm around the trunk, I duck behind the bark before peering out and firing an arrow.

Climbing down from their respective trees, Rosie and Mitch wrap their bows around their chests as they run toward me.

"Which way?" asks Rosie.

"Toward Sean and the others. Fire at the guards coming out of the gates, if need be. If it's unnecessary, stay low and undetected. We don't want to draw any unwanted attention if we don't need to," I answer as I start to sprint toward the vibrant steel mirroring the forest.

A crack echoes beside me. I turn to notice Mitch standing with blood on the end of his bow and a guard at his feet. "Duck!" I shout.

He obliges as I fire an arrow into the neck of a guard directly behind him. Mitch smiles. "Thanks!"

Quickly escaping the shadowed branches canopying our hideout, I look left. There, Sean jumps to his left as his blade pierces the chest of an Elite. Looking right, I notice Marcus screaming— bodies falling behind him. As he sprints toward me with all his might, time slows. Blood drips from his forehead as arrows fly above him. Bodies continue to drop from the sky like a thick mass of hail while screams absorb every ounce of air around us.

"Keep running!" he screams. "Get into Nimbus!" I shake my head as his pace increases and time picks back up. "Keep moving! The doors are closing!"

Pulling my bow back around, I grab an arrow and hold it against my chest. Nearing the doors, I sprint just inside the gate. I turn back and flag Dean and Hannah down from the trees. "Come on!" I yell. Watching as they hurriedly maneuver themselves down, I turn toward Sean. His eyes catch my stare just as Miles collapses beside him. Trying to fend off a guard, Sean punches the man in the face before reaching down for Miles's hand. The guard slowly gets up behind him. I fire my bow. The Elite falls into the dirt with a bloody gap between his eyes. "Sean!" I shout.

Rapidly pulling Miles to his feet, Sean sprints toward the gates.

I remain still with my eyes fixed on everyone trying to get into Nimbus. "Come on!" I yell once more as the gap between the doors starts to grow slim.

Extending his strides like a marathon runner, Marcus crosses into Nimbus as Hannah and Dean follow.

Sean slows and helps Ella to her feet.

"SEAN!" I scream as he holds Miles and Ella at his sides. "Hurry!" With each second, the divide becomes smaller. With each passing moment, his chance of getting into Nimbus grows nearly hopeless. The doors are almost shut.

"RUN!" yells Marcus before he steps outside the gate and hustles toward Sean. Reaching out his arm, he grabs Ella, throws her onto his back, and gallops past the gates while Sean continues to limp with Miles's arm wrapped around his neck.

"He doesn't have much time. I can't go back out and get both of them," exhales Marcus.

Sweat drips down my palms as I clasp my hands together. *I can't watch this,* I think as I turn around. *I can't. I should have ran after him.*

"I'll get them," yells a voice from behind me as I bury my face in my hands.

"Mitch, no!" shouts Marcus.

Unwilling to witness any trauma, I keep my back against the collapsing wall. "Please," I mumble. "Please."

With my face digging further into my hands, I fall to my knees just as the click of the gates reverberates around Nimbus. I shake my aching head while my mind caves into a past nightmare. I can't feel my legs. *Why didn't I help? Why now am I so afraid?*

324

"Elise!" yells Marcus. "Elise!"

I open my mouth to respond, but nothing comes out. I try again, but my vocal chords refuse to exercise volume.

"Elise. Turn around," he says. Placing his warm hand on my shoulder, Marcus exhales loudly next to me. Grabbing ahold of my arm, he tries to lift me up, but I fall. My feeble legs refuse to turn around.

"Elise."

"G-go a-away," I reply to Marcus.

"He's alive," he says.

"If h-he's alive, why isn't he next to m-me?" I cry.

"He's exhausted," says Marcus. "He got Miles through, too."

"What about Mitch?"

"I'm afraid not."

My hands continue to convulse. I anxiously wipe the moisture on my sweatshirt. Slowly standing up, I turn around. Covered in mud with his arms sprawled out on the street, Sean breathes heavily.

"What took you so long?" I cry as I run to him.

"I-it's a long run," he exhales.

"Is everyone okay?" I ask. Looking around the area, I notice everyone either on one knee or sprawled out on the street. They all have the same look across their faces. They all look afraid. I don't blame them.

"We're fine," replies Ella. "But we need to keep moving. We need to find everyone's parents. We need to find Sam and Abby."

Shit, Sam and Abby, I think as I grab Sean's arm and try to pull him up. "We need to keep moving," I say. "We need to g—"

"Watch out!" yells Ella as she pushes Marcus down. "There are still guards up top!"

Bereft of any sense, my mind scatters. I continue to pull on Sean's arm as the guards rain bullets toward us. I watch as Hannah falls onto her chest while Dean drops onto his knees and falls forward. Marcus screams and screams, but no sound crosses into my ears. Pulling Sean up, we run.

"We have to move farther into Nimbus!" yells Marcus. "We have to hide!"

"They're everywhere around us! There's nowhere to hide!" shouts Sean. "Jaxon is still up there."

"Just get inside somewhere!" I yell as a barrage of bullets penetrates the stones surrounding us.

We dash through a barren street; the farther we get from the gates, the quieter everything gets. Occasional shots ring behind us, but nothing nears us. It feels like a ghost town.

"Quick, everyone in here!" calls a voice just ahead of us. "Come on!"

Trying to gain sight of the voice, I arch my neck as I continue to run. "Abby!"

Sean

I take a deep breath as I wipe the blood from my shin. "Where is everyone?"

"We don't know," replies Sam. "Mom and Dad weren't home. Nobody was here either aside from that guard. I don't know where anyone could be."

"Where did the guard come from?" I ask.

"He was here when I got here," Abby quietly replies. "The moment I screamed for my parents, he came out from behind me and put his hand over my mouth. I thought he was going to kill me. . ." she trails off as her focus falls to the floor; the red on her cheeks expanding as she wipes her face.

"Where do you think everyone is?" asks Elise as she presses her back against the wall and sinks to the floor.

"Should we go out and check our homes?" questions Miles.

"It's probably best if we all stay put for now," I say. "I don't think the guards know which house we went into."

"But won't they come looking?" he asks as he props his leg up on the couch, massaging his ankle in the process.

"Probably," says Ella. "We can't hide here forever. We have to find everyone. All of these houses can't be empty. Nimbus can't be dead."

"We saw people get separated; we know that there are still people here," says Rosie. "But we also know something isn't right." Pulling her hair from her eyes, she moves toward Marcus and sits on the arm of his chair. "None of this makes sense."

With everyone scattered around the living room, the blinds drawn and the lights off, silence engulfs us as the light tries to find its way in. It almost feels like we're imprisoned. Shifting closer to Elise, I stretch out my back as I mutter, "Maybe MacMillan knew we were coming."

"So he opened the gates, separated what kids were left, and let us in to receive the same fate as anyone still out there?" says Marcus. "That doesn't make much sense. There isn't really a way he could know we were coming."

"The chips," mumbles Sam. "He always knows where we are. . ."

"Damn," I say. "I didn't even think about that."

"If he can really track us then we need to get out of here," says Abby.

"But where do we go?" questions Sam as he fidgets with his pinky. "He knows our every move. We can't win."

"We can always split up again," I say.

"What good did that do us the first time?" mentions Ella. Shyly chipping away at her fingernails, she continues to speak. "Look around, there are only eight of us left. When we had everyone at the library, we had over thirty. We have eight. We can't afford to split up ever again."

"She's right," says Rosie while Marcus nods next to her. "We have to stick together until the end."

"And when is the end? The end could be now. The end could be tomorrow. The end could be never. We still have a chance to kill MacMillan. We just have to outsmart him," says Marcus.

"How do we do that? You can't outsmart someone who knows your next move," retorts Sam.

"Sure you can. You can go exactly where he expects you with a plan."

"What plan can we have now?" I say.

"You," replies Marcus.

"What do you mean?"

"You don't have a chip anymore."

Reaching my hand toward my scalp, I rub the tips of my fingers against the scar. "That's right," I mumble. "I don't."

"He knows you're alive, but he won't know where you are. If the seven of us stick together, he'll be able to track us, but you can stay off the radar. You're free to do anything."

"But what can I do? What should I do?" I say as I continue to press into the cut. Running my fingers up and down the mark, I turn toward Elise. "What should I do?" I ask again.

"I don't know," she says. "I don't want to split up anymore."

"It might be our only chance at survival," says Marcus.

"What if it doesn't work? What if we lose him like we've lost our families?"

"We won't."

"How do you know that? We don't know where anyone is. We don't know if MacMillan killed our families. We don't know if anyone outside of the Elites still lives in Nimbus. We don't even know if Nimbus really exists anymore. For all we know, this could be a trap. Everything could have been set up to draw us here." Taking a breath, she looks around as everyone's attention remains on the floor. "Why do you think there were so many bodies on our way to Nimbus? That can't be a coincidence."

"But why were they there?" asks Marcus. "A majority of them were Lurkers. And those who weren't were women. It doesn't make any sense."

"Arthur," whispers Elise. "Whatever he was doing, MacMillan knew. They want me."

I bite my lip. "I don't understand any of it and I don't know if I want to understand any of it. There's no reason they should just be targeting you, Elise. All I know is that Marcus is right. We have to split up. We have to do whatever we can to kill MacMillan."

"Even if that involves putting us all in danger again?" asks an irritated Elise. "They just want me."

"How do you know they don't want me, too?" asks Sam. "They tortured me the same way they tortured you, Elise. MacMillan just likes to belittle those who are already on the verge of giving up."

Elise doesn't reply. She just looks around the room.

"We need to face that MacMillan wants us all dead. There's no particular one he wants more than the others. Arthur may have wanted you guys, but we're in Nimbus now. We're all on the same list," says Miles.

"He's right. Until we can kill MacMillan, we're all pinned against the same wall. The only escape is through him. We have to do what we can to end his ways. For God's sake, he's in his eighties," I laugh.

"That's true," chuckles Sam. "He can't be that hard to kill."

"So what do you suggest we do?" asks Marcus. "Where do you think he is?"

"Maybe he's hiding," says Miles. "Maybe he knows we can outflank him."

"That could be it or maybe he's in the open. . .waiting," I say. "What if he's taken our families and expects us to come to him? I mean, if he had any idea we were coming, he might have known what our plans were. That could've led him to taking what we came for."

"That makes sense, but what can he do with that many people? Where can he keep that many people in a place like this?" asks Sam. "Could he imprison all of them?"

"He could, but that wouldn't make sense. There aren't that many cells here," I say as I look around the darkness in search of a clue. "He would need somewhere bigger. Somewhere open enough to hold a majority of the town."

"And where is that?" replies Sam. "This part of town is virtually empty. How can someone hide or get rid of that many people in such a small area? Do you think he sent them outside?"

"Doubtful. They could have found us eventually. He's all about showing his power. Throwing more people outside wouldn't justify it," I say as my mind continues to run in all directions.

"But he threw you out? Wasn't that him justifying his reign?" asks Abby.

"And he threw that girl out when I was eleven," says Sam.

"What girl?" asks Marcus.

"I don't remember her name, but she was Wesley Pearson's older sister."

"I never heard about that," I reply. "I thought I was the first one to be sent back out."

Sam shakes his head. "She created a map of the outside and gave it to Wesley. He showed some kids and next thing we knew, he wasn't at school anymore and she was kicked out the following night."

"So, in a way, these two second separations were his way of showing his power. If he wanted to make a showing with dozens, maybe hundreds of people, he would need a lot of space. He wouldn't want to send them all out together because that would give them a chance to survive. He would need somewhere everyone knows. Somewhere you can see your escape, but you can't get to it."

"What do you mean? I'm not following you, Sean," says Marcus as he leans forward in his seat.

"There's only one place big enough for him to gather the whole city."

"Are you talking about the city we came from on the outside?" Elise asks as she moves closer to me, her eyes fixed on mine before they wander around the room.

"No," I say. "What's the only place in town that's big enough? The one place we go once a year when we're here."

"The Festival grounds?" replies Elise.

"But that's the most open place in Nimbus. If he wants a showing, he'd do it there."

"Are you sure?"

"MacMillan is a madman. If he knew we were coming, he'd want our torment to be unimaginable. Just like Arthur, he thrives on the weakness of others. He preys on the innocent."

"I'm still not entirely following you, Sean," says Ella. "What kind of showing would he have with everyone's parents at the Festival?"

"Do you remember the separation several years ago when half the group tried to run back to their homes?"

"Yea, but I try to avoid thinking about those."

"During that, MacMillan showed the power he wielded by wounding several of the kids and then kicking them out. Before he kicked me out, he starved me nearly to death. I have a feeling he's done something similar to our families," I say as I stand up. Wandering around the room, I pull apart the blinds as a sharp ray of sun beams into the room. "I think he has them on those grounds and is torturing them while he waits for us to be lured into his trap. He wants to break us apart from the inside until we can't even stand on our own two feet. By taking the people we hold closest to us, he can do that. He can kill you without you even knowing you're dead."

Driven to a state of utter disbelief and sheer confusion, Ella shakes her head. "If that's true, what do we do?"

"We go to him," I say.

"Why would we do that?"

"Because that's what he wants."

"Why would we give him what he wants if we know it could kill us?" asks Miles.

331

"Because we have to show him we're stronger than he thinks we are," I say.

"I don't know if I can do that," he cries as he wipes his face. "I don't know if I can endure anymore pain."

"None of us can, but you have to believe in what we've been through. You have to believe in our cause. I know Sean, Sam, Abby, and Elise have gone through more than we have. I know they've seen the ends of the world and back. If they've survived the worst, so can we. We can't let the darkest fears of our imaginations destroy us. If we do that, he wins. We have to be strong," says Marcus as he stands up. "What do you want us to do, Sean?"

"I want you to go to him while I get atop the wall."

"What will you do up there?"

"What do you think?" I say as Elise hands me a rifle.

Sam

Everything's a game to MacMillan. *What better place to hide behind your demonic methods than at the very field where the Founding Festival takes place? What better place to cower behind the fear you've subjected all of us to than the place where everything began? If he knows we're coming, why would he continue to hide?* The farther away he waits, the more of a fool he becomes.

"Are you guys ready to go?" asks Sean as he stands up. Scratching his head, he looks around the room. "Is that a yes?"

"Yea," I nod as a stray tear finds its way down the side of my cheek. I was certain I wouldn't let this plan turn me into a whimpering mess, but a part of me wants to break down.

"I'll be okay, guys. I promise," he replies as he wraps his arms around Elise. Slowly trudging toward them, I fling my arms around their backs. Abby too.

"We'll see you soon," cries Elise. "Very soon."

"You'll see me the whole time," smiles Sean. "But we have to move now."

"He's right," says Marcus. "Why don't you go out first and find a route to the top? We'll head straight to the Festival grounds behind you."

"I love you," mumbles Elise as she presses her lips into his. As much as I don't care to see it, it helps keep me sane. It helps me remember we all have too much to live for. It shows that love will endlessly exist even in the face of death; it proves that no matter what lies ahead, there's always something holding us to the ground.

"I love you, too," replies Sean. Letting go, he looks over at the door. "Let's move."

Hurrying toward the door, he quietly pushes it open before he steps out into the street with his gun held up. Looking left and right, Sean scours the top of the wall before disappearing behind the house.

I run outside behind him, but before I get a chance to say anything, he's gone. Abby runs out behind me and grabs onto my hand. "We have to move," she mutters. I nod.

"Left. Everyone go left," says Marcus as he steps out behind us, closing the door in the process.

Quickly hobbling out onto the road, Miles takes the lead as he limps down the street. "C'mon, guys. We don't know how much time we have. Let's move."

"We're coming," I say. Pulling Abby beside me, I follow Miles.

As I impatiently look back, Sean stands nowhere in sight. I wish I knew where an entrance to the top of the wall was so I could follow his trajectory, but I don't. I don't think any of us do. He's the only one who knows the ins and outs of Nimbus. Really, I doubt many of us know much about this place anymore.

"Keep moving, Sam," says Abby as she pulls me forward.

"Sorry," I sputter. "I'm just lost."

"It's not that far away."

"I mean, I don't understand this place anymore. What happened to Nimbus? For thirteen years it seemed like home. Now, it feels like hell."

"It's always been hell. We just didn't realize it until they threw us out."

"I guess," I say. Spinning in circles, gazing at the vast emptiness that is Nimbus, I end up backward. Abby grabs back onto my hand and pulls me back around. Turning forward, I wipe my forehead as the humidity clings to my scalp.

"Does anyone see Sean?" asks Elise from ahead of us.

"I haven't been able to find him either."

"He can't be that far aw—" says Elise as her words are interjected by the sound of bullets flying above us.

"Get down!" shouts Marcus.

"No!" I yell. "It's not aimed at us! It's Sean. He's shooting guards!"

"Okay, then hurry forward. We can't have Sean alert MacMillan too much."

I tighten my grip on Abby's hand as we start to jog forward. Hustling past everyone, we veer right. Quickly passing various discolored and abandoned shops laden with 'Closed' signs, we jolt left. "Just ahead," I say as we run toward the barren fields once inhabited by the lively people of Nimbus. Hidden behind a wrought iron gate with the words, '*In Harmony We Live. In Peace We Thrive*' written in a semi-circle over the entrance, the fields appear dead.

The instant we step under the rusted black, the sound of bullets in the background disappears. The noise that once ricocheted around our heads has fallen silent as the faces of those we love cry in front of us. With a thick rope around their necks, the floor drops from underneath them. They struggle. Their pale faces become crooked with dread as they blankly stare back at us—the ropes tightening around their pulsing necks the more they struggle. Locked into our places, we watch the horror as they fight to breathe, as they all become nothing. Immobilized by the terror of his reign, our families suffer without any escape. . .without the possibility of our help. *I can't move anything.*

MOVE! I scream in my head. *MOVE!* But I can't. I'm stuck. My legs won't move. My eyes won't blink. My limbs have become nothing more than branches attached to a broken trunk.

I try to go forward, but each time my brain tells my legs to move, they don't. It's like I'm afraid of running toward the inevitability of their demise, like I'm afraid to prevent it. This is the bottom. This is the pit that Arthur threw me into, but now MacMillan has the key. I stand blankly staring at the last glimmer of light as it dies in front of me. *My arms are glued. My legs are cemented.*

"I had a feeling you would show up eventually," echoes the gravelly voice of MacMillan. I shake the only mobile part left on me—my head—in utter confusion as the cruel tone of the devil finds its way into my ears. "What a show, huh?"

With my legs refusing to move, I yell the first thing that pops into my head. "I'm going to kill you!"

"You'd have to get past your weaknesses first, then. All of you. Not one of you had the willpower to come up and stop this. There's nobody up on the stage alive, but me. There aren't any guards. There isn't one single person to stop you, but me. . .and you all fell short," laughs MacMillan as he strides across the stage. "This is why I did this. Weakness will not be tolerated in Nimbus."

"Neither will lunacy!" shouts Elise.

Snidely speaking, MacMillan glares at us. "My methods are stringent upon the necessary skills of survival. No world can survive outside of this wall and no world can survive inside this wall if it's weak."

"There's nothing weaker than someone who hides behind a gun," says Marcus. Taking a half step forward, he holds his knife at his side.

"It's not hiding when you know its purpose. Just like Arthur."

". . .wh-what?" mumbles Abby. "What did he just say?"

"Did he say Arthur?" replies Elise.

"Don't act like you didn't hear me," says MacMillan. Stepping up to the front of the stage, he leans toward us. "I'm surprised you didn't figure it out sooner. How do you think one man could be so ruthless, yet manage to lure dozens of others to work alongside him?"

Trembling in fright, Abby grabs my wrist. "He didn't make Arthur that way," she mumbles. "He did it to himself."

"There's no way he could have done anything," I reply.

Right?

"What are you two bickering about?" questions MacMillan. Stepping back, he pushes against one of the bodies—it motions back and forth before slowing to a halt, the pressure in the rope echoing around us. "Do you think that Arthur was always that way? I mean, how could one man be so selfish, so violent, and so downright unforgiving so easily? That has to take time. Even I'm not that crazy. . .yet."

"You're delusional. You're insane. You're a coward!" screams Miles.

Silence engulfs the field, only to be bothered with the gentle tick of MacMillan's boots. Waltzing across the stage, he arrogantly pokes the dead.

"I might be a little cynical, but that's it. I mean, at least all the weak ones outside the wall are dead now. There's no way they could get the job done without Arthur leading them. Just like there's no way Nimbus could function without me leading it. It's common sense," says MacMillan. Continuing to walk back and forth across the stage as the wide, unblinking eyes of those behind him stare into the sky, he smirks. "Nimbus needs me. Nimbus doesn't need you."

336

Sean

I quickly jump onto a ladder as I climb toward the top of the wall, toward whatever game MacMillan is playing. As my hands grip the cold steel, I turn around, gazing at the lifeless bodies scattered behind me. *Keep moving,* I say to myself as I move into the cold, piercing wind above.

With my feet clinking against the grates beneath me, I run to the north end of the wall. Continuing to look around every direction as I run, the nagging feeling that Jaxon is sitting there waiting for me terrifies me. It makes me feel like everything I've done was for nothing; that what I told everyone else to do was for nothing, but I can't stop. I can't be afraid anymore. I have to keep moving.

Pulling my rifle up and against my chest, I crouch around the corner as I gently lift my head over the wall. "Nothing," I say aloud to myself. Quickly standing back up, I look ahead as I run to the north end. Still nothing. The top of the wall is virtually empty aside from the echoes reverberating off the wall below.

As I lean my ear over the ledge, I hear, "Why do you think it was so easy for Arthur to give you two headaches? He worked for me. I have access to the control panels that control the chips. Put two and two together and there you go, I'm in your head."

"But we were told the chips were only for location purposes," replies Sam.

"Do you really believe everything you're told?" laughs MacMillan. "You kids are terribly easy to fool. You're all so gullible."

I can't stand that man's voice. Every word that comes out of his gin-stained mouth is covered in lies. He can't play this game forever.

Slowly standing up, I peek my head over the edge. With my gun at my side, I look down the scope. Casually wavering in the wind, my eye catches a glimpse of Miles as he lies facedown in the dirt, his hands slamming next to him. Gently shifting my aim to Elise, I notice her glistening eyes as her cheeks convulse. It's almost as if she's grinding her teeth. Shifting my sight once more, I lock in on Marcus. Unlike the others, he seems calm. His hands stand stiff at his sides as he holds his knife against his thigh. His face is utterly expressionless while his eyes stave off any and all fear. He looks lost.

"What's going on?" I ask myself as I set down my gun.

Frantically looking around the field, I catch a glimpse of swaying bodies slowly brushing against each other in the wind. *What?* I think as I pull up my scope once more. Hurriedly changing my focus to the grim horrors beneath me, I try to sustain my quivering fingers, but I can't. I can't see the faces. I can't see who's dead. I can't see anything.

Trying to get a better view of what's going on, I sprint around the wall until I'm lined up with Sam. As sweat trickles down my wrists, I zoom in once more. The pallid cheeks of impassive faces stare hopelessly into the sky as grief attacks my chest. With ill-controlled composure, I fire at MacMillan—missing by several feet. My hands shake as my chest starts to feel weak. . .almost as if my heart's been stopped. Looking down once more, I fire. Missing again.

"It won't be that easy!" smiles MacMillan as he turns his head across the way. "Finish him, Jaxon."

"Finish him?" I mumble to myself. "He never hit me," I say as the pain in my chest grows thicker. Looking down, I notice a vast widening of blood permeating my shirt.

"SEAN!" screams Elise from beneath me. "SEAN!"

What's going on? I think as I start to grow light-headed. With each passing second, my body grows more and more numb as the aching courses through like a river attempting to avoid the inevitable winter. It feels cold. Everything feels icy.

I try to manage another shot at MacMillan, but I can't. My legs lock up as I fall onto the grates. The echoes of footsteps ring loudly around me as a pair of black boots start nearing my blurred vision. I shake my head as the obscurity clears up and the black soles slam into my stomach.

"Just accept your fate, Sean. Nimbus doesn't need people like you."

338

"Nimbus needs serenity," I mutter as Jaxon steps onto my chest. I scream as he presses down onto the wound—blood coursing down my sides.

"You're lucky I didn't shoot you in the heart the first time. I knew that would've been too easy."

"You should've just killed me when you had the chance," I laugh.

"My chance is now. You're dying. You're weak. You have nowhere to go."

"Neither do you," I say as I throw my hands onto his ankle.

"You're too weak to move me. Why even bother?" smiles Jaxon as he presses his foot further into my laceration.

"Because I'm not afraid of this."

"Afraid of death?"

"I'm not afraid," I say as I gather up all the strength in my body and push Jaxon into the air. Quickly standing up, I tackle him to the ground as I throw my fist into his face. Violently, with no regard for my own safety, I pummel my knuckles into his mouth. With each blow, the cold that once consumed me grows warm. With each strike, I feel stronger. Yet, I know it won't last.

"Is that all you got?" laughs Jaxon as he spits up blood. "You punch like a child."

Disregarding my emotions, I wrap my hand around his neck as I squeeze while I cock my right fist back. Instantly delivering a crushing blow to his skull, I pull back and do it again. With two more shots, Jaxon falls silent. "Yea, that's all I got," I say as I sluggishly lift his body up and perch it against the wall. Spattered with blood, his mouth lies agape as his eyes remain closed.

"Sean!" comes another scream from below.

Eager to show that I'm still alive and still clinging to whatever amount of time I have left, I push Jaxon's body over the ledge as the strain forces me back into the wall. *I'm still alive*, I think as a breeze rolls over me. Taking a deep breath, I press my palm into my chest and close my eyes.

Elise

"Sean!" I yell once more as Jaxon's body thuds into the dirt. "Sean!" With each cry for his name, the silence around us grows larger. With each scream pleading for him to shout back, the air grows thick as the wind controls the sound. *Is he okay? Is he alive? How do I get up to him?* I think as my mind runs rampant. Uncontrollable tears slide down my face as I snivel in misery. "Sean!" I scream once more. My knees buckle.

"He's dead, poor girl. You'll be with him soon enough," cackles MacMillan.

"Go to hell!" I shout as I pull an arrow from my quiver and fire it onto the stage. Quickly stepping to the side, MacMillan dodges the lackluster shot.

"You think you can kill me?" he roars. "Nobody can kill me!"

Pulling out another arrow, I fire toward his legs—missing again. This time, he stumbles across the stage and jumps out of the way. Once more, I pull back and miss. Saturated with visions of sorrow, I can't see. I'm choked up and I can't focus.

"Give me your bow," says Abby.

"What?" I sob.

"Give me your bow, now."

Quickly removing it from around my chest, I toss the bow and quiver to Abby. Unable to discern reality from my emotions, I helplessly watch the stage as MacMillan hops down and starts walking toward us.

"This is the end of you. This is the end of every failure Nimbus ever created. This is the end of everything," shouts MacMillan as he hobbles toward us while reaching into his back pocket. Pulling out a pistol, he aims at me. *I'm not afraid*, I think. *I'm not afraid.* Yet, I remain still, with my gaze on the dirt.

340

Slowly pulling my head up, I stare unto MacMillan as he pulls the trigger.

"Nooooo!" screams a voice from beside me. "NO!" "You'll die, you bastard!"

Suddenly, the pace has changed. Time has become a nonexistent thread in an ever-unraveling spool. I try to find the source of the scream, but I can't determine who it is. MacMillan's face goes blank as the raucous cries of sheer horror vibrate my eardrums.

"You'll die!" screams the adolescent voice once more.

Lost in utter delusion, I turn to my left as Sam fires an arrow into the chest of MacMillan. Reaching for another arrow, he fires again. Rapidly releasing arrows into MacMillan's body, Sam continues to fire until his fingers clasp nothing. After firing numerous arrows into MacMillan, Sam sprints toward him. Violently pulling out one of the blades from his chest, he pierces it into MacMillan's skull. Pulling out another, he does it again. The abhorrence of his act sends me into a frenzy. "Sam! STOP!" I yell as I deliberately attempt to grasp onto time. "He's dead!"

"He killed her! He killed her! He needs to suffer!" replies a deranged Sam. "She didn't deserve this. She deserved the world," he cries as he falls beside MacMillan's bloodied corpse. "She deserved everything."

"What, what are you talking about?" I ask as I shake my head, trying to snap back into reality. "What's going on?"

"She's dead, Elise. She tried to protect us. . ."

"Ab. . .Abby?" I cry. "Abby's dead?" This can't be possible. He was aiming at me. He was aimed at me.

"She jumped," softly mutters Marcus. Stepping toward Sam, he looks back at me. "She saved you."

"What. . .what?" I mumble. "Wh. . .what's. . ." I continue to spew nonsense. I turn my head forward; I see Abby's leg, but don't dare look beyond the blood on her shirt.

"You're alive because of her," he says as he pulls Sam to his feet before whispering an inaudible sentence into his ear. "I'm going to go to Sean," he yells as he runs off.

"But she can't be dead. She can't be!" I scream as my arms convulse and my eyes swell. "She never hurt anyone. She shouldn't be dead because of me. I should be. . ." I cry as I trail off and bury my head in between my knees.

"Nobody should be dead," cries Sam. "Nobody!"

Lost in utter disbelief, my mind runs in circles. I can't fathom the inexplicable. *She can't be dead*, I think. *She can't be gone.*

"What. . .what happened? Why did she jump?" I shudder.

Taking a step back, Sam falls onto his backside. "I don't know. She was always stronger than I could ever be. She was always. . ."

"Always what, Sam?"

"She was always everything I wished I could be. This—this moment proves that she wasn't afraid," he cries.

I can't handle this, I think. I close my eyes. "Nobody should die for me," I weep.

"She believed in you, Elise," says Ella from behind me. "She always praised you. You were the older sister she never had."

This isn't helping, I think as more tears wash down my cheeks. "Nobody was supposed to die. Everyone was supposed to live. Only MacMillan was supposed to die. Only HIM!" I yell.

"Nimbus is dead now," says Rosie. "Everything and everyone is dead," she sobs. "What do we do?"

"There's nothing we can do," I reply—my head starting to spin; each second faster than the last. "There's nothing left for us to do."

"Everything is gone. . .the world. . .is gone," says Miles. "Elise is right. We can't do anything else."

"We move on," replies Sam. Wiping his cheek, he starts walking toward me. "We move on even if it kills us to do so."

"How?" I cry as I embrace his arms. "How? Everyone. . .everyone we love is gone."

"Everything is fragile, but the longer you hold onto a broken glass, the deeper the shards will dig. The second you let go, that's when you can be free. That's when you can escape the pain," he whispers into my ear. "Marcus just told me that, and he's right."

"We can't just let go of this, Sam. This is everything we know. This is everyone we know. Our parents are dead. Abby's dead. Sean's. . ."

"He's alive!" shouts Marcus. "He's alive!"

As the words slip from his mouth and bounce around the walls, my mind caves into a fog of disbelief.

Sam

I release my embrace on Elise and gently lay her head against the grass. Rosie sprints toward me and quickly kneels next to her. "Is she alright?" she asks.

"I think she fainted," I say.

A part of me wishes that the same happened to me. At least then, I wouldn't have to deal with everything right now. At least if I was asleep, I wouldn't have any worries. I wouldn't have any sorrows. I wouldn't have a pain I can't decipher.

The one person I could relate to; the one person I could tell just about anything to is gone. Yet, I keep trying to hold onto her; I keep trying to pull her from her sleep. But, the more I cry, the more helpless I become and I can't do that. I can't cave to the deepest, darkest corner of mind because if I do, I might not be able to escape and I can't risk that again. For her, I have to be strong. For her, I have to keep moving. For Abby, I have to keep fighting.

"Ella," I mumble.

"Yea?" she replies, her face a dark shade of red as she wipes her eyes.

"Can you come with me to the top of the wall? I need to check on my brother."

"Y-yea," she stutters.

Grabbing onto her hand, we run toward the luminous steel encircling the city. Quickly sprinting in between different colored houses, we jump over a small picket fence into a pile of mud before we near the route upward. Tucked behind a miniscule kiosk, a ladder to the top stands stowed away in a slim crack.

"You can go first," Ella says, wiping her hands on her pants.

"Okay," I reply. Latching onto the cold steel, I close my eyes and shake my head. *Keep moving.* Stretching my hands upward, I grab onto the next bar as I work my way to the top. With each clink of the steel, the echoes grow softer until nothing but the sound of nature engrosses me.

"Over here," waves Marcus. Kneeling next to Sean with his blood-soaked hand pressing into Sean's chest, Marcus points ahead. "He said there's a first aid kit through the grate over there. It should open right up."

Disregarding my desire to immediately tend to him, I follow Marcus's instructions. Gently jumping over Sean's outstretched legs, I scour the grated floor for a latch.

"Just ahead," says Marcus.

"I don't see it."

"It's next to the wall, he says."

"Where?" I frantically shout.

"You're standing on it now," he laughs.

"Not funny," I say as I step back and pull open the hatch. Quickly stepping into the opening, I kick over empty boxes in search of the kit. Yet, the more I push out of the way, the less apparent a kit becomes.

"It's on top of a locker or something," yells Marcus. "Hurry up!"

Continuously nudging over emptied cardboard boxes into a haphazard pile, I start to grow angry just as my eyes catch a glimmer of white shining next to me. Stowed away atop an open locker sits a white box with a red cross etched onto the front. I grab it and climb out of the space.

"Open up the kit and hand me whatever I can use to pull the bullet out," says Marcus, his eyes jumping toward the box and back at Sean. "Quickly, Sam."

"I don't see anything," I reply.

"Just find something. The bullet didn't get that deep. I can get most of it if you find something. He's losing a lot of blood. Hurry, Sam," he says impatiently.

Emptying the box, I pour everything out. Nothing but gauze, bandages, and various cotton puffs fall onto the grates—some falling through in the process. "There's nothing!"

"Sam! Your knife!" yells Ella. "I have a knife too, it's all we have."

Hastily prying the knife from my pocket, I open it up and hand it to Marcus as Ella does the same.

"I'm going to need you two to hold him back. It's going to hurt a bit," says Marcus as he rips off a piece of Sean's shirt and wedges it into Sean's mouth. "Bite, Sean."

Using what little strength he has, Sean bites. Light streaks of moisture glide down his face as his forest green eyes roll from side to side; his stare tightens as he winces. "Sam," he whispers, though muffled. "Take care of Elise."

"You're not going anywhere," I say tightening my grip on his arm. "You'll be okay."

"Hold tightly, guys," says Marcus loudly as he approaches the wound. "Be steady."

Holding my focus on Sean's face, I watch as he moves his head back and forth before releasing a gruesome howl.

"Hold on, Sean!" shouts Marcus. "I almost have it. Just hold on."

"Look at me, Sean. Look at me," I say. He keeps trying to focus on my face, but each time I speak, his movements grow slower. Each time I cry, I refuse to wipe away the moisture dampening both of our cheeks. "Look at me. You're going to be okay. I'm not going to lose you, too."

"Aghhhhhhh," he shrieks as the tattered shred falls from his mouth. "I can't take much more!"

"Almost there," mutters Marcus.

Refusing to look over at Sean's chest, I turn my focus to the vast steel beside us. The halo wrapped around Nimbus gleams brightly in the sunlight as every curve mirrors the sky—making it look like we're lost at sea. Aimlessly floating around in search of salvation, we fight Mother Nature while she strives to torment our every move.

"Almost," says Marcus. "Just a few seconds."

Feeling hopeless and stranded on a dead island, we fight. We fight for a world where we can be everything we desire to be, where we can escape the oppression we once endured.

"Got it!" yells Marcus. "Ella, apply pressure to the incision. Sam, get Sean some water."

"I have water right here," says Elise as she steps up from the ladder.

"Thanks," replies Marcus. Quickly setting the bloodied knives to his side, he hands the canteen to Sean. "Drink up."

346

Slowly nodding back, Sean grimaces as he splashes the water against his cheeks.

"We need to find something to sew the wound up with. This gauze won't do too much," mentions Marcus as he hands Ella some gauze pads.

"Is he going to be okay?" whimpers Elise. "Is he going to survive?"

"He'll be fine, Elise. We just need to sew it up to avoid infection. The pads will help for now, but we have to get to the infirmary and scavenge for more medicinal supplies or a doctor or something."

"But there's no one here," I say. "It's just us."

"We don't know that yet, Sam. MacMillan could have them imprisoned somewhere. We don't know anything."

"I guess so," I reply as I stand up and reach for Elise. "He's going to be okay," I whisper.

"Thank you, Sam. Thank you for everything," she cries as she gently kisses my forehead.

I sigh as I let go, "Thanks for keeping me alive."

Distressed and exhausted, Elise smiles. "I owe everything to you."

Half-smiling as I reach for the bars extending from the ladder, I turn my back toward the city as I descend back toward the pain from what happened moments ago.

Marcus

"Sam, we need to move back toward the gate. The infirmary is that way," I say as I jump down from the ladder.

"Sounds good," he replies with a solemn look strewn across his face.

"Are you going to be okay?" I ask as I turn my head toward his. I watch as his eyes wander throughout Nimbus, through a town devoid of liveliness, spirit, and everything that once made it a unique colony. What were once boisterous shops overcrowded with smiles of contentment are now unkempt, abandoned buildings overrun with a look of hopelessness. It's an unpleasant sight—one that sends shivers down my legs.

"Y-yea," he mumbles. "I'll be fine."

"I'm not too fond of that word, Sam. Fine is and will always be a middle ground for emotion. Either you're good or great or you're not. Fine is useless. So, what are you?"

"I don't know," he replies as he starts dragging his feet.

"You know she would have done the same for you," I say.

"And I her."

"I know it's hard to get over something like that and it will take time, but you just have to keep your head up. The hardest parts of life are always the ones we least expect. It's not the pains of sorrow that hold you down; it's the weight you thrust on yourself that holds you down. If you bury yourself in a pit of sadness, you'll be stuck in it forever. Always keep your head above the dirt and you'll be okay," I say as I wipe the drying blood on my pants.

"Thanks," he mumbles. "It's easier said than done."

"I know, I know."

"I may be young and not know much about this sort of thing, but I think I loved her."

"And she loved you, Sam. You have to hold onto that. You can't let that go, but if you always think about what could have been,

348

you'll never survive. You know she'll always be with you, so you have to hold onto that feeling. You have to let her live through you," I say.

"I'll try," he sobs. "I'll try."

"That's the first step," I smile as I wrap my arm around his shoulders. "You're the toughest fourteen-year-old I've ever met, Sam. You're going to survive. You're going to lead us beyond Nimbus."

"I don't know about that," he smiles weakly.

"In time."

As we walk along a dirt path parallel with the wall, we continuously move past rows of houses shadowing our way. With each house, the shadows loom larger—almost as if we're in the city again, running down the streets. Still, here, we're not afraid of what lies in the houses like we were in the city. Lurkers controlled nearly everything, but here, nobody's in control. The only beings capable of torturing us now are ourselves. We just have to stay positive and remember that we're still here, that we're still breathing.

"Hopefully," he nods. "Let's just get to the infirmary. Maybe somebody's still there. There's no way this whole place can be empty."

"Yea, it doesn't make much sense," I reply as we cut between two houses toward the main street. Quickly turning back left, a luminous red cross stands tall several hundred feet ahead of us while the gates stand open next to it. "Why is the gate open?" I ask Sam, uncertain of his knowledge of it.

"Did it close? When I ran inside, they were still open," he answers.

"Y-yea," I mumble. "Sean was the last one in."

"Then, how could they open back up?" he asks. "I thought you could only open them from the inside."

"That's what I thought too and none of us opened them," I reply. "Is someone still here?"

"I am," comes a voice from behind us.

"Who are you?" I ask without turning around.

"You know who I am, Marcus," he says. "Turn around."

Taking a deep breath, I turn toward Sam and nod. Together, we slowly turn around as a bespectacled, slender, bearded man stands in front of us. "Kyle?" I ask as I squint to gain a better view.

"Yes," he smiles back.

"You're alive!" I cry as I sprint toward him.

"I am. . .I am," he cries as he wraps his arms around my shoulders. "I can't believe you're here."

"Where is everyone?" I immediately ask as I let go.

"Exiled," he replies. "MacMillan sent them all out the opposite way he sent us."

"So you opened the gates assuming they might find their way back?"

"After hearing gunshots, I thought maybe they'd manage a way back. After MacMillan issued a decree that every non-Elite guard or non-founding blood was to be kicked out, I hid. I had heard from the Young family that Sean Martin had a plan to bring down the tyranny here. I guess I just hoped that he really would," says Kyle as he wipes his glasses.

"So, why was there still a separation?"

"MacMillan had all the kids whose birthdays were this week stay behind. He wanted to enjoy a few more separations before Nimbus was completely cleared out."

"Why?"

"Because he wasn't right," glares Kyle.

Coughing, Sam leans in, "Marcus, who is this?"

Laughing, I look at Kyle as I say, "Sam, this is Kyle Bishop. He's the one who took me in outside the wall. He's the one who upheld the library before I got there."

"Nice to meet you, Sam," smiles Kyle as he reaches out his hand toward Sam.

"You too," says Sam as he shakes Kyle's hand. "Do you know if anyone's outside the wall?"

"I haven't gotten a chance to look. I just opened the gates."

"Let's go have a look, then," I say as I turn back to face the opening.

"We have to be quick though, Marcus. Sean still needs us," says Sam as he starts to run toward the split in the wall.

Quickly picking up the pace, I start to run alongside him. With each step across the stone-slabbed street, the hairs on my neck stand taller. Each stride galvanizes me more than the last.

"Faster!" yells Sam as he sprints ahead of me.

"I'm coming!" I shout as he maneuvers himself around various fallen corpses at the front. "Take it easy, Sam!"

Instantly reaching the wall, he stops in his tracks as dirt drifts off behind him.

"What do you see?" I ask as I steadily step next to him.

"Nothing yet," he says as he steps out into the open before looking to his left. As he shakes his head from side to side, he turns right.

"See anyone, Sam?" asks Kyle as Sam remains still in the open.

"Sam?" I ask.

"Everyone," smiles Sam. "Everyone's here," he cries. "Everyone!"

Eagerly stepping out from Nimbus, I turn toward a group of wide-eyed people as their mouths sit agape. Hundreds of them stare back in awe as we blankly look at each other; each more distraught than the one in front of them. These are the people a society needs to thrive. These are the people a world needs to survive. *I can't believe they're still alive.*

"They're alive," cries Sam. "People are still alive."

Suddenly, the crowd starts walking toward us, as we remain stunned. Several push past us and into Nimbus while others extend their arms in gratitude. What was once an unbearable world governed by a lunatic now has the chance to become something new. I hold my arms out as I embrace the change, as we embrace the joys of others.

"I can't believe the gate is open," sobs a woman as she pats me on the shoulder. "Thank you, boys. Thank you for allowing us to go home."

Another man shouts, "MacMillan is dead! Thank the heroes of Nimbus!"

With each person that passes, the generosity never wanes. Each individual is as thankful as the one before it as we remain awestruck in euphoria. Yet, despite the excitement, there's one thing we still need to do. There's still one person we need to save to ensure Nimbus's fate. Standing tall, I yell, "Is anyone here a doctor?"

Lost amid a crowd of enthused civilians, a woman raises her hand. "I am!" she shouts as she bustles past dozens of ebullient people.

"You're just the person I was looking for," I say as I grab her hand and guide her back home.

18 February 2192

Sam

"I hereby dedicate this day to Abby Young after she gave her life to protect the future of our world. Without her sacrifice, we might not be here today. Without her courage, mankind as we know it could die out. Now, without MacMillan, Nimbus will not be a place where families fade into nothingness and where those who aren't prioritized are exiled. This world will be a place of freedom where you can go as you please, and where nobody will ever be kicked out upon his or her fourteenth birthday. This place will forever get stronger as those who embody the spirit of Abby Young will do everything in their power to continue to thrive in a successful world. With this day, we can now step in the right direction toward the future of mankind and there's nothing anyone can do to take that away from us," says Sean as he looks out upon the people of this city, his arm in a sling next to his chest.

Taking a second to turn his head back and smile, Sean rubs his cheek as a wave of applause shakes the area. Whistles and cheers erupt throughout our new world as we embrace the praise.

Continuing to smile as the applause dims, Sean starts to speak again. "Over the past week, I've seen what this city can do in moments of anger, in moments of sadness, and in moments of grief. I've seen. . .hell, I've felt the pain that MacMillan threw upon Nimbus. I've felt the evils of a madman firsthand, but what I've seen since, what I've felt since. . .it's incomparable. When someone tries to break us, we get stronger. When someone tries to kill us, we band together to form something nobody can defeat. The personal, heartfelt sentiments we've received from each of you," he says as he motions toward us. "They're incredible. It just goes to show how strong we are. How incredibly tough we are in the face of adversity. Yet, nobody. . .absolutely nobody, embodies the character of a hero more than my little brother, Sam. Without him, I wouldn't be here. Without him, we wouldn't be here," he says as he wipes his eyes.

Slowly taking a step back from the podium, Sean sets the microphone down before stepping toward me. Wide-eyed and somber, he wraps his good arm around my back. "I love you, little brother," he whispers, resting his head against mine. "Now, go get 'em."

Turning back toward the podium, he grabs ahold of the microphone and speaks once more. "And now, a few words from my brother, Sam Martin."

I smile as I stand up behind Sean and step up to the stand— the audience standing and cheering. He nods as he takes my seat next to Elise. Slowly unfolding the crumpled paper in my hand, I place it upon the stand before looking out at the eager crowd. Hundreds of wide-eyed individuals look up at me happily while I fumble with my sheet.

"Just breathe, Sam," whispers Elise.

Taking a deep breath, I start to read, "When I was first separated, I didn't know what to do. I had no survival skills and I had no idea what I needed to do to come back here in eleven years. The only things I had were a hatchet, the clothes on my back, and a friend. Abby stuck with me from the beginning until the end. There wasn't a moment outside the wall where I felt completely lost with her. I'll never forget the sacrifice she made for Elise, for me, for Sean. . .for Marcus. . .Miles. . .Rosie, for Ella, for everyone. I will never forget the leap she took when she was the one who was afraid of losing us. Though, in reality, I think I was more afraid of losing her than I was myself," I say. Looking back at Elise, I take another breath. "Deep outside the wall, my mind was always running amok, b-but each time I became defeated, she was there. E-each time, I fell down, she picked me back up," I say as I wipe my face. "Abby Young was more than just my friend, she was a survivor. Just like everyone here. She conquered Separation and because of her sacrifice, nobody will ever have to step a foot outside of that wall again," I say as I slam my fist into the podium—the crowd erupting into applause.

I wipe my eyes as my words become overwhelmed in cheers. Every person in the city stands up as whistles, applause, and screams fill my ears. Yet, I can't help but break down even more as my knees buckle. *I miss her.*

"Sam, Sam, it's okay," says Elise. Stepping behind me, she brings me to my feet. "Stay strong. Keep going."

"It's j-just so hard," I sniffle.

As she wraps her arms around me, Sean stands up and follows suit. Standing up in awe behind me, Marcus and everyone else start to applaud. "You can do this," smiles Elise. "But if you need to sit down, I can take over."

"I'll b-be okay," I whisper, staring up at Elise. "I'll be okay."

Nodding, I wipe my nose on my sleeve before stepping back up to the podium. Instantly, the applause halts as I sniffle. "But just because we're in a new era doesn't mean this is the end of what's outside that wall. When I was out there, I managed to stumble into an abandoned city. There, I was tortured, beaten, and starved to the point that I became senseless. So senseless that I would have rather died than spend another second out there. Yet, I realized that just because I was around merciless vagrants, it didn't mean everyone out there was like that. There had to be others who were sane, who were normal, who just wanted to survive like us. That's when I met Marcus. Marcus, Miles, Ella, Rosie, and many others at the library were like us," I say as I gesture toward Sean and Elise. "They were normal kids just trying to do what they could to survive, but unlike us, they were rebuilding. They were rebuilding a library that stood as a beacon of hope in an empty city. Eventually, that beacon was burned to the ground. And because of that terror, because of the nightmare we lived through, we find it in the best interest of ourselves and the future of this generation to go back out there. Not just to prove that we're stronger than what we endured, but to prove that there's a future for society outside of a giant wall," I say as the applause starts again.

Crumbling up my speech, I shove it back into my pocket and look around the audience. As each cheer grows louder than the one before it, my eyes mist over with joy.

Slowly tilting the microphone up a bit more, I look up at the glistening steel around me. "We'll do this for our families. . .for everyone lost under the cruelty of MacMillan. We've all lost someone, and we plan to search for something that proves the fate they suffered wasn't for nothing. We'll search for something new, something great, something that can't be destroyed. Without the chips monitoring our every move, we'll seek to find all those still wandering outside of these walls. We'll search for others beyond the boundaries created by MacMillan. We'll go farther than anyone in this century has ever gone and we won't come back until we find what we're looking for. Anyone who wants to follow is welcome, and anyone who wants to remain behind and rebuild can." With a quick glance back at Sean, I smile as I say, "In harmony we live. In peace we thrive."

Nimbus isn't the end.

Halcyon is coming.

Made in the USA
Columbia, SC
20 August 2018